D0428197

BY JIM C. HINES

Fable: Blood of Heroes

MAGIC EX LIBRIS

Libriomancer

Codex Born

Unbound

Revisionary

THE PRINCESS SERIES

The Stepsister Scheme

The Mermaid's Madness

Red Hood's Revenge

The Snow Queen's Shadow

JIG THE GOBLIN

The Legend of Jig Dragonslayer

Goblin Quest

Goblin Hero

Goblin War

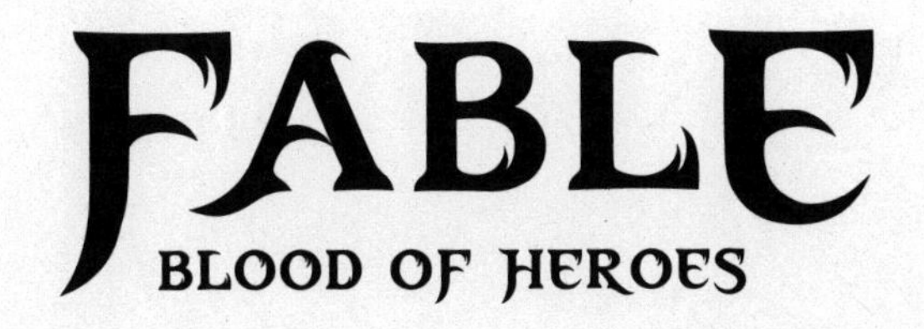
FABLE
BLOOD OF HEROES

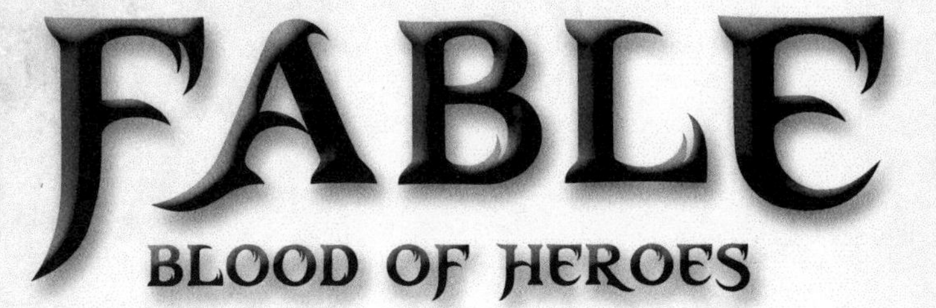

Jim C. Hines

DEL REY BOOKS
NEW YORK

Fable: Blood of Heroes is a work of fiction. Names, places, and incidents either are products of the author's imagination or are used fictitiously. Any resemblance to actual persons, living or dead, events, or locales is entirely coincidental.

A Del Rey Trade Paperback Original

Published in the United States by Del Rey, an imprint of Random House, a division of Penguin Random House LLC, New York.

DEL REY and the HOUSE colophon are registered trademarks of Penguin Random House LLC.

ISBN 978-0-345-54234-2
eBook ISBN 978-0-345-54235-9

Printed in the United States of America on acid-free paper

randomhousebooks.com
lionhead.com

2 4 6 8 9 7 5 3 1

First Edition

Dedicated to the memory of that legendary Hero
Sir Whitefeather Cluckwarbler the Quick, also called the
Courageous, the Strong, the Daring, and the Chicken.
He was an inspiration to generations of poultry to come.

(In the end, Sir Cluckwarbler ultimately came
to be known as "the Tasty" . . .)

Part I

The Return of Heroes

There was a time when Yog would have lit the candle with an act of Will.

Of course, there was also a time when she'd had her own teeth, walked without the assistance of a stick, and didn't wake up four times a night to piss.

These days, she needed to conserve what power she had. Her gnarled fingers eased a lit taper through the open jaw of the centre skull. Inside, a fat tallow candle sat as if in a pool of its own hardened blood, melted and spilled over the past months. A bud of blue flame appeared at the end of the wick. Yog withdrew the taper and sat back as a sweaty, smoky smell filled her hut.

She extended her Will into the candle. The flame sputtered. Tallow bubbled and splashed within the skull. Lines of smoke escaped through square nail holes in the top of the cranium, giving the appearance of ethereal horns. A bit escaped to drip through the nose cavity like rivulets of hot snot. The image was appropriate, considering who was magically bound to this one.

This was the smallest of the three skulls arranged on the wooden table. Like most of Yog's possessions, the skull was strapped into place. Strips of old leather crisscrossed the bone, securing it to her work desk.

Two other skulls bookended this one. The one on the left was slender, blackened by soot and ash. To the right was the largest of the three, broad and strong, with a layer of thickened bone over the brow. Each contained a matching candle, but Yog left them unlit for now.

Once the flame in the centre skull was burning steadily, Yog peered into the eye sockets, concentrating on the small blue glow. The walls of her home faded into shadow. She followed the flame out through the shadows of Deepwood and the marshes of the Boggins, to the town of Brightlodge, a town that appeared not so much planned as vomited onto an isle atop a waterfall, splattering bridges and buildings in every direction. The tower stretching out over the falls—Wendleglass Hall—looked as rickety as Yog herself.

She barely recognised this Albion, so different from the Old Kingdom. This was an Albion just beginning to crawl out of the darkness, like toads digging themselves out of the dirt after a long winter. It was a land where most people lived their entire lives without venturing more than a stone's throw from their villages . . . mostly because venturing farther tended to bring a sudden and painful end to those lives. Often involving thrown stones.

How long had Yog hidden away from the world in her hut in Deepwood? And then word had begun to spread throughout the land: Heroes had returned to Albion.

Yog hadn't believed the rumours at first. Heroes had been lost with the destruction of the Old Kingdom. Gone was the bloodline of men and women who could call lightning from the sky with an act of Will or wrestle a bear and win.

To the average man, Heroes were a foreign concept. Much like hygiene. Their return was as far-fetched a story as the one about the redcap with the enchanted, chicken-drawn sled who flew through the winter skies to sneak down people's chimneys and set their stockings on fire. Preferably while the owners were still wearing them.

Yog looked beyond the blue candle flame onto the streets of Brightlodge, settling her awareness into the senses of a creature who crouched in an alley behind a half-full rain barrel, the same creature whose blood and hair were moulded into the candle. She had never used such measures in her prime, but the candle eased the strain on her Will, just as her stick did for her body.

The sounds and scents of the street filled Yog's hut. A dog barked in the distance. The building to the left smelled like burnt bread. A breeze carried the stink of weeds and dying flowers. As for the creature itself, a redcap named Blue, his scent was enough to make Yog's eyes water.

She felt the single drop of blood that tickled the side of Blue's face. He wiped it on his sleeve, then reached up to adjust the filthy, pointed cap nailed to his skull. Two nails protruded from his brow like the antennae of an insect, while a third jutted from the back of his head.

Redcaps were a miserable, pathetic breed, but this one had shown himself to be surprisingly skilful. Skilful, that is, when he wasn't distracted.

Blue plunged his hand into the rain barrel to retrieve a drowned mouse. He giggled to himself as he fitted the sodden corpse into the pouch of his slingshot and sneaked towards the mud-spattered road.

He drew back the mouse and aimed at a thick-built man arguing with a street vendor over a pair of cabbages. The mouse struck the back of the man's head and dropped neatly down his collar. It was too waterlogged to do any real damage, but the man screamed like a balverine had fallen from the sky and crawled into his undergarments.

Blue giggled and vanished back into the shadows. He paused briefly to study the moon, as if contemplating how big a slingshot he would need to knock it out of the sky. Eventually, he sighed and tucked the slingshot back into the rags he wore for clothing.

"Stupid humans. Stupid town. Stupid dead cow. Stupid mistress, sendin' Blue out to—"

"Hello, Blue," Yog said, projecting her words directly into his skull.

Blue squealed and looked around furtively, as if terrified the shadows might lash out to punish him.

Yog enjoyed startling the redcap. It was one of the few pleasures she allowed herself these days. On a good day, she could make Blue soil himself. "Tell me of your progress."

Blue jumped again, then pulled a skeletal finger on a leather thong from his shirt. The finger had come from the same redcap as the skull in Yog's hut, another crutch to supplement her Will. He brought the finger to his lips and whispered, "Mistress?"

"Have you completed your task?"

"Alehouse. Dead mouse." Blue tended to rhyme when he was anxious. Or manic. Or drunk. Or when he thought it would annoy her.

It was Blue who had brought her the first confirmation of the rumours, letting her know that Arthur Brutus Cadwallader Wendleglass, the self-proclaimed King of Brightlodge, had put out a call for the Heroes of Albion to gather in his little town.

For Yog, the news was like awakening from a dream. Emotions she had thought extinguished lifetimes ago flared hot once more. She might have thanked King Wendleglass personally . . . if the fool hadn't managed to get himself killed by the White Lady in the midst of his own Festival of Flowers.

Wendleglass certainly threw a memorable party, but the man had been an idiot. Even a redcap knew better than to pick the White Lady's roses.

"Show me," she said.

Blue waited until nobody was looking in his direction, then scampered around the bakery and down a darkened street, crossing through Hightown in the general direction of Wendleglass Hall. Someone dumped a chamber pot into the street. Blue jumped, then scampered up the side of the building. He hung from one hand and used the other to pick his nose and flick a nugget at the woman's back.

He scampered over the rooftops until he reached the back of a loud, raucous inn called the Cock and Bard. Shoulders hunched, he crept closer. One hand stretched towards the door, but it swung open before he touched it. Blue yelped and dived behind a pile of empty crates and refuse. He waited, a small slingshot in one hand, as a woman tossed scraps into the street.

Once the woman had gone, and a pair of dogs had emerged to fight over the scraps, Blue tugged open the door. He peered into a kitchen that stank of spilled beer and questionable meat. He pointed to a small wooden keg, the side of which bore a brand in the shape of a dead cow.

After all these centuries, Yog was still capable of surprise. "You did it."

"Aye," said Blue.

"The ale was properly prepared?"

Blue nodded, making the tip of his cap flop back and forth.

"You didn't piss in it this time?"

He shook his head even harder.

"Or put frogs or snakes or anything else, living or dead, into the keg?"

"No bugs, no slugs!"

"Well done. Return to the library and rejoin the others before—" A woman in a stained apron stomped through the kitchen and froze when she spotted the redcap. Yog sighed. "—before you're seen."

The woman drew breath to scream, then hesitated. "Are you here to spend your coin? We serve the twenty-third best ale in Albion."

Blue shook his head again.

"Oh. All right, then." *Now* the woman screamed.

Blue jumped up and fished a snake skull packed with pebbles and dried mud from a pouch at his belt. He loaded his slingshot, aimed, and loosed the missile in one smooth motion. He missed the woman completely but struck the glass lantern hanging on the wall behind her. Blue whooped with delight as the lantern shattered, spraying flame and oil over the wall.

Bad enough Yog was stuck with a redcap serving as one of her three Riders. She had to pick one with a particular love of setting things on fire. It was a miracle Blue had gone two days in Brightlodge without setting the whole place ablaze.

Blue yanked the door shut and scampered away.

Yog extinguished the candle and rubbed her eyes. Blue *had* made sure the keg was delivered safely to the pub. The rest was as much Yog's fault as anyone's. She was the one who insisted he return to the pub so she could see for herself. She might have been better off ordering him to jump from the top of Wendleglass Hall.

Not for the first time, she cursed her fortune. The woods were full of creatures far more powerful and dangerous than a half-mad, bloodthirsty changeling. But her power wasn't what it used to be, and her plans required a redcap, at least for now.

Assuming the pub didn't burn to the ground, it wouldn't be long before she confirmed the ale's effect on the townspeople. Yog and her Riders would soon reclaim their former strength and glory, and Albion would cower at the mention of her name.

If all went well, perhaps she'd let Blue burn Brightlodge to the ground as a reward for his service.

chapter 1

INGA

The new king, Cadwallader Wendleglass, son of the recently deceased King Arthur Brutus Cadwallader Wendleglass, reminded Inga of a blind puppy: clumsy, enthusiastic, and likely to charge headfirst into a wall if you let him run loose. As if stepping into his father's shoes wasn't enough, he had to do it with his dead father occasionally popping in to look over his shoulder.

Young King Wendleglass peered over a table with a map of Albion on it and beamed at the Heroes gathered in Wendleglass Hall. He took a deep breath, straightened his spine, and said, "I've spoken with Beckett the Seer, and I'm delighted to announce the imminent doom of Brightlodge."

Silence.

Wendleglass blinked and reviewed the half sheet of crumpled parchment clutched in his hands. "Right. Um . . . sorry. Delighted, I mean to say, that we have Heroes to *prevent* our imminent doom."

That was better. Inga glanced at her fellow Heroes. Some had come from as far north as the Deadlands. She'd never imagined meeting so many others who shared her determination to protect the people. Growing up, she hadn't even known Heroes existed. To discover what she was, and that she wasn't alone had made her as happy as a four-year-old in a field of mud puddles, as Old Mother Twostraps would say.

"Nimble John and his band of smugglers infest Brightlodge's tunnels," said Wendleglass. "A redcap sets our buildings ablaze in the night. Thankfully, we . . . I mean, the Heroes—"

"There were no redcap arsonists while I *was alive!"*

That last came from the spectral form of Brightlodge's recently deceased ex-king. The ghost of Arthur Wendleglass had been popping up throughout Brightlodge since his death, moaning and wailing and making a right nuisance of himself, if truth be told.

Old King Wendleglass drifted forwards to slam his glowing fist onto the table. Onto and through. The ghost stared at the table, head cocked to one side. He was still getting used to being dead. *"Nor smugglers,"* he added. *"In my day, I'd have outlawed doom, whether it be imminent, impending, or any other flavour!"*

When nobody responded, his shoulders slumped and he retreated to the corner to glower.

"Yes. Well." Young Wendleglass glanced at his notes. "Beckett says to take heed of his portents. Find the criminals who roam our streets, and they shall lead you . . . um . . . to the greater scourge!"

"Where's Beckett run off to?" Inga called out. "What else can he tell us about this scourge?"

"He told me you'd ask." The young king nodded. "Like myself, Beckett is utterly confident that the newly gathered Heroes of Brightlodge will defeat this threat. He reassured me that his decision to take a vacation far from Brightlodge, well out of range of any potential doom, was a complete coincidence. To that end . . . that is, as your king, I ask that you, um . . ." He bit his lip and looked around.

"Perhaps we ought to start by poking around the pub where that fire broke out?" Inga said. "Asking about to find out if anyone saw where that redcap ran off to?"

"Excellent suggestion, thank you, yes!" Young King Wendleglass pointed at three other Heroes, seemingly at random: Leech, a healer in cloak and mask; Rook, the Stranger from the north; and a bull-sized brawler named Jeremiah Tipple. "Perhaps these others can join you to assist with your poking and asking, and ensuring the safety of my . . . um, of *our* town."

"Right," said Tipple. "We'll find the bastard who tried to burn my third favourite pub in Brightlodge."

Leech's birdlike plague mask tilted to one side. "Brightlodge only has three pubs."

"Exactly." Tipple's grin was as boisterous as the slap he planted on Leech's back. "And if Winter hadn't shown up last night with her magic to help put out the flames, we'd be down to two. Can't have that, can we?"

Old King Wendleglass followed them out the door. *"Four Heroes? You're kinging all wrong, son. I was never so overcautious. I'd have sent a single Hero to vanquish these minor villains."*

Young Wendleglass sighed and rubbed his brow. "Good luck, Heroes!"

Inga was still getting used to the sights and sounds of the big town, so different from the hills where she had grown up. Wendleglass Hall stretched out over the edge of the falls, as if it might take flight and soar among the clouds. Old stone pillars supported the bridge to the main isle, where the broad, stone-paved streets were decorated with brightly coloured signs and flags.

"Hello there." She waved to a fellow selling pies in the shade of a Hightown barbershop. "My name's Inga. Have you seen any smugglers about?"

The man shook his head and shoved a chicken potpie at the Heroes. "Fresh-baked this morning. Guaranteed beak-free!"

Someone screamed in the distance. The man jumped, nearly losing his pies.

Inga was already running, her armour and sword clanking with each step. Long before she discovered she was a Hero, Inga had learned to run *towards* the screams. She had grown up fighting the bullies who preyed on the weak, and as she grew older and stronger, fighting the monsters that preyed on . . . well, pretty much anyone they got their teeth and claws into.

Turning the corner brought her face-to-face with a runaway pig charging down the street. Men and women threw themselves out of the animal's path. The ghostly king drifted into the street, pointed at the pig, and cried, *"Stop, foul swine!"*

The pig ignored the former sovereign.

It wasn't as exciting a foe as Nimble John and his band of outlaws, but Inga knew damn well the damage a full-grown pig could do once it worked itself into a fit.

"I've got him," said Rook, raising his crossbow.

"First off, that's a she." Inga stepped between the grizzled veteran and the charging sow. "Second, the poor thing's obviously scared to death. You don't have to shoot everything that looks at you funny, you know."

"I don't *have* to, no." But he lowered his weapon and nodded at her to proceed.

Inga grabbed an apple from the fruit cart on the side of the road and hurled it up the street. The sow skidded to a halt. After a cautious sniff, she snatched it up and gulped half of the fruit in one bite.

Inga moved towards the animal, trying to minimise the noise of her armour. She hardly noticed the weight these days, any more than she did the enormous wood-and-brass shield strapped to her arm, but to a poor, frightened animal, she must be a terrifying sight.

"Where are you running to in such a hurry?" she asked. "Poor girl. You must be starving after all that fussing about."

The pig snorted and lowered her head. Saliva bubbled from her mouth, and she made a popping sound with her jaw. Whatever had sent her racing through the streets of Brightlodge, she was riled up and ready to trample anything that got in her way. The sow was fully grown and probably weighed as much as Inga did.

"Rook, circle around behind her right flank," said Inga. "Walk slowly towards her. Try to herd her my way."

Rook's snort sounded a lot like the sow's, but he did as she instructed. He kept his crossbow ready as he approached.

"Everyone stay calm," Inga called. "Tipple, find us some rope. Leech, take the left flank."

The pig finished scarfing down the apple. Inga smiled and made an encouraging clicking noise with her tongue. The sow's filthy black hoofs clopped against the street as it stepped closer, snuffling and sniffing.

"There you are!" A furious-looking man roughly the same size, build, and cleanliness as the sow stomped up the road, a heavy stick clutched in one hand. The pig emitted an ear-stabbing squeal and fled . . . directly towards Inga.

"What did you have to do that for?" Inga lowered her stance and met the sow head-on with her shield. It was like an ogre had flung a boulder at her, but Inga was the girl who had once knocked out a pain-maddened cow back home to stop it from trampling some village children. She could handle this.

Her boots skidded along the street. The sow pushed her into the fruit cart, which toppled over backwards. Inga shifted her angle and used her shield to shove the sow sideways, then lunged to grab one of the rear legs.

The squeals grew louder. The sow kicked and struggled to break free of her grip. They crashed onto the fruit cart, crushing its spilled contents into jelly, but Inga held tight. "Easy, girl. I won't let anyone hurt you."

Jeremiah Tipple cinched a rope around the sow's neck and added his bulk and strength to Inga's. The sow shrieked and convulsed one last time, then the fight seemed to drain out of her.

"Doesn't look like much of a threat," Tipple boomed. Whereas Rook was quiet and deadly, Jeremiah Tipple was loud, boisterous, and more often than not, intoxicated. But also deadly, in his own way. "Maybe we could put a hat on her head, call her a redcap, toss her in the stocks, and retire to the Cock and Bard?"

Inga stretched out her leg and hooked another apple with her foot, kicking it towards the sow. The animal snorted again but snatched the apple and began to chew.

"You'd need nails to make it convincing," said Leech. "Redcaps don't take chances when it comes to losing their caps. They believe the caps are magic and that a redcap without a hat becomes a deadcap."

He looked to the others expectantly, and his shoulders sank when no laughter followed. The only reaction came from the sow, who shifted and kicked anxiously. Leech had that effect sometimes.

While not a large man, the plague mask Leech wore gave him an inhuman appearance. A leather cone covered his face like an oversized beak. Red-tinted glass lenses were worked into the leather above the beak, like the eyes of an enormous insect. The bulk of the mask was stuffed with straw, mint, and rose petals. The pleasant smell was a sharp contrast to the pouches and jars he carried about his person, filled with leeches and blood and all manner of nastiness. A broad-brimmed hat shaded his head, and a green cloak hung from his shoulders.

"Thanks for catching her," called the man with the staff. His eyes widened. "You're some of them Heroes, aren't you?"

"Right you are," Tipple said.

The man fumbled about his person. "The wife's a big fan. Would you mind autographing Bacon for her?"

Inga's ears were still ringing from the pig's squeals. She reached down to scratch the animal's bristly neck. "You named her Bacon?"

"That's right. Named her after my dear departed mum."

Inga glanced at Rook, who rolled his eyes. To the pig's owner, she asked, "You want us to sign your pig?"

"If it wouldn't be too much trouble."

Leech was already dipping a quill into a bottle of indigo liquid. He drew an illegible scrawl over the pig's rump. The fur caused the ink to smear and run, but the man didn't seem to care. Leech passed the quill to Tipple.

"We're supposed to be searching for outlaws and a redcap," Inga said.

"The redcap?" Bacon's owner scowled. "No good looking around here. The filthy thing busted the gate on my pen earlier this morning, then ran off. Killed three of my animals and set the trough on fire. I've been chasing pigs all morning."

"Did you see where the redcap went?" asked Inga.

"Didn't see it, but I heard it laughing and shrieking." The man pointed eastward.

Brightlodge was spread out over a series of small, interconnected islands, most of which had only a few ways on or off. If they could corral the redcap, trap him on one of the smaller islands, they'd have a much easier time of it. "Thank you."

"Wait, you haven't signed Bacon yet!"

Inga snatched the quill and scribbled her name. The ghost of Old King Wendleglass crouched on the other side. It looked like he was trying to stamp the pig's ear with his spectral signet ring. The pig shook her head in annoyance, and the dead king gave up, vanishing to wherever it was ghosts went when they weren't following Heroes about.

"What about my cart?" A woman was straining to right the overturned fruit cart.

Inga hurried over to help. "We're sorry about the mess. We didn't mean to—"

"Who's going to pay for all this?"

Tipple picked another apple off the ground, wiped it on his shirt, and flipped a coin to the woman. "Put the rest on the redcap's tab."

"Come on," said Rook before the woman could argue further. "Before the trail grows cold."

There was little risk of losing the redcap. It had apparently given up on secrecy, leaving a trail of destruction and chaos like a balverine in a glassware shop.

An old drunk showed them the mouse skull that had struck him in the ear. A pair of red-faced, dripping kids described how they had been snogging on the bridge when a hail of rocks knocked them into the water. A librarian pointed to the fresh urine stain on a tome he was carrying back from the bookbinder, and directed them towards the bridge to Library Island.

Across the bridge, Rook spotted the remains of the creature's breakfast beside a drainage pipe where the island's waste flowed into the water. Little remained but a scattering of bones and seagull feathers on the rocky slope beside the tunnel. Judging from the trail of well-gnawed bones, the redcap had continued to snack as it crawled into the sewer tunnels.

"Smells like the wrong end of an ogre in there," said Tipple.

Leech was picking through the bones. He examined the seagull skull. With its beak, it looked distressingly like a miniature version of his plague mask. "Did you know bird bones are lighter than ours? They're porous like cork, and—oh look, there's still a bit of brain left in here!"

Inga strapped her shield to her back and hunched to peer into the tunnel.

"Oi, Ingadinger," said Tipple. "Are you sure that overgrown slab of wood will fit through there?"

"Bulwark stays with me." The enchanted shield had been her

constant companion since the day she took it off a grave-robbing bandit in Pinescrub.

Even as she spoke, Bulwark stirred on her back. From the metal-bound wood came the shadowy shape of a hand, which twisted into an old-fashioned but obscene gesture, telling Jeremiah Tipple exactly what it thought of his suggestion.

"Same to you, shield!" Tipple returned the gesture with both hands.

Inga had felt oddly protective of the shield from the moment she touched it. It reminded her of a stray mutt, desperate for affection and unfailingly loyal. To judge from the way Bulwark lent her its power, it felt the same way about her.

She stepped cautiously into the tunnel. Bulwark's edge scraped the loose brick overhead, bringing down a sprinkle of what she hoped was dirt. She kept her feet to the edges, where the flow was shallowest. It meant walking like she was straddling a saddle, but it kept her boots out of the worst of the muck.

"What's this forecast of doom and downfall all about, do you think?" she asked as they walked.

"Disease," Leech guessed. "A good plague could wipe out the whole town in less than a month." He followed a little too close for Inga's comfort. She could feel his feet and body brushing against hers. She didn't think he was afraid. Leech would happily confront—or dissect—things that would send most people screaming. Nor was it a clumsy attempt to get his hands on her. She had seen him do this indiscriminately, to men and women alike. Leech simply didn't notice other people's space the way everyone else did.

Tipple shook his head. "You want a real disaster, I heard a rumour Les at the Cock and Bard's started watering down the ale. Any day now, there'll be rioting in the streets."

"Don't waste time with groundless guesswork," Rook said firmly. "Be prepared, and focus on the job."

Inga twisted around. "We're going to need a torch pretty soon."

Rook pulled a brand from his pack. The moss-slimed rock didn't appear to bother him, and he gave no sign of noticing the smell of waste. Then again, you could probably set Rook's beard on fire and carve his pet crossbow into toothpicks, and he wouldn't so much as blink.

Oh, he'd kill you dead for the slight against his beard and his weapon, but he'd be utterly stone-faced when he was doing it.

Jeremiah Tipple, on the other hand, looked green as an unripe tomato as he squeezed his way into the sewer.

"You all right there, big guy?" asked Inga.

Tipple belched. "Let's just get this over with."

Rook brought his torch close to the wall. "Someone's been here."

"We knew that," Tipple snapped. "That's the whole point of us rooting around like sewer rats."

"Not the redcap." Rook pointed to fresh scratches on the bricks. They looked like random white marks to Inga.

"Cellar guards?" she guessed. Before his demise, Old King Wendleglass had assigned a group of town guards to patrol the tunnels beneath the islands, chasing off the occasional creatures who tried to breach the city from below and repairing any damage. A section of cleaner brick up ahead showed where one of the walls had recently been replaced.

"Smugglers. I learned their signs when I was patrolling with the Strangers." Rook traced three parallel slashes with his finger. "They use them to mark their territory. This one's a warning about the guards."

"Do they tell you where a man could find a privy?" asked Tipple.

Rook ignored him.

"Smugglers, eh?" asked Inga. "Looks like the little mite's leading us right to Nimble John's band, just like Wendleglass said he would."

For Inga, this was what being a Hero was all about. Chasing monsters in the darkness, wading through the muck to protect the people of Albion.

The tunnel split a short distance ahead. The left passage was broad and dry, while the right smelled like a swamp after the first spring thaw.

"Left," said Leech. "Redcaps avoid the water when they can. Like cats."

Tipple looked pointedly at the right tunnel. "You think that sludge qualifies as water?"

"Sure. From the smell, I'd say water mixed with faeces, urine, rotting food, algae, mildew"—he adjusted his mask and sniffed—"and just a hint of vomit. None of that matters to a redcap. They're just worried it will wash the blood out of their headgear."

That was good enough for Inga. She turned the corner and caught a glimpse of movement in the distance. Her body reacted automatically, raising her left arm as the filthy, hunchbacked creature with the pointed red cap drew back his slingshot.

Something sharp crashed into her forearm where Bulwark should have been. An animal skull fell into the dirt at her feet. Manic laughter echoed through the tunnel as the redcap scampered away.

"Get back here, you pointy-headed pimple!" Tipple roared. "If you're gonna ambush someone, do it to her face, like a man!"

The tunnels here were larger than the sewer and better maintained, but Inga still felt like a bull in a barrel. She shifted Bulwark onto her arm in case the next missile was deadlier. There was just enough room for her to hold it at an angle across the front of her body.

"Easy," said Rook. "Only a fool charges into the monster's lair."

Inga nodded. The ground was hard-packed dirt, which muffled the redcap's retreating footsteps. The walls were made of irregularly cut stone. Thick timbers helped to support the ceiling. She kept bumping the overhead beams with her shield.

The redcap couldn't have gone far. This was one of Brightlodge's smallest islands, housing little more than the library tower. There might be a few underground storage rooms where he could hide, or perhaps another tunnel running to the foundations of the bridge, but little more.

She couldn't help feeling sorry for the poor thing. Trapped underground, pursued by four armed Heroes. Did he realise how hopeless his situation was?

But he *had* started that fire, a fire that could have killed everyone in the tavern. Not to mention setting that sow free and all the other mischief he had caused. What if next time he attacked a child or an old woman? Worse, once he settled in to Brightlodge, would others follow like rats to a leaking grain sack?

Bulwark shifted of its own accord as she rounded the next corner. An arrow cracked against the wood. Inga glimpsed eight—no, nine—outlaws hunched behind an assortment of barrels and crates. She waved for the other Heroes to stop. The outlaws had been here for several days, judging from the rumpled blankets, discarded food, and remnants of an old cook fire. It looked like she had interrupted their breakfast.

Inga looked pointedly at the arrow on the ground. "I'm willing to pretend that didn't happen." She used the same tone her mother used to take with her when she came home covered in mud and blood. "Put down your weapons, and we can talk things out over some of that fish."

"Forget the sewer fish," Tipple called out. "What do they have to drink?"

A pair of chickens wandered aimlessly through the mess, searching for bugs. The redcap perched atop an empty cage, his manic smile displaying far too many teeth as he rocked from side to side.

"That redcap looks comfortable," Inga said. "Is he with you?"

The man with the bow scowled. "Not by choice."

"Nonsense." Inga inched closer, ready to knock down anyone who so much as twitched. Bulwark's surface rippled like the air over a sunbaked field as the shield gathered its power. "Granny Brody used to say even a fly can choose which cow pat to live on. Why hide away like animals in the darkness when you could fill your purses with honest work? Smithing or baking or—"

"Do we look like bakers to you, lady?" said another outlaw, this one nearly as large as Tipple. He picked up a small barrel and hurled it at her.

The barrel cracked against her shield, spilling fish and seawater onto the floor. The man scooped up a club and charged.

Inga drew her sword. "That was the wrong choice."

chapter 2

ROOK

Rook had begun assessing the outlaws the moment their arrow smacked into Inga's shield. Only a single shot, suggesting a lone archer. He'd heard two distinct voices, plus the redcap, before all hell broke loose.

He jammed the end of his torch into a crack in the wall. "How many?"

"Nine." This was followed by the distinctive sound of a heavy shield smashing a body to the ground. "Eight. Plus some chickens."

Rook leaned around the corner and raised his weapon.

Your regular crossbow packed a decent punch, and probably would have been enough against this band of outlaws.

Rook preferred to carry more than enough. Much more.

That meant the Catsgut repeating crossbow: standard issue for the Strangers who patrolled the north. You could load multiple bolts into the oversized weapon. A series of weights and counterweights used the weapon's own recoil to reset for the next shot. You lost a bit of accuracy, but you could empty a full magazine of bolts into your enemies in the time it took them to piss themselves. When you spent your days fighting hollow men freshly risen from the grave, not to mention the never-ending tide of other nasties, that Catsgut was a better friend than any man or woman.

Rook's first three shots thudded into the outlaw's chest. The man staggered back. He wasn't dead, but he wouldn't be doing much fighting with a punctured lung. The rest of the outlaws froze.

Amateurs. Rook took in the layout of the room in a single glance. Cracks of light from a shuttered lantern near the back illuminated the outlaws, plus the damn redcap. Three looked like your run-of-the-mill brawlers. Nothing special there. The fourth fellow could have been part giant.

"Dibs!" shouted Tipple as he charged into the melee, clocking the giant with a roundhouse punch that sent him staggering.

One of the outlaws swung a heavy club at Inga's head. She raised her shield at the last second. The crack of the impact sounded solid enough to split a boulder, but it was the club that cracked. The outlaw stared dumbly at his broken weapon.

Rookie mistake. Inga punched the back of his hand. A blow to those bones would hurt under any circumstances, but the hilt of her sword gave the strike more than enough power to shatter the man's hand.

Rook searched for his next target. The archer had fallen back to the rear of the room, along with a hunched man covered in feathers and chicken crap. Then there was that crone hiding in the shadows—or was that a bloke? Too hard to tell beneath the vines of greasy hair and the loose layers of clothing. She was holding a human leg bone, to which she had tied strings of glass beads and what looked like a mummified fish head.

From the look of her, she was either the magical firepower for this little band or else she was utterly loony. Possibly both. Rook didn't care to find out which. He stepped out to get a clear shot past Inga and put half a dozen bolts into the crone's chest and gut.

"Careful." Inga lashed out with her sword. "I don't want to spend the day picking your prickles out of my armour."

Tipple scooped up two staves from a broken barrel on the floor. He broke them both over the giant's head with a roar, then unleashed a storm of punches to the fellow's gut and face. Rook kept moving, trying to line up another shot. The archer was his next priority.

Before he could squeeze the trigger, the hunchback shouted a command, and four of the wandering chickens flew into the brawl. Some sort of sharpened steel spurs glinted on their claws and beaks. Rook adjusted his aim and shot one out of the air. "What is it with Albion and all these damned chickens?"

The birdmaster pointed at Rook. "Spike, kill!"

A rooster charged. In addition to the metal spurs the others wore, this one had hammered metal plates around his body, with additional spikes along the back. The bloody bird had better armour than most warriors.

Rook got one shot off, but the bolt ricocheted off the rooster's tiny helmet, then a chicken launched itself at Rook's face. Hooked metal claws reached for his eyeballs. Rook twisted aside and punched the bird out of the air.

The rooster jumped onto Rook's boot and drove the steel beak-spur into his lower leg.

"Bloody hell!" He reached for the rooster, but the spiked armour protected the neck and back. It looked like there were blades strapped to the wings, too. With the way the thing was flapping and fussing, there was no way to get a good enough hold to wring its neck.

"Hah!" said Tipple. "Rook made a friend!"

Rook stepped back and finished cocking his crossbow, then kicked hard enough to launch the rooster into the air. From the pain and the blood, he guessed those beak spikes were barbed, too. He pulled the trigger, and a spray of missiles buzzed through the air to find the gaps in the bird's armour. It hit the ground and didn't move.

Warmth pulsed through Rook's leg, and the pain of his wound

eased. He glanced down. The bleeding had stopped, and the skin scarred over as he watched. Behind him, Leech stood with his hands outstretched. Rook wasn't sure exactly how the man was able to pull life from one body and transfer it into another, but it got the job done. He tested the leg and nodded his thanks to Leech.

An arrow whizzed past. Rook dropped to one knee, sighted between Tipple's legs, and shot the birdmaster in the thigh.

"Oi!" Tipple shouted. "Mind the goods!"

"Mind your own goods," Inga shot back.

He laughed. "Not in the middle of a fight, Ingaling!"

One of the outlaws staggered, pale and off balance, despite the lack of any visible injuries. That would be the source of whatever healing Leech had pumped into Rook's leg. There was always a price to be paid, but sometimes it was nice to let someone else foot the bill. Tipple boxed the drained outlaw about the ears, and he dropped.

Rook stepped forwards to club a chicken off Inga's back. Half the outlaws were down, and the rest looked to be losing their nerve. The archer had fled down the tunnel, and the birdmaster was limping after, howling and clutching his leg. No discipline at all. Rook shot him in the back.

Now, where had the bloody redcap run off to?

One of the remaining outlaws, a bulky man whose rags and mismatched scraps of armour appeared slightly newer than the rest, shouted, "Get back here, you worthless cowards. Don't let them—"

Shadows lurched and danced as the redcap yanked the lantern from the wall and clubbed the outlaw on the head. The outlaw caught the redcap by the wrist and tried to wrench the lantern away, but the little beggar was tougher than he appeared. He kicked the outlaw square in the groin, then went right back to beating him about the head.

"I'm starting to like this fellow," said Tipple.

Again and again, the redcap swung, sparks shooting from each impact as the lantern cracked and broke. Burning oil spread to the man's hair, then to his tattered cape.

Screaming, the outlaw finally peeled his attacker loose and threw him aside. He tried to shove past Inga, presumably hoping to douse himself in the sewer beyond. A thrust of Inga's blade put an end to the man's worries.

With that, the fight was all but over. The outlaws—and chickens—were either dead or fled. Rook was tempted to chase after the ones who had escaped, but they had a head start and knew the terrain. Let them run. Men who panicked left a clearer trail.

"Not bad." Routing a nest of outlaws from the sewers might not be the glamorous adventure most people imagined when they daydreamed about becoming Heroes, but it was all part of the job. Today, that job had been both quick and efficient. Some of his companions were a little short on experience, but they fought well.

"That was fun." Tipple brushed his hands together and belched. "So much for death and doom and whatever."

"Cockiness killed the cat," said Rook.

Leech looked up from examining the corpses. "I thought it was curiosity."

"That too." Curiosity, cockiness, carelessness . . . cats didn't survive long in the Deadlands.

For generations, the Strangers had guarded Albion against whatever the Deadlands to the north cared to throw at them. But you didn't beat back the nightmares with enthusiasm or overconfidence; you did it with skill, a cool head, and a well-kept weapon.

Tipple was a tough old bastard. Looking at the bodies sprawled throughout the room, you couldn't question the man's effectiveness. And there was something to be said for raw, unbridled arse-kicking. But the man lacked the discipline Rook had grown used to among the Strangers.

"Right." Rook pointed his crossbow at the redcap, who was gleefully laughing and jumping about, searching for more things to set on fire. "Where can we find Nimble John the outlaw, and what's with this pending-doom nonsense?"

Inga put a hand on Rook's arm. "He helped us."

"Redcaps can't tell one human being from another." Tipple rubbed his eyes and looked around. "Wait, what were we talking about?"

"Inga's right," said Leech. "He spent the whole fight watching that particular outlaw, waiting for the chance to kill him."

The redcap had begun singing to itself, a high-pitched rhyme about bones and stones. He grabbed a blanket and held it over the burning body of the outlaw until it caught fire, then dropped it and grabbed one of the dead chickens. Singing happily, he began plucking the chicken and tossing feathers onto the flames.

"You think he led us here deliberately?" asked Inga.

Rook's nose wrinkled. The stench of burning plumage was enough to turn even his stomach. "What's your story, redcap?"

The creature set the partially plucked bird on the fire, then scampered about, searching for additional fuel. Leech snatched a book out of his reach, and the redcap hissed in frustration.

"What is it?" asked Tipple.

Leech turned the pages. "Looks like someone's diary. Oh, here's a 'To Do' list dated last week."

1. Unload shipment from Grayrock.
2. Find redcaps.
3. Get paid.
4. Buy beer and second pair of underwear.

He flipped to the last entry. "There's a badly sketched map noting the location of the pubs—"

"Important information," Tipple said solemnly. "When I first got to Brightlodge, I wasted an entire half hour finding the nearest pub!"

"—and a reminder to get out before Brightlodge is overrun," Leech finished.

The others fell silent. Rook stepped sideways, keeping his crossbow pointed at the redcap. Something about this place gnawed at him like a hound with a fresh boar hoof. This wasn't the first criminal lair he had cleared out, and for the most part, it was no different from any other: stolen goods, the smell of lousy cooking, unkempt bedrolls . . . most outlaws were sadly lacking in discipline.

He crouched to examine the empty cage near the back. Muddy feathers and bird crap littered the bottom. This was where the birdmaster had kept his killer chickens. But the bars of the cage were the width of Rook's finger. That was overkill even for these birds.

The bars had corroded. One was broken loose at the bottom. It looked like it had been shoved out from the inside. A bit of red thread hung from the rust near the top.

The redcap went still, all of his attention on Rook. He found this sudden attentiveness far more disturbing than the redcap's earlier madness.

The thread was stiff. Dry blood flaked away on Rook's fingertips. He held it to the firelight, comparing the colour to the pointed hat drooping over the redcap's nose. "They locked you up, too, did they? That's why you killed that outlaw?"

The redcap didn't move.

"'Find redcaps,'" Inga said. "That's what the book said. But what did they do with them once they found them?" She stepped closer. "He wasn't locked up. He was coming to rescue his friends."

"Redcaps don't have friends," said Tipple. "Not like us Heroes. Come 'ere and give Jeremiah Tipple a hug, you!"

While Inga evaded Tipple's embrace, Rook used a knife to sift through the mess in the cage. He found a chipped tooth among the feathers and crap, along with several bloodstains on the floor. "How many, redcap?"

The redcap held up three fingers.

Rook looked at the cage. "That's a tight fit. Especially squeezed in with the birds."

The redcap shrugged and waved his fingers again, then jammed the middle one up his right nostril.

"He led us here," said Inga. "He got our attention—"

"By trying to burn down the bloody pub," Tipple interrupted.

"—and once we reached the tunnels, he left a trail even a blind dog could track." Inga's tone softened. "But you were too late to save them. What's your name?"

Bloodshot yellow eyes narrowed suspiciously. "Blue."

"Blue the redcap?" Tipple chuckled. "How'd you end up with a name like that?"

"Blue flames in the eyes," said the redcap. "Always whisperin' nasty lies." He held a chicken feather over the small fire and stared, entranced, as it shrivelled and blackened.

"What happened to the rest of the redcaps?" asked Inga.

"Bones and stones. Stones and bones. Magic groans."

Tipple threw up his arms. "Well, that explains everything."

"Splintered bone makes a serviceable weapon." Rook searched the ground. It didn't take him long to find a broken chicken bone the length of his finger. The end was dark with blood, though it was impossible to say whether that blood belonged to the chicken or one of the outlaws. "So do rocks."

Blue smiled and rocked back and forth, staring into the distance like he was reliving a pleasant memory.

"I've found the other redcaps," Leech called.

They found him standing over three corpses, a short distance up the tunnel. Old blood darkened the ground. Leech had already unrolled a leather tool kit, and was using a pair of pliers to try to remove one of the nails securing the cap to a redcap's skull. "I want to see if removing the hat causes any changes, postmortem."

Rook studied the bodies. What was the profit in imprisoning redcaps in the first place? It wasn't like you could ransom them back to their families, and keeping prisoners alive was a bigger headache than most people imagined. Especially nonhuman prisoners.

"Bones and stones and groans and crones," Blue chanted.

The outlaws had cut the redcaps' throats. Rook pinched the dirt between his fingers. The dark clumps crumbled under pressure. "There's not enough blood."

"How much do you need?" Tipple asked.

"No, he's right," said Leech. "Three bodies that size, we ought to be standing in enough blood to fill a bucket or two."

Rook turned back to the redcap, his crossbow pointed not so subtly at the creature's leg. "What did they want from you?"

"Give him a drink," suggested Tipple. "Strong ale loosens tongues and morals both. And occasionally bladders."

"Right, because what we need now is a *drunk* redcap," said Inga.

Rook was tempted to just shoot the redcap and head out to track the rest of the outlaws, but experience and instinct both told him there was more going on here. The outlaws had slain redcaps, but this particular redcap hadn't been a prisoner. Had he tricked the outlaws into trusting him, only to betray them?

"Blue, do you know why those humans wanted redcaps?" asked Inga.

Blue shook his head.

People said redcaps were cursed, transformed by changeling magic. In that instant, Rook could believe it. Blue looked almost human, confused and exhausted. And then his expression turned crafty, and any trace of humanity vanished. "Heroes helped Blue. Blue will help you."

"What kind of help?" Rook asked warily.

Blue grinned, showing off crooked, green-stained teeth. "Help kill outlaws. Kill Nimble John. Kill *everybody*!"

Tipple nudged the burning outlaw with his toe. "I take it this ain't Nimble John, then."

"Nimble John? Ha!" Blue spat on the body. "That's Ugly, Stupid Weaselface."

"Who's this one?" asked Tipple.

Blue glanced over. "Ugly, Stupid Dogarse."

With an exasperated sigh, Rook grabbed a coil of rope from beside the cage. The instant he turned towards Blue, the redcap shrieked in dismay and tried to flee, but in his panic, he ran face-first into Inga's shield. He bounced off and fell to the floor like he'd collided with a mountain.

While Blue groaned and clutched his bleeding nose, Rook tied a quick noose and looped it over the redcap's head. He pulled it snug, then coiled the rest of the rope over his shoulder.

"How's a twisted-up wreck like you going to help us?" asked Tipple.

Blue climbed to his feet. His eyes went round as plates. "Magic."

"*You* can do magic?" Tipple folded his arms.

"Very strong Will," Blue snapped. In his enthusiasm for killing, he seemed to have forgotten to rhyme. Rook hoped that lapse continued.

Tipple sniffed. "Very strong stench is more like it."

"Watch, watch." Blue tugged what looked like an old finger bone from beneath the rags of his shirt.

Rook tensed, and even Inga readied her weapon, but the redcap didn't act like he was trying to fight or escape. He seemed excited, bouncing in place and muttering as he gripped the old finger in both hands.

Blue closed his eyes. His forehead wrinkled like a prune. A rotted prune, one that had sat in the mud for three days in the hot sun. Veins bulged beneath his skin, and his muscles trembled.

"Will, Will, can't sit still." Blue rocked faster and faster, his body taut with concentration. Rook rested his finger on the trigger of his weapon. This crossbow was as much a wife to him as any woman could be, and he knew precisely how far he could squeeze her trigger before she spat death from her maw. He brought the trigger to that razor-thin edge, until the slightest twitch would send a series of bolts into Blue's throat. Any hint of attack, and Blue would be dead before he could blink.

Leech, Inga, and Tipple leaned closer. Blue raised the bony finger towards the ceiling. "Here it comes, ugly humans!"

At the end of Blue's pronouncement, a thunderous fart echoed through the tunnel. Blue toppled forwards, as if the force of the expulsion had flung him to the ground. The others staggered back.

Rook kept Blue in his sights, which was difficult, given how badly his eyes were watering. By the old king's ghost, he could *taste* the foulness in the air. "*That* was your 'magic'?"

Blue's eyes were wide, like he was just as surprised as anyone. He sniffed the air. "Nope." He glared at the dead finger, then shoved it back into his shirt. "*That* was bad seagull."

"It smells like a corpse crawled out of his arse," Tipple wheezed.

Blue twisted about, snatching at the seat of his trousers as if to reassure himself that they remained corpse-free.

"We should—" Inga coughed and rubbed her face. "The quicker we escape these tunnels, the sooner we can bring the rest of these outlaws to justice."

"Yes!" Blue whirled and grabbed the rope trailing from his noose. He tugged hard, trying to drag Rook along. His apparent terror from before had vanished like it never existed. "Kill the outlaws. Blue knows where."

"You'll take us there?" Leech asked.

Rook scowled, but for the life of him, he couldn't tell whether or not Leech had made the rhyme intentionally.

Blue nodded so hard, his cap would have flopped off if not for the nails holding it in place. "This way, Heroes."

Rook doubted anyone else saw the way the redcap's eyes narrowed, or the crafty smile that peeled his lips back. The expression vanished an instant later, washed away by madness and mania.

Rook tightened his grip on the rope and followed.

chapter 3

LEECH

They left the outlaws' lair far too soon for Leech's liking. Surely the fall of Brightlodge would wait while he completed a quick dissection or two, or at least long enough for him to cut out a few organs for later study.

He'd barely had time to collect one of the nails from a redcap skull. It looked similar to the ones protruding from Blue's cap: about the length of Leech's index finger, iron with a square head.

When they emerged into the sunlight, Blue stopped abruptly to gather the discarded seagull bones he had left at the entrance. Curious, Leech reached out and tugged the nail jutting from the back of his skull.

Blue screeched and flung the bones at Leech's face.

"Sorry," said Leech. "Did that hurt?"

Rook gave the rope a warning pull. Blue tugged at his noose with one finger and scowled at Leech.

"How'd you get the nails in?" Leech continued. "Did you hammer them yourself, or did another redcap do it? Did they drill guide holes to keep the skull from cracking?"

Leech had examined redcaps before, and there was no logic or consistency to how they secured their headgear. One redcap might have a single oversized nail straight through the centre of the skull, while a more recent specimen he'd dissected had a head like a metal porcupine. In life, the weight of those nails had dragged that redcap's head down, giving him a tendency to run in erratic circles.

"Aw, don't tell me you've never wondered," Leech said. "Like the wise man said, 'Knowledge is half the battle.'"

"The way I learned it," said Tipple, "this here is half the battle." He tightened his right hand into a fist.

"Yes, but the other half—," Leech began.

"Is over here." Tipple clenched his left hand and grinned.

Leech sighed. "I met a man who took an arrow through the head and lived. Scrambled his brain like an egg. He started repeating whatever folks said, cursing up a storm. Forgot half his life, including his own wife, though I think he might've been faking that last bit." He pointed to Blue. "Makes you wonder how much of what makes a redcap comes from those nails, hey?"

None of which explained why someone would bother to drain the redcaps of their blood. Or where the rest of the blood had gone. "They must've killed 'em somewhere else."

"Who?" asked Inga.

"The redcaps. It'd explain the lack of blood. But why bother dragging the bodies back through the tunnels?"

"To keep them from being discovered," suggested Rook.

"Maybe." Leech rubbed his arms, absently trying to restore warmth to the flesh as he walked. It was always like this after he manipulated the lives of others. His power was unlike those of other Heroes. They attacked the body from the outside. Leech reached past the flesh and pulled the very life from its core.

Taking an outlaw's essence and using it to heal Rook had been simple enough. Leech was simply the river through which that energy flowed. What worried him was the fact that, over time, every riverbed began to erode.

It was a shame the dead king had run off before the fight. It would be interesting to see how Leech's ability interacted with a ghost.

A shout yanked his attention back to his surroundings. They had reached the bridge to Hightown. Men and women shied back from the redcap, pointing and crying out.

Blue loved the attention. He grew wilder, leering and laughing and flinging his remaining seagull bones in every direction, until he looked to be in danger of toppling over the side of the bridge and plummeting into the water below.

A young girl threw a rock, striking Blue in the forehead. He shook like a wet dog, then laughed and charged. He had gone only three steps when the noose went taut around his neck. He toppled over backwards, and there was a sharp clink as the nails in his head struck the steps. He rolled about, clawing at his throat for air.

"There's nothing to fear," Inga called, her words booming out over the crowd. "Blue is trussed up good and tight. He's no danger to any of you."

"Sure he is," said Leech. "The fact that he's tied up doesn't change that. It just prevents him from killing anyone until he can escape, that's all."

Inga glared at him.

"Sorry." That seemed to satisfy her. "If you think about it, people are just as dangerous. They say redcaps started out human. We've all got the potential for their savagery. Makes you wonder whether redcaps retain the potential for humanity."

Leech turned to look at Blue, who had climbed onto the side of the bridge and was getting ready to piss over the edge. Rook yanked him down, fortunately for everyone on the boat passing below.

The crowd grew as they reached the top of the stairs and entered Hightown proper. Shops ringed the plaza. Merchants shouted over one another, competing for the attention—and more important, the money—of potential customers. Weapons and clothing, food and potions, exotic hairstyles, everything was available for the right price.

Leech's body tensed. He had never appreciated crowds, and the assault of colours and noise and smells made him twitchy. He straightened his spine and deliberately stilled his hands. A handful of other people were like campfires scattered across the landscape; this was a kaleidoscope of multicoloured bonfires, bright and overwhelming and threatening to break into a forest fire. His muscles pulsed with the itch, the *need,* to move and respond.

Blue darted towards a hat shop. Rook pulled him up short, but not before a man with a walking staff broke away from the crowd. "Is that the monster that's been stirring up so much mischief?"

"The Heroes have brought him back for justice!" called a woman.

"Someone get the feathers and hot tar!"

"We're all out of tar."

"My brother has some syrup. Would that work?"

"What kind?"

"Treacle. Fresh, too!"

"Right," said the man with the walking staff. "We'll treacle and feather the redcap!"

Inga positioned herself between Blue and the crowd. "The redcap stays with us until we've finished our quest and saved Brightlodge."

"Saved it from what?"

"We . . . well, we're not really clear on that part yet," Inga admitted.

"What about my pigs?" That was the man whose pig they had stopped earlier.

"And my fruit cart?"

"And my pub?"

While Inga tried to calm the crowd, Leech saw the man with the walking staff hobbling sideways, out of her line of vision. He raised his staff and lunged towards Blue.

Leech stepped in and kicked him in the side of the knee. The man went down hard. His staff clattered away. He looked up to find himself face-to-face with Blue. His eyes widened and his face paled—typical panic response. Before he could recover, Blue sank his teeth into the man's arm.

"None of that," Rook said sharply, giving the rope another tug.

The man waved his bloody arm in Leech's face. "The thing bit me!"

"He sure did. You'll want to get a bandage on that." Leech grabbed the man's arm and pressed his fingers to the edge of the wound. Bright blood welled and dripped to the ground. "Redcaps aren't venomous, but any bite wound can be nasty. When this gets red and swollen, use a hot blade to drain the pus. If dark streaks begin to spread, I'll be happy to amputate it for you."

"You . . . you'll what?"

"It's a simple enough procedure. We could do it now if you'd like. You start by tying a tourniquet just above the wound. Cut through the skin and muscle, then saw through the bones. Stitching up the skin flaps afterwards can be tricky. The secret is to peel back some extra skin before you do the bone. Took me a few tries to figure out that trick. When it heals, you should have enough of a stump for a hook."

Inga gently tugged Leech back. "It's little more than a scratch," she said. "I've had worse roughing around with the youngsters back home. Spill a bit of the good wine over the cut, keep it bandaged, and you'll be good as new in no time."

"There's a lot to be said for a good hook," Leech called. "Durability, grip strength . . . if you change your mind about that amputation, you can find me at Wendleglass Hall!"

"We're in a hurry here," said Tipple.

"Right." Inga raised her voice. "The redcap is in our care. You'll leave him alone, or I'll knock your block off, got it?"

The crowd fell back. There was no further talk of punishment or syrup and feathers. They gave Leech a particularly wide berth.

Blue laughed and leered as they walked.

"Do you think redcaps and people could interbreed?" Leech mused.

"I don't know what you're thinking," said Inga, "but count me out."

"Oh, no. I didn't mean—I just think they have more in common with us than we realise."

"He set a man on fire," Tipple pointed out.

"For revenge," said Leech. "What's more human than that?"

"Thin man with the ugly mask is nice," Blue announced, swivelling his head to look at Leech. "Blue will eat you last."

Tipple burst out laughing.

Leech ignored him and turned his attention to the redcap. He had never been good at casual conversation, but he was determined to show them the possibilities. "Condolences on your dead friends back there."

Blue shrugged and scratched absently at his crotch.

Leech searched for another approach. "You know, biting a man on the outer forearm like you did back there isn't the best way to go."

Blue's eyebrows rose.

"You'll get more bleeding from the inside of the forearm." He pushed up his sleeve and traced the veins that stood out on his pale skin. Blue crept closer, suddenly attentive. "The inner arm's more sensitive to pain as well."

Blue nodded hard. He examined his own arm, then touched a finger to his teeth. "Need to sharpen them. Sharp as steel. Make them squeal!"

"Not a good idea," Leech said. "Let me tell you about this one fellow, a minor merchant. Not the brightest coin in the bank. He refused to let me extract a broken tooth. Three months later, half his mouth had rotted. It was fascinating to watch, and one of the most foul-smelling things I've ever come across. He died shortly thereafter. All from a chipped tooth."

Blue's shoulders slumped, momentarily transforming him from a bloodthirsty killer to a disappointed child.

"How long did the outlaws have your friends captive?" Leech asked.

"Never. Forever." Blue adjusted his trousers. "Always, always throats to sever."

"First redcap I've seen with a flair for the poetic," said Tipple.

"Any chance you could end that flair?" asked Rook.

"Depends on the cause." Leech studied the redcap's skull. "The rhyming might be part of his personality, like Tipple's drinking or your scowling. It could also be a response to stress, or an effect of those nails. He's far more intelligible than most redcaps. Adding or removing nails in just the right location might let us change his patterns of speech. There's no guarantee it would be an improvement, though. More likely, it'd make him worse."

"Forget I asked."

The wind was rambunctious today, carrying the spray of the falls like horizontal rain as they crossed the bridge leading out of town. Leech peered over the rail. He had no fear of heights, but he respected the water's power. He had seen the bodies of the drowned, their lungs bloated, their skin pale and wrinkled. Not to mention the waterfall itself. From time to time, someone would take a boat too close to the edge and get caught up in the current. The bodies were rarely recovered. Which was a shame, as Leech would have loved to study the damage inflicted by such a fall.

"What do these scoundrels have planned for Brightlodge?" asked Inga. "Do you know why they were stealing redcaps, or how they mean to destroy the town?"

Blue didn't answer. He tugged at his rope, keeping to the centre of the wide bridge and disrupting traffic in both directions.

"Do you even know where to find Nimble John?" demanded Rook.

Blue smirked. "John be nimble, John be smart. John, who stinks like herring farts."

Rook pulled the redcap close. "If you're wasting our time . . ."

"Quiet, stupid humans," yelled Blue, apparently uncaring of his own volume. "They'll hear you from their boat. Kill you all."

Leech lowered his voice. "You're leading us to a boat?"

"Big boat." Blue chuckled. "Full of ale and hats and rats."

"How many crewmen?" asked Rook.

"Lots."

Leech nodded. "Good."

Tipple stared at him, an odd expression wrinkling his brow and tightening the corners of his eyes. "That's good how, exactly?"

"It's obvious, isn't it? It's one thing to beat a weaker force, but once we start crushing a larger group, their morale will shatter like old bones." Leech shrugged. "Should make it easy to get the truth out of the survivors."

Blue led them several miles upriver to a spot just south of the Boggins. The ground squished underfoot, and the air smelled of decaying vegetation. Insects buzzed about their heads.

Leech wiped moisture from the lenses of his mask. It was a shame they were in such a hurry. Hopefully he'd have time to collect some frogs and leeches on the way back. He was starting to run low on a few species.

The redcap pointed through a curtain of reeds to a large wooden riverboat anchored on the far side of the water. At first glance, there was nothing unusual about the boat. Flat and wide, it sat relatively low in the water, suggesting a full hold. Faded paint on the side traced the outline of either a snake or a dragon, but too much had peeled and flaked away to be certain. Leech guessed the boat could carry a crew of twenty-some, with room for cargo. A peaked roof covered much of the deck, providing shelter from sun and rain. A series of rusted metal oarlocks were secured to the lower railing. Crates and barrels were stacked and tied down near the aft.

"She's seen some action," said Rook.

As he peered closer, Leech began to make out signs of battle. The side bore numerous scars that looked to have been made by axes or hatchets. More telling was the row of faded red caps nailed to the roof, possibly as warnings. Leech counted nineteen such trophies.

Blue turned large, hopeful eyes towards his captors. "Kill them now?"

"Only if we have to," said Inga. "My parents raised me to be a Hero, not an executioner."

Blue stomped his foot and spat. "Stupid parents."

"We don't even know if anyone's home," Tipple pointed out.

"They're here." Leech stared at the boat, feeling the faint tug of the lives moving about belowdeck. He shivered, trying to quell the shadow stirring inside him. There were times when his power left him feeling stained, like his blood had been replaced by cold and darkness, though there was no physical change. He'd taken enough samples of his own blood to be sure.

"You and Rook stay here," said Inga. "Tipple and I will swim out and board the boat. Keep an eye on Blue and give us cover if we need it."

Rook pointed to the dark, narrow windows about a foot above the waterline. "They'd be fools to not have someone on watch." He tied Blue's leash to a nearby tree and began checking his weapon.

Tipple removed his pack and kicked off his boots, then waded barefoot into the water. "I'll be yanking leeches off my skin for the rest of the night," he grumbled.

"Oh, good!" said Leech. "Save them for me, please?"

Inga strode after him, armour and all. By all logic and reason, she should have drowned immediately, but her shield appeared to float, despite its size and weight. Inga used it as a makeshift raft, paddling with her free hand and kicking towards the boat.

They were halfway across when the first outlaw popped up with a short bow and arrow. Rook shot first, catching the outlaw in the throat.

"That was a lovely shot," commented Leech. "He'll be dead in less than a minute. Faster if you hit the carotid."

A second outlaw followed. This one ducked behind a low crate and managed to put an arrow into Inga's arm.

Leech looked at the crouching archer, at the fragile life flowing through her skin and bones. He had never found words to describe the perception, a blend of sight, smell, and taste. Colour seemed to drain from the world, the green of the ferns and reeds fading to grey, the paint on the boat turning the colour of ash. Everything dulled save his target. Her form shone like a lantern at midnight. The sweat on her face, the quickness of her breath, the drumbeat of her heart. The human body was little more than a complicated puppet.

Leech cast his Will like a fishing line, lodging a hook through the woman's life and pulling until it tore. He directed her strength and health towards Inga. The arrow remained lodged in Inga's arm, but the bleeding slowed as the flesh healed around it. The archer dropped her bow and fell backwards, her strings cut.

"Thanks, Leech," called Inga.

"Bloody hell," Tipple shouted. "I think a fish just crawled up my breeches!"

Two more outlaws joined their companions on deck.

"I've got the ugly one," said Rook.

"Can you be more specific?" asked Leech.

A spray of bolts from Rook's crossbow cleared up Leech's confusion. He weakened the second outlaw, then Inga and Tipple were at the boat. Tipple simply reached up to grab the rail and hauled back hard, tilting the craft just enough to ruin the outlaws' balance, while Inga pulled herself one-handed onto the deck. "All right," she said, "like Old Nanny Smith used to say, we can do this the easy way or the bloody painful way."

This had been the riskiest part of the attack. Now that Inga and Tipple were on board and able to fight back, they should be more than a match for the remaining outlaws.

Behind Leech, Blue began to laugh. He pointed at the caps nailed to the boat. "Humans' turn to die now."

Leech sat on a half-rotted stump, his attention never wavering from the boat. Everything was going smoothly so far. Blue had led them to the outlaws, and from the sound of things, Inga and Tipple were laying waste to the boat and her crew alike. It made him nervous. There was no way this band of outlaws could have brought about the doom of Brightlodge, at least not on their own. If the seer's prediction was right, the true threat was still out there, waiting.

On the bright side, he'd soon have plenty of bodies to study.

chapter 4

TIPPLE

Inga would have done well on the tavern brawling circuit. She was a fine figure of a woman. Strong as an ox to boot. It'd been years since Jeremiah Tipple met anyone, man or woman, who could go toe-to-toe with him for more than a single round, but Inga was tough enough to give him a run for his money. If she'd been a few years older, or he a few years younger, he'd have tried to find out if they were a match in other ways.

"On your left," Inga shouted.

Tipple spun. Something smashed into his back, between the shoulder blades.

"I said *left*!"

He roared and spun around, backfisting the fellow behind him. "Come 'ere, you!" He followed up with a haymaker that knocked the man arse over ankles into the river. "Right. Now who's next?"

"That's everyone on deck," said Inga. "I hear the others scuttling about below."

They moved towards the trapdoor in the centre of the deck. Inga positioned herself to one side and nodded. Tipple gripped the metal ring with one hand and yanked the trapdoor open so hard the hinges bent. An arrow flew up from the darkness to splinter against Inga's shield.

"Oh, so that's how it is?" Tipple's blood pounded like a drum, and red edged his vision. A fair fight was one thing, but trying to shoot a man—or a woman—while cowering in the shadows? He searched the deck for large, heavy things, eventually settling on one of the overturned crates. He hefted it overhead and returned to the hatch. "Which one of you rat-faced, pox-sacked, flea-scabbed cowards took that shot?"

He heard the creak of a bow being drawn. He smashed the crate down with a roar. A cry of pain told him he had hit his target.

"Watch the shore," Leech shouted from the far shore.

Tipple stepped back from the hatch. The deck was clear, but something was moving in the trees beside the boat. Branches rustled, and he glimpsed a flash of red. He tromped to the starboard side of the deck as the first wave of redcaps leaped from the treetops. One landed heavily on the roof. Another struck the edge and toppled back onto the rocky, root-gnarled beach.

"That's more like it!" It wasn't a real brawl until the bystanders started jumping in from the sidelines. In true tavern-fighting tradition, he had no idea whether these redcaps were here to kill him and Inga or if they were out for revenge against the surviving outlaws. Keeping with that same tradition, he didn't particularly care. "Come on! Who else wants to fight?"

Tipple ducked behind a stack of crates as a rain of rocks, bones, and other missiles flew at the boat. No wonder most of the outlaws stayed below, where the redcaps couldn't pelt them from the trees.

"I've got this lot, Ingadinger," he shouted. "Go crack some heads down below."

He ripped open the closest crate, which was branded with what looked like a dead cow. A broad grin spread across his face at the sight of the bottles and jugs packed neatly inside the straw-padded crate.

"Ha! The universe rewards a good man." He pulled out a pair of bottles, bit the cork from one, spat it over the side, and took a drink. His smile faded. "Pah. What kind of reward is this? The label says ale, not this . . . fermented horse piss."

A pale, filthy head peeked upside down from the edge of the roof. Tipple smashed the first bottle against the side of the redcap's head. He set the second bottle down for later. Horse piss or not, there was no sense in wasting the stuff.

He ducked another barrage from the trees and listened to the sounds from the roof, trying to guess where the next one would pop out. The clumsy footfalls combined with the endless chatter made the redcaps easy to track.

"Mind the water, lads!"

"Gi' him a knife right in the lug!"

"Shut yer gobs. We're *sneaking*!"

"Wait, wot? I thought we were goin' fer supper. Ye promised me pudding!"

Tipple picked up a jug of what looked to be mead, waited for the closest of the voices to reach the edge, then leaned out to toss the jug up to the redcap. The creature reacted instinctively, dropping its weapon and catching the jug . . . which overbalanced it and sent it toppling headfirst into the water.

Tipple scooped up an oar and snapped it over his leg as more redcaps landed on the roof. There was an angry shriek, and one fell off the roof, a handful of bolts from Rook's crossbow peppering its chest and face. Another jumped onto the deck, and Tipple clubbed him on the side of the head.

The redcaps were getting smarter, sticking to the starboard side of the peaked roof as cover against Rook and his crossbow. Others jumped directly from the trees to the rail, scrambling onto the boat faster than Tipple could knock them down.

He cocked an ear towards the ladder that led into the darkness below. The sound of steel hitting shield and shield hitting flesh told him Inga had matters under control. "You almost finished down there?"

"Like Old Mother Twostraps used to say, you can do a job quick, or you can do it well!"

"Wait, whose mother did what now?" Another redcap slammed into Tipple's side, trying to knock him down. He clubbed the creature on the back, tossed the broken oar aside, seized the redcap by the waist and collar, and hurled it at one of its companions.

He took out two more before murderous laughter alerted him to the trio who had sneaked in behind him. Instead of attacking, they crowded around an open crate. One had broken open a tinderbox and lit a length of what looked like hand-spun cotton. They were dipping the makeshift fuse into a jar of what looked like lamp oil.

"Oh, balls."

"Drink this, ye keech-faced stechie!" Cackling with delight, the closest redcap lifted the jar with both hands to hurl it at Tipple.

Tipple was quicker. He snatched up the broken oar and threw. The jar shattered in the redcap's hands, splashing its contents over him and the deck. Yellow-blue flame spread with a *whoosh*. The redcap shrieked and leaped into the river, his fear of the water overpowered by having accidentally set himself on fire. His partner whooped and smashed a second jar into the flames before following. The others fled as well, laughing at the misfortune of their fellow.

Tipple tried to stomp out the fire, and when that failed he ripped open one of the remaining crates and hurled jugs of ale at the flames. Even good ale didn't have enough alcohol to burn, and this stuff was anything but good. But the fire was spreading too quickly.

He cursed and returned to the hatch. "Last call!"

"I've got a bit of a snag down here, and—is that smoke? Jeremiah Tipple, did you set the bloody boat on fire?"

"Not all of it." Not yet, anyway. The fire had spread over a quarter of the deck, and was climbing the posts to the roof. The redcaps had all retreated, though. That was the silver lining in this bucket of puke.

From below came the crack of breaking wood—or possibly bone—and an unfamiliar shout of pain.

"All right, let's get this over with." Teeth clenched, he jumped through the hatch into the belly of the boat.

Even a normal-sized man would have had to crouch to avoid striking his head against the thick, square-cut beams below deck, and Jeremiah Tipple hadn't been normal-sized since age nine. He felt like a dog chasing rats through their nest. How Inga had managed to manoeuvre both herself and her shield down here was beyond him. Hunching his head and shoulders, he squeezed past barrels, hammocks, rope, and the bodies of both humans and redcaps.

Inga stood towards the bow, where a single lantern hung from a metal hook. She had squared off against the skinniest man Tipple had ever seen. The light reflected from his sweaty face and from the small, curved sword he pointed towards Inga. Behind him, a woman lay crumpled against the wall, a chain around her neck.

"Oi! Tell me the next time you have a party!" Smoke curled around the edges of the hatch, wisps spilling in after them. He could see firelight through the cracks overhead. Sparks dripped like dust between the deck boards. "Who's the bird?"

"Ask Nimble John here," said Inga.

"That's Nimble John?" Tipple smothered a cough. "Aw, he's no masterman—no mistermind—He's no Outlaw King."

"I am so!" It would have been more convincing had his voice not cracked. "You think a man needs to be a lumbering ox like you to command respect? Brute force is nothing against my cleverness."

"Put that pigsticker down before you hurt yourself," said Inga. "Whatever trouble you're mixed up in, there's no point dying over it."

One semiconscious crewman groaned and reached for a belaying pin. Tipple absently kicked it out of reach, then seized the man's collar and tossed him into a barrel full of pickles.

"I'm not afraid of you," said Nimble John, his defiance undermined only by the quavering of his blade.

"Then you've got the brains of a turnip," Tipple roared.

"You'll never take me alive!" He thrust his sword at Inga, who knocked it out of the way with her shield. She hadn't even bothered to draw her own sword. Instead, she simply clocked the man in the jaw, knocking him onto his backside.

"Be careful!" cried the girl behind him. She cowered against the wall, pulling a ragged blanket around herself. "He's trying to make you underestimate him. It's how he defeated my bodyguards and murdered my husband."

One of the crossbeams cracked, and sparks showered them all. Tipple kicked the side of the pickle barrel. Brackish green water spilled out, extinguishing the embers on the floor. The outlaw he had stuffed into the barrel gasped for breath.

Tipple glared at the man. "Even if you're as good as the girl says, you're no match for the two of us. So drop the damn sword and tell us about the fall of Brightlodge and whatever it is you're smuggling . . ." He coughed, then scowled. "Wait, what was I saying?"

Inga stepped back and lowered her stance. "You're right."

"Great. About what?" Tipple stepped back as the power of Inga's shield stirred. The front of the shield had been carved to suggest the visage of a man. As Inga braced herself, the face blinked and looked about, first at Nimble John, then at his prisoner. A spectral double of the shield swelled forth like an expanding bubble.

"What are you doing?" cried the girl.

At the last moment, Inga turned to face the girl. The shield's shell of force broke free and sped forth to slam into the girl, flinging her against the hull like she'd been thrown by a giant.

Nimble John looked on uncertainly. He looked like an animal waiting for the trap to spring shut and snap his neck.

The girl's angry shout held none of the fear she had shown before. Inga seized the man's wrist, twisted the sword from his hand, and hurled him towards Tipple. By the time she spun back around, the girl had recovered enough to point a small crossbow at Inga's chest. Her chains fell away into the water beginning to lap at their feet. Whatever Inga had done had damaged the boat as well as the girl, and the river was seeping through cracks in the hull.

"You can't change a sheep into a wolf." Inga coughed, but the sword in her hand never wavered. "Not even with a crossbow hidden away and pointed at his back. That's how you forced him to square off against us, hoping we'd kill him and 'rescue' you. Isn't that right, Nimble John?"

The girl snorted. "Johanna, if you don't mind. And you should know that the poison on this crossbow bolt is enough to bring down even a Hero. So if you don't want to die screaming in agony, you'll step aside and let me out of here."

Tipple covered his head as another board gave way overhead. He moved closer, but the crossbow whipped around to point at his face. "Shoot me, Inga runs you through. Shoot her, I stuff you into the nearest porthole. Shoot me, and Inga will—"

"She gets the idea," said Inga.

"No one has ever captured Nimble Johanna. No one ever will."

"Fair enough." Tipple studied at the floor. With a crooked smile, he raised his hands higher, as if in surrender. Johanna brought the crossbow back towards Inga.

Tipple pressed his palms to the hot ceiling, braced himself, and stomped his right foot hard, directly where the floorboard ended. The other end of the board ripped free to strike the underside of Nimble Johanna's arm. Her shot went wide and thumped into the far side of the ship.

Inga jumped forwards, shoving her shield into the outlaw and the outlaw into the wall. She slammed the shield twice more, until Johanna's protests changed to groans and she slumped to the floor. Inga's boot crushed the crossbow to splinters.

"Thank you." The man's skin was pale, and he was shaking. "They ambushed me by the river. I was—"

"Run now, talk later." Tipple started towards the hatch, his boots splashing through the water. He reached the ladder, then jumped away as a section of the burning roof crashed down, blotting out the daylight. More smoke flowed in, burning his lungs. "Hell. Never thought I'd die like this."

"Trapped in a burning riverboat?" asked the man.

Tipple shook his head. "Sober."

The heat was like a living thing now, a wall battering him from all directions. He covered his mouth and nose with his sleeve, but it made little difference. It was like he was trapped in a forge.

"Get behind me." Inga's words were hoarse and strained. She wedged her shield up above her head. "Bulwark will protect us from the flames."

The man mouthed, *Bulwark?*

Tipple ignored him. The shield's magic swelled outward again, pressing the flames and the boards back, but it couldn't clear a path for their escape. The question was would the smoke choke them to death before the fire barbecued them. Given the choice, he was hoping for the smoke.

Tipple rubbed his eyes and stared at the thin sprays of water coming through the hull. "New plan." He coughed again. "Get outta the way."

"What are you doing?" asked Inga.

"There's an old saying. 'Better hungover than hanged.'"

They both stared at him. "What's that supposed to mean?" asked Inga.

"Don't ask me. Just seemed like something to say." He held his breath, lowered his head and shoulder, and charged.

Tipple awoke to the smell of smoke and mint, and a dull throbbing in his right shoulder. That was odd. Usually when he woke, the pain and pounding were in his head. His stomach wasn't happy with him either, but he'd grown accustomed to that over the years.

He cracked open one dry eye, then the other, and found Leech standing over him, the tip of his mask so close Tipple went cross-eyed trying to focus on it. Inga and Rook were here as well, along with that blasted redcap.

"What happened?" His voice was little more than a hoarse croak.

"You sank ship!" Blue crowed.

"With your face," added Inga. She sounded as bad as Tipple. Her skin was blistered, her clothes blackened, and she had lost a bit of hair. "You're lucky you cracked the hull instead of your skull."

"It worked, didn't it? Besides, you and Bulwark weakened it for me." The bed creaked in protest as he sat up. "Last time I was in bed with this many people staring at me, it was a much better party." He glanced beneath the sheets. Someone had taken his jerkin and sandals, but he still had his trousers. Definitely not as good as that other party. "How'd I get back to . . . wait, where are we?"

"The Cock and Bard," said Leech.

Tipple grunted. "I thought I recognised that smell."

"I dragged you to shore, and then we used Bulwark as a sled to haul you to town like a side of beef." Inga didn't sound happy about that.

"Right, right. What about the ale I tossed off the ship?" No one answered. Tipple groaned. "The blasted redcaps have probably made off with it by now. What a waste."

"I couldn't get Johanna out," Inga said. "I damn near drowned trying to make sure you and Sam escaped that bonfire with your hides intact."

Tipple blinked. "Who's Sam?"

"Johanna's prisoner." Inga sighed. "The one you and I rescued? Thin as a broomstick. Remember?"

"He's resting in the next room," added Leech. "He's half-starved, burnt, and still coughing from the smoke. He swallowed a fair bit of river water. I could have that out as quick as you'd like if I drilled a hole into his lungs to drain—"

"No," Rook said flatly.

"Smuggled alcohol and dead redcaps." Tipple looked at his fellow Heroes. "What's all that got to do with the fall of Brightlodge?"

"We don't know yet," said Leech. "Young King Wendleglass is in talking to Sam now."

"The poor fellow needs his rest," Inga added with a frown. "Rest and a good draught of mustard tea, strong as snakebites, just like Granny Duckworth used to make for kids with the sniffles."

"Pah. What kind of medicine is that?" Tipple stood and cautiously stretched his arms. His head and shoulder didn't hurt as much as he'd expected. Leech must have been busy putting his insides in order. Tipple grabbed his jerkin from the floor and squeezed into the still-damp leather. His sandals were stiff and covered in muck. He clapped them together a few times, then jammed them onto his feet. He got halfway to the door, then stopped to turn around. "Wait, where was I going?"

"To interrogate Sam," said Rook.

"Right." He swung open the door and stomped into the hall. "And who's that, again?"

Blue shook his head. In addition to the rope around his neck, someone had bound his wrists in front of him. "Dumb as a bum full of rum."

"Keep it up, redcap, and you'll find out why they call me the

Haymaker. I'll rip that stupid cap off your head and feed it to you. Got it?"

Blue nodded sharply.

"Right. Now, someone point me towards this Sam fellow."

Sam yelped in surprise when Tipple and the others barged through the door. He was sitting in bed, knees hugged to his chest, with a blanket wrapped around his shoulders. Young Wendleglass sat on a chair at the foot of the bed.

"Ah, there you are." Wendleglass looked Tipple up and down, and his nose wrinkled. "You smell of smoke and pickles."

Tipple sniffed his jerkin. "Yep."

"Have you learned anything from Sam?" asked Rook.

"Oh, we've had a lovely chat," said Wendleglass. "Sam was telling me about the ducks that live by his home. They have the most peculiar cry, like rusty hinges."

Rook's expression didn't change. "Have you learned anything about Nimble Johanna or the threat to Brightlodge?"

"Oh, yes. I mean, no. That is, um, he hasn't said anything—not about that. Not that I asked, really." Wendleglass looked down at Sam. "Do you know anything about Nimble John—Johanna—or our impending doom?"

Sam pulled himself tighter. "It was like a nightmare."

"Nightmares are for people who can't cope with the real world," said Tipple. "And by cope, I mean starting a tab. Sam, isn't it?"

"That's right, sir."

In the sunlight streaming through the window, Sam was . . . well, just as unimpressive as he'd looked back in the outlaws' boat. Young, skinny, and filthy, not to mention bruised as an apple that bounced down a mountainside, but otherwise intact.

Tipple yanked the blanket away. "Come with us, Sammy. The last thing we need is peace and quiet after everything we've been through today."

He escorted Sam down the stairs and into the pub, drawing the others in his wake. He sat down at the bar and guided Sam onto the stool next to him. Normally Lester Mead manned the bar, but today it was Nelly Flagon herself serving up drinks. "Nelly! Your finest for me and my friends, to celebrate our victory over Nimble John's outlaws."

"Anything for you, Jeremiah Tipple." Nelly Flagon crossed her arms and leaned forwards. She snapped her fingers, yanking Tipple's attention back to her eyes. "S'long as you pay up front."

Tipple brought a hand to his chest, trying to convey how deeply wounded he was by such unwarranted distrust. "I'm sure my friend Leech will be more than happy to cover the tab." He glanced at Leech. "As a fine healer and surgeon, your purse must be overflowing with coin. What better way to support the struggling entrepen—enterpruners—the struggling business people of Brightlodge who lost so much to Nimble John's villainy?"

Leech sighed and dropped several coins onto the bar.

"Surgeon, eh?" asked Nelly. "I appreciate a man who's good with his hands."

Tipple laughed and clapped Leech on the shoulder, then turned his attention to Sam. For the next hour, he did his best to loosen the man up. Tipple regaled him with stories of brawls that had left not a single piece of furniture intact, and of the glorious bouts at the old village bars where Tipple had first begun boxing for money. "Trouble was, it was a small village, and all too soon I ran out of people to fight. No bouts meant no money. No money meant it was time to move on. Fortunately, I ended up in Brightlodge. The Hero business isn't much rougher than tavern brawling, and the payoff's better. Usually."

He raised his mug in a toast and waited for Sam to follow suit. "Come on, Sammy my boy. Drink cleanses the soul as well as the palate." He drank several swallows, wiped his lips, and added, "Of course, some stains are harder to get out . . ."

"Thank you." Sam gestured at the drink. "For this, and for saving me."

"He finally found his tongue!" Tipple wrapped his arm around Sam's shoulders and gave him a friendly squeeze. "Where are you from, and how did you end up in that den of filth?"

"Grayrock, but I'm not going back there." Sam took his mug in both hands and stared into it like he was trying to see the future. Or the past. He shuddered and shook his head. "The smell reminds me of the boat."

"That's an insult to this fine establishment. Nimble Johanna was loaded down with third-rate swill. Nelly here serves only second-rate stuff."

"How did they catch you, Sam?" asked Inga. "What did they want redcaps for?"

"I don't know about any redcaps, ma'am. Johanna kept those monsters tied up, then one day she just killed them. Cut their throats, as cold as she was butchering cattle. I didn't ask questions. I was afraid she'd do the same to me. As for how they got their hands on me . . ." He flushed. "I was . . . chasing a lady."

"Ha!" Tipple pounded him on the back hard enough to make him spill most of his drink. "You're far from the first to follow that path to ruin. Who was she? Not Nimble Johanna?"

"No, not Johanna." Sam's cheeks were red, from drink or embarrassment or both. "Nobody knows who she is. They call her the Ghost of Grayrock."

"A ghost?" Wendleglass perked up. "I've learned a thing or two about ghosts, since my father's . . . um . . . return."

"I don't know about her being a ghost, but her money's real enough," said Sam. "She's the one who hired Nimble Johanna. I never overheard exactly what she wanted, but Johanna was scared of her. Lots of people were. Men who crossed the ghost's path tended to disappear."

"And yet you sought her out?" asked Rook.

Sam turned a deeper shade of red. "Well, they say she's very beautiful."

Inga rolled her eyes.

"I found her at the docks," Sam continued. "Cloaked in smoke and fog. I crept closer, but that's when Johanna's men spotted me."

"You walked right into the outlaws' hands," said Tipple.

"That's right. They said they meant to ransom me. If my parents couldn't pay, they'd put me to work as one of their crew."

Tipple was only half listening. Johanna had been parked on the river with a boat full of ale and dead redcaps. She'd sent a handful of her people ahead into Brightlodge, along with three more dead or soon-to-be-dead redcaps. On a hunch, he leaned over the bar and searched the shelves. "Hey, Nelly! How about another drink of that dead-cow ale?"

"Can't get enough of my foaming jugs, can you?" Nelly winked and brought a new mug to the bar. "There you go, love."

"Dead cow?" Inga covered Tipple's mug with one hand. Had he been in a fouler mood, that would have earned her a good uppercut right there. Inga leaned forwards. "Where did you get that keg?"

"Came in just last week."

"The crates on Nimble Johanna's ship had the same mark," said Inga.

"What is it?" asked Wendleglass.

"Horse piss, best I can tell." Tipple belched. "I sampled some of Johanna's stock during the fighting."

"You were supposed to be keeping redcaps off my back," said Inga.

"A man can do two things at once." Tipple tugged his mug free and sniffed. Anger clouded his vision. "Hey, that's right. Where's the good stuff? Why are Sam and I sitting here drinking horse piss?" He took another sniff, then hurled the mug across the room. "Horse piss gone bad!"

"Bad how?" asked Inga.

"If there's one thing I know, it's alcohol. Alcohol and brawling. Right, that's two things. The point is, this stuff is tainted somehow."

"Tainted with death," muttered Blue.

Tipple spun. "What do you know about it, redcap?"

"Dead cow." Blue went very still. "Dead Grayrock. Dead Heroes."

"You think they poisoned the ale?" asked Inga.

"If they did, we'd be dragging corpses out of the pubs by now." Tipple stood and brushed his hands together. "But we need to conficaste—confi—we need to take every barrel with that dead cow on it. And some samples of Nelly's other stock. Just to be safe. Wouldn't you agree, Wendleglass?"

"Um, yes. I suppose that would be wise."

"King Wendleglass," said Inga, "maybe you ought to ask some Heroes to travel to Grayrock to investigate this ghost."

"Dead and red." Blue rocked in place. "Bled and fed."

"Right." Tipple leaned over the bar. "I think we're going to need a drink for the redcap as well."

chapter 5

GLORY

Grayrock was a pit. Literally.

The unimaginatively named town was northeast of Brightlodge, on the edge of the forest past Talondell. Generations of quarry workers had dug the town deeper and deeper into the base of a mountain in order to supply much of Albion with bricks, cobblestones, and high-quality throwing stones for the short-lived sport of rockball, which had been very popular about ten years back until the high rate of concussions put an end to the first season during the Rockball Cup Finals.

It was a town blanketed in grey dust, surrounded by grey stone. Glory was starting to forget what colour looked like.

To the north, a tall, grey dam stopped the river from turning the town into a lake. From either end of the dam stretched a stone wall (also grey), protecting the people from the outlaws and worse living in the woods beyond. Even the people were grey. When the quarry workers returned from a hard day of cutting and shaping rock, the dust made them look like living statues.

The only exception to the colour scheme was the statue of an oak tree in the centre of town, carved to commemorate something or someone terribly important that everyone had forgotten about years ago. It too was grey stone, but flecks of pink quartz gave it a bit of a sparkle, making it immeasurably better than the rest of this pockmark in the earth.

Shroud and Winter had taken Grayrock in stride, but that was no surprise. Shroud preferred greys and blacks. They were part of his image as a self-proclaimed master assassin. As for Winter, she ran about barefoot and clad in furs. Her idea of fashion could only be improved by a layer of dust and dirt.

Then there was Sterling, who had spent the entire time brushing off his brightly coloured, ribbon-slashed sleeves, his flamboyant trousers, and his gleaming boots. He was fighting a losing battle, but he hadn't surrendered yet.

On the bright side, blood stood out quite vividly on the grey stone road, making it easy to see the site of the most recent death.

"It's the fourth suicide this month." The Mayor of Grayrock was a rectangular man who wore a faded sash with an embroidered image of an oak tree to mark his importance. "No need for Heroes to concern themselves. Some people simply can't handle the stress and pressure of the rock business is all."

"The fellow our friends rescued, Sam, talked about the Ghost of Grayrock." Winter was an odd one, always laughing and chatting with everyone she met, as if her lifelong goal was to befriend all of Albion. At first glance, she looked like an uncivilised girl from the mountains. A second glance pretty much confirmed the first.

The wolf pelt she wore revealed as much as it covered, and the fur trim made her look like an ill-sheared sheep. There were hints at a sense of fashion or style, from the thick collar to the cinched waist and the high leather belt, but it was all second-rate work. To top things off, tattoos covered her hands and her bare feet. Winter said they helped her to focus her power.

Glory sniffed. She herself had never needed anything beyond her own strength of Will.

"The so-called ghost, yes." The Mayor scowled. "Look, these are people who hit rocks for a living. They get suspicious of anyone who isn't covered in dust and calluses, but as long as this ghost isn't violating any laws, her business is her own."

"What business is that?" asked Winter.

"I wouldn't know. Let me be clear. Any *minor* problems in Grayrock are completely under control. There's certainly no call for outsiders who don't know nothing about Grayrock to come tromping in and stir things up."

"I understand. Clumsy, ignorant buffoons are so frustrating, aren't they?" Glory continued before the Mayor could figure out how to respond. "Sam said the Ghost of Grayrock was hanging about the docks, but we didn't find anything there. Where do you think we might locate her?"

"I couldn't say. I've not seen her myself."

The man was as useful as a trapdoor on a rowboat.

"What happened to the dead fellow?" Shroud peered up from the shadows of his black hood. He was crouched on the edge of the road, sketching and measuring the splattered blood. Glory couldn't have said whether he was asking about the body because he wanted more information or if he simply wanted to admire the artistry of the broken corpse.

The Mayor grimaced. "I'm sorry, what was your name again, sir?"

Shroud stood and offered the Mayor a half bow. A cream-coloured card appeared between his index and middle finger, as if by magic. The card was embossed with the seal of the Conclave, and read:

~SHROUD~

CONCLAVE-TRAINED SOLVER OF PROBLEMS

OBSTACLES REMOVED, INHERITANCES ACQUIRED,

SUCCESSIONS FACILITATED, FEUDS RESOLVED

Present this card and receive a 15% discount!

If this card was the same as those he had distributed to Glory and the others in their little band of Heroes, there would be a note on the back indicating that this month only, the assassin was offering a two-for-one deal on twins. Shroud had also passed out a series of informational pamphlets to his fellow Heroes back in Brightlodge.

"I ordered the remains taken out to the cemetery for burial," said the Mayor. "I didn't want the sight of a dead body upsetting my people. It's my duty to care for them, after all."

"Very thoughtful," said Glory. "And I'm sure the bloodstains all over the road won't bother them in the slightest." She had met his type back home, cocksure and arrogant, having inherited their power instead of earning it through their virtues and their actions. Glory had inherited certain privileges from her well-off father, but she had long since surpassed any advantages his wealth had given her.

The man refused to answer to anything but "Mayor" or "Your Honour." Given the rumour around town that he had been born Frankfort Snogsworth Mudwater III, Glory couldn't really blame him for that. "You're sure this was a suicide?"

"That's right," the Mayor said decisively. "Just like the others. Poor soul jumped to his death. If only he'd come to me for help instead."

Glory glanced at Sterling, who rolled his eyes. With a weary sigh, she gestured towards the buildings to either side of the road. "None of these rooftops are more than ten feet high. How exactly do you think he managed to splatter himself from such a height?"

The Mayor's forehead wrinkled. He scowled at the closest home. Glory could almost see his thoughts crawling along, like insects with half their legs plucked off. Then his eyes lit up. "He must have brought a chair onto the roof and jumped from that!"

"Excellent thinking, my good man!" Sterling slipped an arm casually around the Mayor's shoulders. "If that's the case, the chair couldn't have gone far. Why don't you search the area while we see what we can figure out here? Together, we'll soon uncover the truth of this terrible tragedy."

Once the Mayor scurried off, Shroud crouched on his heels to examine his sketch, comparing it to the street. "I've measured the shape and width of the blood splatter on the cobblestones. Assuming this fellow was of average height and weight, if he did jump from a chair, it would have to have been a chair seventy-five feet high. Even jumping from the town wall shouldn't have made a mess this size."

From outside Grayrock, the town wall stood roughly twelve feet tall. Inside the town was another matter. The early settlers had dug deeper and deeper, until most of the town was roughly twenty feet lower than the land outside.

"How do you know that?" asked Winter.

"Research." Shroud tucked his notebook away in his cloak. "Death is an art. It takes a lifetime to truly understand and master its many forms." He pointed to the top of the roof. "You throw bodies down from various heights and study the results. I worked out a formula for the height of the fall based on the diameter of the splattered blood. I'm not one to boast, but I can lay out a tarp, toss a man from the top of a tower, and leave not a single drop of blood to stain the road. In this case, the more likely possibility is that the victim didn't jump at all but was thrown down by someone or something incredibly strong."

"Interesting schooling you had," Sterling commented.

Shroud pulled his black cloak more tightly around his shoulders. "This was more of an independent study."

"Right." Glory stepped away from them both. "Four deaths. Hardly the kind of thing that threatens the very survival of Brightlodge."

"All four deaths were men," Shroud pointed out. "All quarry workers, too."

"Ninety percent of the men in this town are quarry workers," Glory said. "And most of the women."

"It's a place to start." Sterling stepped between them and brushed another layer of dust from his shirt. "Unless you'd prefer to stick around here and help the Mayor look for a seventy-five-foot chair?"

By the time they reached the quarry that occupied the eastern quarter of the town, dust coated the inside of Glory's mouth and nostrils. She could literally *taste* the grey.

A broad pit spread out at the base of a curved cliff. Wooden scaffolding clung to the rock face. From a distance, it looked like an enormous arena with oversized stone steps descending to the bottom, where tiny men waged a never-ending battle against the mountainside.

Given what Glory had seen of the townspeople thus far, her money was on the mountainside.

"It's the Ghost of Grayrock all right," said an older worker when they asked about the deaths. Like most of the others, he wore tight, layered clothing, with a head wrap to cover his mouth and nose. He was currently setting a series of small fires atop a broad block of stone. "To look upon her is to pay a terrible price. Longing fills your every waking moment, and your dreams are haunted by her beauty. Desperation turns to despair, until you welcome death."

"I'm sorry," said Winter, "but what are you doing?"

"I'm a fire-setter," he said, as if that explained everything. He gathered another pile of sticks and lit it with a brand from the previous fire. When nobody spoke, he pointed to the line of fires and said, "The heat cracks the stone."

"Aren't hammers and chisels easier?" asked Winter.

"Sure, but this is tradition. It's all for our protection, don't you know. See, as long as Grayrock's been cutting stone, we've had a fire-setter. And in all that time, not a single worker has been eaten by dragons!"

"They say dragons are all but extinct," said Shroud.

"That's what they say, but why take chances?"

"Did any of the victims say they had actually seen the ghost?" Glory asked, trying to drag the interrogation back on topic.

"Well, no. Not exactly." He poked one of the fires, sending up a geyser of sparks. "It's not really the kind of thing one talks about. More of a private experience, if you know what I mean. Like those feelings you get around a really good-looking cousin."

Good-looking cousins. Well, that would certainly explain a lot about these people. Glory looked around for another worker to question. Any other worker. She pointed to a man hitching a pair of mules to a cart stacked with cut stone. "You. Can you tell us where this ghost came from?"

"Nobody knows." He leaned against one of the mules. "They call her the Smoking Huntress."

"Why?" asked Sterling. "Is she a huntress who smokes a pipe or cigar, or is she literally on fire?"

The man stared blankly. Behind him, another worker looked up from the stone he was shaping with hammer and chisel. "Her *true* name is the White Ghost of the Sky. I saw her myself as she was flying over Grayrock not three days ago."

"You were drunk, and that was a cloud," snapped his partner.

"A *ghost* cloud!"

A young man, barely more than a boy, said, "I heard she rose up from Founder's Hill to kill us all. I call her Lady Death."

"Why Lady Death?" asked Glory. "If you're looking to give her a scary name, why not just Death? If the ghost was a man, would you feel compelled to call him *Mister* Death?"

The boy stammered something unintelligible, then hunched his shoulders and turned back to his work.

Glory raised her voice. "Has anyone here actually seen or spoken with the Ghost of Grayrock?"

They murmured uncomfortably to one another, but nobody answered. The man who had dubbed her the "White Ghost of the Sky" started to raise his hand, but his partner punched him in the shoulder, and he lowered it again.

Glory tried again. "Forget the ghost. What can you tell us about the man who died yesterday?"

"Good worker," said the fire-setter after a long pause. "Showed up every day, did his job, didn't complain."

A woman sharpening chisels looked up. "That's not true. Billy walked off the job yesterday. I bumped into him on the way home after finishing my shift. He said he couldn't work for the Mayor's new foreman anymore—"

"The Mayor hired a new foreman?" Glory jumped down and made her way to the woman.

"Oh, yes. The Mayor took a team of twenty men off the quarry. Something about an exciting new business prospect. We haven't seen any of them since, except for Billy, and he was only back for a day before his tragic death."

Glory glanced at the other Heroes. The Mayor had told them the ghost was here on business. "When the Mayor talked about this new prospect, did he happen to mention a partner?"

The woman shook her head.

"What about the foreman? Where can we find him?"

"Dunno." She sighed. "Will said Big Rob was right."

"Big Rob?" asked Sterling.

"Another victim of the White Ghost of the Sky," said the man with the hammer and chisel. "Poor fellow shot himself."

"How exactly did he do that?" Glory asked.

"With a longbow."

She folded her arms, waiting.

"Indulge my curiosity, my good chap," Sterling said slowly. "We were told only that these men had killed themselves and we weren't allowed to see the bodies. Where, precisely, did the arrow strike Big Rob?"

"The first one—"

"He shot himself more than once?" Glory interrupted.

"That's right, miss."

"With a longbow?"

He nodded. "First in the belly, then in the side."

Glory looked around. Most of the gathered workers had pushed back their head coverings, so she could see a few dusty faces wrinkle as they realised something about that story wasn't quite right.

"What about the others?" asked Winter. "How did they die?"

Several men responded at once, pressing closer to Winter. "Connor tied himself up and jumped off the dam. He'd bound rocks to his feet to make sure he'd drown. A fisherman hooked him two days later, in the shade where the dam meets the mountainside. Good fishing there. I once caught a trout big enough to feed a family of four."

"Little Rob cut off his head with an axe."

"If the rest of you are any indication, he won't miss it." Glory sighed. "Did Billy say anything about what he was doing, or where this new foreman had taken him?"

"They were all sworn to secrecy." The woman spat in the dirt. "I noticed his boots were muddy, though. It's not rained in five days."

So they were working somewhere wet and presumably hidden from view. "The other men who died—Connor and the Big and Little Robs—they were on this secret project as well?"

"That's right."

"Thank you for your help, milady." Sterling captured the woman's hand and brought it to his lips, leaving a kiss-shaped smudge in the dust on her skin. "The truth is a powerful weapon, and we shall use it to strike down all who threaten Brightlodge. And Grayrock too, of course."

"I don't know about all that, but if you need any other kind of help, you know where to find me." She winked and blew Sterling a kiss.

"Keep your sword in its sheath," Glory snapped. "We've work to do."

The Mayor had lied to them. As a Hero, she intended to build such a reputation that no one would dare try to play her for a fool. That meant letting the world know what happened to those who tried.

Sterling cleared his throat and nodded towards her hand, where red light shone through the cracks between her fingers. "On you, dear Glory, even rage is like the beauty of a fresh-bloomed rose. I've no doubt you could make a man welcome death. But before you bring the Mayor's tower down around his head, keep in mind that it's difficult to extract information from a corpse."

"Difficult, but not impossible." Glory quenched her magic and flashed a brilliant smile. "I'm not interested in killing him. Merely in persuading him to tell us the truth."

The Mayor's tower was a round, two-storey building on the edge of the town square, with a single wooden doorway and a series of arched windows on the second floor.

"You really think the Mayor's plotting against Brightlodge?" asked Winter. "He doesn't come across as the evil-mastermind type."

"Oh, Winter." Glory gave her a too-friendly smile. "You of all people should be careful about judging others by their appearance."

Winter matched her expression. "Oh, but I judge for so much more than just looks."

"The door's locked," said Sterling. "I don't see movement through those windows."

"Allow me." Shroud pulled out what looked like a small knife handle with a series of metal rods folded into the hilt. He unfolded one of the rods and crouched in front of the lock.

"Excellent," said Sterling. "Winter, why don't you stay to assist Shroud in his endeavours, while Glory and I visit the Mayor's home."

Subtlety was not one of Sterling's strengths. Not that there was any need for him to play peacemaker. Winter might be an unmannered rube, but she was still a Hero. Not a particularly impressive one, perhaps, but presumably useful nonetheless.

The Mayor and his family lived two streets over, just north of the square. Their house was twice the size of any other in Grayrock, which wasn't saying much. Smoke rose from the chimney, and Glory heard children arguing inside.

The woman who answered the door had a face like creased leather. She wore a dark green bodice and skirt over a white chemise. Nothing fancy, but a far sight nicer than the average quarry worker. "What is it?" she asked warily.

"Is the Mayor home?" Glory smiled. "We had a few more questions about the Ghost of Grayrock."

"Haven't seen him. He usually gets in after me and the boys have gone to bed, and lately he's been out the door before the rest of us have had a chance to rub the sleep grit from our eyes."

"Missus . . ." Glory waited for the woman to provide her name.

"Mrs. Mayor, please."

"Really?" Glory looked past her into the house. "Is there a Mayor Junior running around back there? Perhaps playing with his sister Mayora?"

Her eyes narrowed. "What do you want with Mayora? Has she been snogging with that no-good rock-for-brains Kris again?"

"What my fellow Hero means to say is that your husband is obviously a gentleman of fine taste." Sterling's bow included so many flourishes it was practically a dance routine. "Where might we find him at this hour, to seek his wisdom and counsel?"

"I couldn't say." The woman was clearly nervous, fidgeting and refusing to meet anyone's eyes. But was she nervous because she knew what her husband was up to, or simply intimidated by the two Heroes who had shown up at her door?

Glory folded her arms and waited, stretching out the silence before finally saying, "Mrs. Mayor, your husband lied to me. I find this upsetting. How upset I become depends on how long it takes me to find him, and how many obstacles I have to overcome in the meantime."

The woman drew herself up. "Are you threatening me, missy?"

"Yes." Glory opened her hand and concentrated. Mrs. Mayor leaned closer, curiosity overpowering fear, as tendrils of red and orange light blossomed from Glory's palm and spun themselves into the shape of an apple. Flames danced eagerly along the surface.

She tossed the glowing red apple into the air, where it exploded into flames with a sound like a miniature thunderclap. Heat washed over Glory's face, and Mrs. Mayor's hair whooshed back as if blown by a powerful wind.

"You and your husband are important people. Possibly the most powerful people in all of Grayrock." Glory made a show of wiping the dust from her hand. "We aren't from Grayrock."

"Now, now." Sterling winked at the Mayor's wife. "You'll have to forgive my companion. She gets terribly jealous whenever I pay the slightest attention to another beautiful woman."

"Keep it up," commented Glory. "I'll make sure you're unable to gift a woman with your . . . attention . . . ever again." She peeked past Mrs. Mayor to the small wooden bench sitting on one side of the entryway. A drying puddle of grey mud outlined a pair of boot prints. The people at the quarry had mentioned Billy's boots being muddy too. "Does your husband have an office in his home?"

"He does, but he doesn't let anyone else in, not even me or the children."

Glory strode past, ignoring her protests. A pair of young children played beneath the kitchen table, while a young woman—another daughter, or perhaps a servant—roasted quail over a fire. Two doors in a back hallway opened into bedrooms. The third was locked.

Sterling turned to go. "I can bring Shroud to—"

"No need." Glory conjured a smaller apple and tossed it onto the door. The explosion splintered much of the wood and part of the surrounding wall. The smouldering latch fell with a dull clunk.

"Oh dear." Mrs. Mayor stomped on the tiny, smoking embers on the floor. "He's going to be so angry about this."

Glory paused. "If he threatens to lay so much as a finger on you, kindly tell him I'll be along to burn it off."

"You can do that?" She looked over her shoulder. "Tell me, have you ever done babysitting work?"

Glory didn't dignify that with a response. She stepped into the small office and looked about. There wasn't much here worth guarding: a small pouch of coins, an old sword desperately in need of oil and a whetstone, and a map of Grayrock spread out on a wobbly table. Crude sketches showed plans for what appeared to be a tunnel beneath the dam.

"What are they digging for?" asked Glory.

The woman took a step back. "All he told me was that we'd finally have the lives we deserved."

"Either money or power," she guessed. It always came down to one of the two. "Whatever he's doing, he doesn't want anyone else finding out. That's why he killed those men, to protect his secret."

"To be fair, we don't *know* the Mayor was behind those deaths," said Sterling, but he sounded dubious.

Mrs. Mayor shook her head, her face pale. "He wouldn't—you're lying. It was the ghost."

"No doubt she's involved too, whoever she is," Glory said. "And we'll deal with her as well. But your husband is helping her."

"You're wrong." The Mayor's wife folded her arms and steeled herself. "She's the true evil. That woman is worse than a ghost. She's a creature of death and smoke and darkness. She steals the innocent from their beds and lures good people to their destruction. If my husband has done these things, it's only because of her."

Glory had grown up watching her father negotiate with customers and fellow traders. She'd learned more than he ever imagined, including when to push and when to offer kindness. "You might be right," she said gently. Having taken the woman's mental balance, it was time to reel her in. "If so, riches won't be enough to stop her. The ghost, whatever she is, will continue to endanger Grayrock. Your friends. Your children. You said she destroys good people. Is your husband a good man?"

"He's . . ." She hesitated. "Well, I suppose he's a pretty good man. Doesn't hog the blankets. Doesn't usually miss the piss pot in the middle of the night."

"How charming," Glory said flatly. "Mrs. Mayor, the fact is, four of the men he's working with have turned up dead. If not by his hand, then that means the ghost is killing them off one by one. Eventually, it will be his turn."

"They call us Heroes," Sterling said, swelling up like a rooster about to crow. "But it falls to you to save your husband's life. Find your courage and lend us your aid, my dear lady. Tell us what it is your husband seeks and prove yourself a Hero. Rescue the man you love. Rescue all the people of Grayrock. Indeed, from your ruby lips could pour the knowledge that rescues all of Albion."

Glory rolled her eyes, but his overblown words worked.

"I heard him talking in his sleep a few nights back," Mrs. Mayor whispered. "He said there was gold buried in the foundation of the dam."

Glory rubbed her brow. "The Mayor of Grayrock has taken a team to dig away at the dam's foundation. The dam that's the only thing stopping the river from flooding this town like an enormous bucket."

"A little water never hurt anyone," said Mrs. Mayor. "You've seen these people. They could use a good bath."

Glory turned to leave. "I don't know whether or not your husband is a good man, Mrs. Mayor. But I can state with certainty that he is a very *stupid* man."

chapter 6

SHROUD

Shroud carefully fitted the "Shadow Whisperer" beaver-fur silencer into place. It looked like a fat brown caterpillar trying to engage in unnatural acts with the upper portion of his bowstring, but the fur had proven the best thing for muffling the distinctive *twang* of his weapon. He finished securing the second silencer to the lower part of the string, tested the draw, and nodded to himself.

As was often the case, he found himself silently repeating the lessons and advice of his Conclave masters. He had memorised every word they spoke. His memory was one of many gifts that had propelled him to the top of his class and set him upon the path to becoming the top assassin in all of Albion.

Know your environment. If you're venturing into caves or tunnels, you'll often be dealing with a lot of moisture. Traction will be an issue, and too much humidity can harm your bow. Beeswax rubbed into the wood should minimise the damage.

He had already treated the bow. From his pack, he pulled out a pair of what looked like oversized black sandals with leather ties. He stepped onto the first, placing the sole of his boot in the centre of the print, and looped the ties around his foot and ankle. "Sharkskin. Good gripping power, and unlikely to be affected by dampness. They're useful for climbing, too."

"We'd like to get inside before sunset," Glory said.

"A rushed job is a botched job." He tied the second piece of sharkskin to his other boot and took a few steps to make sure everything was secure. Next, he double-checked the various knives and other tools strapped to his body and tucked away in his cloak. "Proper planning is one of the things that separates the amateurs from the professionals."

"What are the others?" asked Winter.

"Training. Discipline." He adjusted his black hood and smiled. "Style."

He stepped back to assess the dam, which was essentially an oversized curved wall of grey blocks. Darker streaks marked where water had spilled over the top, filling a shallow pond at the base of the dam. Moss and weeds clung to the blocks, thickest near the edges. To one side, the dam merged smoothly into the mountain. To the other, it sheared away to join the wall around the town. A small guard tower stood at the intersection.

The Mayor had tried to hide what he was up to, but it hadn't been difficult for Shroud to discover the fresh tracks through the gardens at the eastern edge of the pond, or the dying branches piled up to cover the tunnel where the dam met the mountainside.

He pulled a random arrow from his quiver and checked the tip.

"We don't even know for certain that the Mayor is in there," said Winter. "And you're already planning to kill him."

"I'm already *prepared* to kill him. There's an important difference." It was a difference drilled into Shroud by some of the deadliest men and women in all of Albion. Only a select few were selected for initiation into Albion's oldest order of assassins. Of those who proved themselves worthy to be trained by the Conclave, fewer than half survived the training process.

Shroud had not only survived, he had excelled. He knew the

twelve best knots to use when preparing a garrotte. He could demonstrate all twenty-six techniques for killing a man with his own soup spoon. As an archer, his marksmanship had impressed even the shadowy masters of the Conclave.

"Is there anyone you aren't prepared to kill?" asked Winter.

"Certainly." He made a show of studying each of his companions in turn. "Me."

Shroud had no intention of killing his fellow Heroes—not unless they gave him good reason to do so. Or if someone paid him. Or if he saw the opportunity to inflict a truly memorable and impressive death, one that would significantly add to his reputation. Regardless, he rather enjoyed the sidelong looks they gave him, as if he were a serpent, sleek and deadly and unpredictable. He turned and gestured "after you" with one arm.

Sterling was the first to step through that jagged crack into the darkness. He was the only one of the group who seemed comfortable turning his back on Shroud. Foolish man. But it would make killing him easier should that become necessary.

Sterling came across as a stuck-up, overly romantic peacock, but the man could fight. Shroud had seen him in action, his blade jumping from one foe to the next, striking so quickly his enemies didn't have time to realise they had been slain. If there ever came a day when Sterling needed to be removed, Shroud would be better off doing so from a distance. A single well-placed arrow, probably a broadhead. Or else he would simply arrange an "accident" to divert suspicion.

You'll always be a suspect. Members of the Conclave wear death as a second cloak.

That was true enough, but suspicion was a far cry from proof.

Shroud followed Sterling into the cave. The air was cool and damp. Water dripped in the distance. The tunnel was broader than he would have expected. Had he been the one digging for treasure, he would have kept the entrance as tight as possible to better conceal it.

Glory was next. Her magic made her a very different challenge than Sterling, but the Conclave had trained him to eliminate the most powerful targets, including both those with great Strength or Skill and those who used their Will to manipulate the supernatural. Magic was a dangerous weapon, but like any weapon, it had limitations. In a straightforward fight, Shroud was confident he could plant a blade in Glory's chest faster than she could summon her magic to use against him.

Of course, a straightforward fight was always a last resort.

Shroud moved soundlessly ahead. By the time he was five steps in, it was too dim to make out anything but shadows and shapes. After ten steps, vision was useless.

Torchlight would alert the Mayor to their presence, but darkness presented dangers of its own. A single misstep could lead to a twisted ankle, and they had no way of knowing what other creatures might have taken up residence in a place like this. And to Shroud's ear, the footfalls of his companions might as well have been an army marching in full plate armour.

"Allow me," he whispered, slipping past Sterling. He brushed the man's shoulder with one hand, using the other to follow the roughness of the wall. He tested each step before shifting his weight.

How many months had he spent training to fight while blind or deaf? He touched his face, remembering the rough linen blindfold his teachers had tightened around his eyes. His opponent for those bouts had been an old master known as the Poisoned Violet, who took great pleasure in beating the tar out of him day after day until he learned to hear the softest footfall, to feel every disturbance in the air. Ah, the good old days.

The path sloped deeper underground before veering to the left, towards the dam's foundation. They hadn't gone far when he began to hear the clink of metal on rock.

"Idiots," Glory said softly. "All it would take is for a single block to shift, and the water rushing into the tunnel would drown them all."

"More likely they—and we—would be crushed in the cave-in," said Shroud. Once the structure of the dam failed, the weight of the rock would flatten anyone caught inside like mosquitoes.

"You two suck all the fun out of exploring dark, dangerous tunnels," whispered Winter.

Winter was as deadly as anyone else in their little band. She fought using her Will to conjure ice and cold. Unlike Glory, her technique was more instinctive. Winter's power could slow or even immobilise an enemy. To take her out, it would be best to divert her attention and trick her into expending that arctic power in another direction. Perhaps a whistling arrow, shot into the distance to simulate the approach of some shrieking creature . . .

He nodded to himself, satisfied that he could dispose of any of his companions if necessary. Not that he expected to have to do so, but it was better to be prepared. Planning kept his mind sharp. It was one of the things that had always given him the edge over others in his classes.

His eyes began to discern the distant glow of a hanging lantern, illuminating jagged walls, glassy puddles, and bat guano. "Wait here."

He crept silently ahead. A short distance beyond, a second lantern hung on a metal spike in the rock. Farther in, roughly twenty men worked in a small cavern. They had exposed three of the great stone blocks that formed the foundation of the dam, and were slowly chipping away at the centremost stone. Four others were piling dirt and rubble into wagons. Shroud wondered idly where they were taking the waste rock.

And then what he had assumed to be another rock pile trudged away from the wall, and surprise chased any other questions or concerns from his mind. He didn't see the Mayor anywhere, but they had a bigger problem: The Mayor's new foreman was an ogre.

Most ogres couldn't supervise themselves, let alone a crew of twenty, but this one was not only shouting orders, she—Shroud was 70 percent certain the ogre was female—was even using complete sentences. Mostly.

The ogre resembled a boulder herself, round, grey, and craggy. She made the workers look like little dolls. A trio of daggers hung from her left ear like jewellery. In one hand, she carried an axe that looked capable of splitting the dam all by itself. The top of her head was bruised and bloody where it had scraped the low rock ceiling again and again, but none of the injuries looked serious enough to slow her down.

A pair of ogre heads hung from her belt like enormous, hairy grey prunes. A third was suspended by a rusty chain around her neck and sat in the chasm of the ogre's cleavage. A fourth was tied to the end of a stick slung over her back.

Four noggins. Strange . . . most ogres only carry one.

One of the reasons ogres were so tough to kill was that their anatomy was so thoroughly ridiculous. Cut off the head, and the body would eventually stop trying to kill you, but the head would keep jabbering away. Their vital organs—the heart and what passed for a brain—were both housed in their rocky skulls.

Ogres were generally born in pairs. When they grew up, the stronger twin killed the weaker and took his or her head as a trophy, companion, and source of advice. Those unfortunate noggins tended to be smarter than their full-bodied brothers and sisters, perhaps because they had nothing to do except think and talk. This allowed the victorious ogre to worry about more important things, like eating and killing.

Go for the soft targets: belly, throat, groin, and eyes.

One of the heads on her belt blinked. "Hey, who said it was time to rest?"

The ogre marched towards a worker who had slumped against the wall to mop sweat from his face. He snatched up his hammer and attacked the rock with newfound vigour, while the various heads chuckled to themselves.

"*That* is no ghost," Winter whispered. The clang of hammers helped to muffle her voice.

"Not yet." Shroud allowed himself a small, unseen smile. He spied a fifth head strapped to the ogre's opposite hip, though this one wore a gag of rope and old rags.

"There's another one in the corner," Glory whispered, pointing to an older-looking head nested among a pile of rocks.

Using the noggins to keep watch in every direction at once. Clever.

He could have shot the ogre from here, but arrows were a gamble. A perfect shot to the eye *might* penetrate through the socket to the brain, but this was an ogre. Piercing the brain might just make her mad.

Perhaps a flash bomb to blind the noggins. That would nullify much of the ogre's advantage. If Shroud and his companions struck quickly, they could take her down in the confusion. A standard-issue Laird-Eastman Eyeburner Bomb would work best in this confined environment. He plucked a black egg from a padded inner pocket in his cloak. "You'll want to shield your eyes."

Shroud pulled his cloak around his body, transforming himself into shadow. He shook the egg gently, feeling the contents warm as they mixed together. A sharp impact against something solid—like an ogre's skull—would be more than enough to crack the shell and trigger the reaction. He double-checked that his bow and arrows were ready, raised his arm—

A gravelly shout erupted mere feet from where he was standing. A seventh noggin stared up at him from the shadows. He had mistaken it for a rock. This one had braided pigtails, of all things. "Oi, Headstrong! Visitors!"

Headstrong the ogre spun around, raised her weapon, and bared enormous yellow teeth.

With a curse, Shroud snatched the noggin off the ground and

crammed the Eyeburner into its mouth. The head squawked in muffled protest as Shroud grabbed both pigtails, spun around, and hurled it at the approaching ogre.

Headstrong reacted in typical fashion for her kind, swatting the noggin away with the flat of her axe.

The blow was more than enough to set off the flash bomb, and the resulting explosion reduced the number of noggins to six, as well as effectively blinding all those who hadn't covered their eyes. Even through his hands and closed eyelids, it was like Shroud had stared at the midday sun. He blinked rapidly as he nocked an arrow—a hardened bodkin tip had the best chance of penetrating the ogre's hide. He sighted in on the blurred form and released the string.

Cold wind caught the end of his cloak as Winter launched her own assault. Sterling bounded past with sword drawn, eliciting a curse from Glory, who had to smother her magic to avoid hitting him.

"Fear not, good people of Grayrock," Sterling cried. "Sterling, Hero of Albion, has come to free you from your tormentor. Behold the legend!" He thrust his sword, jabbing Headstrong in the thigh.

The ogre spun to the side and swept her axe through the air, but Sterling had already danced out of range. The wound didn't slow her down. She continued to whip her axe to and fro, drawing unpredictable patterns of steel all around her as a noggin with a ragged scar through the remnants of her left eye and ear barked orders.

"Keep moving! Don't let 'em get close. Chop that one like a melon!"

Another noggin, this one with a snot-covered ring through his nose, said, "Chase 'em into the tunnel. Make 'em trip over each other. Forget the axe. Yer stench will drive 'em back!"

"Watch it, Schemer." Headstrong yanked the noggin-on-a-stick from her back and used it like a club in her off hand, working to corral the Heroes. "I'll gag you like I did Big Mouth."

"I'm already gagging," the noggin named Schemer replied.

"Are you seeing this?" asked Glory.

"Seeing, yes." Shroud fired two more arrows. One lodged in the ogre's belly. The other ricocheted off a noggin, leaving a thin cut along the scalp. "Still working on understanding."

Few of the workers showed any interest in joining the battle. One man who tried was flattened by the accidental backswing of Headstrong's makeshift club. After that, the rest stayed as far out of range as possible.

Headstrong continued to chase Sterling, swinging her axe like a farmer with a scythe. A drunk farmer. One who was less intent on harvesting her crop than on reducing it to a bloody pulp.

"Step to your right," shouted Glory. Both Sterling and Shroud moved out of the way, and an orb of crackling flame hit the ground between Headstrong's feet. The ogre howled as the fire exploded, burning her legs.

"Well done, my Lady of the Apples!" Sterling darted forwards to score another cut to the same leg he had hit before.

"Watch the ones in back," shouted another of the female noggins. "Forget the peacock with the steel toothpick. And stop missing!"

"You don't like it, Thinker?" Headstrong growled. "Help me kill the meat sacks!"

Thinker didn't respond. Winter had encased the head in a layer of ice, a glassy mask that shone in the lantern light.

"Get outta dere." That was the noggin called Schemer. "You're outnumbered. I'm not dyin' for some dirt and rocks."

With a growl of frustration, Headstrong turned to flee, tossing human workers behind her to slow pursuit. Shroud put two more arrows into her back before she shoved her way into another tunnel. He started to follow.

"Shroud, wait," Winter said. "We have to help these people."

"Do I look like a healer? More important, imagine the injury my reputation will suffer if my enemies begin surviving their encounters with me."

"We're here to find the Mayor," Winter pressed. "These people might know where he is."

"Headstrong might know too," Shroud countered, trying to duck around her. "I know a hundred and twelve ways of persuading her to tell us."

"You really think an ogre is the best source for intelligence on the Mayor? Or intelligence, period?"

Shroud hesitated. "That's a fair point."

Sterling climbed onto the nearest rock pile and rested one arm on his bent leg. "Fear not, good villagers. Your imprisonment is at an end! And now, if you could tell us where your villainous Mayor is hiding, we'll make certain his evil is vanquished from Grayrock for all time."

"Ain't seen him today," said an older man, leaning heavily on his hammer. "Most days, he comes round with the Ghost of Grayrock to inspect the work."

"Excellent," said Sterling. "We're interested in speaking with her as well."

"What can you tell us about the ogre?" asked Shroud.

The old man shuddered. "Not much to tell. She's an ogre. Big. Mean. Ugly. Rumour has it her job was to kill anyone who refused to work or who tried to leave these caves before the job was done. All I know is those few who walked off never came back." He looked at them expectantly.

"Yes, yes. Your friends are dead," Shroud said. "Where do you think Headstrong might have run off to?"

"None of us wanted to chat up an ogre," said another worker.

The clank of a hammer cut off Shroud's response. He stared at the man who had resumed his work on the dam. Two more moved to join him. Shroud looked at his companions, who appeared baffled.

"What are you doing?" asked Shroud.

"There's still treasure to find," said the old man, shouldering his hammer. "With rockhead gone, that gold will be all ours."

"What gold?" asked Glory. "You're digging into the *foundation of the dam.*"

"Right," he said. "That's where the treasure's buried."

"Keep digging and you'll flood the entire town," said Sterling.

"Ah," answered one of the men loading the wagons. "That's what makes it such a clever place to hide a treasure. You'd have to be a fool to dig here."

Sterling blinked. "Well . . . yes."

"You need to stop before you wipe out the entire town," said Winter.

"We know what you're about," said the wagon worker. "You think you're so clever, scaring off old granite-face and 'rescuing' us. Then once we're out of the way, you'll take the gold for yourselves." He grabbed a rock and raised it in what he doubtless believed to be a threatening manner. "We've earned this treasure. There's nothing you and your gang here can do to make us leave."

Shroud smiled. "Is that a challenge?"

"I vote we leave them," said Glory.

"Why am I not surprised?" Winter asked.

"You can't save people from their own stupidity," Glory shot back.

"Sure you can." Shroud unshouldered his pack. He pulled out a curved, double-edged dagger with an ivory handle and made a show of inspecting the long blade in the lantern light. "I received this weapon from an assassin who trained in the Deadlands. He taught me thirty-nine ways to kill a man with it. I've come up with a dozen more since then."

His smile grew. "Who wants to stick around and help me find number fifty-two?"

chapter 7

WINTER

"Why would Headstrong, the Mayor, and the Ghost of Grayrock want to flood the town?" Winter asked, once the last of the workers had left. None of them had provided any useful information.

"Why indeed?" Sterling rubbed his chin and examined the shadows, as if his piercing eyes could pry the truth from the darkness. "Neither the Mayor nor the ogre strikes me as the evil-mastermind type. The ghost must be the one behind this."

Winter jumped onto a pile of broken stone and balanced on one foot. "Maybe someone really did bury gold here when they built the dam. These people don't exactly put a lot of thought into their actions."

Glory smiled. "No wonder you've seemed so comfortable here."

"I enjoy life no matter where I go. It's so much nicer than walking about like you've got an icicle up your—"

"Does anyone have any *useful* suggestions for finding our foes?" asked Sterling.

A blackened noggin landed on the ground between them. "Let's ask the ogre," said Shroud.

Winter would have thought a flash bomb in the mouth was

more than enough to kill an ogre head, but this one had survived. Mostly. The noggin was missing some teeth, and the jaw looked like it was broken, but the yellow eyes burned with hate. One of the braids had burned to a stub, adding to the stink.

The jaw flopped open. "If I had arms, I'd crush you like—"

"But you don't," Glory interrupted. "Do you have a name?"

"Watcher." The thing's voice was slurred and difficult to understand. Winter wondered briefly how it spoke without lungs.

"Where can we find your master?" asked Sterling.

"If I knew where to find old Headache, I'd tell you. Long as I got to watch you gut her. Or watch her gut you. I'm not picky." The noggin's red-veined eyes studied each Hero in turn. "Any of you runts in need of a noggin?"

Winter sat cross-legged in front of the oversized head. She grabbed the remaining braid and turned it to face her. "Why does Headstrong want to destroy Grayrock?"

Watcher snorted, spraying the ground with bloody green snot. "Same reason she does anything. She likes killing stuff."

"Nothing wrong with that," said Shroud.

Glory yanked the head back around towards her. "What about the ghost?"

"How should I know? She don't talk to noggins. She just left us in this dung-hole with the humans."

Winter tugged the head by its less-burnt ear. "How did Headstrong end up with seven noggins?"

"Who cares," snapped Glory. "We need it to tell us where to find the ghost."

"She isn't exactly a normal ogre, is she?" Winter countered. "I'd like to know exactly what we're up against." When the noggin didn't answer, Winter flicked her fingers, and frost spread over the tip of the bulbous nose. "That was your cue, noggin."

"In the beginning, it was just her and Scratcher," said Watcher.

"That's the chump on the end of the stick. Then she took Night Axe, thanks to—" Watcher's eyes went round, and her mouth snapped shut.

"Thanks to who . . . ?" asked Winter. "The ghost?"

"Every moment we waste with this talking lump helps the ogre to escape," said Glory.

"You heard the grumpy witch." Winter snapped her fingers, and the frost crept over the rest of the noggin's nose. "Talk fast."

"Night Axe helps Headstrong fight, s'all. Since then, she picked up me, Schemer, Hard-Arse, Big Mouth—he was the one with the gag, and Thinker. You got questions, Big Mouth's the one to ask. He does the remembering."

"Who did she take Night Axe from?" Winter asked. "Cooperate, and I'll buy you a nice hat when we get back to town. Maybe even some earrings to go with—"

"Tell us where to find her," Glory interrupted.

Yellow eyes twitched towards the tunnel where the ogre had fled. "Before we came here, Headstrong liked to sleep in the hills, on the rocks. Never in the same place."

"A cunning precaution," said Shroud.

"S'not it. She'd just forgot where she'd been from one night to the next."

Winter grabbed the noggin by its remaining braid. "Where do we find the ghost?"

The noggin bit its lip and stared at the wall.

"You can play with the head while we hunt the ogre," Glory said.

Sterling started towards the tunnel. "We should make sure none of the townspeople try to sneak back in to have another go at that gold."

"I'll take care of that." Shroud rubbed his hands together. "What kind of deterrent would you like? Are we talking cuts and bruises or decapitations and impalements?"

Winter flinched. "We're here to help these people. Try not to kill anyone."

"Every killing helps someone. Oftentimes that someone is me, but the point remains." Shroud shrugged and turned to study the tunnel behind him. "On the other hand, a couple of maimed workers dragging their bloody bodies back to town ought to scare the rest off. There's a snare trap with barbs and explosives I've been itching to try."

Winter shook her head. The man desperately needed to lighten up. Maybe an evening out dancing, followed by a good, long night with a woman. Or a man. Winter had no idea what Shroud's preferences were. Most of his conversations were about how best to change living things into dead things.

Speaking of which . . . Winter glanced at the noggin and sighed. Ogres were tough, but there was a limit to the damage they could take. She tossed the expired head to Glory, who flinched.

So much for buying her that hat.

The first thing they saw when they emerged from the tunnel was a pair of goats munching a small thornbush. Both goats paused to watch Winter wipe dust and cobwebs from her face, then returned to their snack.

Smashed bushes and droplets of blood showed exactly where the ogre had fled into the hills, but the dirt and shrubs soon changed to bare rock, and the trail vanished.

Winter turned to look out over Grayrock. The great pit of the quarry stretched out below to her left. The dam stretched out to the right. Moonlight reflected from the river, and the lanterns in town glowed like fireflies. She hadn't realised how high they'd climbed. "Look at that view!"

"We're back to square one." Glory folded her arms and glared at

Winter. "The Mayor and the ghost are both still out there, and we're no closer to learning their plans."

"Oh, relax," said Winter. "We're on square three, at least. We might not know their full plan, but we stopped them from bringing down the dam. We don't need to keep looking for them. Once Headstrong finishes licking her wounds, they'll come after us."

"Winter speaks the truth," said Sterling. "The forces of darkness now know what it means to face Sterling and his fellow Heroes. Their schemes will come to naught while we remain in Grayrock. They will be forced to give up their plans, or else to face us in battle."

"Exactly," said Winter. "In the meantime, we should be celebrating. There has to be somewhere in this town people can go for a little fun."

"What about the workers we saved?" snapped Glory. "Shouldn't we be questioning them instead of wasting our time on childish frivolity?"

Winter grinned, refusing to let Glory's sour tone melt her good mood. "Childish frivolity is *never* a waste of time."

"The workers believe we're here to steal their treasure," said Sterling. "They're unlikely to be of any help. We can check to see if the Mayor has returned, but if not, I second Winter's suggestion. We fought well today, and it's time to toast our victory! Tomorrow we hunt the ghost and put an end to this threat."

There was no sign of the Mayor. After checking both his house and office, they headed across the square to the Broken Blade Tavern, where a pleasant-looking bald man named McCullough served up overcooked meat he swore was chicken, along with mugs of watered-down wine.

"The Mayor will return sooner or later," Sterling said. "The man has invested too much time and work to simply abandon Grayrock."

They could see the Mayor's home and workplace from the window. No surprise there. Politics and alcohol often kept very close company.

Winter tilted her mug, concentrating her Will to freeze the wine as it poured forth. She broke the blood-red spike from the edge of the mug and munched on the tip as she bounced back to the bartender. "Back in Brightlodge, there were these twins who'd march into the street and perform a musical duel on their mandores." She smiled, remembering how their feather-tip picks flew over the strings, weaving rhythmic spells that drew all within earshot to dance. "What kind of music do the good patrons of the Broken Blade enjoy?"

McCullough jerked his chin towards an older, heavyset woman in the back. "Sarah over there is known to play a few songs on the bladder pipe."

"Excellent!" Winter spun away and slapped three coins on the table in front of Sarah. "How many songs will that buy me?"

Sarah's eyes widened. "For that, I'll play all night."

Winter grinned and added two more coins to the pile, then dragged Sterling from his chair.

Sarah pulled out an instrument with an air bladder the colour and shape of a giant onion attached to the top of a wooden pipe, similar to a flute. The music was low and rich. What Sarah lacked in polish and precision, she made up for in enthusiasm, just the way Winter liked it. Soon, Winter was spinning and stomping and laughing with Sterling, while others in the tavern clapped along.

When the first song ended, she pushed Sterling towards an attractive-looking woman at the bar and snatched another man from the crowd. "My name's Winter." She shoved her hair back as she spun, and "accidentally" stumbled, pressing close to her new partner. "Whoops! I'm so sorry. I don't know this dance."

He stammered and took her hands, guiding her through the steps.

"Thanks!" She grinned. "I've never been to Grayrock before. How long have you lived here?"

"All my life." He was red-faced and sweating, whether from the exertion or from Winter's more energetic dancing was impossible to say.

"Then you know about the ghost?"

"Oh, sure. She arrived about two months back. I saw her once, from a distance. By the time I caught up, she was gone. She left burnt footprints in the dirt."

The song came to a close, and Winter gave her partner a quick kiss on the cheek before grabbing another. For the next few hours, she danced and flirted and gathered what information she could.

"They say she rose up from Founder's Hill," said an elderly but surprisingly energetic man with an impressively thick beard.

"First anyone heard of her was about two months back." This was the woman Winter had seen loading a sledge down at the quarry. She seemed far livelier now as she and Winter took turns twirling one another to the music. "She stays in the woods outside of the wall. Nobody knows exactly where."

Winter was dancing with McCullough, the bartender, when she noticed the girl watching from the corner. She looked perhaps twelve or thirteen years of age, and she was staring directly at Winter. Seeing that she'd been noticed, the girl bit her lip and turned away.

"Who's that?"

"Her name's Greta," said McCullough. "Her father works at the quarry. Mother is a seamstress. Her brother disappeared a few days ago."

"The ghost?"

"Nobody knows. Ben was always a little odd. It's possible he just wandered off, but . . ."

"You don't think so." Winter finished the dance and walked arm-in-arm back to the bar with McCullough. "Could you get me two mugs of that delicious hot honey lemonade?"

A short time later, she carried the steaming mugs towards the corner where Greta was lurking. The girl looked like a frightened rabbit preparing to bolt. Like most of the townsfolk, she was filthy, covered in grey dust. Her hair was a tangled mess, and her clothes were little more than rags. But she didn't strike Winter as a beggar or a thief. Her eyes held a different kind of desperation.

Winter held up both mugs with one hand. "You look thirsty."

Greta hunched her shoulders and looked away.

"I agree," said Winter. "I never understood why they served this stuff hot." She dipped her finger into her own mug and stirred until the surface brimmed with ice. "I prefer my drinks chilled."

"How'd you do that?"

"Practice." Winter grinned and waved her free hand, showing off her tattoos. She pursed her lips and blew a minor enchantment, just enough to raise goose bumps on the girl's exposed arms.

Normally, such tricks elicited giggles and demands to "Do it again!" from children, but the girl looked like she was about to cry. Winter lowered her hands and stepped closer. "What's wrong, sweetie?"

The girl didn't answer.

Winter looked through the crowd. Glory had finally thawed enough to join the fun, performing some elegant and overly stiff dance while three men tried to shoulder each other aside for the chance to join her. Winter eventually caught Sterling's attention. She shifted her head to indicate the girl. He nodded his understanding.

"Why don't we step outside?" Winter asked. The air was refreshingly cool on her skin. Sunrise lightened the sky to the east. No wonder she was fighting yawns. How long had it been since she danced through the night like that? "My name's Winter. You're Greta, right?"

"You're a Hero," she said flatly. "You and your friends. Even the scary one."

"Even Shroud, yes." The assassin had returned halfway through the night. "We came to protect Grayrock from the ghost."

"You can't."

"McCullough told me about your brother. Do you think the ghost took him?"

Silence.

Greta was lucky Winter had been the first to notice her. Had she gone to Shroud, the man would be threatening her life to find out why she was watching them and what secrets she might be keeping. Glory would be lecturing in that irritatingly condescending tone, and Sterling would give one of his speeches about courage and duty and how people can be True Heroes if they only try. None of which would hold a candle to teenage stubbornness.

Winter, on the other hand, knew exactly where to take the girl. She had memorised the layout of the town on her first day. Not that there was much to learn. The poorest homes were in the eastern part of town, close to the quarry. The more money you had, the farther you could get from the dust and noise.

Winter grinned and pointed west. "Let's go shopping."

They started with food. Winter bought a pair of fruit-topped tarts from the baker and handed one to the girl, who looked like she was going to cry again. Winter cloaked her confusion with an easy smile. "If you're not hungry, I'm happy to eat them both."

"No." The girl hastily nibbled the edge of the crust and whispered, "Thank you."

"You're welcome!" Winter plucked a cherry from her tart and popped it into her mouth. "Next up, Roderick's Robes and Garments." She hurried across the street to a shop with a sign showing a well-dressed couple, both of whom looked like walking corpses thanks to the ubiquitous grey dust.

"I know what you're doing," said Greta.

"I'm shopping." Winter slapped her hands against her fur leggings. A cloud of dust rained from her legs. "Fur and dust are a horrid combination. I'm hoping to find something to repel the worst of it. Preferably in blue."

"You're trying to make me like you so I'll tell you about the ghost."

"Well, yes. That too." Winter looked pointedly at the half-finished tart. "How is it working so far?"

Greta flushed and looked away, but not before Winter saw the quickly smothered smile.

"Did you or your brother know a man named Sam? He vanished from Grayrock too, but another group of Heroes rescued him. He's safe in Brightlodge."

Winter waited, but Greta's stone mask had already fallen back into place. Winter didn't want to push, so she walked into the shop and began browsing through Roderick's meagre stock of cloaks, capes, and robes, trusting Greta to follow.

Winter pulled out an emerald-green cape with brown fur trim. "What about this one?"

"It's too small for you," said Greta. "And I thought you wanted something in blue."

"Not for me, silly." Winter winked and tossed the cape at Greta, who barely managed to catch it in her tart-free hand. "Try it on."

Winter smiled to herself and turned to study a deep blue cloak. It was beautiful, the colour of the sky just before sunset, with gold embroidery and rabbit-fur lining. She brought it to her cheek, luxuriating in the softness of the fur.

"Are all Heroes rich?" Greta asked bitterly.

Winter laughed. "I'm not rich, girl." She checked her purse. "If we buy these, I'll have just enough for a meal later today. Possibly breakfast tomorrow morning too, if I'm not too picky about the ingredients."

"And you're wasting your last coins on clothes?"

"You can't wear treasure. Well, I suppose you can . . . there was a belly dancer in Greenwall whose entire outfit was made up of copper coins. But when you deal in ice magic, the last thing you want is a lot of metal touching your exposed skin." She took Greta's cape and the fur-lined cloak to the shopkeeper and laid out a handful of coins. "This will go well with the brown of your eyes."

"What will you do tomorrow after you run out of money?"

"Do you know what's outside that door?" Winter pointed.

"Merchant Street."

"Not that. Beyond the wall. Beyond Grayrock." She waved her hand, painting an imaginary picture. "There are monsters and outlaws and haunted woods and battles to be won. More important, there's treasure. So much treasure, all waiting to be found and spent."

Greta didn't speak again until they left the shop. She carried the folded cape in one arm, but didn't put it on. She kept looking down at the material longingly, like she was trying to persuade herself it was all right to keep it. "You're really bad at this," she said.

"Bad at what?" Winter fastened the cloak's clasp over her shoulders and tried an experimental twirl.

"If you're trying to bribe someone to talk, you shouldn't pay them until after you get the information you need." Greta held up the cape. "What's to stop me from running off?"

"Nothing at all." The clasp rode up a bit, until the metal edge was digging into Winter's neck. She adjusted the shoulders, trying to find a comfortable balance. Perhaps if she wore it with one side tossed back. "How would *you* convince a frightened girl it's safe to tell you the truth?"

"I'm not frightened."

"That's good." Winter brightened. "Oh, look. It has hidden pockets on the inside!"

"How did you become a Hero?" Greta asked a few steps later.

"I wanted to see the world." Winter shrugged. "When Old King Wendleglass announced the return of Heroes and put out his call, how could I pass up that chance? There are other ways to travel, but nothing else comes close to the excitement. Or pays near as well."

"No, I mean—the way you froze that honey lemonade, and made the air colder with your magic. Can anyone do that? Who taught you?"

Now it was Winter's turn to look away. "I didn't learn what I could do until I was seven years old." Her cheeks burned at the memory. "I . . . accidentally froze our dog to the wall."

Greta laughed, the first sound of genuine pleasure Winter had heard from her. "How do you 'accidentally' freeze a dog?"

"I sneezed, and the cold just kind of exploded out of me." Winter smiled ruefully. "The dog was fine once Dad melted him free and gave him some hot soup to drink. But after that, any time I got sick, he'd run and hide for days. The dog, I mean. Not my father."

They had come to the ramp leading up to the main gates. Winter turned left, following the well-trod path along the inside of the wall. "Mum and Dad, they were like me, though they kept their magic hidden. When they learned what I was, they helped me learn to use my powers."

"They were Heroes too?"

Winter chuckled. "No, they were fur trappers. That's how they ended up in our village. They never used their powers when I was little. They wanted a quiet, peaceful life."

She shrugged. She had never understood her parents, but they had been good enough people to let Winter make her own choices. To allow her to become whoever she wanted to be.

"Did you have any brothers or sisters?"

"My parents had enough work on their hands with just me."

"My brother's name is Ben," said Greta. "He's nine. We call him Hedgehog, because of the way his hair sticks out."

Winter nodded but didn't speak, afraid that words might break the spell and send Greta back into her shell of silence.

"We were playing in the woods, out by Founder's Hill." She

stopped walking and stared at the mountains. "That's where Skye found us."

"Skye?"

"That's the ghost's name. She smelled like an old woodstove. Smoke swirled around us, until I could barely see Ben in front of me. I grabbed his hand, but I couldn't see which way to run, and we were both coughing. I heard Skye laughing. Ben screamed when she pulled him away from me."

"I'm sorry," Winter said quietly. "Do you have any idea where she took him? My friends and I can—"

"She promised he'd be all right, as long as I did something for her."

"What's that?"

"She said there would be Heroes coming to Grayrock, and once they got here, I was to let her know." Tears painted glassy lines through the dust on her cheeks. She thrust the cape at Winter. "I'm sorry. I just wanted my brother back."

Winter pushed the cape back. "What did you tell her about us, Greta?"

"Everything I could. That there were four of you. What you looked like, and what kind of weapons you had. Who you were talking to. But Skye didn't give Ben back to me. She said he had been cursed, and she couldn't undo the spell herself. She said the one who could free him would want payment."

"Did she, now?" Winter could guess the answer to her next question, but she asked anyway. "What kind of payment?"

Greta wiped her nose on her sleeve. "The four of you."

chapter 8

STERLING

Their course of action was clear. Villainy threatened the town. This child, Greta, had lost her brother to a monster. More important, she knew how to find that monster. Their duty as Heroes was to go forth to vanquish this so-called ghost once and for all, rescue the boy, and return triumphantly to the grateful people of Grayrock.

And had they set out five minutes sooner, Sterling had no doubt things would have gone exactly as he envisioned.

But instead, Sterling first had to return to the Broken Blade to wake up Glory, who'd fallen asleep in the back. Winter needed to drop her new cloak at the inn. Then Shroud had to finish counting and sorting his arrows. By the time they were finally ready to go, the Mayor had returned, and he didn't look like a happy man.

The Mayor marched up the road, surrounded by half a dozen armed guards. "There they are," he sputtered when he spied the Heroes gathered in the square. "Arrest them all!"

"Oh, good," said Glory. Sterling didn't have to look to know she was smiling and probably a heartbeat away from launching a magical assault in the middle of the town. "Where was he yesterday when we *wanted* to find him?"

Sterling spread his arms in welcome and deliberately stepped in front of Glory. With a well-polished smile, he said, "Fear not, Your Honour. We four have vanquished the ogre that was tormenting your people and sent her fleeing from the good town of Grayrock. Your workers have returned safely to their homes and families, and I trust there shall be no further 'suicides.'"

The Mayor hesitated. He had obviously come prepared for a confrontation, and Sterling's politeness had taken him off guard. Sterling could see the man rethinking his approach.

"I question your idea of safety," said the Mayor. "The traps in those tunnels are deadlier than any ogre."

"Then the solution should be obvious even to the most dim-witted mind," Shroud commented.

Sterling smiled broadly. "So long as your people avoid the tunnels, they shall be safe. In the meantime, would you be so kind as to answer our questions about the ogre, Headstrong? Rumour has it she was working with you. That the two of you served the Ghost of Grayrock."

"How dare you! You claim to be *Heroes.*" The Mayor spoke the word like a curse. "But you're nothing but bullies. You believe you can go wherever you like, do whatever you choose. You've threatened my people. Broken into my home. Frightened my wife. This is *my* town, and I'll not allow you to—"

"That's enough, sir!" Sterling had grown up among society's high-minded elite. While his family might not have been mayors or kings, they were upper-middle snooty, at least. He had learned politics with his letters and could adopt a mask of friendly concern or righteous fury, with the ability to switch between them from one breath to the next. He advanced on the Mayor, pretending to ignore the spears of his men. "Let us discuss instead what *you* have done. You've allowed monsters to prey on the innocent men, women, and children of Grayrock, all so that you might claim a share of some nonexistent treasure!"

He turned so that all of the men and women who had begun to gather might hear his words. "What did the ghost promise you, Your Honour? Gold? Magic? What price to sell your own people into slavery?"

The guards looked uneasy. Well, most of them. One was watching Sterling with a rapt expression, his face flushed, his pupils dilated. He looked to be in his early twenties, with a strong chin and long black hair tied back at the neck. Sterling made a note to chat him up later on, assuming they didn't end up killing each other.

"These baseless accusations are outrageous," the Mayor sputtered. "It's good that the Heroes of legend died before they saw such pretenders running about—"

The Mayor's last word ended in a mouselike squeak as Sterling's sword seemed to leap from its sheath to his hand. The end of the blade rested on the Mayor's dusty shoulder before his guards could do more than blink. "This sword is named Arbiter. It has tasted the blood of many a villain and has defended my honour against all those who would tarnish it. You wouldn't be attempting to tarnish my honour, would you?"

The Mayor's eyes were wide and unblinking, unable to look away from Sterling's sword. The blade was narrower than most, but the lighter weight allowed him far better control. With this sword, Sterling could carve script into his opponents' flesh or slice their garments to tatters without breaking the skin.

"Not at all," the Mayor stammered. "'Your Bitter,' you say? A peculiar name for a weapon, but of course I'm a peaceful man with little knowledge of such things. Named after a favourite drink, perhaps?"

"Arbiter," Sterling said impatiently. "As in judge, or decider."

"Right," said the ponytailed guard. "So it does things arbitrary-like?"

Sterling sighed. The man had been so pretty before he opened his mouth. "My point, Your Honour, is that you've turned your back while the forces of evil terrorised your town. You've done nothing to prevent the kidnapping and murder of your people. You, sir, are a disgrace to your office."

"I am the rightfully elected ruler of Grayrock, and you will address me with the respect I deserve!"

"That's precisely what I've done," said Sterling. "Out of curiosity, when was this election held?"

The Mayor puffed out his chest. "I was voted in at the age of twenty, upon the retirement of my father, rest his soul."

Glory looked him up and down. "So, about fifty years ago, then?"

His face darkened. "I am forty-one years old."

"And the people of Grayrock chose *you* to lead?" Sterling pressed.

"Of course they did," the Mayor shouted. "Father and I tallied the votes ourselves!"

Sterling let that statement hang in the air, but none of the townspeople seemed to find anything peculiar about it.

"It's a miracle these people manage to get dressed in the morning without accidentally hanging themselves," Glory muttered.

"I wonder," Sterling said loudly, "if the people realise that a man elected to power can be elected *from* power if his people feel he's failed in his duties."

"The smugglers and bandits have only grown worse since the Mayor took office," a man near the back said tentatively.

"My uncle was one of the men digging at the dam," called a woman. "He says the ogre would have likely eaten them all if not for the Heroes."

"I've seen the Mayor dance, and he's not half as graceful as Winter, nor as easy on the eyes!"

The Mayor raised his hands. "Don't you see what he's doing? He's turning us against one another."

Sterling slowly withdrew Arbiter, pausing only to flick the

Mayor's forelock with the tip of the blade. He made eye contact with each of the guards in turn, waiting for them to lower their own weapons. His eyes lingered on the ponytailed guard, and he threw in a quick wink. Maybe if the fellow refrained from talking . . .

"Words can end a man as effectively as any blade," Sterling said quietly. "Tell us what you know, support our efforts to protect Grayrock, and save face in front of your people." He sheathed his sword and stepped closer. "Otherwise, I will cut you down where you stand. Oratorically speaking."

The Mayor looked at Sterling and the Heroes, then at the crowd beyond. "Perhaps I've been hasty in my—"

"Sterling for Mayor!" someone yelled.

Sterling froze. "Excuse me?"

Several more people took up the cry, which caused the Mayor's face to turn a fascinating shade of red.

"Let's not be hasty with such important political decisions," said Sterling.

"Conniving, treacherous, usurperous snake!" Spittle sprayed from the Mayor's lips.

Sterling raised his index finger. "I'm fairly certain 'usurperous' isn't a real word."

Off to one side, Winter was covering a laugh with her hand. Glory rolled her eyes. Shroud simply slid a hand towards one of the many weapons concealed upon his person, presumably looking forwards to the pending chaos.

Sterling turned to the crowd. "My apologies, good people, but I must decline your kind nomination. A Hero must serve all of Albion, not just a single town. Though there are a few of you I'd be happy to service in private, once our work here is done."

"But Grayrock would be safer with a Hero in charge," said a man.

"Grayrock would be safer with a chicken in charge," Glory shot back.

To the Mayor, Sterling whispered, "Ask yourself which is more valuable. Your position as Mayor of Grayrock, with all of the power and respect you've gathered over the years, or the empty promises of a ghost."

"Skye," the Mayor mumbled in a voice only Sterling could hear. "Her name is Skye."

"Yes, we know." Sterling beamed and wrapped an arm around the Mayor's shoulders. The Mayor tried to pull away, but years of sword work had strengthened Sterling's grip, and it took only the slightest pressure to still the man's struggles. "Now tell us something we don't."

"I can't. If she believes I've betrayed her, she'll kill the boy. Do you know what that could do to my approval ratings?"

Sterling's fingers tightened. "I wasn't planning to tell her. Were you?"

"No! But she's spread her spies through Grayrock!"

Sterling glanced at the crowd. All it would take was a single whisper in Skye's ear and Greta's brother was dead. He wanted to crack the Mayor like a walnut, to spill his secrets and his betrayal for all to see. But to question him now, in public, could cost an innocent boy his life. Nor could they simply drag the Mayor off somewhere private without arousing suspicion.

"We are going to save that child," Sterling whispered. "When we come back, you will tell us everything. If you try to run—"

"You'll kill me?" The Mayor seemed to have regained a bit of his bravado.

"Not me." He pointed to Shroud. "Him."

The Mayor swallowed.

"Also, I'm terribly sorry about this. It's almost entirely for the sake of Skye's spies." Before the Mayor could respond, Sterling backhanded him across the face, knocking him into his guards. Raising his voice, he said, "Very well, you black-hearted rat. Keep your secrets. We *will* uncover the truth!"

With that, Sterling stomped away. Two sounds jumped out at him as he left. The first was the Mayor's outraged shouts. The second was a woman who, from the sound of things, was doing her best to get one of her chickens nominated to be the new Mayor of Grayrock.

"How do we know we can trust the girl?" asked Shroud. They had been hiking for roughly half an hour. The dirt trail was well used, and the greenery to either side had been grazed short by goats and other livestock. Pine trees hid Grayrock from view. "The ghost said to bring the Heroes to her, and here we are, marching into her parlour. Seems a little too convenient to me."

Greta had hardly spoken since leaving Grayrock. She stayed close to Winter and kept looking at the others, then looking back towards town. If not for the occasional howl of a distant animal to remind her of the dangers awaiting solitary travellers, Sterling suspected, she would have bolted by now.

"She told me the truth about spying on us, and about Skye," said Winter. "I trust her."

"I'm sure that will be a great comfort to us all when we're fighting for our lives," said Glory.

"I didn't tell Skye you were coming," Greta insisted. "Even if I wanted to, I only have one way to contact her." She pointed to three ordinary-looking sticks bundled together and strapped over her shoulder. "Once we reach the spot where my brother was taken, I'm to light a fire and burn these. That's the signal that I have news of the Heroes."

"Don't worry, child," said Sterling. "We shall rescue your brother, stop this creature of smoke and death, and get to the bottom of this mystery."

"Careful," said Glory. "If you puff and preen about any more, someone's liable to mistake you for a peacock."

"What troubles you, my lady Glory?" asked Sterling. "Your wit and charm have been particularly barbed since we left Grayrock."

"Since we let a murderer go free, you mean? You *know* the Mayor was behind those so-called suicides."

"Do we?" Sterling countered. "Justice requires proof, and all we currently have are suspicions. Perhaps Skye will be able to give us the proof we need."

"Or perhaps feathers will magically sprout from your backside."

"The people of Grayrock have consistently described Skye as a creature of smoke and death," said Shroud. "We should be prepared to counter a magical assault."

"We're almost there," Greta said softly. A short distance ahead, a shelf of dirty rock jutted out from the mountainside.

Sterling dropped to one knee and put a hand on Greta's shoulder. "I know you're afraid, but your brother needs you. We will be watching though you won't see us. I'll not allow this woman to harm you. You have my word."

"Once Skye shows up, just get out of the way," Winter said. "You and your brother will be back home before you know it."

Greta nodded and hunched her shoulders beneath her green cape, then marched onto the ledge. She glanced back, and Sterling gave her an encouraging smile. Greta took a deep breath, then sat down to start a fire.

Shroud slipped away between the trees. Despite having seen him go, Sterling was hard-pressed to follow the assassin's movements as he scaled a tree and readied his bow.

"I hope she does have some sort of fire-based power," Winter said with a grin. "This could be fun."

Sterling ducked behind a recently fallen tree. The branches

should hide him from view while letting him keep an eye on Greta. Winter and Glory followed suit.

Greta's small fire was soon crackling away, devouring pine needles and small twigs. She set the three sticks over the flames. They caught quickly, as if they had been soaked in lantern oil. The flames turned red. Smoke blotted a black river through the sky.

It wasn't long before a second trail of smoke rose in the distance, as if in response. It moved swiftly, closing towards them like a deer sprinting through the woods. Greta saw it too. She was breathing faster now and kept looking back as if searching for reassurance that they hadn't abandoned her.

"Pretend we aren't here," Sterling whispered. "Else you'll give us away."

Winter pursed her lips and blew, sending a gust of cold air towards the ledge. For some reason, that seemed to comfort the girl. She shivered, then smiled and turned to await Skye.

She didn't have to wait long. The so-called ghost, when she arrived, was barely larger than Greta. Her hard, barklike skin marked her as a nymph though she lacked visible wings. Her features were darker than those of any nymph Sterling had previously encountered. Her face made him think of a wooden mask charred black in the embers of a fire.

A heavy gown of deep green velvet covered her body. Smoke poured from the hem and sleeves, obscuring her hands and feet. A long gold cape hung from her shoulders, rippling like ocean waves. Skye had a knife tucked through her belt, and several pouches rested against her hip. A knucklebone hung from a black cord around her neck.

There was no sign of the boy, Ben.

"You have information about the Heroes?" The nymph's words rasped like those of a crone though her features were youthful. Smoke trailed from her mouth when she spoke. Sterling wondered briefly what it would be like to kiss such lips.

"She's done one better." Sterling stepped out of hiding. Greta scurried out of the way, leaving Sterling and Skye to face one another over the fire.

"Greta told me there were four." Skye's fingers moved towards the bone on her necklace.

Sterling pulled Arbiter from its sheath. "Where's the boy?"

She smiled. "What if I tell you it's too late for him?"

He heard Greta whimper. His hand tightened on the hilt. "Then you'll die."

Sterling moved closer, studying the bone. It was too old and yellowed to have come from Ben.

"You'd kill me anyway," Skye said lightly. "It's what you do. Slaughter the people of the forests. Burn our homes to the ground."

"Only if I must." Sterling flashed his most charming smile. "I can think of far more pleasant ways to pass the hours. Give us the boy, and tell us why you're plotting against Brightlodge and Grayrock, and perhaps we could discover just how hot the fire is that burns within you."

Skye rolled her eyes. "Hot enough to burn your little sword to ash. As for Grayrock, I do what I'm ordered to do."

That wasn't the answer he had expected. "Ordered by whom? Who commands the nymph, the ogre, and the buffoon?"

"You'll meet her soon enough." She reached for one of the pouches on her belt.

Sterling levelled his sword, prepared to leap over the small fire and run her through. But the wooden doll she removed appeared harmless. Small, crudely carved limbs twitched.

"This is the child you seek. Surrender to me and I'll let him return to his sister. Resist and poor Ben will suffer terribly." Smoke rose from Skye's fingers, and the movements of the doll grew more frantic.

"Give me back my brother!" Greta ran at the nymph.

Sterling stepped sideways, cutting her off. At the same time, an arrow flew silently from the shadows into Skye's shoulder. The doll tumbled to the ground, dangerously close to the campfire.

Skye ripped the bone from around her neck and the flames grew taller, belching black smoke. Sparks swirled together, jumping into the branches beside the trail. When the smoke cleared, small creatures made of what looked like smouldering sticks jumped at Sterling.

Arctic wind rushed past him to envelop the closest of the magical constructs. Frost smothered the embers, and the thing collapsed in a pile.

"Not very sturdy, are they?" asked Winter.

Skye hurled the bone directly at Sterling. He turned to the side and swatted it away with Arbiter.

The instant steel met bone, the bone exploded. The light of the sun and the heat of a forge washed over him. He kept his sword pointed in Skye's direction while blinking and rubbing his eyes with his free hand, trying to restore his vision.

"Mind the ledge, Sterling," shouted Shroud.

Through smoke and the sparks still flickering in his eyes, Sterling saw the blurred shape of Skye reaching for the fallen doll. He switched Arbiter to his off hand, pulled a dagger, and sent it spinning through the air. It missed, but the blade stabbed the ground in front of the nymph's hand, making her jerk back.

Before he could follow up with a second dagger, another of Skye's minions seized his leg. His boot protected him from the worst of it, but the thing reached two sets of flaming arms up to burn through Sterling's pants and sear the skin beneath.

"Oh, no. You won't slay me that easily." He slashed Arbiter downward to cut through the construct's body. Most of it fell away, but the arms continued to cling and burn. "Have a taste of Sterling silver!"

Glory groaned. "Your wit inflicts more pain than your blade."

Cold washed over his leg before he could come up with a suitably cutting response. He reached down to break the blackened sticks free and nodded his thanks to Winter.

"They're not sturdy, but they're quick, and if you cut them apart, they just keep fighting," complained Glory. She hurled a green orb at one of the constructs. It shattered, covering it in dark, viscous ooze that slowly smothered the thing's flames. It fell into a pile of black, gleaming sticks.

Skye did something to the clasps on her shoulder, and her cape billowed outward like the throat of a bullfrog. Smoke filled her cape and lifted her into the air.

As the flames spread to the shrubs and brush, new creatures arose, like hellish mockeries of woodland creatures. Their movements were quick and random, almost panicked. A hunched ball of fire and thorns darted right past Sterling and vanished over the ledge.

"So be it," Skye called out, her body all but invisible in the smoke. "Then let Grayrock's death come not from flood but from fire!"

More of the constructs arose, baking the air like an oven. They assailed the Heroes while others scampered towards Grayrock.

"I was doubtful when the girl told me Heroes had come to Grayrock," Skye continued. Sparks and smoke flew down like meteors, raising new creatures wherever they landed. "Perhaps she was correct. Yog will be disappointed to lose you to the fire, but there are others—"

Sterling stomped a construct into the dirt, jumped free, and hurled a dagger into the smoke.

There was a meaty *thunk*. "Oh, *rot,* that hurts!"

Skye flew higher, avoiding the next dagger. One of Shroud's arrows disappeared into the smoke but hit nothing.

Sterling glanced about. Many of Skye's constructs had collapsed into normal flames. "Forget the minions. Focus our assault on their mistress, and victory will be ours!"

Winter walked to the edge. The fire died as she passed. Frost spread over the ground. She raised her hands, and cold wind poured forth, clearing the worst of the smoke.

Shroud's next arrow hit Skye in the stomach. Glory reached out, summoning two more of her green apples. But Skye fell away, gliding towards the treetops.

The remaining constructs fell apart. Sterling ground the nearest beneath his boot, while Winter used her magic to extinguish those that had fled towards Grayrock. By the time they brought the fires under control, Skye was gone.

"I don't know where she got that cape," Shroud said, "but I want one."

"It's not the cape," said Glory. "She's using the smoke, controlling it with her Will and using it to lift herself about."

"I tried to extinguish it." Winter was sweating. "There was too much. It's a part of her, burning her up on the inside."

"Power isn't everything, and we've triumphed once again. We've met our foe and saved the boy. Assuming the lady of smoke and fire was telling the truth." Sterling picked up the fallen doll. It was a simple thing, twice the length of his hand, made of hand-carved wood. Iron nails held the limbs in place. Wisps of dirty yarn were glued to the scalp for hair. The face had been painted on. The body was slightly blackened but didn't appear seriously damaged.

"Is he all right?" Greta asked, pushing closer.

The head turned, and inky eyes looked up at them both. The painted mouth opened. "I want to go home."

"And so you will, Ben." Sterling tried not to let the living, moving doll in his hands disconcert him. This was a child in need of aid, and Sterling meant to help him . . . no matter how creepy his current form might be. "But first, what can you tell us of this Yog, and why does she plot against Brightlodge?"

"She wants to destroy Grayrock first," said Ben. "And then she means to go to Brightlodge to hunt and kill the Heroes."

"Which Heroes?" asked Sterling.

The doll looked up at him with black, expressionless eyes. "All of them."

Part II

The Green Storm

There was no question anymore. Yog had watched Skye's defeat through the nymph's own eyes. Heroes had indeed returned to Albion.

She eased down on her stool and relit Skye's candle, then brought the taper to the ogre skull. She far preferred communing with Skye, or even with that ridiculous redcap. Headstrong's candle smelled like boiling sweat, and seeing the world from the ogre's point of view always left Yog feeling fuzzy in the head, like a hangover of idiocy.

She reached out to Skye first. "You lost Grayrock. You lost the boy."

Yog couldn't see the nymph's face, but the candle flame shivered with echoed fear. "Forgive me, mistress. I can sneak back into town after nightfall to—"

"By now the Heroes will have secured both entrances to the tunnels. They'll be searching for you, and the stink of burning trees will draw them to you before you've stepped inside Grayrock's walls."

All plans required flexibility, or they would shatter like poorly tempered steel. Her late husband had taught her that. It wasn't the loss of the dam that made Yog want to crush Skye's skull with a rock and extinguish the nymph's fire forever. "You tried to send your sparklings to burn Grayrock. Do you think I would have wasted weeks sending you and Headstrong to chip away at the dam if I could have simply set it ablaze?"

"I didn't—"

"You know what I seek," Yog continued. "What the item is made of."

"Wood," Skye whispered.

"Fire devours all in its path. Had your impetuous attack succeeded . . ." She breathed into the skull, and the blue flame danced higher.

Skye screamed.

Yog left her to her suffering and, reluctantly, turned to check on Headstrong. She found the ogre in the midst of a shouting match with . . . was that a goat standing in the middle of the trail?

Headstrong raised her axe with both hands. "*Nobody* arse-butts an ogre!"

The goat responded with a lazy bleat, then went back to munching on the thistle growing from a crack in the rocks.

"What are you doing?" Yog demanded.

The ogre jumped and spun, slashing the axe through the air behind her before realising who was addressing her. "The goat attacked me!"

"Shut up!" whispered one of the noggins. Probably Schemer. That one was a little smarter about recognising when Yog was in a mood. They couldn't hear her voice as clearly as Headstrong did, but they all picked up on echoes of her voice. And her wrath.

The nymph's cries were growing tiresome. Yog waved a hand and the candle flickered down to its natural flame. "Chaos has begun to spread through Brightlodge."

"Time for the storm?" That was Night Axe.

Another noggin, Thinker, answered before Yog could speak.

"Can't use the storm on Brightlodge, bonehead. Not 'til Grayrock falls."

"Bloody Heroes," muttered another.

"The ale Blue delivered to Brightlodge is potent enough for ordinary men and women, but the Heroes are proving resistant," Yog said. Resistant, but not entirely immune. Yog adjusted both skulls to face her. "Meet me in the Boggins. Once I've prepared a stronger mixture, the two of you will transport it to Grayrock and prepare the storm."

The Heroes in Grayrock would be hard-pressed to counter this assault. She had hoped to use the storm against Brightlodge, to spread panic and chaos that would make the surviving Heroes easy targets. That was before the ogre and the nymph had failed her.

"The Boggins?" asked Headstrong. "What about the humans? I wanna get my hands on them and—"

Yog picked up a slender iron hook and pressed the point onto the top of the skull. Applying gentle pressure, she scraped the tip over the bone.

Headstrong dropped her weapon and clutched her head, howling in pain. The goat trotted away.

"What of the redcap, mistress?" whispered Skye.

"Blue has been taken by the Heroes." Not for the first time, Yog questioned her choice of a redcap as her third Rider. The creature was skilful enough, and far smarter than most of his kind. Yog had enhanced those traits, but there was only so much she could do. You couldn't forge a blade out of dung. She had to make do with the materials she had.

Never in her youth had she settled for such flawed Riders. A clever but half-mad redcap, a powerful but tormented nymph, and that idiot of an ogre.

"We'll retrieve him for you, mistress," said Skye. "I will rain fire upon Brightlodge while Headstrong—"

"You'll do as I say," Yog snapped. "Bad enough I've lost my Rider of Skill. I'll not risk the two of you."

Oh, for the days when her body had been capable of containing her full power. The days before a desperate man's curse had reduced her to *this,* forcing her to pass so much of her abilities into the bodies of her Riders.

"I will see to Blue's return myself," she said. "My outlaws are wiped out, so you must transport the storm's ingredients to Grayrock so I can wipe out those pathetic rock workers myself."

She extinguished both candles with a wave of a hand. The people of Grayrock would die, and after so many generations, her curse would at last be washed away. She would finally reclaim her power.

All it would take was the eradication of a town or two.

chapter 9

INGA

"What do you mean, you're taking my ale?" Pale Pete, owner of the Hack and Cough Pub, was not a happy man. Built as solidly as one of his larger kegs, he stood with folded arms between the Heroes and his stock. A thick cudgel hung from his hip.

"Every keg with that hideous dead cow on it," Inga confirmed. "You haven't had any yourself, have you?"

"I taste test every barrel that comes through these doors." He grimaced. "Can't say I could stomach more than a sip of that stuff. But I got a great bargain."

"I'm sure," Inga said. "But like Old Mother Twostraps used to say, if you pay for rough linen drawers, you can't expect 'em to feel like silk. Sure, outlaws and smugglers are happy to cut prices. They're just as happy to cut throats. That ale is poisoned."

"That's preposterous!" Pete looked at Tipple, and his eyes narrowed. "I see what this is about. Old Jeremiah Tipple claims to be a Hero, but nothing's really changed. He can't pay his tab, so he's spun a story about tainted drink as an excuse to steal my stock, is that it?"

"Tipple wouldn't do . . ." Inga hesitated. "Well, maybe he would, but that's not why we're here."

"Besides, if I were planning to swindle you, I'd steal the good stuff." Tipple's face shone with sweat, and his pallor was the yellow-green of an old bruise. He had been complaining of a sour stomach all morning. It had taken two potions and a bit of Leech's power to get him up and about this morning.

"Look at him," Inga said. "This is what your ale did."

"Prove it."

"Very well." Inga folded her arms. "Go ahead and drink a pint of that dead-cow ale. One pint and we'll leave you in peace."

Pete looked past Inga to the patrons seated at their tables, many of whom were watching the exchange. "I told you, that stuff tastes like—"

"I'm sure you've had worse," said Inga. "One pint. I'll pay." She pulled a coin from her purse and slammed it onto the bar. "You can keep the change."

Blue chuckled softly. "Risky ale makes you pale." He tilted his head to one side. "And dead."

"That redcap gives me the creeps," muttered the owner.

"You're not alone, friend," said Tipple.

"What's wrong?" asked Inga. "Not thirsty anymore?"

Pete's shoulders sagged. "Take the damn kegs, blast it all. Both of them. I was thinking about closing this place anyway. Mother always said I'd no head for business. But if a fifty-percent-off sale's good for profits, shouldn't a hundred-percent-off sale be twice as good?"

Inga patted him on the shoulder. "Always listen to your mother."

"Can I get a bottle to go?" Tipple asked as he grabbed the nearest keg. "Wine, not that poisoned sewage."

Inga sighed. "Are you sure you should be drinking that? You're already sick as a dog."

"If the dog felt like this, he'd want a drink too." Tipple looked back longingly as they left the tavern, seemingly unbothered by the weight of the keg balanced on his shoulder.

Inga carried the second keg. To her left, Blue played idly with an earthworm he had dug up from the side of the road earlier in the day. A length of rope secured him to Inga's wrist. "Blue, what do you know about this poison? Why would Nimble Johanna want to kill innocent people?"

"Not innocent people. Heroes."

Inga frowned. "She wanted to kill us?"

Blue nodded so hard the tip of his cap slapped his eye, making him yelp in surprise.

"Why?" asked Tipple.

"Because Heroes are big and stupid and smelly!" Blue sniffed Tipple, then made a show of toppling over. He bounced back to his feet. "Yog will kill them all!"

"Who's Yog?" asked Inga.

The redcap's eyes went round. "How do you know Yog?"

With great difficulty, Inga swallowed her first retort. Blue wasn't trying to be difficult . . . probably. Depending on which rumour you believed about where redcaps came from, Blue might even have been human once. With those spikes he had driven into his skull, it was a wonder he could talk at all. "Is Yog an outlaw? Another redcap?"

This triggered a bout of laughter. "Yog is bone and stone and iron chain. Flying death and deadly rain."

Tipple looked around. "Am I the only one who can't make a lick of sense out of that?"

"Did Yog work for Nimble Johanna?" asked Inga.

Blue hunched his shoulders and pulled out the skeletal finger he had shown them before, the one he claimed was magic.

"Yog . . . is a finger?"

Blue kicked her in the shin. "Stupid Heroes. Stupid outlaws. Stupid redcaps."

Beneath his obvious anger and disgust, Inga heard something more. Pain and longing. "We thought you might have been a prisoner of those outlaws. You weren't, were you? The redcap bodies we found. Did Yog tell you to betray them, and to help the outlaws deliver their poison to Brightlodge?"

"Maybe." Blue looked away. "Not telling."

"You helped to kill your fellow redcaps," said Tipple.

"Maybe," he said, more quietly than before. His eyes were glassy. He blinked and swiped a filthy hand over his face. Could a redcap actually be feeling guilt over betraying his own kind?

If so, that guilt vanished the instant he spotted their destination. Rook and Leech had dragged three more kegs to the edge of town, where they were dumping the contents into the sewers that flowed into the falls.

Blue's eyes went round. "Fish will be drunk on ale that's sunk!"

From the angry shouts of the crowd, the Heroes might as well have been tossing babies over a cliff.

"They say it's the start of a prohibition!" cried one man. "We won't stand for it, do you hear?"

"Wendleglass can have my ale when he pries it out of my cold, dead belly," said another.

"*Real* Heroes wouldn't march into my establishment and steal my kegs without as much as a how-do-you-do!"

Inga shoved through the crowd, set her own keg on the ground, and raised her voice. "The ale is poison!"

"But it's *cheap* poison!"

"Not to mention it tastes like sewage," added Tipple.

"*Cheap* poisoned sewage!"

"My brother had a pint of the stuff last night, and he was just fine when he left. Mostly fine. Not dead, at any rate."

"And how is he this morning?" asked Leech.

"Now look here, just because a man takes mysteriously ill after a good, honest night's drinking doesn't mean—"

"Enough," shouted Inga. They were like stubborn children. Tell them they couldn't have a treat and they grew more determined than ever to gobble it down the instant you looked away. "Listen here. Anyone so much as touches these kegs, I'll toss you in after them, got it?"

Rook smashed the butt of his crossbow into another keg, hard enough to crack the wood. Tipple lifted the keg and hurled the whole thing into the sewer. The crowd roared in response.

"Stand aside!" The crowd split to open a path for a pair of Brightlodge guardsmen. They were sweating and out of breath, and one had blood on his spear and uniform.

Inga's gut tightened. "What's wrong?"

"You're to return to Wendleglass Hall immediately!" said one.

Rook folded his arms.

"That is . . . I meant to say, Young King Wendleglass has asked that all Heroes join him at the hall," the guard amended. "If you don't mind."

The other shifted his weapon to point at Blue. "Redcaps have invaded Brightlodge."

Poor King Wendleglass had been in a panic. Inga and the other Heroes had smiled and nodded reassuringly until they could get him out of the way and get down to the business of planning their defences, planning which was complicated by interruptions and criticism from the king's dead father.

Even now, Old King Wendleglass wandered the streets of Brightlodge while Heroes searched for the intruders in groups of two and three. Inga could hear him shouting, *"Redcaps at our walls! Redcaps in our streets! Redcaps in our privies! Brightlodge was never invaded by redcaps when* I *was king!"*

There were reports of redcaps popping up all over Brightlodge. Inga had been partnered with Jeremiah Tipple, but they hadn't gone far when Tipple paled, clutched his stomach, and raced to the nearest privy.

Inga pounded on the door. "Will you hurry it up in there? We're supposed to be protecting people."

The only answer was an inarticulate shout. Tipple sounded like a cow in labour. Inga winced to imagine what was drawing such sounds from the man.

Blue crouched close to Inga, hiding behind her bulk as the townspeople alternately fled into their homes and came back out to see what was happening. He appeared to be enjoying the panic and occasional screams.

"Do you need me to fetch Leech?" Inga called to Tipple. He and Rook were working several streets over.

Something slammed against the outhouse walls from the inside, hard enough to make the entire structure jump several inches. The wooden planks creaked.

"Tipple?"

The door exploded from its hinges. Inga instinctively yanked Bulwark up. Flying shards of wood thumped off the shield. A body tumbled into the dirt. Tipple stomped out after it, one hand holding his trousers up, the other balled into a fist. Blood dripped from parallel scratches on his face. "The pipsqueak was hiding in the roof like a damn spider," he roared. "Waited for me to sit down and settle in, then pounced on my blooming head."

The creature was unlike any redcap Inga had ever seen. It appeared to be female and was superficially similar to Blue. Pups from the same litter, as old Lottie Dragonbreath used to say. But the skin lacked the sickly pallor of a redcap, and while she did have a hat pulled tightly over her head, it appeared to be a damp nightcap, the laces tied tight beneath the chin. The hat was the deep green colour of decaying swamp muck. A single nail through the forehead held it in place.

The creature—the greencap—jumped to her feet and pounced at Inga, who bent her knees and braced herself. The greencap bounced off Bulwark and went sprawling.

Before the greencap could recover, Tipple seized her by the back of her nightgown, hefted her into the air, and threw her headfirst into the outhouse. She smashed through the back wall, hit the ground, and didn't get back up.

The outhouse swayed, and for a moment Inga thought it might survive the abuse that had been heaped upon it. Then, with a series of loud cracks and bangs, it collapsed into a heap of broken boards. A foul-smelling cloud of dust spread outward from the wreckage. Blue pinched his nose in disgust.

"Where do these things get their caps?" Tipple rubbed his head with one hand. "Is there some deranged hatter running around selling red hats and iron nails to new-formed redcaps?"

"Her cap was green," Inga pointed out.

Tipple shrugged. "Maybe this one wasn't ripe yet."

"She smelled ripe enough to me."

"Ha!" He snorted and wiped his nose. "That's a good one, Inga-dinga." He reached out as if to hug her.

Inga swiftly interposed Bulwark between them. The man had just been in a privy brawl, and he had the stink to prove it. She tugged Blue around the collapsed privy to examine the fallen greencap. "How many more of you are roaming the streets of Brightlodge?"

"Not one of us." Blue crept towards the greencap and nudged her with his toe. "She's broken."

"Tipple has that effect on people," Inga agreed.

Another redcap—greencap—galloped past, riding a pig like a steed and stabbing a pitchfork at anyone who came too close. Inga hoped it wasn't the same pig she had helped catch the day before. That poor animal had been through enough.

She turned her attention back to the greencap who had attacked Tipple. "Do you know what happened to her, Blue?"

Blue glanced down. "Big, pickle-smelling human threw her through a privy."

Inga scanned the street and adjusted her shield. "You said she wasn't one of you. What is she?"

Before Blue could answer, she heard Leech shouting from one street over, calling for backup.

Inga ran towards the sound, dragging Blue behind. They found Rook trying to get a clear shot at a greencap inside a barbershop. A group of four angry townspeople crowded around Rook.

"Leave her alone," yelled a heavyset boy, swinging an iron skillet at Rook's head. "That's my granny!"

Rook easily dodged the blow. The boy staggered back, though nobody had struck him that Inga could see. Leech stood in the background, draining the strength from Rook's attackers.

"We don't have time for this nonsense." Inga bulled her way to Rook's side and slammed Bulwark down in front of her. The old face on the shield came to life, and a trio of spectral shields spread out in a half circle. With a flash of light, the shields shot forth, knocking the townspeople to the ground.

A middle-aged man started to get back to his feet. Inga tugged her sword free. "Stay there. Otherwise I'll just have to knock you down again. Now what's all of this fussing about?"

Another greencap jumped down from the roof of the barbershop. Inga waited for it to approach, then calmly clubbed it on the side of the head with the flat of her blade. Rook raised his crossbow to shoot down the other.

"Please," said the man. "She don't mean no harm."

Inga looked at the unconscious greencap, a short man with a boyish face. He could have been handsome if not for the blood covering much of his clothes and the twisted snarl on his face. Her stomach knotted.

She put a hand on Rook's crossbow. The greencap hiding in the barbershop was as old as dirt, with wrinkled skin and a hunch so severe she resembled a walking horseshoe. To the boy, she asked, "What did you mean when you said that was your granny?"

The boy sat up, clutching his chest with both hands. "She came back from the pub last night saying she had a stomachache. When we woke up this morning, we found her like this. She was trying to eat our dog."

"Broken, broken, broken," said Blue.

"What about the other one?" asked Inga.

"Him?" The older of the humans—the boy's father, perhaps—waved a hand. "That looks like our neighbour, Clump. You can go ahead and kill him. He's a complete arse."

The granny charged, waving a wooden cane about with both hands.

Inga sheathed her sword, caught the cane on her forearm, and yanked it away. The old greencap wobbled and fell.

"Stop it!" yelled the boy.

Inga crouched to look Blue in the eye. "What happened to these people?"

Blue shrugged and stared at the road.

"They say redcaps were once ordinary humans," said Leech. "Rumour has it, if you drink the blood of a redcap and spend the night under the light of the full moon, you become one of them."

"I thought it was if you mooned a redcap in the middle of the night," said the man.

"The redcaps beneath the library," said Leech. "They'd been drained of blood."

"Someone's transforming the people into these things." Inga glanced at Blue. "This isn't an invasion. How much did you know about this?"

Blue turned to flee. Two paces later, the rope went taut and he landed hard on his back, clawing at the noose.

Tipple stumbled up, one hand clutching his gut. "If Blue was trying to poison people, why'd he try to burn down the tavern?"

"Redcaps aren't known for well-thought plans," said Rook.

Across the road, a man screamed as a greencap chased him out of his home. The greencap was dressed in pyjamas and was swinging a broken, burning chair about his head.

Rook sighed, raised his crossbow, and shot the greencap in the hip.

Inga grabbed Blue's rope and lifted. *"What did you do to these people?"*

"Hard to talk without air," Leech pointed out.

She lowered the rope until Blue's toes touched the road. He twitched and squirmed like a fish on a line. He had been tied up throughout the night and had never left the Heroes' presence. "How did you do it, and how many people—"

"Can't say!" Blue squealed. "Can't say or Yog will flay and slay!"

Inga glanced at the boy. "You said your granny was at the pub," she whispered. "Did Clump go to the pub last night too?"

The boy nodded. "He went most nights."

"The ale," said Rook.

"It wasn't poison. It was something worse." Inga spun back to Tipple. "How much of that stuff did you drink?"

"A pint, maybe?" He grimaced.

Leech studied Tipple, checking his pulse at the wrist, then standing on tiptoes to examine his eyes. "Drink this," he said, handing over a small flask. "It'll help heal whatever war's ripping through your guts."

"Thanks." Tipple downed the contents in one gulp.

"An' if it doesn't work, at least I'll get the chance to dissect you."

"How are you feeling?" Inga asked, jumping in before Tipple could answer.

"Like I swallowed a balverine, and the bastard's trying to dig his way out from the inside." He looked down at the moaning greencaps. "Am I gonna wake up tomorrow morning and nail a bloody cap to my skull?"

Leech circled around, continuing to poke and prod Tipple's body. "Tomorrow? I want to know why you haven't changed already. I guess it could just be your greater mass, hey?"

"What's that supposed to mean?" Tipple whirled, one hand going to his gut, the other balling into a fist.

"Blue, what's happening to them?" Inga demanded. "Can it be cured?"

Blue touched a finger to his cap and held it out. Red blood smeared the skin. "Blood gets tainted, caps get painted."

"People are dying, dammit!" Bulwark began to glow, responding to Inga's anger. Throughout Brightlodge, families were watching their loved ones twist into monsters. In that moment, she could have killed Blue for his role in this.

Blue licked his lips. His whole body was trembling, and his eyes were moist. He had dug that old bone finger out of his shirt and was clutching it with both hands the way a frightened child might cling to a favourite doll. He even seemed to be whispering to it.

Pity dulled the edge of her rage. "Why is their blood tainted, Blue? What else was in that ale?"

"Don't know. Have to go." Blue tugged weakly at the rope.

"Enough." Rook pointed his crossbow and pulled the trigger. A series of bolts ricocheted off the cobblestones between the redcap's feet, making him squawk and dance away as far as the rope would allow.

"Don't know!" Blue squealed. "Have to go! Have to go!"

Inga crouched to speak to him at eye level. "Is there a cure?"

"Moonwort bud," he whispered. "Human blood. Mixed with sun and other mud."

"Other mud?" asked Leech. "What does that mean?"

"Don't know." He watched Rook warily, moving closer to Inga as if using her as a shield. His eyes widened, and he tugged Inga's sleeve. "Nimble Johanna knows."

"Fat lot of good that does us," said Tipple. "Nimble Johanna is fish food. Toasted fish food."

Blue's eyes narrowed, and he spoke in a whisper Inga had to strain to hear. "Johanna had a secret place. With secret door. Secret potions, and lots more."

Hope made Inga's heart pound harder. "If you help us cure my friend—and if you swear to leave Brightlodge in peace—we'll let you go when all this is done. You'll be free."

Blue stared at her, barely breathing. "Free?"

"You have our word." She glared at the others, daring them to argue. Rook shook his head, but said nothing. Tipple shrugged and took a drink from a bottle he'd been carrying somewhere on his person.

With his blood-smeared hand, Blue yanked the bone finger from around his neck. "Free."

"I promise," said Inga.

Arm shaking, Blue flung the bone away. "Follow me."

chapter 10

ROOK

"Well done, Heroes!" Old King Wendleglass floated through the streets of Brightlodge, congratulating everyone he encountered. For the moment, those streets were empty save for Heroes and the occasional groaning greencap. Most of the people had retreated to their homes, hoping to find safety behind locked doors. As if safety was anything but an illusion, a luxury bought with the blood of men and women like Rook and his companions.

"My kingdom is saved, thanks to you." The old ghost spread his arms, and for a moment Rook thought he might try to hug them.

"Not yet," said Rook. There couldn't have been more than thirty greencaps running about town, and most of them had been cut down or locked up within hours. This had been nothing. A feint, or perhaps a test. The true threat was out there waiting.

He stepped past the ghost, heading purposefully towards the bridge out of town. He kept one eye on Blue and the other on Jeremiah Tipple. There was no telling what damage even a small dose of redcap blood might do to a man. Rook had never bought that whole "Anything that doesn't kill you makes you stronger" philosophy. There were plenty of ways to break a man without killing him. Just look at the survivors from that hollow man attack in the Deadlands a few months back.

Tipple's ability to imbibe inhuman amounts of alcohol and still function were legendary, and that healing potion might have helped, but there was always the chance he would succumb and change into one of those green-capped killers before they found Nimble Johanna's cure. If it even existed.

The good thing about Rook's crossbow was that it would allow him to put down both Blue and Tipple in short order if it came to that.

"Wait!" Young Wendleglass ran after them, flanked by his guards. "I was hoping you might, um . . . report back to the hall." He stopped to catch his breath. "I'm told you were the ones . . . who discovered the cause of this plague. We need you . . . to share what you've learned."

Son and dead father glanced at one another, but neither spoke. The ghost looked vaguely annoyed, and the young king just looked uncomfortable. Theirs was an odd relationship if ever there was one.

"We will," said Inga. "Just as soon as we return."

"Oh. You have another quest? I don't remember anyone mentioning—"

"Jeremiah Tipple drank blood-tainted ale," said Leech. "We're hoping to cure him before we have to kill him."

"I see." Young King Wendleglass took two steps back, while his guards shifted nervously. The man had all the confidence and spine of a wet dishcloth. "Do you think it might be better—I mean, if you'd like, I could ask my men to, um, take him into custody?"

"He's our friend." Inga stood like a boulder, hard and immovable. "We're going to take care of him. If something happens, we'll subdue him ourselves. We *won't* be killing him." That last was aimed at Leech.

"But—"

"The lad's with us," said Rook. "The longer we stand here gabbing, the more likely he is to start pounding nails into his head and trying to kill everyone. If that's to happen, I'd rather it be outside of Brightlodge, wouldn't you?"

The king swallowed, then nodded.

"Right. Let's be off." He shouldered his crossbow and started walking.

Young Wendleglass wasn't wrong. Rook would have been happier with Tipple locked away for everyone's safety. But he knew Inga wouldn't go for that. The lass had a heart of gold when it came to protecting her friends. Rook could respect that kind of loyalty. He just hoped it didn't get them killed.

"How far to Nimble Johanna's hideaway?" asked Leech.

"Always three lives away," said Blue.

Rook's jaw twitched, but he said only "Quiet." They were nearing the Boggins. This region was home to threats both magical and mundane, and if anything tried to get the drop on them, he wanted to be able to hear them coming. "This could all turn out to be a trap."

"You think everything's a trap," said Tipple.

"That's why I'm still alive."

"What's it like up north, anyway?" asked Tipple. "They say half the men who set foot in the Deadlands never return."

"They say a lot of things."

"Is it true a band of Strangers fought off an entire swarm of . . . what were they . . . ?"

"It's true." Mud squished underfoot as he moved ahead. A low hum filled the air, a combination of buzzing insects and the guttural yawp of frogs.

Rook had never regretted the choices that led him to the Strangers and a brutal life on the edge of the Deadlands, guarding the rest of Albion against things pulled right out of their worst nightmares. A life of constant battle and vigilance had forged him into the man he was today.

Blue tugged Inga's arm and pointed to a clearing up ahead, where a yellowed fence surrounded a rickety wooden hut. Blue began muttering to himself and playing with the point of his cap.

The hut was raised on thick stilts, placing it about two feet above the damp ground. No smoke rose from the stone chimney. The fence was poorly constructed, little more than old bleached sticks wound together with black cord, topped with larger stones.

"Doesn't look that secret to me," said Tipple.

"Oh, sure." Leech shrugged. "Anyone could find it, s'long as they were wandering hours out of their way through the swamp."

Rook approached the edge of the clearing, ignoring the insects that swarmed like a buzzing cloud, drawn by his breath and sweat.

Any man who claimed to feel no fear was a liar or an idiot. Strangers learned to listen to fear, to heed its warning . . . and then to tie it up and toss it into a pit so they could get on with doing what needed to be done.

Rook examined the empty hut, trying to understand what had roused that tickle of fear in his gut. The oak walls were dark and dry with age but showed no trace of the rot that should have crept from the swamp to consume it.

"What's the holdup?" Tipple grumbled.

Rook raised a hand but said nothing. He brought his crossbow to his shoulder and moved slowly into the open, testing the ground before each step. The gate rattled though the air was stagnant and heavy. He peered more closely, then swore. "This is no smuggler's hideaway."

What Rook had taken to be wooden sticks topped with stones were in fact bones and skulls, lashed together to form the crude fence. More ominous was the fact that the skulls had begun to move. Each one rotated to and fro, their empty sockets searching for intruders. One by one, they turned towards Rook.

Rook pointed his crossbow at Blue. "What is this place?"

The redcap clung to Inga's leg. "Bones and crones," he said, his voice an octave higher than normal.

Bones and crones. Blue had babbled about that before. "Bloody hell. You've brought us to Yog."

Rook shouldered his crossbow and spun, searching the shadows and the trees. Inga joined him, shield and sword at the ready. Leech and Tipple stayed behind. No point in exposing them all to whatever trap or ambush Blue had led them to.

"What's she waiting for?" whispered Inga.

Rook didn't answer. The perfect opportunity for Yog to strike had come and gone. Could the hut be abandoned? Something might have drawn Yog away, something more important than trying to kill four Heroes.

"Maybe she saw us coming and fled," said Tipple.

Rook glanced at Blue. The redcap was trembling, but his attention wasn't on the Heroes he had betrayed. He was focused entirely on the hut. Rook could have drawn a knife and placed it to Blue's throat and it wouldn't have broken the redcap's attention.

"I don't think so." Rook started towards the gate.

The skulls followed his movement, like animals waiting for the right moment to pounce.

"Bugger this." He yanked the magazine from his crossbow, swapped in a different set of darts, and banged it home. "We've come this far. Might as well knock."

Gripping the weapon with both hands, he pulled the trigger and emptied the magazine. The bolts thudded into the wall and door, then exploded into small orange fireballs. Blue-black, metallic-smelling smoke filled the air.

Rook was already slamming another magazine into place. Inga moved to cover him with her shield.

Black circles of soot and ash pocked the door, but the hut was otherwise undamaged. The thing was tougher than it looked.

"You taught that house a thing or two." Tipple's normally raucous voice was strained. "I hear there's a shack over in Saltcliff that's been giving people trouble. Maybe you oughta go there next and give it what for."

Rook ignored him. Azure fire flickered in the eyes of the closest skulls. One by one they rose from the gate.

He tracked the first and fired. The skull exploded, scattering blue sparks and shards of bone.

This was more like it. Give him a real fight any day. "Inga, Tipple, smash the rest before they get airborne."

Rook shot two more skulls out of the air. A third sneaked past him. It swooped towards Inga, but instead of attacking, its jaws snapped down on the rope binding her to Blue. The redcap fell back into the mud and scrambled away on all fours.

Inga's sword cleaved a skull in half, and Bulwark's power smashed outward hard enough to rattle the entire fence. Rook kept shooting as skulls swarmed towards him, jaws clacking like some sort of obscene musical instrument.

Blue was racing towards the hut. Where the hell was Jeremiah Tipple? He should be helping Inga or taking down the redcap.

A skull shot towards his face. He tried to twist aside, but it struck him above the left eye. His vision flashed white. Blood trickled down his face, stinging his eye. Another latched onto his arm. The teeth punched through his leather armour like blades. "Tipple, get your arse over here!" Heavy footsteps squished through the mud behind him. "About time you—"

The first punch clipped Rook on the ear, spinning him in a full circle. Rook raised his crossbow, using the stock to intercept the follow-up. "That bloody hurts!"

Tipple simply roared and waded after him. Every blow Rook blocked jarred him like a hammer striking an anvil. Damn, the man was strong.

Another skull flew at Rook. He ducked, then swung his crossbow like a club, knocking the skull into Tipple's face with a burst of blue sparks. Tipple wiped his eyes and shook his head.

"Over here, you big ox!" Inga smacked a skull with her sword, sending it through the air to strike Tipple in the ear.

Tipple let out an inarticulate yell and charged. Inga ran to meet him head-on. Not the strategy Rook would have chosen. Inga was strong, and that shield of hers was impressive, but Tipple still outmassed her.

At the last moment, Inga dropped low, bracing herself and sliding through the mud, shield raised. Bulwark struck Tipple in the knees. With a howl of pain, the man toppled over her. Inga spun around, and a phantom shield shot forwards, hitting Tipple like a battering ram and tossing him to the edge of the clearing.

"Well done," said Rook. "Leech, can you do anything about these skulls?"

"I'm trying."

"Try harder!" Rook rejoined Inga, standing back-to-back for protection. He reloaded his crossbow, moving with the cool efficiency his years with the Strangers had drilled into him.

Tipple pushed himself to his feet. He looked dazed. Blood dripped from his nose where Inga had flung him to the ground. One unsteady step at a time, he walked into the swarm of skulls.

"Where's he think he's going?" asked Inga.

He wasn't acting like the greencaps they had fought in Brightlodge. Rook saw no madness in Tipple's eyes. He saw nothing of Tipple at all. The man was a hollow puppet with no awareness of his own, stumbling towards the hut.

"He's enchanted," said Leech. "He's got a second life inside him, thin and dark, like a shadow."

Rook had come to the same conclusion, and it was a good bet Yog was behind it. Which meant they *really* didn't want him getting to that hut. Rook double-checked he had loaded nonexplosive bolts, then sent half of them thudding into the backs of Tipple's knees. Enchanted or not, Tipple wasn't going anywhere without working legs.

"Enough of this," Rook snapped. "Inga, give me a path."

Inga raised her shield. Rook shot two more skulls off her back as she did whatever it was that summoned Bulwark's power. That shield had knocked Jeremiah Tipple on his arse. Floating skulls didn't have a chance. They were flung out of the way like draughts from a flipped board.

Rook sprinted towards the hut. He switched his crossbow to his left hand and slammed his shoulder into the door. It opened without resistance. He fell to the floor, rolled, and bounced to his feet with his finger on the trigger.

Nobody was home save for Blue, who cowered in the corner. Rook kicked the door shut behind him to keep the skulls from following. "When did you sneak in?"

Blue didn't answer.

Rook looked around, ready to turn the redcap into a bloody pincushion should he so much as twitch. The hut was a cramped, crowded place. The clutter had an organic feel, like a carefully constructed nest of furniture, ancient woven rugs, drying herbs, and assorted bones. The floor creaked as he walked. The whole place felt ready to break apart and sink into the swamp.

Shelves peeked from behind mismatched wall hangings, offering glimpses of coloured bottles and satchels. An iron pot hung in the small fireplace. Dry lines of red crawled down the side of the pot, left behind by whatever had simmered there. The floorboards in front of the fireplace were warped, darkened by soot and age.

"You said there's a cure." Rook turned his full attention to Blue. "Was that a lie?"

Blue shook his head.

"Where is it?" Bones rattled against the door and walls like oversized hailstones.

Blue pointed to a shelf near the fireplace. Rook yanked a heavy curtain aside to find a small wooden box strapped to the shelf. Most everything in this place was tied down. Odd, but no deterrent to a sharp knife. He cut the box free and brought it to a stained and scarred wooden worktable.

"Open it." Rook had seen too many inexperienced and overeager rookies fall prey to old traps.

Blue got to his feet and opened the chest. Inside, five small glass flasks were arranged in a wooden rack, padded with straw and rags.

Rook lifted one free and studied the contents. The potion looked like a blend of blood, swamp water, and sea foam. He held it towards Blue. "Drink up."

The redcap's eyes went round. He shook his head frantically.

"Trying to poison us, were you?" Rook asked.

"No!" Blue covered his mouth with both hands and spoke through his fingers. "Cure smelly human. Kill *real* redcap."

The hut trembled. Rook scowled and opened the door a crack to see what was happening. As he did, the entire building tilted to one side, tossing him back into the worktable. The door swung inwards. Before he could regain his balance, the hut shifted like a seesaw. Rook snatched the chest by the open lid, dragging it with him as he spilled out onto the muddy earth. "Bloody hell."

With a creak like old, arthritic bones, the hut rose up on four thick, stilted legs. There was a wet slurping sound as they pulled free from the mud.

"I'm getting too old for this." Rook tried shooting the hut in the leg like he had done to Tipple. The bolt lodged in the gnarled, knotted wood but didn't affect the hut's movement.

The fence of bones went mad, ripping free and swirling about the hut like a tornado. Skulls battered Rook, forcing him to retreat.

The hut began to walk into the woods like an overgrown, lumbering, wooden bear.

A stone thumped into Rook's gut, hard enough to bruise. Blue stood in the open doorway, a slingshot in one hand. Rook scowled. Blue yelped and tried to hide his crude weapon behind his back. Rook aimed his crossbow, but the door slammed shut before he could return the favour.

He watched with frustration as the hut fled, gaining speed with each step. Rook had been thrown out of people's homes before, but this was the first time the home itself had been the one to evict him.

"Did you get the cure?" Leech called.

Two of the flasks had fallen onto the ground, but they were intact. He gathered them back into the chest. "I hope so. If not—what's the matter, lass?"

Inga stared after the hut, her normally ruddy face pale. Save for a few bloody bites and scratches, she had come through the fighting unscathed. "I know who Yog is."

Curious as Rook was to know the truth about their enemy, there were a few things to take care of first. He took his time binding Jeremiah Tipple's hands and feet. The man was strong, but Rook knew a thing or two about securing prisoners. Between this and the wounds to his legs, Tipple wasn't going anywhere.

Tipple groaned and looked up at them. "Where are . . . Oi, you shot me!"

"You're welcome." Rook checked the perimeter, making sure none of Yog's flying skulls had remained behind to spy on them. By the time he returned, Leech was bandaging Tipple's knees.

"Don't move." Leech swatted Tipple's bound hands away from the crossbow bolts embedded in his legs. "Leave 'em. They'll plug up the bleeding while I get to work."

"What do you remember?" asked Rook.

"Not much." Tipple winced. "I was . . . my head felt like it was on fire. I couldn't move. S'like when you dream you're running, but it feels like you're slogging through a swamp."

Rook looked pointedly at their surroundings.

"Right." Tipple blinked. "Wait, what was the question?"

Rook rubbed his forehead. At least the man didn't look ready to rip free and attack them again. He turned his attention to Inga. "Well?"

"There's a story Old Mother Marguerite—we called her One-Armed Maggie—told to frighten the young ankle-biters, about a woman who long ago roamed the forest in a walking hut, stealing children and devouring Heroes."

"Devouring?" asked Tipple. "As in eating?"

Leech shrugged. "People should be just as tasty and nutritious as beef or pork. And Heroes are likely to have a lot of meat on 'em."

"Go on," said Rook.

"Maggie called her by a different name. Baya, not Yog." Inga ran a hand over her shield, as if for comfort. "Baya held power over death and transformation. She lived alone, constantly moving through Albion. In the beginning, if your courage and honesty impressed her, she might help you or give you a gift. But over time, she began to see people as nothing more than animals.

"She set out to punish humanity for abusing her gifts. She would fly through the night sky, and she could sniff out her prey from five miles off. She commanded three Riders, sending them to bring the strongest Heroes and the naughtiest children for her cauldron. I . . . used to have nightmares about Baya swooping out of the darkness to snatch me up, like an eagle catching a rabbit."

"You're saying a witch from an old wives' tale is mucking about with redcaps and flying bones, trying to destroy Brightlodge?" Tipple said dubiously.

Rook cocked his head. "Right. This is probably a completely different enchanted hut tromping through the swamp."

"They say Baya took the children's beauty and the Heroes' might for herself," said Inga.

Tipple snorted. "Some Heroes have plenty of beauty too, you know."

Leech picked up one of the broken skulls. "Eating not just the meat, but the power as well. I imagine it'd have to be done quickly, before the life drained from the flesh."

"You mean she'd eat us alive?" asked Tipple.

"It was just a story." Inga rubbed her arms. "If Baya was real, she'd have died ages ago."

"Unless eating Heroes' power extended her life as well," said Leech. "Or maybe someone found her old hut and moved in."

Rook stood and walked to where the hut had stood. The stilts had left deep impressions, but water already seeped into the tracks, and the mud sagged inwards, filling the holes. The hut had been moving too quickly, and even if he managed to follow the trail, he doubted the others would be able to keep up.

Heavy footsteps squished through the mud behind him. He recognised Inga from the sound of her armour. "You all right, lass?"

"I believed Blue would help us, but all he wanted was to get back to Baya. To Yog."

"Maybe." From the sound of things, Inga had shaken off the fear of old nightmares, just as he'd known she would. She was too tough to let such things cling to her for long. He glanced over his shoulder at the chest. "But if those potions can cure whatever's happened to Tipple, then he gave us fair trade. Better than fair."

"Better?"

"He gave us knowledge. Now we've a better idea what we're fighting." He returned to the chest, took one of the vials in his hand, and carefully removed the stopper. Whatever this was, it smelled vile, like blood and decay and foul beer. "No point wasting any more time."

"What if it poisons him?" asked Leech. "Blue could've lied."

Rook thought—he hoped—the redcap had been too frightened to lie. But if not . . . "Then Tipple's no worse off than he is now."

He put one hand behind Tipple's neck and helped him sit up. It was like lifting a fully loaded wagon.

Tipple sighed. "Bottoms up!"

Rook only let him drink one swallow. If it *was* poison, he'd have a better chance of fighting off a smaller dose.

"Now can we get rid of these blasted ropes?" Tipple held up his bound wrists.

"Not until we know you're cured." He shoved the stopper back into the vial, returned it to the chest, and hoisted the whole thing onto one shoulder.

"Well, let's get to it then." Tipple gestured towards his legs. "It's not like I can walk back to Brightlodge."

Both Rook and Leech turned to look at Inga.

"Oh, hell." With a resigned sigh, she laid Bulwark on the ground beside Tipple and set about converting the shield into a makeshift sled.

chapter 11

LEECH

"Look at this jawbone." Leech held the L-shaped shard of bone in front of Tipple and poked at one of the large, yellowed teeth protruding from the groove along the top. "There's a clean break along the centre where Inga hit it with her sword, but you can see it's too long to be human."

He placed it next to Tipple's cheek to demonstrate where the jaw would connect to the rest of the skull. The end of the bone protruded a good two inches beyond his chin. The teeth were unusually large as well, and the bone was thicker than human jaws. Not large enough to be a balverine, though. An immature balverine might have a jawbone this size, but the teeth would be sharper, and there would be more of them. These teeth were worn smooth with age. Some kind of redcap, perhaps? He set it down and moved on to a curved fragment of skull.

Leech had gathered every broken piece of bone he could find from the site of Yog's home. The intact bones had traipsed off with her walking hut, but they seemed to lose their magic when damaged. Bones covered the entirety of Leech's primary dissection table, sorted according to function and size.

Tipple was laid out on the other table, which groaned and

creaked every time he shifted position. Leather straps secured his limbs, with additional ropes pulled tight to keep him from escaping. Tipple didn't seem to be getting worse, but Leech refused to take chances.

"This place is . . . well, it suits you," Tipple commented.

"Thanks." Leech had rented the one-room home shortly after he arrived in Brightlodge. Officially, he lodged at Wendleglass Hall with the rest of the Heroes, but people could get so worked up when they barged in and found you dissecting a goodfellow on the floor. Besides, he liked having a place he could go for quiet and solitude.

Carefully labelled specimens covered the shelves on the walls, from bones to hides to jars containing preserved organs. A stuffed shrew peered down at them from the topmost shelf. Leech had set a tiny black hat on the shrew's head a few days back, when he was feeling whimsical. It gave the place a sense of fun.

The shutters were open, providing additional light and ventilation. The tools of his trade—saws, knives, pliers, and drills—were arranged on a narrow countertop. On the opposite side of the room, a pile of blankets were neatly folded against the wall, beside the hearth. Everything in its proper place.

"My legs still hurt," Tipple said.

"That's 'cause I didn't fully heal them." Leech had removed the crossbow bolts and given Tipple a healing potion to seal the worst of the wounds but had deliberately watered down the potion. The torn, swollen tissue would slow Tipple down if he somehow broke free and tried to attack Leech or run off.

"Can't say I blame you." He stared up at the ceiling. "I'd be dead if not for you lot."

"Aw, not necessarily. You'd probably just be a greencap, or maybe still walking about as Yog's slave."

"And you, working t'fix me up again. I love you guys." He

belched quietly. "How long before I piss the rest of Yog's ale out of my system?"

Leech picked up another piece of skull. "Don't worry. By the time Rook and Inga get done helping to round up any remaining greencaps, you'll be good as new. If not, we can always try another round of leeches to speed things along."

Tipple grimaced. "What are you looking for with those bones?"

"Anything they can tell me about Yog and her power." He brought the shard of bone to Tipple. "This came from a redcap. You can see where the nail went in." The skull had split along that nail hole, leaving only a triangular gouge in the bone.

Tipple stared, his red-veined eyes blinking blearily. "How d'you know it's not a human skull someone put a nail through?"

"Look at the edge of the bone. See how it's thickened and rounded around the nail hole? That's where the bone knitted together. Healed right around the nail. This hole was there for years before the creature died." He waved a hand at the other bones. "But there are skulls here that look human, as well as balverines, ogres, goodfellows, and some I don't recognise."

"And that tells you what, exactly?"

"Yog's just scavenging for bones, not using any particular creature. However she controlled 'em, that power came entirely from her, not from the bones themselves."

"You have the creepiest hobbies."

"Nothing creepy about it." Leech set the fragment back in the skull section of the table and picked up a femur. "We're all made up of the same basic bits and bobs. Once you know how the parts work, you can take down a man twice your size."

He grabbed a fibula and a tibia, held them together in his other hand, and showed where the two lower bones would join with the femur at the knee. "Ever tried to break a man's thigh? You're probably strong enough, but it's one of the toughest bones in the body.

Much easier to take out the knee instead." He bent the bones at the joint to demonstrate, then set the femur down.

"These two connect the knee to the ankle. The tibia's pretty tough, but land one good kick to the fibula . . ." He returned the larger bone to the table, took the fibula with both hands, and snapped it in two. "Doesn't matter how strong you are. Dislocate the right bones, and you're not going anywhere."

He reached out to brush a splinter of bone off Tipple's face. "Joints and organs are even better. Have you ever looked at an elbow or a knee beneath all that skin and blood? They're just bands of muscle and cartilage holding things together. Much easier to tear and destroy. I once measured how much weight it took to dislocate a human elbow. Go on, guess."

Tipple's complexion had turned slightly pale.

"Still nauseated?" Leech asked cheerfully. "I can loosen the rope around your neck if you need to vomit again. Let me grab another bucket. I can compare this to your earlier mess. There might be a way to measure whether the bloody ale in your gut is decreasing."

He waited, but Tipple didn't answer.

"Thirteen pounds," Leech said. "To dislocate the elbow, I mean. A lot depends on the angle. But with the right training and a little luck, even a child could do it."

Tipple shifted his chin towards a bandage knotted around Leech's forearm. "What happened t'you? I thought you stayed back from the fighting."

Leech glanced at his arm. "I drained some of my blood. I wanted to compare it to the blood of a greencap. And to yours. Don't worry, I learned how to stitch myself up one-handed years ago." He set the broken fibula in the leg-bone pile. "How are you feeling? Any strange urges to kill me or nail a cap to your head?"

"Feels like someone already did." Tipple groaned. "Do those bones tell you how to kill that witch?"

"Not yet. But I can tell you she's travelled all over Albion." Leech scooped up a flattened skull with large eye sockets and pointed teeth. "This looks like a seal. Big one, too. You don't see those until you get up near the Divide."

He grabbed another bone, a vertebra larger than his fist. "And you know what this is?"

"A bone?"

"Yes, yes. But what *kind* of bone?"

"Oh hell, Leech. I don't know."

"Neither do I!" Leech grinned and turned the bone over in his hands. "The closest I've seen came from a horse, but this is longer and heavier. Not thick enough to be an ogre vertebra, though."

"You're a peculiar man," Tipple said. "Smartest fellow I've ever met, but peculiar."

Leech nodded. People had said far worse to him. It didn't matter. And Tipple's teasing was never edged with cruelty. That was just how he acted with people he considered friends.

Leech had tried to reciprocate once, but his attempt at friendly teasing had fallen flat. Apparently, calling someone an ugly drunk who smelled like the inside of a goat's arse was an insult no matter how cheerfully you said it.

He turned back to his work. Sorting and identifying the various bone fragments was an interesting distraction, but what he really wanted to figure out was how Yog had brought the bones back to life. Traces of Yog's power remained, but in most cases, too little for him to work with. He had set aside several pieces that felt promising. He picked up the largest, a mostly intact thighbone, and carried it over to Tipple.

"What now?" he asked.

"Shut up and let me concentrate." Yog hadn't been present to command each individual bone. Even if she had, Leech doubted anyone could directly control so many flying minions against multiple opponents. It would be like a general giving orders to every individual soldier. More likely, Yog had simply animated the bones and sent them forth with a general set of commands.

Leech wrapped one hand around the bone. Cold seeped into his blood, like shadows worming through his veins, seeking his heart. It was a familiar sensation but disconcerting nonetheless. He wondered idly what would happen the day those shadows finally reached their target.

While some tendrils worked their way inwards, others stretched from his body deep into the bone, tugging at the faint embers of life trapped within. He touched his other hand to the scabbed wound on Tipple's right thigh. The redness faded slightly.

"Not bad, hey?" Leech pulled free, allowing the bone to clatter to the floor. "It wouldn't fix more than a scraped knee, but that's not the point. Plenty of living opponents to use for healing. But the next time Yog throws her bones our way, I should be able to drain 'em in midair. Probably."

Someone pounded on the door hard enough to rattle it in its frame. Leech wandered over and opened the door a crack, then turned to Tipple. "Have you felt anything weird since we left the Boggins? Anything tugging you towards other greencaps, maybe?"

"My britches've been riding up something awful, but that's about it. Why?"

"Just curious." Leech peeked out again at the cloaked figures, hunched and giggling on the street in front of his house. They had a dog on a leash who was cloaked as well, but the dog had shaken off the hood to reveal a lopsided green cap. "Either they were drawn here by your presence or else they just decided my home looked like a good place for mischief."

He picked up a scalpel from the table and donned the leather apron he used when working with hazardous substances and specimens. It should serve as makeshift armour.

"What's out there?" Tipple asked. "Let me up, and I can—"

"No need." Leech opened the door. "There's only five of them."

Leech returned a short time later and dropped the scalpel into an open jar of diluted alcohol. The clink sounded louder than usual in the otherwise-silent house.

He untied his leather apron and sighed. One of the greencaps had cut a gash along the front. Two others had bled all over him. The leather was treated to repel fluids, but getting the blood out of the mask and his favourite hat was another matter.

Certain venoms were particularly effective at dissolving bloodstains. In living victims, the venom turned the blood watery and prevented it from clotting. Sea-serpent venom worked the best. Deadly, but great for laundry. He'd have to see about picking some up.

He set his hat on the table and went to drag one of the bodies inside. Tipple watched him intently, hardly even blinking. His intensity was enough to make Leech reach for another scalpel. Once armed, he visually inspected Tipple's bonds. "What is it?"

Tipple jerked his chin towards the door. "You just took apart a pack of greencaps with a blade the size of my little finger."

"I only killed two," said Leech. "The rest ran away. Including the dog."

In truth, Leech had allowed the dog to escape. He preferred dogs to most people. They were so much more honest. If the dog liked you, it wagged its tail. If not, it growled and tried to bite you.

At the same time, it would have been fascinating to dissect a dog who had been transformed into a greencap. To the best of Leech's knowledge, redcap blood only turned humanoids. What had Yog done to her mixture to make it affect dogs, too? And what was a dog doing drinking tainted ale in the first place?

"You ought to think about cutting me loose," said Tipple. "Anything gets inside, there's not much I can do to protect myself like this."

"That's why I didn't let them in."

Tipple laughed. "You're not intimidated by anything, are you?"

"Should I be?" He returned to the door to fetch the fallen greencap.

"You're hurt."

Leech glanced at his side, where blood soaked his shirt and the top of his trousers. "One of the greencaps caught me with a cleaver." In the heat of the fight, he'd barely felt it. He touched the cut, and pain flared through his side. He pressed a hand over it to slow the bleeding.

"Why didn't you just heal it?"

"I am." He dug through one of the cabinets until he found a healing potion. He pulled the cork loose with his teeth, spat it onto the floor, and downed the contents.

"I meant that thing you do. Like when you stopped my knee from bleeding all over the place."

Leech tugged the shirt away from his side. The skin was pink and tender, but the bleeding had stopped. "It doesn't work on me."

Tipple pursed his lips. "Where'd you learn how to do that, anyway? I've met Will users before, but never one who could steal the life out of his enemies."

Leech used a knife to cut away his shirt and used it to wipe up the worst of the blood from his side. "I used to be a barber."

That elicited a barking laugh though Leech hadn't intended it as a joke. "Like that fellow down by the Port who keeps trying to talk me into colouring my hair ginger?"

"That's right. I'd cut hair, pull teeth, stitch wounds, lance boils, splint bones, apply leeches, and more. I learned how to amputate limbs and cut people open. Most of 'em even survived. Once you've seen people from the inside, you realise we're all pretty much the same. Humans, hobbes, balverines, redcaps . . . I could lay out the spleens of a dozen different species, and aside from a little variation in size and colour, you'd never guess which one came from which."

"That doesn't explain the power," said Tipple. "Don't tell me they teach tricks like that in the Barbers' Guild."

Leech pulled on a clean shirt, then finished arranging the greencap on a tarp. "Nope. Though they did teach the importance of a razor-sharp blade. The rest came along after an encounter with a shadowblight."

Tipple whistled. "What happened?"

"I killed it, obviously." If he hadn't, he wouldn't have been here. "I'm sure I've told you this before."

"I get the occasional gap in my memory these days."

Leech wasn't surprised. Between the drinking and the fighting, Tipple's body had taken a lot of abuse over the years. "I was living in Whitehollow at the time. I'd been out working in the graveyard—"

"Working?"

"Collecting samples," Leech explained. "The shadowblight surprised me in the woods on the way home."

The sun had been setting, turning the sky a darkening shade of red. He remembered the shadowblight swooping towards him like a strip of midnight torn from the blackest sky, with eyes like red flame. It moved quickly, circling Leech and cutting off his escape. Deep in the woods with nobody else around, armed only with the tools of his trade, Leech had expected to die. "I think the body parts I'd harvested confused it, scattering its power like a crystal to sunlight. I sliced its neck with a bone saw and stabbed it in the shoulder with a pair of scissors."

"Ha! Good on you, Leech. Everything's a weapon when you're desperate."

"It wasn't enough." The shadowblight had fought viciously,

shrugging off its wounds and biting and clawing at Leech's flesh. At the same time, the creature had continued its efforts to reach into Leech's soul, ripping the heat and life from his body. He remembered hearing his weapons fall away, and the forest whirling around him. He must have fallen, but he didn't recall hitting the ground. Only the darkness, blotting out the sky, the trees, the feel of the air, the smell of the leaves.

In the silence that followed, nothing existed but the shadowblight tearing at his soul like a carrion bird.

"We were connected," Leech said. "I should've died. But while it was busy ripping the life from my body, I reached out and did the same to it."

Few people saw a shadowblight and lived. Leech knew of none who had fallen into the shadowblight's darkness and escaped.

"You're walking around with part of a bloody *shadowblight* inside you, and you've got me tied up for drinking a little poisoned ale."

Leech grabbed a knife and carefully used the tip to clean the blood from the thin white crescents of his nails. "It's certainly given me a useful skill set. Fixing you lot, draining our enemies. And then there's this."

Leech wiped the knife on his sleeve, then set it aside. Through the lenses of his mask, he peered not at Tipple's flesh, but at the life pulsing within. Smaller flickers of life glowed like dying embers from the bones arranged through the house. Shadows reached out, but instead of drawing on those lives, he simply wrapped the darkness around himself like a blanket. He felt himself becoming *thinner,* while at the same time growing beyond the bounds of his human body.

Tipple flinched. "By the king's balls. I'll never get used to that."

Leech allowed his phantom form to fall away. "It's fascinating to perceive the world of shadows. I always feel cold afterwards. But you should've seen the way those greencaps ran when I showed them my shadow face."

"Makes that bloody mask of yours look downright friendly." Tipple was breathing faster than usual. "Don't you worry about losing yourself to that thing?"

"Occasionally." Leech checked Tipple's colour, then pressed a hand to his throat to feel his pulse. "You seem to be getting stronger. Time for another dose of Yog's antidote. If all goes well, we'll have you up and about by nightfall."

"And if all doesn't go well?"

"In that case, would you mind if I kept your liver? For study, of course."

chapter 12

TIPPLE

Jeremiah Tipple had never been one to worry about things he couldn't control. He'd either recover or he wouldn't, and so far, it looked like he'd gotten off lightly. That said, he hadn't been thrilled about getting hauled back to Brightlodge on Inga's shield twice in as many days. And Leech's poking and prodding was getting old.

Leech kept adjusting Tipple's bonds to keep him from stiffening up and helping him to eat and drink—nothing stronger than goat milk, sadly. But the sooner he was out of these ropes and able to use the chamber pot without an escort, the better.

It wasn't so much the indignity of Leech helping him with his trousers as it was the running commentary on the colour of his urine.

The door swung open, and Inga stepped inside. "How's he doing?"

"Well enough to travel," said Leech. "I was just getting ready to set him loose."

Tipple waited while Leech unbuckled the straps holding him in place. Inga helped him to sit. He stretched and cracked his back, then rotated his arms to work the stiffness from his limbs.

Rook stood in the doorway, one hand on his crossbow. "You're sure he's not going to turn on us?"

Leech looked about. "Let me show you. When we first brought

Tipple back, his urine smelled like molten copper. That'd be the poison getting expelled from his body, of course. This morning, the scent is more—"

"We'll take your word on it," said Inga.

Tipple massaged his forehead, pressing his thumbs hard against the upper edges of his eye sockets. The poison might be out of his system, but he hadn't yet pissed away his headache.

"We brought three vials of the cure to the captured greencaps," said Inga. "It didn't change them back, but they've calmed down a bit. Any luck cooking up more?"

Leech grabbed a scrap of parchment. "I've jotted down my best guess as to the ingredients. Haven't had a chance to test it yet. If nothing else, it shouldn't make the greencaps any worse."

The small house felt uncomfortably cramped with the four of them—plus one partially dissected greencap—crowded inside. "Enough standing around and talking," said Tipple. "It's far more civilised to *sit* around talking. Preferably in the pub. I need something to drown the goat milk I've been belching all day."

Tipple squeezed past the others and stepped onto the street, where he breathed in the smell of the morning air. The scent of fresh-baked rolls was a welcome change. Heck, after being cooped up inside, even the musty smell of the mud was refreshing. He started walking, trusting the others to follow. "Have you lot learned anything else about Yog and her plans?"

"We've spoken with the other Heroes," said Inga. "But so far, we've got little more than old tales."

"I been thinking," said Tipple. "If it's Heroes she wants, Brightlodge is the place to go. But why harass Grayrock?"

"You have a theory?" asked Leech.

"Nope! But when it comes to unanswerable questions, there's only one man in Albion to talk to." Tipple didn't say another word until they reached the pub. He pushed open the door and bellowed,

"My good friend Rook here will pay five gold to anyone who can tell us where to find Beckett the Seer!"

The consensus in the pub was that Beckett was likely hiding out in Rosewood, south of town. He couldn't have gone too far, as he'd come back to Brightlodge twice so far to stock up on supplies. Most of which came in bottles. Rosewood was still a lot of land to search, but it was a start, and they had Rook to sniff out his trail. Strangers were supposed to be as good as hounds when it came to tracking, and far less likely to sniff each other's arses.

Tipple'd first met Beckett in the tavern, where the older man had been attempting to tell a particularly buxom barmaid about his vision of the future, a vision that had apparently involved Beckett, the barmaid, and the barmaid's sister. Alas, that particular prediction had ended with Beckett drenched in drink and Tipple pounding the table with laughter.

Beckett had been an adviser to Old King Wendleglass. He claimed he'd tried to warn Wendleglass about his coming demise, but seeing the future was one thing. Persuading a king to listen was a much bigger challenge.

Beckett had disappeared after Wendleglass's murder. Some said he was searching for clues about the king's killers. Others believed he was on the run from a group of bruisers who hadn't taken kindly to Beckett's using his gifts to cheat them out of their gold at the chicken races.

Either way, he'd gotten himself into a spot of trouble, and Tipple had been one of the Heroes to come to his rescue. Hopefully, that would be enough to get him to share some answers about Yog in return.

"Have you found him yet?" Tipple asked.

Rook didn't answer, though his shoulders tightened. He moved slowly and silently between the trees, stopping from time to time to examine a bit of scuffed dirt or a broken branch.

"Let the man work," said Inga. "Like Old Mother Twostraps always said, you can't eat the chicken before it's hatched."

"Beckett's not the only one to wander these woods." Rook pointed to a bright green fern at the side of the trail. To Tipple's eyes, it looked exactly the same as a hundred other bright green ferns they'd passed since leaving Brightlodge. "But if you think you can do better, you're welcome to take point."

A shrill scream echoed through the trees. Tipple grinned and punched his fist into his palm. "I think I will, thanks!"

He heard the others readying their weapons behind him. Tipple merely unhooked one of the mugs strapped to his pack. He'd commissioned this three years back. Reinforced with iron bands and pointed rivets, a blow from this mug could crack stone and still hold a drink when it came time to celebrate victory.

Pipe music floated through the trees, lively and alluring. Perfect! All fights went better with a good tune in the background.

"By the river," he shouted. With the noise he was making as he tore through the woods, there was no use worrying about surprise.

He jumped into the shallow water of the riverbank, giving him a clear view of three pucks surrounding Beckett the Seer. A fourth lunged at Tipple from the shore. Dark claws slashed at his throat.

Tipple barely broke stride as he blocked the blow and delivered a backfist that sent his attacker reeling. The puck disappeared before Tipple could follow up.

Two more of the goat-legged creatures broke away from Beckett. Dark fur covered their legs. Their chests were bare, revealing lean muscle. Pucks were tough for their size. Thick horns curved from their skulls. This crew wore wooden masks decorated with green leaves and pine needles. They spread out, brown tails lashing from side to side.

Rook dropped one of the pucks with his crossbow before they

knew what was happening. Tipple roared and charged the next, who turned invisible. Tipple stumbled right past and smashed his mug into the face of the third, hard enough to split the puck's mask in half.

Tipple looked about. "I meant to do that!"

Another puck reappeared to one side. Claws slashed Tipple's arm. He caught the thing's hand and squeezed until the fingers broke. Without letting go, he brought the mug down like a hammer, sending the puck to the ground.

"Where are the pipers?" shouted Inga.

Tipple searched the trees. The music surrounded him, making it impossible to pinpoint the music's origin.

Glass shattered behind him. He spun to see a puck staggering back, his body covered in leeches and small cuts. A roundhouse/uppercut combination knocked him out cold. Tipple looked over to see Leech standing on the shore, another jar ready in his hand.

"Nice throw!" Tipple enjoyed brawling with goodfellows. Like him, they enjoyed good drink, good song, and good fun. Unfortunately, they were also cruel, sadistic killers, gleefully tormenting and murdering whoever crossed their paths.

The pucks liked to sneak in, cut you up with them claws, then turn invisible, but the pipers were a whole other matter. The sneaky bastards hung back in the shadows, weaving spells and illusions to torment the mind.

Inga grabbed Beckett by the arm and hauled him around behind her. "I've got the seer!"

Tipple looked around for the source of the music. The song mingled with the air, filling his body with every breath. He spied movement by a fat oak to his left. The piper ducked behind the tree, but when Tipple followed, it had vanished.

"You want to play games with Jeremiah Tipple, do you?" He spun and slammed his fist into what he thought was another goodfellow but turned out to be the all-too-solid trunk of a tree. "Come 'ere, you!"

The air around him blurred. He heard whispers and giggles from the woods. Women stepped shyly from behind the trees, clothed in wisps of cloud that left just enough to the imagination. They were strong, too. No dainty damsels these, but broad-shouldered lasses capable of taking whatever life threw their way and punching it in the face.

Tipple raised his mug in salute. "Hey there, ladies. Any of you seen . . ." What was it he'd been hunting?

The women formed a ring around Tipple. Their strong, bare arms reached out, stopping just short of touching him. He frowned. There was something he was supposed to be doing, someone who needed a sound thrashing . . .

They began to sing one of his favourite songs, an old folk tune about a mythical drink of the fairies.

"Won't you take this lovely lass
To your home down in Thistlecrown?
To that fine little cottage by Crowsgate Pass
To share a jug of brown-brown.

"Ha, ha, hee, hee, just you and me,
And a fine old jug of brown-brown.
We'll go for a walk in the evening sun,
And drink 'til we both fall down.

"Brown-brown, brown-brown,
Together in Crowsgate Pass.
Brown-brown, brown-brown,
It'll knock you on your ass!"

He tried to catch the hand of the closest of the young ladies. Her fingers turned to smoke in his grasp. She ducked away with a flirtatious grin, beckoning for him to follow. Step by step they led him away.

He laughed and raised his mug to his lips.

"Wait, where the hell's the brown-brown?" Not a single drop of the fairy brew darkened the bottom of the mug.

"From old Sam Sykes we stole the still
And brought it here to Thistlecrown.
A week we brewed that fairy swill,
The magic drink called brown-brown."

He was as fuzz-headed as if he'd been drinking through the night, but the mug was bone-dry. What was wrong with him? First his blackout at Yog's hut, and now this.

Yog's hut. He squinted and looked around. "This ain't Thistlecrown."

His body felt numb. He searched clumsily about his person until he found one of the bottles he had brought along for the hike. The woods spun around him, women dancing in and out of focus.

The song faded, replaced by the haunting sounds of a goodfellow's pipe. Tipple tugged the cork from the bottle and drank deep. He filled his mouth until his cheeks puffed like the throat of a frog. A hand touched his arm, trying to draw him back into their spell.

Tipple sprayed the contents directly into the faces of the closest women. They shrieked and fell back, coughing and wiping their eyes. Illusion fell away, revealing slender, sharp-toothed forest sprites.

"Sorry, ladies. You're not my type, and all the drink in the world isn't going to change that." Tipple searched for the source of the music. One of the pipers stood half-hidden behind a pine tree. Tipple filled his cheeks a second time, then flipped the bottle in his hand and hurled it through the air to smash against the piper's brow.

He saw his companions standing entranced, mumbling softly to whatever illusions the pipes had created. He sprayed this mouthful at his friends. Their contented murmurs changed to cries of disgust and protest, but they looked to be shaking off the spell.

The remaining piper played more frantically. Music assaulted Tipple's senses, but he had spent most of his adult life fighting while the room seemed to spin around his head. He roared and charged. The piper raised his instrument, but Tipple snatched it away and broke it over the piper's head, then laid him out with a left hook.

Bolts from Rook's crossbow thudded into the trees, sounding like an angry woodpecker. The piper Tipple had stunned with his bottle cried out in pain. Tipple moved in and finished him up with an uppercut that lifted the piper off the ground. The piper hit the dirt hard and didn't move.

Tipple stomped the fallen pipes and turned around. "About time you lot joined the party," he said. "Do I have to do everything around these parts?"

Inga wiped her face and grimaced. "That was foul."

"The pipers created a potent illusion," said Leech. "How'd you break through it?"

"Pah. You want potent, stop by the Drunken Dragon in Crowsgate and ask Blind Becka to mix you a Hollow Man's Spirit. After a couple of those, a little magic music is nothing."

He was curious what the others had seen, particularly Leech. What kind of vision would entrance that man? But he could ask about that later. He strode towards the shore and helped Beckett the Seer to his feet. "We were hoping you might answer a couple of questions."

"Whatever it is, you don't want to know." Beckett had brought them back to his campsite, a small hollow between two fallen trees, with a bit of canvas stretched over the top for shelter. "Answering questions about the future is nothing but trouble."

"We can handle trouble," Tipple said.

Beckett stared. "I didn't mean trouble for *you*. People don't like the answers, so who do you think they blame for their future mistakes and misfortunes?"

"It's important," said Rook.

"It's *always* important." Beckett sat on a log and began poking the ashes of an old fire. He blew on the embers until he roused a small flame, then fed it a handful of dried pine needles.

"Are you sure this place is safe?" asked Inga.

"For three more days, yes. A bear was sleeping here before I came, and her scent is strong enough to scare off most threats."

Rook gave a grunt that could have been a sound of approval. It was hard to tell with Rook.

Tipple sat down beside Beckett. "What can you tell us about Yog?"

"What part of 'you don't want to know' do you not understand?"

"Forget the future," said Inga. "Tell us about the past. Is this truly Baya? If so, how did she survive for so long? Are the stories about her true?"

"All stories are true." Beckett dug out a jug from his small pile of belongings, took a drink, and offered it to Tipple. "Baya, eh? That makes sense. Given how many lives she devoured, it's possible she's survived all these centuries."

"Devoured?" Tipple repeated. "You mean it's true she'll try to eat us?"

Beckett snickered. "Maybe she prefers her meat well pickled."

"If Yog is so powerful, why muck about with greencaps?" asked Tipple. "Why waste her time on Grayrock?"

"Don't know." Beckett took another drink.

Tipple dug through his things, producing two more bottles.

"Where do you keep them all?" asked Inga.

"Don't ask." He clapped Beckett on the back. "What say we refresh your memory?"

Half a bottle later, Tipple's lingering headache had faded, swept aside by a warm, tingling sensation. "So there I was in the outhouse. No sooner had I dropped my drawers when the damned greencap dropped on my . . . on my . . ."

"On his head," said Inga.

"S'right! Tried to bite my ear clean off!"

"Only you, Jeremiah Tipple." Beckett laughed. "And don't think I don't know what you're doing, trying to soften me up with drink!"

Tipple grinned. "Course you do. Probably planned it this way to get me to bring you something worth drinking. What are you doing out here, anyway?"

"Hiding." Beckett pointed his bottle at Tipple. "There's a storm coming, and I don't want to be anywhere near when it hits."

"So give us some answers and let us stop it."

Beckett leaned back and belched. "Everyone says they want to know their future. The 'truth,' whatever that means. They hassle and chase and pester you until you finally give it to them, and are they grateful? Never. Doesn't matter how kindly I phrase the news, either. 'The nice thing about being mauled to death by balverines is that it will be quick.' 'Yes, he's going to cheat on you, but he'll be thinking of you when he's with her.'" He shook his head. "They ask for the truth, but they pay more for a good, comforting lie."

"Yog poisoned the people of Brightlodge," said Inga. "She tried to flood Grayrock."

"Grayrock. Pah." Beckett downed the rest of the bottle and tossed it into the river.

"Tell you what," said Tipple. "Give us both the truth and the lies about Yog! We'll guess which is witch. Which witch is . . . wait, what was I saying?"

Beckett snorted. "You'll die sober."

"Lie," Leech said before Tipple could react.

"You'll live longer if you stay away from Yog. Keep chasing her and she'll end up lashing your bones to her gate and mounting your thick skull on the gatepost."

"Is that true?" asked Tipple.

Beckett merely grinned. "Pass me a new bottle and I'll tell you everything you want to know."

"Lie!" Leech matched Beckett's grin, clearly enjoying the game.

Tipple pulled another bottle from his pack. "Why'd you flee Brightlodge?"

"Because I'd make an ugly greencap." He jerked his chin at Tipple. "More to the point, you saw how she turned this mountain of muscle against the rest of you. Imagine what'd happen if she got her poison into someone who could see the future."

"Truth." Leech nodded to himself. "You gave more detail that time."

"Oh, it's detail that separates the lies from the truth, is it?" Beckett leaned closer. "Your daughter, Leech, has an enormous wart on the tip of her nose. The other kids call her a witch. Milk makes her so flatulent, the dog leaves the house. She's bright, though. Memorises all the songs after hearing them just one time, and sings them at night when she's supposed to be sleeping."

"That's obviously a lie," said Leech. "I don't have a daughter."

"You sure about that?"

Leech started to respond, then frowned. He sat back and folded his arms. "You're a cruel man, Beckett the Seer."

"That's what they tell me." Beckett chuckled.

"How d'we kill her?" pressed Tipple. "Yog, not Leech's repulsive daughter."

Beckett studied the bottle for so long, Tipple thought he had forgotten the question. "I don't know."

"Lie?" guessed Leech.

"If only." He shook his head. "I see towns falling. Sometimes it's Grayrock, sometimes Brightlodge. But I can't see Yog. She's . . . dispersed. Her life's hidden away where even I can't find it. The only thing I'm certain of is the coming storm."

"What storm?" asked Tipple.

"The *coming* storm. Pay attention." Beckett sighed and set the bottle on the ground. "Yog's desperate to regain her former might, but she's not ready yet. Something prevents her, something in Grayrock."

"What's that?" asked Inga.

"Who knows. Maybe a magical weapon. Maybe the only remaining copy of her recipe for spicy Hero sausage."

"We just saved your life," Tipple snapped. "The least you could do is give us some straight answers."

"You think that would make a difference?" Beckett shrugged. "I warned Old King Wendleglass of his impending death. Didn't do much good, did it? You think knowing the future is the key. Sure, I knew if I hung around here, the goodfellows would find me, but I also knew you'd show up and start giving me drinks. I could tell you what's coming to Grayrock. You'd just go running off to join the others, and like as not get yourselves killed."

"You're saying we *shouldn't* join the other Heroes in Grayrock to help stop Yog from destroying the town?" Tipple asked.

Beckett started to laugh, an erratic, slightly hysterical sound that ended with a sudden and potent belch. "You poor, blind fool. Who do you think brings about Grayrock's downfall?"

chapter 13

GLORY

"He's kissing a chicken," said Glory.

Winter giggled as she watched the chicken flap its wings in protest.

"What better way for the Mayor of Grayrock to win back the hearts and minds of his people?" asked Sterling.

"Hearts, anyway. I think minds are a lost cause in this town." Glory looked out at the crowd gathered around the Mayor. "The town is in danger, and its ruler and elected protector is out prancing like a prize pony. We don't have time for this nonsense."

"I've found that people often confess their darkest secrets on their deathbed," commented Shroud. "If we really want him to tell us what he knows, I could—"

"We didn't come back here to assassinate the Mayor of Grayrock," Sterling said firmly.

Shroud shrugged. "Well, no. But there's always time for a little freelance work."

They had returned Ben and Greta to their parents, who had been overjoyed to have their children home safe though the father was horrified at his son's condition. His mother was more accepting, saying with Ben's new size, they were going to make a fortune in the chimney-cleaning business. Ben had been less than thrilled about this idea.

The last Glory saw, he had been trying to train the family dog to carry him around like a little wooden warrior on a floppy-eared horse. If the boy wasn't careful, the mutt was going to use him as a chew toy.

"Maybe Sterling *should* get himself named Mayor," Winter suggested.

"Don't say such things." Sterling glanced around, as if afraid someone would leap out of the shadows and stab a badge of office to his chest.

"Do you know the mortality rate among elected officials?" asked Shroud. "They're three and a half times more likely to die of unnatural causes than your average man on the street."

"Do not be afraid," the Mayor said, raising his voice. "The walls of Grayrock have stood strong and proud since the days of our great-great-grandparents. Our people have weathered difficult times before, and we will do so again! Do not let yourselves be ruled by fear."

Sterling chuckled. "I suspect the Mayor found himself a bard to write a pretty speech."

Glory gave him a sidelong glance. "That's like the balverine calling the ogre ugly, considering the purple prose that comes out of your mouth."

Sterling winked. "This mouth is good for far more than florid speech, my lady Glory. Perhaps you'd care to—"

"No, thank you." Glory wrinkled her nose. "I know where that mouth has been."

She strode out of the shadows before he could respond. She weighed and discarded her options as she approached the Mayor. The temptation to simply drag the incompetent old fool off somewhere and pry the truth out of him was strong, but it would mean getting past the ring of ten armed men. None looked particularly skilled or strong, and Glory had no doubt she and her companions could overpower them, but there was always the chance one of them would get in a lucky thrust.

The crowd was the larger problem. In a town this small, everyone knew one another. Heck, half of them were probably related. Hurt one guard and you'd immediately be set upon by his brother, cousin, great-uncle, nephew, and half sister. A fight would become a riot, and she'd end up having to destroy half the town to pacify the remaining half. There were simpler ways to get what she wanted.

The Mayor's smile grew strained when he spotted Glory and her fellow Heroes. "You're back," he said. "All of you still alive. How wonderful."

"We vanquished the Ghost of Grayrock and sent her fleeing to her mistress, a witch named Yog," Sterling called out. "The kidnapped boy is safely returned to his family."

Glory had to raise her voice to be heard over the cheers. "Have you heard the news from Brightlodge? Yog has been twisting the townspeople into monsters and sending them to spread panic and death."

"If Brightlodge had a stronger leader, he would protect them from such threats," the Mayor shot back.

Glory pulled a folded piece of parchment from her pocket, glanced at the message from Brightlodge, then used it to fan herself. "Beckett the Seer believes Yog will attack Grayrock. He spoke of a coming storm." She looked to the sky, where a mass of dark, green-edged clouds had been gathering over the woods since sunrise. "What has Grayrock's leader done to protect his people?"

The Mayor raised his hands. "A little rain is nothing to worry about."

"The clouds are a portent of doom," said a woman. "Just like the omen my sister Peg saw last week, when her cat gave birth to a two-headed lamb! Evil is coming to Grayrock!"

Glory groaned. They had investigated that story their first day in town. As it turned out, Peg also happened to be a taxidermist, and they'd found a very suspicious row of stitches around that stillborn animal's second neck. Which hadn't stopped people from lining up to pay for the chance to see the dead "monster sheep."

"Beware, good people," said Sterling. "For the Ghost of Grayrock was but one of three Riders, servants of Yog. Yog herself is said to be a creature of legend, one who would feed on your helpless children and bathe all of Albion in blood!"

He was laying it on a little thick, but it certainly captured people's attention. Glory pushed her way through the crowd. Sparks tickled her palms as her annoyance grew, but she kept her power to herself and settled for using some well-placed elbows to clear a path. "Why did Skye want to flood the town? Why is Yog intent on destroying Grayrock?"

"Grayrock is peaceful," said the Mayor. "We've no feuds with anyone."

"Well, someone has a feud with Grayrock." She stopped just beyond the range of the guards' spears. "Yog is coming. You can either help us put an end to her plans, or we can go on our way and leave the defence of Grayrock to you. What do you think Yog will do when she learns Grayrock is unprotected?" She glanced at the closest of the guards. "No offence."

Sterling stepped up behind her and whispered, "We can't abandon these people."

Glory pushed the spears aside and approached the Mayor. The guards tensed, but the Mayor held up his hand for them to wait. The man lacked the courage for a fight. Not here, with him trapped in the middle. "You have two choices, Mayor. One: You and I go somewhere private so you can tell me everything you know about Skye, Yog, and their plans. Or two: We leave you to fend off the coming storm on your own."

The Mayor looked down at her from his place atop an old crate.

It was a cheap theatrical trick designed to force everyone, including Glory, to look up to him. "I have no idea what you're talking about. I know nothing of these villains."

Glory countered by lowering her voice to a whisper, making him bend down to hear. "You're going about this all wrong."

"I don't think so." It was his smile that did it. That smug, gloating smile was as irritating as a sliver buried beneath her skin.

Glory gave the Mayor an answering smile that would have chilled even Winter's blood. "This treasure the ghost claimed to be looking for. What guarantee did you have that she would have shared it with someone like you?"

The Mayor's grin cracked ever so slightly. Glory moved closer. "Did she tell you she'd split the treasure? That it would be an equal partnership?" She shook her head like a disappointed tutor. "There's no such thing. Every partnership has a leader and a follower. Tell me, Mayor, which were you? Do you command the Ghost of Grayrock? Does she respond to your summons?"

He wasn't smiling anymore. "Well, no, but—"

"You were in over your head. I understand." The crowd pressed in, but their desire to avoid impaling themselves on the guards' spears outweighed their eagerness to eavesdrop. At least for the moment. "Sterling would see you stripped of your office for your part in things, but I understand that people sometimes stumble. I'm offering you a chance to redeem yourself and retain your power, such as it is."

"I was working on a plan to rid Grayrock of the ghost's influence when you and your friends arrived and disrupted everything."

"A plan," Glory repeated. "I assume your plan involved betraying her the moment you got your claws on this mythical treasure?"

The Mayor had the decency to blush.

"Skye used your greed to lead you about like a dog on a leash. You were never in control." Glory's smile grew. "Would you like to be?"

"What . . . what do you mean?"

Sterling stepped closer. "Glory, what are you doing?"

"Like it or not, this is the Mayor's town. If we want to get anywhere, we need him." She waved Sterling away and turned her attention back to the Mayor, who had puffed up at Glory's acknowledgement of his importance. The man couldn't have been easier to manipulate if he'd been a puppet. "Skye is only a servant. Whatever is about to happen, it's happening by Yog's command. She wants something. Something Skye failed to bring her. Something she's willing to do anything—or *pay* anything—to get. Negotiating with the nymph is a waste of time. We should be focusing our efforts on the one holding the nymph's leash."

"We?" he repeated.

"I'm not the Mayor of this town. I have no way of contacting Skye." They had tried burning the last of the sticks Skye had given to Greta, but if Skye had seen their signal, she had chosen to ignore it. "I suspect you might, though you've been too frightened to use it."

"You propose a partnership?" The Mayor's smile began to return. "And which of us would be the leader in such an arrangement, woman?"

"You're learning," Glory said approvingly.

Sterling grabbed her by the arm and pulled her around. "Glory, you can't—"

Power flowed instinctively through her limbs. Sparks flew from her fingertips. Sterling took an involuntary step back.

"Never lay hands upon me without my permission." Glory swallowed and balled her fists, crushing both her automatic anger and the half-formed flaming apple. Orange sparks burst from between her fingers.

Sterling started to reply—probably a flirtatious quip about where he could lay those hands—but something in Glory's expression must have made him reconsider. He nodded and stepped back. "You're right. My apologies."

Glory took a breath, gathering her composure. "What do you say, Mr. Mayor?"

"You need my power and my connections." He folded his arms. "Why do I need you?"

She looked at the smoke rising from her fingertips. "To make sure you walk away alive."

"I don't trust you," the Mayor said as he led Glory up the stairs of the tower.

"You shouldn't. Trust is what got you into this mess in the first place." Well, trust and greed. And stupidity. Not to mention a heap of unjustified arrogance. Glory kept those thoughts to herself as they reached the top of the spiral staircase, where the Mayor unlocked the door to his personal office.

One of the many lessons Glory's father had shared growing up was to never trust a tidy office, and the Mayor's was immaculate. The furniture was all wood, without a speck of the grey dust that covered the rest of the town like dirty snow. Wooden shelves held old tomes and scrolls, interspersed with rock samples of various shapes and sizes. A citation hung beside the door, complete with wax seal and purple ribbons. Glory skimmed it just long enough to confirm that the Mayor had awarded it to himself, for "Servisse and Dedicashonne Beyonde the Calle of Dutye."

The Mayor had brought four of his guards into the tower with them. Two took up positions to either side of the door. A third stood by the window. The last remained outside, at the top of the staircase.

"My men will say nothing," the Mayor assured her. "My gold keeps their families fed and their children out of the quarry." He sat behind the desk, a move no doubt intended to remind her who was in control here. In certain situations, with a different opponent, it might have worked. But in sitting down, he had sacrificed the advantage of height. Glory ignored the proffered chair and rested her hands on the edge of the desk, looking down at him.

The Mayor spoke first, another small victory for Glory. "*If* I had the means to summon Skye, how do we force her to bring us to Yog? What's to stop her from slaying you for ruining her plans?"

"From slaying *us,* you mean?" Glory waited a beat, just long enough to convey her disdain at such a foolish question. "She's just a nymph. We've humiliated her once. We can do so again."

The Mayor snorted. "She's a creature of flame and smoke and rage."

Glory walked over to study the shelves, forcing him to turn to follow her. He was so easy to control and utterly blind to the strings she was pulling. She glanced at a map of Grayrock and the surrounding woods. "Doesn't it strike you as odd that a being of the forest would come to embrace fire? How did she gain the Will to master the element she most feared?"

She didn't give him time to answer. "Smoke fell from her lips when she spoke. Her body was blackened by flame. She's a nymph of charred trees and ash-covered earth, of smoke that blackens the sky, and she carries that horror within her."

"You paint a tragic picture," said the Mayor. "But even if that's true, how does it help us?"

"By showing us the true nature of our enemy. She spoke of people burning the forests to the ground. You saw only Skye's rage, but that rage was born of despair."

He chewed his lower lip for a moment, his brow furrowed. "It seems to me that fires born of despair will kill you just as dead as those that come from rage."

"True enough," said Glory. "But the power of a strong Will and disciplined mind should defeat them both."

He made a show of rubbing his chin and considering. "You can do this?"

"Of course."

"Can you get us past the traps your friend set at the dam?"

Glory took a scroll from the shelf and unrolled it. This was another map, though this one was many years older. The quarry had expanded a great deal since this map was drawn. "If you still believe there's gold beneath the dam—"

"Not gold," he said quietly. "But there *is* treasure buried in Grayrock. That's what Skye was searching for."

"What kind of treasure?" She set the scroll aside and opened a book that turned out to be a journal of some sort.

"A magical artefact. The very first Mayor of Grayrock buried it hundreds of years ago. Only a select few know of its existence." He raised his chin, obviously proud to belong to such an elite line.

Glory turned back to the old map and frowned. "Was the dam here when they founded Grayrock?"

"No, that was built later, to divert the river and allow us to expand—"

"Then how could that first Mayor have buried anything in its foundations?"

He opened his mouth, but nothing emerged.

Glory sighed. "Do you at least know what this artefact is supposed to do?"

Silence.

"Naturally." Glory turned to study the crest of Grayrock painted on the wall. She had assumed the treasure was a lie designed to trick the Mayor and his workers into destroying the dam and wiping out their own town.

Skye was no fool. If there was truly an artefact hidden away in Grayrock, she would know it couldn't be in the dam. So why not simply sneak into town, retrieve the treasure, and escape?

Skye must not know where it was either. Killing off the people would let her search at leisure, without interference. But it was hard to search a town underwater.

"Perhaps the artefact is hidden somewhere that could only be uncovered by flooding?" suggested the Mayor.

"That . . . is not a completely awful theory." Given the layout of the town, the worst of the flooding would hit the quarry, another area that hadn't existed when the artefact was supposedly buried. "Did Skye share anything at all about this object?"

"Only that it was powerful."

"And what did you intend to do once you had it?"

His face reddened, from the tips of his ears all the way down his neck. "I was hoping that it would be enough . . ." The rest was unintelligible mumbling.

"Enough to what?"

"To become a Hero," he blurted.

She stared at him. *"You?"*

He stood so quickly, his chair toppled over. The guards tensed. "Why not me?" he demanded. "If Heroes are truly returned to Albion, why should you and your friends be the lucky ones?"

He was shouting, assailing her with pent-up pain and outrage, along with the occasional spray of spittle. It was as if she had killed his beloved pet dog, then used the body to kill his other, even more beloved dog.

"Luck has nothing to do with it," said Glory.

The Mayor waved a hand at her. "Look at you. Your clothes. The way you talk. You're the very portrait of a rich brat from head to toe. You probably had money and power handed to you on a silver platter."

"Is that what you believe?" Glory whispered. The closest guard took a quick step back.

"What makes you think you're so much better than me?" snapped the Mayor.

"Do you want the complete list? If so, you'd best clear your schedule for the rest of the day."

"You're a spoiled child. Your parents probably—"

"Think hard before you speak of my parents." Glory snapped her fingers and summoned a flaming red apple. The Mayor flinched back, nearly tripping on his own chair. "My father was like you, a preening rooster in a small coop. He lacked the courage and ambition for true greatness. When he saw greatness in his own daughter, he tried to stomp it out. First with threats. Then with force."

She caught herself and forced a smile. She hadn't expected the Mayor to twist a knife into that particular wound.

"What happened?" he asked.

"He failed." She clenched her fist, extinguishing the threat before the guards had the chance to do something stupid. "I spent years honing my skills, sneaking out of the house and risking my life time and again to battle hobbes around our village. I fought for what I became, making choices and sacrifices you can't imagine."

She turned away, pushing back memories of her father's voice commanding his guards to teach Glory a lesson. She hadn't thought about that night for years, and she couldn't afford to let it distract her now.

"You think that makes you better than others?" asked the Mayor. "You fought a few hobbes and ran away from a mean father?"

"I didn't run." Glory cursed herself for letting him gain control of the conversation. She searched for a way to retake the reins, and her attention settled on the crest on the wall.

The seal of Grayrock was a blue circle bordered in gold. A crossed hammer and pickaxe formed an X in front of a grey brick wall. A pair of children, a boy and a girl, played near the bottom of the crest. Between them stood a bare tree, the same oak statue that stood in the centre of town.

The text beneath the seal had faded over the years, but if she was reading correctly, the official motto of the town of Grayrock was, *"In Tymes of Woe, Go Ye Forthe and Hitte Peopel Wit Rockes."*

She pointed to the crest. "What's so special about this stone tree?"

"Nothing," said the Mayor. "People say it was planted by William Grayrock, so they make a big deal out of protecting and celebrating it. There's a dance every summer, and—"

"Wait. Who was William Grayrock?"

"Our founder. He was born William Fisher, but changed his name one day after almost drowning. An enormous pike took his line and pulled him into the water. They say that pike dragged him four miles upriver to the site of what would become Grayrock. His first act as Mayor of Grayrock was to outlaw pike. I'll have you know that in my time as Mayor, we've captured and executed more than six hundred pike."

"Naturally." She pointed to the children. "That girl looks like she's playing with a doll."

"Yes, and the boy is getting ready to hit her with a rock. So what?"

"Do you have records going back to William Grayrock's time? Anything that might explain the origin and meaning of this seal?"

"I'm afraid not," he said. "For the first fifty years, the town flooded every spring. The records office included. That's when they started building the dam."

Glory could feel the seeds of a headache throbbing directly behind her eyebrows. "It took them fifty years to realise they needed a dam?"

He had the decency to look embarrassed. "The town leaders kept drafting orders for the construction of a dam, but they filed those orders—"

"—in the records office," Glory finished, massaging her forehead. "You said William Grayrock planted that tree. Do you know how it turned to stone?"

"There are rumours and stories, but nobody really knows. The original tree could have died centuries ago, and someone just erected that statue in its place."

"It's on your sash, too." Glory moved to the window to look out at the stone tree. "Yog turned Ben into a wooden doll, just like the one in that seal. It might be coincidence, but we need to dig up that tree."

"You can't," said one of the guards. "Legend has it that's where William Grayrock buried his dear departed brother."

"Nah," said the one by the window. "It's the grave of his father, a drunken old sot who died after picking a fight with a horse."

"A donkey," said the first.

"A *horse.* And once a century, the tree comes alive and grows fermented fruit. A single bite is as potent as a whole barrel of mead."

"William's father won that fight," said the third guard. "It's the horse they buried that day. The tree drops horseshoes on anyone of the Grayrock bloodline. That's how the horse takes his revenge from beyond the grave."

The Mayor rolled his eyes, and for the first time Glory almost felt sorry for him. "Has anyone ever witnessed any of these feats?" she asked.

"My sister hit me with a horseshoe once," said the first guard after a long pause.

Glory counted slowly until she could answer without violence. "Is your sister a tree?"

"Well, no."

"Then I don't think that really applies, do you?"

"These are simple folk," the Mayor said. "They have legends about everything, from the dam to the mountain to the privies."

"That's true," said the guard at the window. "If you duck into the privy south of the butcher's and drop two coppers into the pit, you get a blessing of sorts for the belly, powerful enough you can eat three bowls of Old Marion's chowder without suffering the runs."

"I usually drop a silver in, just to be safe," said the first.

"But the privy isn't painted into the town seal, is it?" Glory had meant the question to be rhetorical, but having asked, it occurred to her that these people were entirely capable of adding such artwork to their official seal. She double-checked to make certain. "There's a good chance the treasure we want is connected to that tree."

"That makes sense." The Mayor's words were edged with triumph and satisfaction, neither of which had been present a moment before. He signalled the guards with one hand. "You said I needed you to keep me alive, and I admit it would be useful to have a Hero or four to protect me if I were to face the Ghost of Grayrock again. On the other hand, once I have that treasure, I can hire my own Heroes. Which means I've got no further need for a partner."

Glory smiled as the guards closed in. "That's funny. I was just thinking the same thing."

chapter 14

SHROUD

Most of the homes in Grayrock had simple wooden shutters or sheets of animal hide for windows, but not the Mayor's tower. His windows were brown glass, tall and relatively narrow, with diamond-shaped panes. They made a right and proper crashing sound when someone tossed a body through them.

The Mayor tumbled out of the second-storey window. His frightened shrieks ended with a thump that made even Shroud wince. The Mayor clearly had never learned how to roll with the impact or absorb the jolt with his knees. He absorbed most of it with his face.

A fall from that height was potentially fatal. Of course, you could kill yourself just tripping over a rock, depending on the ground and the angle of impact. But Shroud was an expert in these matters, and he hadn't heard the hollow-melon sound of a broken skull, which meant there was a good chance the Mayor had survived. Pained gasps affirmed his guess moments later.

The people of Grayrock stared in silence. Shroud loosened his shoulders and eased his hands closer to his knives. Winter's breath turned to fog as she readied her magic. Sterling reached for his sword.

Glory peered out the broken window and waved. Smoke and

sparks rose from her fingertips. "Everything's all right. The Mayor tripped and fell."

Shroud looked from the window to the point of impact. In order to land that far from the tower, the Mayor would have had to be running full speed through his office before "tripping." But nobody argued the point. The guards on the ground moved to surround their groaning leader and looked about uncertainly.

The townspeople broke into cheers.

Shroud sniffed. "They think that's impressive? I'd have hauled him to the rooftop and tossed him in a double somersault into the trough out back."

"Three cheers for Mayor Glory!" shouted someone.

Glory leaned out the window. "What?"

"Hip, hip, hooray!"

"Did they call her Mayor?" Winter's mouth and brows were crooked, as if she couldn't decide whether to be amused or aghast.

A middle-aged woman, still carrying the chicken the Mayor—ex-Mayor?—had been kissing a short time before, said, "Grayrock prides itself on its democratic process. That was what's known as a Motion of No Confidence."

"She threw him out a window," said Sterling.

"He tripped!" Glory shouted.

The woman nodded. "In my great-grandfather's time, they held a Recall Referendum in the streets for Mayor Flotsam, complete with pitchforks and torches. This was two years after Flotsam impeached his mother with an axe. Politics were simpler in those days."

Shroud allowed himself a small smile. Political conflicts were one of the Conclave's biggest moneymakers. He'd settled a few disputed elections himself.

"Why Sterling, you're not jealous of the new Mayor, are you?" Winter teased.

"Not at all," said Sterling. "I just—Glory can't be Mayor of Grayrock."

"What've you got against democracy?" the woman demanded, raising her chicken as if she intended to beat Sterling about the head with the bird.

Three caws in quick succession, repeated again a few seconds later, tore Shroud's attention from the spectacle to a crow perched on the edge of the tavern roof. He slipped away and whistled six notes from an old drinking song. The crow flew to Shroud's arm, and the two of them disappeared into the shadows.

Let the spoiled and pompous elite use their gorgeously plumed hunting hawks and exotic messenger birds, while the commoners made do with clumsily inked letters tied to trained chickens. The Conclave preferred nobody notice their servants. Crows were the perfect bird: dark and dangerously clever, capable of recognising and remembering countless songs and commands, but common enough to travel anywhere in Albion without drawing attention.

The best trained of the Conclave's birds were weapons as well as messengers. By strapping poisoned needles to a bird's talons, you created an animal that could swoop down in silence and kill with a single scratch.

Shroud had once experimented with strapping small explosives to the birds for more dramatic assassinations. It was effective enough, assuming you cut a proper length of fuse, but the Conclave had objected to the loss of so many crows.

He slid the message free from the black tube around the crow's leg. After double-checking that nobody could see, he unrolled the parchment. The message was written in red ink.

ELIMINATE THE OGRE. GRAYROCK'S FATE UNIMPORTANT.

He tore the last word off the parchment and swallowed it. The rest he rolled up and returned to the tube. Removing the end of the message signalled his assent. Had he chosen to refuse the Conclave's assignment, he would have torn off the first word instead. He would have then spent the remainder of his life looking over his shoulder, waiting for the blade that would communicate the Conclave's disappointment with his choice. He suspected the wait would be measured in days.

Red ink meant this went beyond a simple assassination. The target was to be eliminated at any cost. All other assignments were put on hold. And if possible, the target should know who it was that killed them.

Only the highest-ranking members of the Conclave could issue a blood order. Generally, red ink was reserved for internal matters—vengeance against those who had betrayed the Conclave. The fact that Shroud had been entrusted with such a job was a sign of the Conclave's confidence in him. But what had an ogre done to earn a sentence?

You know better than to ask questions. Curiosity killed the cat, remember? Killed it slowly. Painfully. Probably by sneaking in one night when the cat was sleeping, throwing a bag over its head, and dragging it out to the woods, where nobody could hear its screams.

Shroud whistled a different melody, and the crow launched into the air. It flew fast and hard, as if it was eager to escape the clouds roiling in over Grayrock. He watched the crow disappear into the distance, then rejoined the others.

The Mayor lay forgotten on the cobblestones. Glory stood at the centre of the crowd, where she looked to be enjoying her new role. "Gather your best diggers and tools by the oak statue," she called. "And you there, bring me a drink. Cider would be nice."

"You can't seriously intend to become Mayor of Grayrock," said Winter.

"It would appear I already am. Besides, me running things can only help our quest."

Shroud pointed to the tree. "Why are you so interested in that statue?"

"We won't know until we dig it up." From the clipped impatience in Glory's words, Shroud wasn't the first to ask that question.

"Glory thinks this is where we'll find what Skye was really searching for," Winter explained.

Shroud checked the sky. "I don't like the idea of being out in the open when Yog starts raining magic on our heads."

"We don't know those clouds are magic," said Sterling.

"True. Could be poisoned." Shroud looked past Sterling to where a kindly citizen was helping the Mayor to his feet. He looked to have broken an arm, and the dazed expression on his face suggested he might be concussed.

The Mayor pulled free, doubled over, and vomited. Definitely concussed, then.

Shroud studied the clouds. If Yog intended to slaughter the town, a contact poison would be the way to go. Anything needing to be ingested would first have to make its way into the wells and lake, which would dilute most poisons too much to kill any but the sick and frail.

Poisoned clouds. There's no art there. No precision. It's simple slaughter.

If Yog's magic could control clouds, could that power be refined, tightened to manipulate only a single small cloud? A wisp of poisoned fog could be sent through the tiniest cracks, leaving no evidence of intrusion. Nothing but a corpse lying untouched behind locked door and sealed windows. If he could figure out how Yog had done it, this would be a technique to pass along to the Conclave when he returned.

But how to deliver the poison to the clouds in the first place? Skye could fly, but the clouds were so high up. He doubted it was as simple as flying into the clouds and dumping out vials of poison. Perhaps Yog had simply transformed the clouds from the ground, using Will. If so, she was more powerful than they had realised.

The townspeople were returning with shovels and pickaxes.

Such tools were easy enough to find in a town that made its living by carving great big holes in the earth. Under Glory's direction, they attacked the ground around the tree, tearing up the cobblestones and gouging the dirt below.

Lightning stabbed the sky to the west. Thunder rumbled through Grayrock at almost the same moment.

Sterling took up a shovel and began digging at the base of the tree while Glory examined the tree itself, pressing a hand to the cold bark as if feeling for a heartbeat. Sparks jumped from stone roots as Sterling jabbed the shovel deeper. Winter grabbed a second shovel and joined him.

Rain darkened the sky in the distance. Many of the bystanders began to disperse, and Shroud was eager to do the same. "Whatever's here will wait until after the storm."

"Not now that the old Mayor and the townspeople know about it," said Glory. "If they think there's gold or other riches buried here, they'll swarm over the site the instant we turn our backs. They'd be mobbing us right now if they weren't afraid of what we could do. If you're so worried about the rain, pick up a shovel and help."

Shroud pulled his hood over his head. The cloak was waterproof—all the better for removing bloodstains—which should provide protection against whatever was coming. Of course, if it was a contact poison, he'd have a difficult time removing said cloak without getting it on his hands.

It could be acid instead. That would be nasty. Acid from the clouds . . .

Come to think of it, Yog might not be directly targeting the people of Grayrock. Certain kinds of stone could be dissolved with simple vinegar. Maybe Yog planned to erode the dam from the sky and complete the work her nymph began. A little cloak wouldn't save anyone from that.

Shroud snatched a shovel and started digging.

The first raindrops reached them right around the time the first shovel thunked against the small chest buried in a tangle of stone roots three feet belowground. Unlike the clouds, the rain itself had a faint reddish tinge, as well as an odd metallic smell. The stone branches and leaves provided a bit of shelter, but that wouldn't last when the rain started falling in earnest. Most of the workers had left, despite Glory's calling for them to stay and see the job through. Apparently there were limits to what the new Mayor could command.

"The tree has quite the hold on this thing." Sterling jammed his shovel against another root and tried to lever it free, but the root was as thick as a man's wrist. The shovel's handle bowed and cracked. Sterling stumbled back. "The chest appears to be carved from stone as well, though the hinges are metal. A worthy challenge, but it shall not defeat—"

"Move." Shroud tossed his shovel aside and pulled a small, flat crowbar from his pack. He dropped prone and reached into the hole, jamming the bar beneath the largest of the roots. He didn't worry about precision or style, not with haunted clouds darkening the sky.

"You don't have the leverage to break the roots from that angle," Glory said.

"I'm not trying to break the roots. But metal hinges stuck in the damp earth all these years?" Shroud pulled the bar upwards, and one of the old hinges snapped. He moved the crowbar to the left, hastily repositioned the end below the second hinge, and repeated the process. Once both hinges were broken, he shifted his angle and wedged the bar into the crack beneath the lid, trying to shift it to the side.

Glory picked up one of the smaller pieces of broken root and held it out, displaying the striated rings in the centre. "This was once a living tree. The roots must have grown around the chest before it turned to stone."

"You think whatever's in the chest changed the tree?" asked Winter.

Shroud jerked his hands back. *Never allow haste or fear to make you careless.*

He set his crowbar aside and pulled on a pair of deerskin gloves. If they started turning to stone, hopefully he'd be able to yank his hands free before the spell spread to his flesh.

A woman screamed in the distance, somewhere near the town gates. Shroud cast a furtive glance at the others to see if the rain had begun raising welts on their skin or transforming them into monsters or stone statues. They seemed unharmed and relatively dry thus far.

He squeezed his hand through the gap in the chest. Whatever was inside, it wasn't gold. He felt a hard, rag-covered bundle, about the size of a dagger. He shoved the lid with both hands, opening up more space.

Was he imagining the stone roots tightening around his wrist, trying to stop him?

"What is it?" asked Winter.

Shroud yanked the object free. "Shelter first," he said, scurrying across the street towards a small cobbler's shop.

Another shriek carried through the town. "I think you're right," said Glory.

They reached the overhang in front of the shop just before the rain began to assault the town in earnest, as if the clouds were a dam that had suddenly crumbled. More shouts followed: cries of pain and calls for help. Sterling put a hand to his sword and started forwards. Shroud and Glory caught him by the arms, holding him in place.

"The people are in danger," Sterling said. "They need a Hero!"

"Will you be fighting the rain with that sword, then?" asked Shroud. "Because I'm pretty sure the raindrops outnumber you."

He waited for Sterling to stop pulling, then turned his attention to the bundle from the chest. The rags were old and brittle, caked in dust. They cracked like plaster as Shroud pulled them aside.

Inside lay a simple doll, similar in size and shape to the boy they had rescued, Ben, but made of stone. Faint lines along the surface suggested wood grain. The doll, like the tree, might have once been wood. He turned it over. Unlike Ben, this doll was hairless, but the simple features inked onto the face remained. "Another one. Maybe Yog's just a very dedicated doll collector."

"Is it alive?" asked Winter.

Shroud poked it in the eye. Nothing happened. He tested the arms and legs. They swivelled stiffly on their stone pegs.

"All this fuss is over an old doll?" asked Glory.

"I wonder if the boy's going to end up like this," said Shroud.

Winter snatched the doll from his hands. "We're not going to let that happen."

"None of us understands how this transformation occurred," Sterling said gently. "But fear not, Lady Winter. Once we've vanquished Yog and her servants, we shall find a way to restore Ben to his proper form."

Motion caught Shroud's eye. He turned and nocked an arrow to his bowstring before his mind fully registered why. The figures down the street were too far away to see clearly, but their movements were wrong.

Shroud had spent years studying movement, learning how to disappear in plain sight, to become just another sheep in the herd. Movement told you if a person was anxious or confident, strong or weak, alert or distracted. This group moved with a determined stride through the rain, but their body language wasn't quite human. They were too twitchy.

The whisper of steel sliding from its sheath told him Sterling had seen them too. Glory swore and said, "Is that who I think it is?"

The Mayor hurried towards them, surrounded by a dozen men. At least, they had once been men.

The rain had stained their clothes a watery red. They had tied rags around their heads like crude bandages. Their shoulders were hunched high enough to touch their ears, and their exposed skin had taken on a sickly pallor, like they were covered in old bruises.

"I think he's contesting the recall," said Shroud.

Three to four opponents for each of the Heroes. Not an impossible fight by any means, but potentially painful, and in addition to watching out for those spears, they also had to worry about Yog's cloud-borne assault.

The spears give them the advantage of reach, but they're walking in mud and water, which means their balance will be poor. Stay together as a group. They can't all attack at once, though the ones with spears can thrust past their comrades.

Shroud pulled the bowstring to his cheek and waited. Even for citizens of Grayrock, the approaching fighters were disorganised and chaotic. The Mayor barked orders but seemed as eager as the rest to wade in and lay about with the short club he had acquired. His broken arm hung limp against his side. "They're moving like redcaps."

"How is that possible?" asked Sterling. "The man was human when Glory threw—when he fell from his office window an hour ago."

"The letter from Brightlodge said the greencaps were created by blood-tainted ale." Glory pointed to the sky.

"It appears Yog has improved her formula. Stay out of the rain." Shroud loosed the bowstring and shot the nearest guard. The razor-edged Trollfang Broadhead arrow dropped the man where he stood. Unfortunately, that seemed to be the signal for the rest of the mob to charge, shouting and laughing incoherently.

They didn't bother trying to avoid the flaming apple Glory

lobbed into their path, and the resulting explosion sent two guards to the ground.

Winter's magic turned the road to ice, and three more fell hard. "This is *not* proper parliamentary process!"

Shroud tossed a handful of six-pronged caltrops into the street. These were the new M. Cole variety he had picked up two weeks ago in Brightlodge. The barbed tips ensured that not only would they stab through the thickest soles, they'd stick and inflict more damage with every step.

"Try not to kill them." Sterling's sword slashed out, removing the tip of a spear. He slammed the hilt into his opponent's jaw.

"Now you tell us," said Glory.

Try not to kill them? What kind of suicidal, bleeding-heart nonsense is that? A man comes at you with a weapon, you leave his corpse on the ground as a warning to others. In fact, you could argue that by killing the first fellow, you were saving *the lives of everyone who ran away.*

With the ethics sorted out, Shroud shot a second guard at point-blank range. The remaining men pressed in around them, leaving him no room to shoot properly. He snatched a knife from his sleeve and stepped forwards, moving inside the range of the spears and jabbing the tip of his blade at exposed limbs.

There was an artistry to this kind of fighting, a constant movement not dissimilar to a dance. Shroud flowed from one partner to the next, leaving each with a kiss of his knife that blossomed red. He kept Sterling's sword in the edge of his vision to make sure he didn't inadvertently dodge into the way, and did his best not to block the magic Winter and Glory flung.

The dance ended abruptly when the butt of a spear struck the side of his skull, knocking him to the ground. Shroud rolled back towards shelter, pausing only long enough to hamstring another guard. Unfortunately, that pause gave the Mayor time to snatch up a discarded spear and close in. Shroud waited as the Mayor raised the spear overhead, then rolled to one side. The tip sank into the ground beside him. Shroud wrapped his arm around the spear for support and slammed the heel of his boot directly into the man's groin.

Whatever magic had changed these people, their anatomy remained human enough. The Mayor's eyes bulged, and he hobbled backwards, squeaking like a wounded rat.

The remaining guards fled, laughing and bleeding. All total, seven men lay scattered on the ground, the majority of them still alive. For the moment.

That one with the knife wound to the belly won't last long. Kinder to put him out of his misery.

Shroud stood and brushed himself off. The rain was thinning, and the drops falling from the sky had begun to lose their unnatural colouration. Reddish mud stained his cloak. Some of it had splashed his shirt and skin. Where the water touched his body, the flesh itched like a healing sunburn.

"How many others do you think . . ." Winter trailed off, gesturing at the dead and wounded guards.

"That depends on who among these people had the sense to come in out of the rain," Glory said sourly. "Which means half the town could be transformed by now."

"Now, now. You shouldn't speak that way about your constituents," Winter said. "Is everyone else all right?"

Sterling had lost a bit of skin from the knuckles of his left hand, and Winter was sporting what would soon be an impressive black eye, but they were otherwise unharmed.

"I most certainly am *not*."

Shroud spun, knife ready to throw. The voice had come from the stone doll, which must have fallen into the mud during the battle. Shroud grabbed it around the waist and wiped it briskly against his cloak to clean the worst of the mud. The doll responded by kicking him on the wrist.

"Rubbing me into your armpit is hardly an improvement, you arse-faced goon," the doll snapped. The stone head turned with a grinding sound, and the doll surveyed the carnage on the street. "A magestorm. I assume Yog is behind this?"

"That's right," said Sterling. "What do you know about her? Why was she searching for you?"

"Who *are* you?" Shroud interrupted.

"My name is Kas the Undying," said the doll. "I am . . . I *was* . . . Yog's husband."

chapter 15

WINTER

"You're cute, but aren't you a bit small for her?" asked Winter.

Kas studied each of them. His head turned stiffly, like that of a man crippled by arthritis. Every time he moved, the grating of stone against stone made Winter's teeth clench. "She did this to me."

"Why?"

"Because I finally saw the truth of what she was. What she had become. I tried to stop her. Yog didn't take kindly to that." He glanced at the moaning guards. "She's improved her mixture since then."

"What kind of poison did she use?" Shroud demanded.

"Not poison." The doll chuckled, a sound like rattling pebbles. "Not exactly. It's a potion she devised. She wanted a way to break the minds of Heroes, to reduce them to animals she could manipulate and control. She was always tinkering, trying to find a more effective blend. She never used to be able to deliver it in a magestorm, though. Last I remember, she was experimenting with frog secretions, thinking that might let the potion be absorbed through the skin."

"We believe she's using redcap blood," said Shroud.

"That's right. She once told me the first redcaps were a result of a bad batch, back when she was young."

Winter stared. "Are you saying Yog *created* the redcaps?"

Kas made a shrugging motion with one arm. "Hard to say. She'd been around a long time when I met her, and her memory wasn't the most reliable."

One of the guards pushed himself to his hands and knees and reached for a spear. Winter casually froze his hands to the ground. "We thought you were dead when we dug you up. Or broken."

"I was napping," the doll snapped. "Until this buffoon dropped me in toxic muck."

Shroud folded his arms. "If you've got a problem, I'd be happy to bury you and let you get back to your dirt nap."

"Yog won't stop now," Kas continued. "The magestorm is only the beginning, to soften up her enemies. Next, she'll send her Riders to attack the town."

Winter nodded. "The nymph and the ogre."

Kas stared. "An ogre? She's fallen hard indeed."

"We've sent them running once before," said Sterling. "Should they dare to return, we'll do so again!"

"Aye, but you weren't fighting all these townsfolk last time, were you? Not to mention whatever other forces she might have gathered." Kas looked around. "There should be a third Rider. Yog always said three was the number of power. She sought one with great strength of body, one who was the most skilled of their kind, and one with an indomitable Will. They held the spillover, the power she couldn't contain within her own body."

"We've received word from Brightlodge that the third Rider is a redcap," said Sterling.

"Oh, Yog. What have the years done to you?"

"Does she really eat Heroes?" asked Winter.

"You've heard about that part, have you?" Kas nodded. "Heroes for their power, and children for their youth. I should have seen it sooner, but I didn't want to believe. By the time I accepted the truth, she was almost unstoppable."

"Almost?" Winter pressed.

"Her final meal was a Hero named William Grayrock. Bravest man I ever knew. He and I worked together to end Yog's evil. William sacrificed himself, letting me take him to Yog as a prisoner. A 'gift' for my beloved wife. I poisoned him, cursed his very blood. When Yog feasted that night, she took the curse into herself. It weakened her body and splintered her power. But it wasn't enough to stop her from doing this to me."

Winter frowned. "How did you end up buried in the middle of Grayrock?"

"I don't honestly know. I remember fleeing from Yog and her Riders, but these little legs don't get you very far. I tried to use my magic to capture a mount. A hawk would have been ideal, but at that point, I'd have settled for a rabbit or a squirrel. I couldn't do it. Preparing that spell for Yog had exhausted me. I passed out from exhaustion. Someone must have found me and assumed I was dead. I wouldn't have been the first one Yog had done this to." For the first time, Kas sounded uncertain. "How long was I buried?"

"Let's just say you had the world's best nap," said Winter.

"Long enough for people to forget about Yog, and for Heroes to fade into legend until very recently," added Glory. "Were you . . . awake that whole time?"

Kas shook his head. "Only in the beginning. I tried to call out, but the chest was too thick, and warded against magic. They must have been afraid Yog's spell on me could spread to others like a disease. I realised I was likely to be down there a good long time. Long enough for wood to begin to rot. I used what power I had left to transform my body to stone, hoping that would preserve my body until someone dug me up," said Kas. "After that, I mostly slept."

Glory nodded. "Your power leaked. It changed the tree to stone as well. And the chest."

"Interesting." Kas looked around, as if searching for his former tomb. "If the wards on the chest were keyed to me personally, that connection could have caused it to transform."

"Can you change yourself back?" Winter asked, thinking of Ben.

"You think I haven't tried?" Kas raised his little stone arms in exasperation. "I saw Yog reverse this spell once, long ago. Thankfully, it's not something she can do from a distance. Otherwise, had she suspected I still lived, she could have removed the spell and left me to be crushed to death by the roots of that damned tree. If we defeat Yog, if I could search through her hut to learn how she cast this curse, I *might* be able to restore myself."

A child screamed from the quarry side of town. People were dying out there. Winter peered at the clouds. "Is the rain safe?"

"Yog's magestorms expend most of their power in the first minutes," said Kas. "But the dregs of her toxin will linger in the clouds and the rain a while longer. Probably not enough to transform you, but it could make you sick as dogs."

"We can't keep standing around waiting for the weather." Winter spread her hands towards the sky. A chill crept through her veins, as if her blood had been replaced by water from the coldest mountain streams. She had pushed herself in the battle with the guards. But she should be able to provide a bit of safety without suffering full-blown iceburn. Hopefully.

She stepped out, and the falling rain around her slowed. The droplets turned to flakes of snow, which she brushed from her body. She could do this. Freezing the rain was a simple matter of freeing the cold inside her. "Much better. Now, let's go save Grayrock!"

The town was in chaos.

Thankfully, it looked like most of the people had taken shelter from the storm, so few were affected as strongly as the Mayor and his guards. But enough had suffered the same fate to slow the Heroes' progress. Winter maintained her sphere of cold the best she could while the others fought off twisted and raving men, women, children, and worse.

"Remember, these are innocent victims," Sterling said.

"Innocent victims who are doing their best to kill us," Shroud shot back. "Admittedly, their best is rather amateurish. No style at all."

Glory set off a series of magical explosions in front of a trio of children. "Ex-humans are one thing. Do you expect me to hold back against *that*?"

That was a large donkey charging drunkenly down the street, the fur of its scalp matted and bloody. Foam dribbled from its lips.

Shroud's arrow took the animal in the throat. It stumbled and slid to a halt a short distance in front of them. "I vote no."

"Back in the day, the toxic soup Yog brewed in her cauldron only affected people," said Kas. "I'd love to know what she's changed."

From the rooftop ahead, a rain-soaked rooster let out a cry like an angry, flatulent trumpet. Bloody wings spread, it charged along the gutter towards them.

Winter dropped her protective sphere long enough to freeze the bird's feathers. It stiffened, then toppled off the roof. "Too slow, little bird."

Someone peeked out of a window as they passed. Sterling waved them back. "Stay inside your homes!"

To the west, part of the town appeared to be on fire, despite the rain. A pair of redcaps—true redcaps, not the partially transformed residents of Grayrock—chased a dog through the street. Winter froze the road directly in front of the redcaps. The first slipped, and the second tripped over the first, allowing the dog to scurry to the relative safety of a nearby home. Glory finished off the redcaps before they could rise.

"How did they get inside the walls?" asked Sterling.

Winter turned towards the distant flames. "They're burning the buildings closest to the gates." If redcaps had broken through, or if someone under Yog's influence had opened the gates, it might be too late to stop them. "We have to get over there."

Snow swirled around her as she ran. Yog's storm had faded to little more than a drizzle now.

"Yog will know I'm free," said Kas. "She's got a vindictive streak as wide as the sea. If she gets her hands on me—"

"She won't," said Winter. "We'll find a way to change you back. You and Ben both. Though you might be a bit wrinklier than you used to be, given how old . . ." She trailed off as she turned a corner and saw the source of the smoke and fire.

The metal gates were intact, but the stone wall of Grayrock was burning. The nymph, Skye, stood behind the gates, wreathed in flames. Directly in front of her sat what looked like a small catapult, manned by a pair of redcaps.

"That'd be Yog's Rider of Will," said Kas, twisting about to watch as more fire flew through the gates to ignite a nearby stable. "The core of the power comes from the Rider, but Yog will have strengthened her Will, making her even more dangerous. Yog can also see through her Riders' eyes if she chooses."

Shroud was already fitting an arrow to the string of his bow. Before he could shoot, one of the redcaps triggered the catapult, sending three missiles arcing over the wall.

Their flight was oddly slow and irregular. It wasn't until they reached the apex of their arc that Winter realised Skye wasn't launching rocks, but redcaps. They stretched out their arms and howled with laughter. They looked to be holding thick "wings" of woven pine branches, which they flapped with ever-increasing vigour as they plummeted towards the street.

"That looks like fun," she commented.

"Wait for it," said Shroud.

The makeshift wings didn't do much. Two of the redcaps slammed to the ground, while the third bounced off a stone wall. That one didn't get back up. Another scrambled out of sight behind a house. The last redcap pushed himself upright, wobbling from side to side. Blood dripped from his nose. "Gonnae nae do *tha* again!"

More catapults went off, launching redcaps into Grayrock in groups of three and four. Many had tied pine branches to their bodies in addition to their wings. They didn't achieve anything close to true flight, but the branches did provide a little padding against the impact. Not every redcap survived, but the majority did, and they were roused to madness by the flames and the chaos.

"This age's style of warfare is very different than it was in my time," Kas said. "Are these common tactics?"

"If only," said Winter.

One of the redcaps flew too low, and the flames on the wall touched his pine-branch wings. He survived the landing, but was too busy trying to extinguish the branches tied to his torso to present any immediate danger.

Shroud shot the next redcap in mid flight.

"Not bad." Glory sniffed and tossed a red apple at another. The explosion flung the redcap backwards, and Skye had to step to the side to avoid being flattened by her own falling monster. Glory smiled.

"Nice . . . if you're only going after one at a time." Winter began to manipulate the raindrops, freezing them into tiny knives and flinging them at the closest redcaps. But for each one she stopped, two more flew over the wall and scampered into town.

Bells rang out from the Mayor's tower. The remaining inhabitants poured from the nearby buildings, carrying whatever they could on their backs. One woman dragged what could have been her husband. He had obviously been affected by the cursed rain, and was bound hand and foot, with a gag stuffed into his mouth. But she hauled him along like an oversized sack of potatoes.

"What are you lot waiting for?" shouted a boy following along behind them. Their son, from the looks of him. "Don't you hear the bells? That's the Mayor giving the order to flee."

"I did no such thing," Glory said indignantly.

"Maybe someone impeached you while you were busy showing off," said Winter.

"Whoever sounded the alarm might have had the right idea," said Sterling. "Removing the civilians from the field of battle allows us to better concentrate on vanquishing our foes."

Shroud glanced down at the doll. "Why is Yog so intent on destroying Grayrock and capturing you? Vengeance is one thing, but this seems excessive, and that's coming from me."

"Because of the curse," said Kas. "I told you how William and I broke her power. Our spell was bound to the life and blood of William Grayrock, and this town was his home. His bloodline lives on in these walls. This place and its people are what keep the curse alive. So long as Grayrock is home to William's descendants, Yog shall remain a shell of her former self, unable to consume the power of any Hero."

"How many descendants?" asked Glory.

Kas chuckled. "Knowing him? I'd guess half the town traces their ancestry to his loins."

"And now they're abandoning Grayrock." Winter studied the wooden ramp leading up to the gates, and to Skye. "The rest of you, keep the redcaps away from me."

"What are you going to do?" asked Sterling.

"Beckett predicted Grayrock's fall. I mean to prove him wrong." Winter grinned. "Also, I want another shot at that nymph."

"Take me with you," said Kas.

Sterling frowned. "No slight intended, but you're no longer the warrior you once were."

"Aye, but I'm the only one among you who won't be hurt by fire," Kas snapped. "I know Yog and her power. I can aid the lass in this fight."

"I agree with the doll," said Glory. "You know it's a bad idea letting Winter out unsupervised."

"This from the girl who threw the Mayor of Grayrock out a window."

"*Ex*-Mayor," Glory snapped.

Winter simply grinned and snatched Kas with one hand. She ran towards the gates, sending blasts of cold to extinguish the small fires that had broken out on the ramp. Redcaps surged towards her from both sides. She froze the road ahead and put on a burst of speed, sliding between the two groups and leaving them to scramble on the ice like overturned turtles.

The planks of the ramp shuddered with her footsteps. On the opposite side of the gates, Skye stood silhouetted by smoke and flame. Fire crackled over the exposed skin of her face and hands. Steam rose from her clothes. Any of Yog's tainted rain that might have fallen on her would have evaporated instantly.

Winter reached deep into memories of her home, of snowdrifts as tall as her parents and icicles that sparkled in the sun like glass stalactites, some so large they stretched from the edge of the roof to the ground in solid, unbroken pillars. Of flowering patterns of frost spread across frozen lakes. Of snowfall so thick, the world around you disappeared. She gathered that cold and flung it directly into the heart of Skye's fire.

The flames weakened, giving her a better view of the nymph. Skye stumbled, and a heavier cloud of smoke belched forth from her gown.

"Nothing burns like the cold!" Winter shouted gleefully.

"Focus, child," snapped Kas. "The nymph was chosen for her strength of Will. Her power is bolstered by Yog. Your Will must be stronger!"

"Don't you worry your little gravel head." Cold flowed through the swirling tattoos on Winter's hands. Lines of frost clung to her skin, tracing the veins below. She poured that cold into her assault, sending serpents of ice and snow racing through the air to devour Skye's fires.

Another batch of redcaps flew over the wall, and the ramp trembled as one charged up to attack her. Winter did her best to ignore them, just as she ignored Shroud's shout of "Mine!" and the thump that followed as he picked the redcap off with a shot from his bow.

Powerful as Skye might be, she had been pushing herself hard, and her exhaustion gave Winter the edge she needed. She felt the moment her own Will began to overpower the flames. It was like cresting a hill. Everything shifted, and the cold poured faster. She stumbled closer to the gates. "I've got her."

The words emerged from her mouth in puffs of frost.

"Be careful," said Kas. "Yog's Riders aren't so easily conquered."

"You think this was easy?"

Skye broke off her assault and whirled in a circle. A thick curtain of smoke billowed from her body. The flames continued to die, but Winter's power could do little to combat the smoke, which crept through the gates to sting her eyes and sear her lungs.

Winter pressed one arm over her nose and mouth. Eyes watering, she forced herself forwards, trying to overwhelm the nymph, to freeze her where she stood. Tears blurred her vision. "What's she doing?"

"Just because I'm stone doesn't mean I can see through smoke."

Winter tried to answer, but the smoke had crawled into her mouth and chest. Each breath was like swallowing embers and ash. Coughing and half-blind, she had no choice. She retreated, hating each step.

Sterling met her at the base of the ramp. Shroud and Glory provided cover, though most of the redcaps had already been driven back by the smoke. Those who hadn't broken their legs upon landing.

"Drink this," said Shroud, pressing a potion into her hand. "Smoke inhalation's a nasty way to die."

Winter swallowed the potion and nodded gratefully as it cooled and healed the burning in her lungs. "I had her."

"You fought well," said Kas.

"We have to fall back." Sterling pointed to the north. "It sounds like another group has broken through at the dam. We can—"

"It's time to face the truth, lad," Kas said firmly. "You might destroy Yog's foot soldiers and chase her Riders away, but Grayrock is lost. Her storm has soaked the earth. It's in the wells. The soil. The crops will drink her poison. Anyone who stays will end up like those twisted wrecks."

"That's impossible. No poison is that potent." Shroud paused. "All right, it's *theoretically* possible, if you have a strong enough toxin. Iocaine, for example. But this isn't—"

"Behind you, Mr. Shroud." The doll pointed past Shroud's left shoulder.

Shroud spun, shooting another arrow in one smooth motion to take out the approaching redcap.

"We could rally the survivors," said Sterling. "Never underestimate the strength of ordinary men—"

"Or women," said Glory.

"—or women, fighting to defend their homes."

"Their homes are on fire," Shroud pointed out. "Drenched in poison and overrun by redcaps. Those who haven't been involuntarily conscripted into Yog's service are fleeing for the hills."

Winter wondered if Greta and Ben had made it out, or if they had been caught in the storm.

"Turn me over to Yog," Kas said quietly. "Trade me for the safety of Grayrock's survivors."

Sterling shook his head. "A Hero doesn't surrender his companion into the hands of evil."

"Besides," added Glory, "what makes you think Yog would keep her part of the bargain? She doesn't sound like the upstanding, honourable type."

"The refugees are vulnerable. If Yog gets the opportunity"—Shroud paused to kill another redcap—"to hunt down and eliminate William Grayrock's descendants, she'd be a fool not to take it."

Winter's body ached. The skin under her nails had a blue tinge, and her hands felt numb and swollen. She clapped them together anyway. "Then we make sure she doesn't have that opportunity."

"That's the spirit," cheered Sterling. "And how exactly did you mean to do that?"

She stepped into the middle of the street. "Shroud, I'll need you to cover me. Glory, you and Sterling escort the remaining survivors out of Grayrock and into the hills. You wouldn't want to abandon any of your constituents, would you? Take Kas with you."

"I'm staying with you, lass," Kas insisted. "I don't know what you're thinking, but I mean to spit in Yog's eye and make her pay for what she did to me."

"What *is* your plan?" asked Sterling.

"It's a surprise." Winter forced a smile and rubbed her hands together. "You didn't think that little fight at the gates was all I had in me, did you? That was just to get Skye's attention."

She climbed up the nearest home that wasn't on fire. Her fingers struggled to find holds between the bricks. Back home, she used to sneak out to go climbing all the time, but generally not after spending the day running from one fight to another. Once she reached the roof, she raised the stone doll over her head.

"Easy now," said Kas. "What do you think you're doing?"

"Causing trouble." Winter grinned and raised her voice. "Hey, Skye! Tell your mistress I've got her husband!"

It was like throwing rocks at a hornets' nest. Redcaps swarmed out of the smoke, converging on the house. She looked around for Shroud, but he had disappeared.

"If it's trouble you wanted . . . ," said Kas.

Winter leaped to the ground and fell, but bounced quickly to her feet and began to run. The hungry, rasping laughter of the redcaps energised her muscles.

Behind her, mocking laughs turned to shouts of pain and anger. She glanced over her shoulder to see a pile of fallen redcaps clawing at one another. She spied the trip wire a moment later. As the redcaps struggled to regain their feet, Shroud calmly stepped into view and put one arrow after another into them. Half of the redcaps charged after him. Shroud gave her a two-fingered salute and vanished.

Winter dodged around a corner, laughing like a little girl playing tag. A small skull flew past her head, chucked by a redcap slingshot. She glanced over her shoulder. "You brought party favours, did you? Well then, let's get the dancing started!"

She froze the ground ahead of her and spun in a slow circle as she slid along the ice. Cold flowed from her tattoos and into the air as she conjured an ice shield behind her. Normally, she used such shields to protect herself or her friends from attack, but this time she placed it directly on the ground behind her like a wall.

The redcaps hit the icy patch on the road. Their arms windmilled wildly as they tried to stop, then they slid into her ice shield one after the other.

"At wis a helluva dunt!"

"Get aff o' me, ya bampot!"

The shield eventually cracked and broke from the impacts, but it had accomplished two important goals: It had slowed Winter's pursuers, and it made her laugh.

A partially transformed townswoman lurched from between two houses. Winter grabbed Kas by the legs and clonked the woman on the head, sending her reeling.

"Sorry about that, Kas."

"I'd be grateful if you never did that again."

"But I thought you wanted to be a part of the battle," Winter teased.

"She's over here!" The cry came from an ogre head perched atop a bakery. Headstrong must have set her noggins out as sentries. How in blazes had she sneaked into Grayrock? Winter couldn't imagine Skye launching *her* over the gate in a catapult.

The ogre's answering bellow was close, maybe one street over. Winter ran faster.

"They're heading for the dam," the noggin shouted.

"Big mouth." Winter could see the dam now, along with the makeshift barricade Shroud had put together to keep anyone else from entering. Planks and poles formed a crude wall, but she could also make out wires vanishing into the darkness and the gleam of blades waiting to spring.

"Look to the left," said Kas.

Redcaps jeered from the watchtower at the western edge of the dam. Thick ropes trailed down into the street. "That must be where Headstrong got in. They took control of the tower and lowered ropes on both sides of the wall."

"Why keep launching them over in catapults, then?"

"Probably because the redcaps enjoy it," guessed Winter.

Winter avoided Shroud's barricade and began climbing. The bottom of the dam was little more than a hill of broken rock, deposited by years of flooding and digging. When she reached the point where the hill met the true base of the dam, she turned to check her pursuers.

From this height, roughly ten feet up, she could see redcaps and changed townsfolk closing in from all directions. The ogre was lumbering towards her as well, stopping only to collect her extra noggins. A cloud of smoke to the west marked Skye's position.

She saw no sign of anyone else. The people of Grayrock might not be the brightest or strongest in Albion, but they knew when to run away.

"This is as good a place as any for a last stand, but I don't see what you've gained," said Kas. "You can't possibly beat them all."

"Last stands are for people like Sterling. And I bet you five gold that I can."

A rock struck the dam to her right. Another hit her shoulder hard enough to bruise. She craned her neck. Freezing the dam below her would slow them down, but if this was to work, she couldn't afford to waste any more of her strength.

She climbed faster, abandoning caution. Her fingers cramped and her toes protested as she forced them into the narrowest of holds. Twice she slipped, leaving scraped skin and blood on the dam.

An animal skull shattered beside her, and the shards cut her face. Atop the dam, a redcap laughed and loaded another round into a makeshift slingshot. Winter was out of time.

She looked to either side. Orange and white stains down the front of the dam showed where water had seeped through the stones in the past. Many of the leaks had been patched over the years, some better than others. Winter scrambled sideways, hunching her shoulders against another barrage of rocks and bones, until she found a crack where a trickle of water flowed down the dam. There was no discolouration here, suggesting this was a relatively new leak, likely a result of all the digging below.

She pressed a hand over the crack. The water froze, turning to rippled glass.

"What are you doing?"

"Stone is strong." Winter grinned and sent the cold deeper into the leak. "Ice is stronger."

Many times she had seen how water would fill the cracks in cobblestone roads, or flow between broken shingles. In the winter, that water would expand into ice, pushing inexorably outward to split wood and rock alike.

She climbed higher and repeated the process at an older leak.

"Watch it!" shouted Kas.

A stone the size of a human head slammed into the dam, and she almost fell. Headstrong had arrived. The ogre was yanking more rocks from the pile below.

"Keep an eye out," Winter said. "Tell me when to dodge."

The iceburn was back, worse than before, causing her vision to sparkle like falling snow in the sunlight. She pushed her Will deeper, driving a wedge of ice between blocks too massive for anyone to move on their own.

"On your left."

Winter swung to the right, avoiding the rock that would have crushed her spine. Her hands and wrists were starting to cramp. She hadn't climbed like this in years. She dragged herself back and continued her assault on the dam.

Beneath her, the stone wall that had held back an entire lake for so many generations shifted ever so slightly.

New rivulets of water sprayed forth. Redcaps cried out in anger and alarm. Winter risked another look down. Headstrong—or more likely, her noggins—must have realised what was about to happen. She was running as fast as she could. The rest of Yog's creatures remained. They dodged the arcing spouts of water and continued to hurl whatever they could find towards Winter.

"Did we ever tell you the rest of Beckett's prediction?" Winter redoubled her efforts. She froze the new leaks, dislodging the blocks further. "I said that Beckett the Seer had predicted the fall of Grayrock. What I forgot to mention was that he implied it would be Heroes who made it happen."

Her fingers slipped again. She froze her own hand to the rock to keep from falling. The shouts below grew louder. "We can't save the town. We can't stop Yog. But I can make sure she doesn't have an army to send after the survivors."

She hauled herself up, then slammed one final burst of power into the dam.

The stones to her left shifted outward. Ice water spouted forth. Stone and mortar cracked with a sound like thunder. The redcaps yelled furiously but still didn't seem to recognise the danger.

Winter hung there and watched the growing breach. Her arms were heavy with ice and exhaustion. There was no way she could make it off the dam in time. She wasn't sure she could go another inch without falling. "Well, that was fun."

"Impressive," whispered Kas. "If we're to die here, I'm honoured to meet my end alongside such a Hero."

As far as Winter knew, the stone doll didn't breathe. He might sink, but it wasn't like he was in any danger of drowning. All he needed to do was walk through the water to the edge of town and climb out through the gates. But before she could point that out, the centre of the dam gave way and a flood of stone and water rumbled forth.

chapter 16

STERLING

"Come along now." Sterling stood atop a boulder ahead of the column of people marching into the hills. He placed one hand on his hip in a jaunty pose, one guaranteed to increase morale and inspire courage in all who looked upon him. "Fear not. Your town may be under siege, your homes on fire, your neighbours twisted into monsters, but hope remains! Adversity builds strength, and with that strength we shall—"

A sound like an earthquake rumbled past them, and in its wake came a cold mist, deceptively gentle. Sterling stared in disbelief as the Grayrock dam disappeared beneath a waterfall that hurled stones the size of wagons down onto the town. The roar of the water quickly drowned the cries of Yog's forces.

Within seconds, Grayrock was gone.

Moans spread through the refugees. Children cried, as did many of the adults. For once in his life, Sterling found himself at a loss for words.

For generations, that dam captured the annual spring runoff behind a wall of rock, until the lake was larger than the town below. And Grayrock had dug itself deep into the earth like a giant basin.

Sterling shielded his eyes with one hand, searching the muddy, swirling water for survivors. Bodies bobbed along the surface with the rest of Grayrock's flotsam. "We weren't supposed to lose," he whispered.

"Do you think Winter survived?"

Sterling whirled, yanking his sword free before recognising Shroud's voice. "Sneaking up on people is a good way to get yourself run through, especially after a day like this."

Shroud jumped nimbly onto the rocks beside Sterling. "Winter told us she had a plan." He cocked his head towards the dam. "It's not a plan I would have chosen, but she's kept the redcaps off our tail, and I'd challenge anyone to match her body count."

"This isn't what was supposed to happen," Sterling said, quieter this time. For the first time since arriving in Brightlodge all those weeks ago, eager to spread justice and wisdom throughout all of Albion, he felt uncertain.

Sterling had come to think of himself as the compass of their group, reminding them of who and what they could be. He liked to think that by striving to be a Hero worthy of the old stories, he inspired others, Heroes and non-Heroes alike, to reach a little higher. To be *more.*

Now look where Winter's reach had taken her. "We don't know she was caught in the flood."

"You think she was in a position to escape that?" Shroud shook his head. "She and that doll are probably at the bottom of Lake Grayrock by now."

"*This* was her plan?" snapped Glory. "To drown herself and the town?"

"I think it's more accurate to say she planned to drown Yog's forces," said Shroud. "Drowning herself was an unfortunate side effect."

Sterling crushed the urge to punch Shroud in the face.

"She's like a child," Glory continued, her voice rising. "Charging off with no thought of tomorrow, no awareness of the consequences."

"She knew the consequences," said Sterling.

Glory stabbed a finger towards Grayrock. "She destroyed a town—finishing the job Skye started!—and for what? Yog's still out there, and now she's even closer to breaking her curse and slaughtering Heroes and children throughout Albion. Winter was a damn fool."

Sterling clenched his jaw, barely stopping an angry retort. Winter and Glory had grated on each other from the day they met, but this was more than Glory's usual sniping. Her insults were louder and harsher, as if they masked genuine pain.

"She bought these people time to escape," Sterling said quietly. "If she hadn't brought down the dam, these hills would soon be swarming with redcaps and greencaps."

Winter's plan had been heroic and triumphant, there was no doubt of that. But dammit, Winter was too young to die, and to die alone.

And there it was, the thing that truly gnawed at Sterling's heart. They all knew and accepted the dangers they faced. They had seen the carnage left behind by the creatures of the forest, from travellers killed by outlaws to the crippled survivors of balverine attacks to the victims of the White Lady's servants. Most Heroes bore the scars of their own encounters, both visible and hidden.

They all understood that they might die. All Heroes masked their fears and their scars in their own ways, through a seemingly heartless exterior, or by embracing death and turning it into an art form. Or by concentrating on the rewards of heroism, the glory and honour and companionship.

Winter battled the darkness through an indomitable sense of fun, but even she recognised that each time she set out might be the last.

They fought together, despite their differences. If—when—they died, it was supposed to be among friends and comrades. "We should search for her."

"There's no damsel in distress for you to rescue this time," said Shroud. "Just a body."

"Then we retrieve her body!" Several townspeople jumped in alarm. Sterling forced himself to speak more calmly. "We bring her back to Brightlodge for a proper burial."

"Or we join her." Shroud pointed to the lake. "Add two more corpses to the soup."

Sterling turned towards Grayrock and began walking.

"I thought you were all about leading the people to Brightlodge," Shroud called after him.

"Glory can lead them. It's her duty as Mayor, right? I'm not leaving Winter behind."

"That water's a good thirty feet deep in places."

"Bodies float." Sterling's throat felt like stone. He swallowed hard, forcing the pain down into his chest where it gnawed at his ribs. There was also the matter of Kas. The flood shouldn't have killed the stone doll, but Yog's Riders would be searching for him. "The water flows west, through the town gates. Where the gates used to be. It will create a bottleneck. You can see the debris already starting to pile up. I'll search there."

"What about Yog?" asked Glory. "With the town destroyed and William Grayrock's descendants dead or here in the hills, what's to stop her from feasting on Heroes?"

"All the more reason to get Winter's body away from there." Sterling's jaw tightened. "Glory—"

"I'll keep them safe," she said.

"There may be more redcaps, or worse," said Sterling.

Glory opened her hands, summoning apples in each hand. One gleamed red, burning with inner fire, while the other was a sickly green. "They've not seen 'worse.'"

Without another word, Sterling began making his way back down the trail.

Shroud checked his bow and followed. "If we keep Yog from getting her hands on Winter, she'll likely just try to make one of us her dinner."

Sterling dropped a hand to Arbiter's hilt, taking comfort in the familiar, solid feel of the weapon. "I hope she tries."

They passed three more survivors on the way back to Grayrock. Two were townspeople who had managed to cling to an overturned wagon and ride out the worst of the flooding. Sterling sent them on to catch up with the others. The third was a redcap, which he despatched with a single thrust of Arbiter.

Their retreat from Grayrock earlier in the day had taken them over a wooden drawbridge into the mountains proper. Now water filled the chasm where the bridge had been.

The water here was disconcertingly quiet, rippling in the breeze. The eastern edge of the dam stretched out perhaps ten feet before falling into rubble. Over time, storms and the seasons would finish what Winter had begun, smashing the remnants of the dam until nothing of Grayrock remained.

Sterling tugged off his boots. He removed his jacket next, and after a brief internal debate, his sword as well. He bundled his things together and tucked them behind the bushes on the edge of the trail. He turned to speak, then stared.

"What?" asked Shroud.

"I've never seen you without your cloak before." It wasn't so much the lack of the cloak as it was the glaringly white ankles peeking from the hems of Shroud's trousers. This was not a man who spent much time exposed to the sun.

"Wait." Shroud pulled him down and pointed to the far side of the lake. A group of redcaps had gathered atop the wall, which put them only a few feet above the water.

"What are they doing?"

"Looks like they're fighting over some buckets. Wait, no, now they're hitting each other with rocks."

As Sterling watched, one of the redcaps fell into the water. Or maybe it was pushed. It held a bucket over its head, but that didn't stop it from sinking out of sight. Another redcap followed, then a third.

"They've got rocks tied to their limbs to drag them down," said Shroud. "I once killed a man like that. A stonecutter with questionable business practices. I chained him to one of his own shoddily made headstones."

Sterling crept towards the edge of the water. "They're searching for Kas. The buckets are for air, and to protect their caps from the water."

"I wonder how she got them into the lake. Redcaps don't like water."

"They're more terrified of Yog." Sterling waited until most of the redcaps had disappeared, then hurried into the water. Shroud dived in a moment later. He cut through the water like a razor, sending only the smallest of ripples to mark his dive. Did the man have to be so sneaky and quiet about everything?

Shroud shoved a floating bottle out of his way and looked around. "Remind me, we came here to *protect* the town of Grayrock, right?"

"Shut up and try to look like a corpse." Sterling allowed the current to pull him along. If Winter was dead, she'd likely be at the gates, where a handful of redcaps were laughing and shouting after their submerged companions.

He hadn't gone far when Shroud grabbed him by the shoulder. One hand covered Sterling's mouth. He barely had time to fill his lungs before Shroud yanked him beneath the surface.

Sterling twisted, reaching instinctively for Arbiter before remembering he had left the sword behind. He grabbed Shroud by the wrist, using his greater strength to pry his hand loose.

When they surfaced again, Sterling tried to kick free, but Shroud put a finger to his lips, then pointed to the sky. Sterling stopped struggling.

Circling high over Grayrock was what looked like an old woman sitting in a heavy black cauldron. She appeared to be using some sort of wooden spoon to guide her flight. "That's got to be Yog."

"Probably searching for Winter and Kas."

Sterling forced himself to relax as Yog swung back in their direction. He didn't move. They were just two more bodies floating along.

Smoke lingered in the air, obscuring the details of the woman who had attacked both Brightlodge and Grayrock. Yog leaned to one side, and Sterling glimpsed a hunched silhouette and tangled grey hair. He wanted to call out a challenge, to force her to face him in combat so he could finish what Kas had begun so many generations before and cut her evil from the world.

Instead, he waited as the cauldron flew to and fro. The next time her back was to them, Sterling hastily scanned the surface. With Yog searching overhead, they couldn't afford to stay in the open. "That barrel over there."

They ducked underwater and swam together. Sterling caught the open side of the barrel and pulled it upright over his head and arms. Shroud squeezed in on the other side a moment later. If Yog looked down, she should see nothing but a bottom-heavy barrel drifting with the rest of the flotsam.

The interior smelled of salted fish. There was some awkwardness as Sterling and Shroud adjusted positions. They ended up with their faces pressed cheek to cheek, each gripping the opposite edge of the barrel to keep it upright. Shroud's hair tickled his ear. He smelled like leather and oiled metal.

"Together in the dark, both of us cold and soaking wet," Sterling joked. "What *ever* shall we do while we wait?"

"Really?" Shroud said quietly. "Logistics aside—"

"Oh, the logistics are part of the fun. I remember one night in the rafters of a barn with a farmer's sister. Surprisingly acrobatic, that one. I was sore for three days, but it was well worth it."

"How do you intend to die, Sterling?"

He slipped a hand between them to wipe the water from his eyes. "Easy, my good man. A simple no would suffice. I'm not one to force my attention where it isn't wanted."

"Winter's death bothers you a great deal," Shroud continued. "Why?"

The words were like a blade piercing Sterling's stomach. "The fact that you have to ask such a question—"

"I understand grief, but your reaction is something more. It's personal."

Sterling didn't answer.

"Death is nothing to fear. Neither one of us is likely to die of old age. If Winter is dead, she died kicking Yog in the arse. Letting your own pain overshadow her victory does her a disservice. Her accomplishment deserves to be celebrated."

Surprisingly, the man had a point. "I give you my word that nobody will forget what Winter did today."

"All people are forgotten in time. Heroes were gone from the world for so long, people began to question whether they truly existed at all. Yog terrorised Albion in her day, but over the years, memories withered until nothing remained but old stories."

"I should have been there," said Sterling. "I left Winter behind, turned my back on someone who needed my aid."

"Bollocks," said Shroud. "Our job was to keep the people of Grayrock alive. We did that. Most of 'em, at any rate."

"But Winter—"

"Made a choice. As deaths go, I'd say this was a good one, and I've seen plenty. Are you so arrogant that you'd take that choice from her?" He clucked his tongue. "And you didn't answer my question. How do you mean to die?"

Sterling sighed. "Heroically, I suppose. I've never given it much thought."

"You should. It's important. Potentially the most important moment of your life."

"You're a very morbid person."

"Goes with the job," said Shroud.

A chill crept up Sterling's legs. "Did you feel that?"

"I felt nothing, and I'd prefer to keep it that way, so mind your right hand."

"Stay here." Sterling slid free of their awkward embrace and dived. Muddy water stung his eyes. The sun shone overhead, but he couldn't see more than the murky shadows of the buildings below. He kicked harder, confirming what he had felt, then returned to the barrel. "The water's colder just behind us."

To Shroud's credit, he didn't waste time with questions. He unwound a slender black rope from his belt and gave one end to Sterling. "Tug twice if you find something. Three times if you need help. I'll stay with the barrel to make sure it's still here when you come back up."

Sterling knotted the rope around his wrist, held his breath, and dived again. He followed the icy water until his hands touched the stone tile of a slanted rooftop. The tiles were so cold, he jerked his hands away. This couldn't be natural, and Winter was the only one he knew who could create such cold. But was this something she had done deliberately, or a side effect of her death?

Hope hammered in his ribs. He grabbed the edge of the roof and pulled himself down, searching for a door or window. He found the door open, but a table blocked the way just inside. His chest was beginning to hurt, like the ribs were squeezing his lungs and heart. He'd have to go back for air soon.

Instead, he kicked the table aside and dragged himself through. It felt like he had fallen into a mountain pool in the middle of winter, and he barely managed to stop himself from gasping in shock. He kept his hands in front of him, shoving past chairs and floating clothes that tangled his limbs like seaweed in the darkness.

Fingers clasped his collar, and this time he did try to shout, losing some of his precious air. Before he could tug Shroud's line for help, he was dragged up into a pocket of frigid air.

"Who's there?"

Sterling was gasping for breath so hard, it took him three tries to respond. "Winter?"

"Sterling! You were supposed to get out of town before I broke the dam!"

"We did." Sterling found her shoulders and pulled her into a hug. Her body was like ice. "And then I came back to look for you. Shroud and I both did."

"We had to hide from Yog," said Winter. "I was too exhausted to make it to land. If she found us, I wouldn't have had the strength to fend her off."

Sterling yanked the line twice. "We saw the dam come down."

Winter chuckled weakly. "Glory was Mayor of Grayrock for less than a day, and you see what happened?"

"How did you survive?" His teeth were chattering.

"The dam was falling apart. The rocks and water smashed the closest buildings to gravel. I held on as long as I could, but when I felt my section of the dam start to give way, I jumped." She laughed again, the sound strained and weary. "That was fun, like cliff diving, but I landed in a mass of panicked redcaps. They were screaming and flailing and trying to drag me down. I finally dived as deep as I could until I found a house with air bubbling out of it. I froze the roof to keep the rest of the air from escaping, and we've been hiding here ever since."

Sterling's hands found the underside of the roof. Icicles hung from the slats between the rafters.

"I planned to wait until nightfall, then try to sneak out," said Winter. "Assuming the air lasted that long. But I'm not sure I can keep this up. You can hear dripping of melting icicles. I used everything I had to bring down the dam. I can't—"

"You can." Finding Winter alive had eradicated every trace of doubt or despair from Sterling's heart. "You didn't single-handedly stop Yog's army just to meet your end here."

"So her plan worked?" Kas's voice came from the rafters behind Winter.

"Brilliantly. Glory is leading the townspeople to Brightlodge." He could feel the tension ease from Winter's body. She rested her head on his shoulder.

"I admit it," said Kas. "I'm impressed, lass."

"As am I." Sterling reached up, searching for something to grab on to in order to help keep him afloat, but the ice covering the ceiling made that both impractical and painful. He took the dagger from his belt, stabbed it into the ceiling, and clung to the hilt. "You've done well. Now let's get you out of here."

"How are you planning to do that?" asked Kas.

"Simple." Sterling flashed his most confident smile before remembering neither of them could see him. "We walk."

The water had a strange effect on the sounds of the world, muffling some but amplifying others. The occasional collapsing building sounded like distant thunder, and it was impossible to tell exactly where the noise came from.

The same was true of the underwater redcaps. Their shouts and laughter grew gradually louder as they neared the icy house, as did the grinding noise of the stones they dragged along like makeshift anchors, but Sterling couldn't pinpoint the direction of their approach. He kept one hand on the door frame as he squinted through the murky water. The dirt and mud had settled somewhat, but he still couldn't see much beyond his own hand.

He pulled himself back inside to the noticeably staler pocket of air where Shroud and Winter waited. "They're close."

"Good," said Shroud. He had joined them a short time before. He and Sterling spoke in low whispers, uncertain whether the redcaps would hear. "We're running out of time."

Winter shivered uncontrollably, one hand on the icy ceiling. Sterling wasn't sure how much longer she could hold on.

"The Conclave taught us to fight underwater," Shroud commented. "The water will take your speed and power. The thrust is the most effective strike."

"Understood. Are you ready?"

"Always." Shroud's hand touched Sterling's shoulder. A moment later, Shroud pressed a metal pan into his hand. "I found one for me, too."

"Excellent. Let's make some noise." Sterling pulled his dagger, held it and the pan underwater, and rammed the metal pommel into the pan. Shroud did the same.

Sterling tilted his head so that one ear was underwater. The ring of metal on metal sounded like a series of muted clicks, but they worked. Soon the muffled voices of bucket-helmed redcaps grew louder.

"It's oer here!"

"Di ye bang yer skull? They're in tha hoose there."

"Yer both bampots!"

It wasn't long before the first redcap reached the house. The dragging stones sent vibrations through the walls, and the flow of the water was subtly different, echoes of the redcap's movements pressing against Sterling's skin.

"On three," Sterling breathed. He pressed one finger to Shroud's shoulder, then two. When his third finger touched Shroud, they both pushed, held their breath, and ducked below the water.

Sterling could just make out the shadowy form of the redcap standing in the flooded dining area. Sterling reached out and rapped his knuckles against the oversized bucket protecting its head. The redcap spun towards him, and Shroud struck from behind. Moments later they were back with Winter and Kas.

"Not the most honourable approach, but one does the best one can," said Sterling. The bucket was about two feet wide, with a rope handle that could be fitted beneath the chin like the strap of a helmet. The redcap had tied sacks of stone to each ankle to keep him submerged.

"Come on," said Shroud. "We've got two more buckets to fetch."

The bucket over Sterling's head limited his vision even more than the muddy water. He could see nothing save his own feet trudging along the ground. No wonder it had been so easy to surprise the redcaps.

Sterling and Shroud supported Winter's arms as they walked. The rocks tied to their feet stirred swirls of dirt with each step. It was slower going than Sterling had expected. The air in his bucket had grown intolerably hot and stale by the time they reached the edge of the quarry. Sterling's body was numb, and his limbs were tingling. His breathing was quick and shallow. Twice he almost lost his grip on Winter.

"We're close," he said, seeking to rally the others. Neither Winter nor Shroud responded.

They were almost to the cliff when Shroud stopped moving.

Sterling swore and reached past Winter to shake Shroud by the arm. There was no response.

Sterling fumbled to unsheathe his dagger. It took him three tries to cut the stones from Shroud's ankles, and he was pretty sure he slashed the man's legs in the process. He grabbed Shroud with one hand to keep him from floating away, then cut himself and Winter loose as well.

The air in the buckets pulled them up. The instant Sterling reached the surface, he tilted his own bucket back and gasped, filling his lungs with the cool evening air. He lifted the edge of Winter's bucket and listened to make sure she was still breathing. He took care of Shroud next. Shroud was mumbling to himself about a job for the Conclave and didn't appear to know where he was. Probably hallucinating.

Only a sliver of sunlight remained above the horizon. They were at the eastern edge of the lake, a short distance from safety. A few buckets bobbed on the surface behind them. Redcaps coming up for air, presumably. Yog was still flying to and fro. She had expanded her range and was now searching the woods beyond Grayrock's boundaries.

"Come on," Sterling whispered.

"To where?" Winter's words were slurred.

"First we catch up with Glory and the others," said Sterling. "Then we go after Yog."

"The curse might be broken, but she'll remain weak until she's had the chance to feed on Heroes," said Kas.

"Her twisted appetite will draw her to Brightlodge," guessed Sterling. "The town will be one big, Heroic buffet."

"Yog won't strike right away," Kas continued. "Winter hurt her badly. She'll need time to rebuild her forces. For the moment, she's vulnerable. And Yog has lived too long to let impatience push her into foolish risks."

"That means we still have time to stop her."The thought brought warmth to Sterling's muscles as he dragged himself onto the trail. They had lost Grayrock, but they had survived, and who knew how many lives they had saved from Yog's monsters and her poison. That was a victory worthy of celebration. Just as soon as the feeling returned to his extremities.

By the time they reached the safety of the bushes where he and Shroud had stowed their things, Sterling was shivering so hard he could barely walk. Never had he so envied Shroud the heavy cloak he snatched from behind a bush and wrapped around himself. As for Winter, she simply lay back and closed her eyes.

"None of that." Sterling shook her by the shoulder, and was rewarded with a groan and a halfhearted punch to his arm.

He pulled on his boots, then reached for Arbiter. His fingers touched an empty sheath. His fatigue vanished instantly. "Someone's been here," he whispered.

"I know." Shroud was patting down the various pockets inside his cloak. "Took some of my favourite toys."

Sterling hauled Winter to her feet, though his own muscles protested. He felt like his own limbs had turned to stone.

They had gone a short distance into the hills when something large and white flew from a ledge up ahead. Sterling sidestepped and smacked it aside with his left hand. The missile—a skull of some sort—shattered against the rocks.

"Clever Heroes."The singsong words dissolved into mad laughter. A redcap, then. Either one of the partially transformed survivors of Grayrock, or one of Yog's minions who had survived Winter's flood. "Up, up, up they crawl, but which one has the doll?"

A stone hit Shroud's hip. He grunted, then hurled a small, spinning blade into the shadows. Metal struck stone, and the redcap giggled.

Sterling started towards the sound, but Shroud caught his arm.

"Most of my caltrops are missing. If he's smart, he's spread them across the trail. Step on one of those and you won't walk for a week."

Winter was too exhausted to help. It looked like it was taking all of her strength simply to remain conscious.

"Trade!" the redcap shouted. The sound came from higher up the trail. Perhaps one of the scraggly pine trees that clung to the hillside. "Give Blue the doll. You get broken skull."

"Is that a threat?" Sterling asked.

"I think he means the skull he threw at you."

Sterling eased forwards, sweeping his boots across the path with each step before shifting his weight. He had taken only three steps when something splashed onto the ground in front of him.

"What was that?" asked Winter.

"Could be poison," laughed Blue. "Could be redcap piss. Who knows! Give Blue the doll, or else you fall." A fist-sized rock hit Sterling in the shoulder. He staggered back.

Sterling glanced at the doll. "Yog is quite determined to get you back."

"Aye," said Kas. "She hoards grudges like a dragon with her gold."

Shroud tossed a small ceramic pot to Sterling. "The redcap didn't take all the good toys. Just light and throw. Land it within five feet of him and he's in trouble."

A twisted hemp fuse protruded from the corked top. "Light it with what?"

Shroud patted his cloak pockets. "Dammit, redcap! That was a brand-new Ackerman Quick-Starting fire-flint!"

Blue's laughter spilled down the trail.

"In my youth, I'd have tossed fire from my bare hands to deal with the likes of this nuisance," said Kas. "Alas, this form has stolen the better portion of my power."

Sterling took the doll from Winter and dropped to one knee. "My apologies, good sir." Before Kas could protest, Sterling scraped the doll's head against the steel of his knife. Kas yelped as sparks flew from his petrified scalp. A few more tries and Sterling managed to land the sparks on the fuse, which began to hiss and burn. He dropped Kas, scooped up the pot, and hurled it towards the sound of the laughter.

Flame exploded among the rocks and trees, silhouetting a single redcap huddled in the branches. The redcap squealed and jumped back, a move that sent him tumbling out of the tree to land hard on the trail below.

"Forget the trade!" Blue shook his head and staggered to one side. "Keep the skull. You keep the skull!" He threw another rock at Sterling's chest, but it was a feeble attack, too weak to leave more than a faint bruise.

"Nobody cares about the blasted skull." Sterling raced forwards, ready to throw the redcap into the lake with his bare hands. He froze when he saw the small, steel caltrops fly from Blue's hand to litter the ground. "Where is my sword?"

Blue laughed and fled down the trail, singing, "Hero lost his blade. Didn't want to trade. Now he's sore afraid!" Shroud chuckled. "Catchy tune."

Kas was massaging the side of his head where the steel of Sterling's knife had left white scratches on the stone. The blade was scratched as well. "If you *ever* do that again," Kas said firmly, "I will personally crawl into your mouth while you sleep and choke you to death from the inside."

"Understood." Sterling picked up a caltrop and handed it to Shroud. Most of their things were probably near the redcap's hiding spot. Blue hadn't been carrying Arbiter when he fled. "Did he truly expect to beat the three of us with nothing more than rocks?"

"He's a redcap," said Winter, as if that explained everything.

Sterling picked up one of the broken pieces of the skull the redcap had thrown at him. Offering to trade an enchanted doll for a bit of old bone? Yet another thing that only made sense if you had nails in your—

He frowned and turned the skull towards the dying flames of Shroud's bomb. There were letters scratched into the bone.

"What is it?" asked Shroud.

"I'm not sure." Sterling knelt, searching for other fragments.

"We can't stay here," Winter said wearily. "There will be more stragglers, and Yog may have seen that firepot go off."

Sterling picked up another shard of bone. "We were unable to save Grayrock, but we *will* protect Brightlodge. The closest Yog will come to feasting on Heroes is when she tastes my steel."

"You mean that steel?" Shroud smirked and pointed to the top of the pine tree where Sterling's sword hung like a broken branch.

With a sigh, Sterling dropped the skull pieces into a pocket and began climbing . . .

PART III

THE RISE OF YOG

Yog ran her heavily scarred tongue over her teeth. The scars had dulled her sense of taste, and there were times she longed to be able to enjoy a bowl of beet-and-onion soup the way she had in the distant haze of her youth, but such was the cost of survival and old age.

Skye, Headstrong, and Blue stood silently in front of the hut, waiting for her orders. Yog took another bite from her crust of dry acorn bread. She chewed slowly and deliberately, wanting to prolong their discomfort.

The ogre had lost another noggin. That was Schemer and Watcher both gone, each taking a portion of Headstrong's knowledge and skill with them. Of the remaining five, Night Axe was the most valuable. Each loss diminished Headstrong's usefulness . . . though Yog wouldn't mind seeing Big Mouth dead at the bottom of the lake.

Skye appeared shaken by her battle with the human girl at the gates and her narrow escape from the flood. She had been nibbling at her fingers, chewing the dark, flaky skin until threads of smoke rose from her hands.

And then there was Blue, rocking on his heels and examining a scab he had picked from his scalp. When he saw Yog watching him, he hastily flicked the scab onto Headstrong and giggled softly.

"Do I ask too much of you?" Yog wiped the remaining crumbs on her apron. Her stomach gurgled at the memory of the last time she had tasted the untainted power of a Hero. To Skye, she said, "I rescued you from the blaze that consumed your forest. I gave you the power to heal your burns, to take the flames into yourself and turn them against your enemies. Headstrong, I gave strength beyond that of any ogre. You could rule as queen over your people. And Blue, thanks to me, your mind is sharper than any redcap's."

Blue pulled his finger from his ear and examined a small lump of wax, seemingly oblivious to Yog's words. Yog sighed and gestured to Headstrong, who kicked Blue in the back of the head hard enough to send him sprawling.

"I gave you my redcaps," Yog continued. "I turned the town of Grayrock against itself, and still you failed to bring my husband to me."

"How were we t'know they'd flood the town?" That was Scratcher, the noggin Headstrong kept tied to the end of a stick.

"Shut up," Thinker whispered frantically.

Yog summoned one of the skulls from her fence. It flew past her and into a tight orbit around Headstrong. Skye and Blue backed away. Headstrong spun like a cat chasing her own tail. Yog brought the skull to a halt directly in front of the impudent noggin, allowing Scratcher to recognise it as having once belonged to an ogre. Headstrong swallowed and stuffed the poor noggin into her armpit, muffling any further commentary.

"Not only did you lose Kas, you failed to capture a single Hero. Just one, and I would have the strength to assault Brightlodge directly. Instead, I stand here having exhausted my supply of redcap blood, without the strength to create another magestorm for at least a week. I am revealed, and unprepared to fight the Heroes of Brightlodge. What will you do to atone for your failure?"

Headstrong raised a pair of enormous axes. "I'll cut them down and serve the muscle-bound warrior to you on her own shield," she snarled.

"I will burn them all," whispered Skye.

Blue nodded eagerly. "I'll hit them with rocks." He looked from Yog to his fellow Riders, and his shoulders sank. "Lots of rocks?"

"All in its proper time," said Yog. "Blue, step closer. Your role is key in what is to come."

Blue stuck out his tongue at the other Riders.

"There is a large band of redcaps who have retreated into the caves in the Needles, to the west. You are going to lead me to them. Headstrong, you will accompany us."

"Redcaps again?" Skye looked pained. "Their warriors are little better than children."

"No warriors. Just their blood and their bones." Yog smiled. The loss of Kas and the Heroes was a setback, but after so many centuries, Yog's curse was lifted at last. "As for you, Skye, I have another task in mind . . ."

chapter 17

ROOK

The inhabitants of Brightlodge welcomed the Grayrock refugees in their traditional fashion: by hiking prices and milking the newcomers for every last coin.

A sign at the pub advertised a hearty lamb-and-potato stew, JUST THE THING FOR THE WEARY TRAVELLER, for only three times the usual price. Signs in front of half the homes in town proclaimed rooms for rent, though more often than not, those rooms turned out to be nothing but a hastily cleared closet or a cot shoved into the attic with the rats and cobwebs.

The meeting room in Wendleglass Hall was as full as Rook had ever seen it. Both kings were here—the living and the ex-living—along with all of the Heroes who had come to Brightlodge in recent months. The eight of them who'd been chasing after Yog and her minions sat closest to Young King Wendleglass.

The team from Grayrock didn't look all that Heroic at the moment. They were tired and filthy, with shadows under their eyes and dirt staining their clothes. Winter was on her third mug of tea and looked like she wanted nothing more than to rest her head on the table and sleep for a week. Glory slashed a plate of roast pork so viciously, Rook expected the plate to crack. As for Shroud, who knew what was going on with him, hidden away in the shadows of his cloak and hood?

"Winter's actions saved most of Grayrock's people," Sterling was saying. "She drowned Yog's redcaps and bought us much-needed time."

"Bought it by destroying the town you were supposed to be saving." That was Malice, one of Wendleglass's odder recruits. There was no physical body beneath the heavy armour and horned helm, but that didn't stop the cursed ex-villain from gleefully slaughtering every outlaw and monster he could find.

Glory set down her silverware. "You think you could do better, Malice?"

"It'd be hard to do worse." Malice's words conveyed his sneer.

"And yet I have complete confidence that you'd find a way," Glory said sweetly.

"How much time?" the young king asked. "How long before . . . before Yog and her Riders attack Brightlodge?"

"Not long." Kas was the strangest of the refugees, a doll of living stone who claimed to be Yog's former husband. He wore a blue linen napkin as a makeshift cloak. "From the moment Grayrock fell, she turned her efforts to hunting Brightlodge's Heroes. As soon as her forces are strong enough, she will come for you."

"And Grayrock's fate will be Brightlodge's." That was the *former* king. The man was much more depressing since his death. "Doom comes for us all!"

"Nonsense," said Rook. "I've been through bad times before. Life goes on." He took a drink, then added, "For the survivors, at least."

He looked about. Jeremiah Tipple was whispering to Evienne, a slender, energetic lass with a sword nearly as big as she was. Leech had barely eaten his quail, preferring instead to pick at it with knife and fork, dissecting his meal and losing himself in his work. Inga was listening intently and looked ready to go running out of Wendleglass Hall to bring Yog down once and for all.

"Enough talk." Inga pounded the table. "There's nothing left to discuss. We protect Brightlodge, and we put an end to Yog."

"Yes, we've established that," Glory said without looking up. "The question is how to defend the town without destroying it in the process."

"Yog doesn't care about Brightlodge," said Sterling. "She wants us."

"She wants to *eat* us," said Tipple. "Don't forget that part."

"Some of you, yes." Kas paced along the centre of the table. "But you mustn't forget the potion she's been working on. You told me of its effects on Mr. Tipple. Given this potential feast of Heroes, I imagine she'll consume the most powerful while transforming the rest. Three will become her Riders, and the others her greencap slaves. You've seen what she did with an army of redcaps. Imagine her strength when the Heroes of Brightlodge fall under her spell."

"The answer seems simple enough." Rook tossed back another swallow of ale. "We hunt her down before she can regroup. Hit her on the road, away from Brightlodge, and end her."

"And how do you mean to do that?" asked Tipple.

Rook patted his crossbow.

"If only it were that simple," said Kas. "Yog may not be at her full strength, but she's no easy target. I'm the one who taught her the secret of undeath. Her essence—her life, if you will—is locked away someplace safe. That's how she survived my curse, how she's lived all these years. You'll have to find her life and destroy it, and that's no easy task."

"According to the stories, Baya kept her spirit in a wooden box," said Inga.

Rook shrugged. "Then we shoot that too."

"How do we find her?" asked Leech.

"Be patient." Sterling kept looking over his shoulder towards the main doors. "In the meantime, would someone be so kind as to fetch one of the Grayrock refugees? A boy named Ben. He also goes by 'Hedgehog.' He's currently about this tall and made of wood. You'll likely find him with his family. I have an idea, but we'll need his aid."

"Were you planning to share this idea with the rest of us?" Glory asked.

Sterling merely smiled. "All things in good time."

The man had something up those ribboned sleeves of his. He'd been distracted from the moment they sat down. Rook didn't like it.

Sterling reminded him of a lad who'd signed up with the Strangers about ten years back. All proud and cocksure, more worried about looking good than doing good. He'd been sent home not three months later. Most of him had, at any rate. Unlike that boy, Sterling's skill had lived up to his boasts. So far.

"Eight of us have fought Yog's Riders," said Rook. "We should be the ones to hunt her down, while the rest of the Heroes protect Brightlodge."

"That sounds wise," said the king. "Why don't you, um—oh, what is it now?"

The sound of weapons being readied throughout the room almost overpowered the indignant shouts from beyond the main doors. Sterling jumped onto the table and waved his hands. "Hold your blades, my friends. There's no danger here."

A familiar redcap stood in the doorway. Blue clutched a pair of curved swords, and he clearly had no idea how to use them. He flailed them about like out-of-control kites on too-short strings, as much a danger to himself as to anyone else. Though it did keep people from approaching him too closely. How in the blazes had he sneaked into Brightlodge, let alone into Wendleglass Hall?

Rook raised his crossbow and waited for a clear shot. Blue spotted him a moment later, but instead of hiding, he tossed his swords to the floor and ran towards Rook, laughing and shouting, "Found them! Blue found the stupid Heroes!"

Inga put a hand on his crossbow. "He's unarmed."

"No, he's still got both arms," said Rook. "Give me a minute and I can fix that."

Sterling stepped past them. "Don't hurt him."

"Why not?" asked Glory.

Blue collapsed in a sweaty, gasping heap at Sterling's feet. He held out both hands and said, "Look! No rocks this time!"

Shroud slipped past Rook like a shadow, knife in hand. "Give us one reason not to kill you where you stand, redcap."

Blue laughed. "Two reasons. First, Blue isn't standing."

"He's got you there," said Tipple. "What's the second reason?"

It was Sterling who answered. "Because he's going to help us."

Rook's eyes narrowed. "Help with what?"

"Heroes will help save redcaps from Yog." Blue bit his lip, then blurted, "And Blue will help Heroes kill Yog."

"I hate this bloody plan," Rook muttered as he crept through the woods. Sterling, Winter, and Tipple followed along behind him. Kas rode in Tipple's front pocket.

"It's foolish to trust him," Kas agreed. "He's a redcap, and one of Yog's Riders. She can peer through their eyes, listen through their ears."

"Fart through their arses," Blue had agreed, nodding hard.

"Blue contacted me on the outskirts of Grayrock," said Sterling. "There, he delivered a message etched onto a skull. A message, and also an obscene doodle of a farmer and a pig."

Blue chuckled.

"Didn't you say he also tried to smack you about the head with that skull?" asked Tipple.

"If Yog can see what Blue sees, then this has to be a trap," said Winter.

"Yog sleeps. Asleep in a heap." Blue darted ahead and beckoned impatiently for them to follow. "Blue poisoned her drink. Yog will be mad when she wakes. Flay Blue alive. Flay and play and run away."

Blue could be telling the truth. Anything was possible. But even if Blue meant to help, there was the minor problem of not actually knowing where Yog's life was preserved. Without that, they had no way of killing her. Which meant they had to find a way to search her hut.

"How many redcaps in this cave of yours, again?" asked Tipple.

Blue stopped to count on his fingers. His forehead wrinkled. Eventually, he nodded to himself and said, "Lots!"

According to Blue, Yog meant to slaughter an entire tribe of redcaps hidden somewhere in the mountains. Their blood and bones would fuel the assault on Brightlodge.

Rook paused. The hike had been uneventful so far, but a subtle change in the air suggested that was about to change. He signalled the others to wait.

The trail ahead was empty, but the woods were too quiet. The wind was against them, so their scent shouldn't have carried forwards to warn men or beasts of their approach. The scent of the outlaws waiting in ambush around the bend, on the other hand, carried quite well. Specifically, the smell of sweat, tobacco, and campfire smoke.

"Amateurs," he muttered.

Rook studied the bend, where a clump of trees grew up between a pair of wind-smoothed boulders. He readied his crossbow and walked onward.

The first outlaw jumped out from behind the boulders. He opened his mouth to bellow what would have doubtless been a well-rehearsed threat, had Rook not shot him in the throat. The hooded woman hiding in a tree's upper branches fell next, her partially formed spell fizzling into sparks as she hit the ground. The biggest of the outlaws required Rook to empty his crossbow, but once he went down, the rest lost their nerve and fled.

By the time the other Heroes caught up, it was all over. Blue moved furtively towards the fallen outlaws, his face alight like a child's with a new toy.

"How much farther to these caves of yours?" asked Rook.

Blue pointed to the hills. "Not far."

"Strange thing, trying to save redcap lives," commented Tipple.

"Human lives," Rook said. "I'll lose no sleep over any incidental redcap casualties."

"Incidental?" Blue jabbed a finger into his nose, pulled it out, and flicked the results of his excavation in Rook's direction.

"Blue's right," said Winter. "These redcaps weren't hurting anyone. Let sleeping redcaps lie."

"Blue, what do redcaps eat?" Rook asked.

Blue shrugged. "Rats and bats. Bugs and slugs. And also Bob."

"Bob?" asked Sterling.

A sly smile curled Blue's lips. "Bob was running from outlaws. Tried to hide in the caves." He patted his belly. "Bob tasted like chicken. Oh—redcaps also eat chickens!"

After that, they walked in silence.

The path into the cave was well travelled. Rook spotted the deeper indentations left by Yog's hut, as well as larger prints that meant the ogre was with her. "The entrance looks clear."

"Are you sure about this?" asked Tipple.

"Sooner or later, all Heroes must enter the shadows to confront their enemies," said Sterling.

Tipple frowned. "Was that a yes or a no?"

"Do you have a better way of getting inside Yog's hut?" Winter grinned. "Maybe Sterling should try to seduce her."

"I wouldn't advise that," said Kas. "It didn't end well for me."

Rook searched the hillside. He saw no guards or lookouts, nor any sign of an ambush. He studied Blue, trying to understand what was going on in that iron-pierced brain.

Sterling trusted the twisted little wretch, and dammit, Rook was inclined to trust Sterling. The man believed in his ideals, but he wasn't one of those useless blue blood romantics who'd grown up in a tower with no idea what the world outside was all about. He was a man whose actions backed his words. Sure, Sterling's plan was likely to get them killed and eaten, but it also had the best chance of letting them destroy Yog.

"Well, hell. Let's do this." Tipple brushed his hands together and raised his chin, allowing Sterling to knot a rope around his neck. They tested the knot twice, making sure it wouldn't slide or tighten, then handed the other end to Blue.

Blue laughed nervously as he wound the rope around his wrist. "Noose on the moose. He can't get loose!"

Rook pulled a single crossbow bolt from his quiver and held it in front of Blue's face. The redcap's eyes crossed.

"If you betray us, the last thing you see will be a bolt like this puncturing your left eye. Got it?" He tapped the tip against Blue's scalp.

Blue swallowed and nodded hard.

"Good." Rook replaced the bolt and double-checked his weapon. "Let's go."

Blue headed into the darkness, pulling Tipple along behind him. Rook and the others followed at a distance, far enough to hide if necessary but keeping Blue in sight. The occasional burning torch jammed into the dirt provided flickering light, but also attracted swarms of buzzing, bloodsucking insects. Rook ignored the stings, keeping his attention on Blue and the tunnels beyond.

They hadn't gone far when a pair of redcaps came around a curve. Rook raised his crossbow, but before he could shoot, Blue tugged the rope hard enough to make Tipple stumble.

The manic laughter of the two redcaps made Blue sound almost sane. One pulled out a knife and advanced.

"*My* human!" Blue smacked the redcap with the end of the rope. "Get your own."

The other redcap snarled and grabbed a spiked club from her belt.

Blue yanked the rope again. "Ugly human. Kill that redcap!"

Tipple smiled and stepped forwards. He let the redcap swing first, then moved in to grab her arm above the elbow. With his other hand, he caught the back of the redcap's trousers and slammed her into her companion, knocking them both against the wall. Their laughter changed to groans, and neither redcap rose.

"Not dead. But good enough." Blue kicked one of the redcaps in the rump, then dragged Tipple along. "Hurry. Not far now."

Blue was good to his word. A short distance ahead, the tunnel opened into a broad cavern with a pond at its centre. Yog's hut stood on stilted legs in the water, a stone's throw from the edge. The location made sense. Redcaps distrusted water. If through some miracle they found the courage to fight back against Yog, the pond would keep them at a distance.

"It's been a long time since I laid eyes on that monstrosity of a home," said Kas.

A narrow beam of sunlight pierced a crack in the cavern high overhead. Water trickled through one edge of the crack. The drops hitting the lake created a never-ending series of expanding rings on the surface.

"There must be at least fifty redcaps down there," whispered Winter.

The redcaps had created a . . . Rook couldn't dignify it with the word "town." A primitive camp, perhaps. Scattered piles of dirt, rocks, and rags seemed to serve as beds. They looked like nests created by oversized, clumsy birds with very low standards. Bones were scattered everywhere, and the smell of old meat and redcap waste made his nose wrinkle.

One redcap squealed as the ogre, Headstrong, grabbed him by the neck and dragged him to a shallow indentation in the dirt on the far side of the lake. A wooden bucket sat in the middle of the depression. Other redcap bodies were piled to one side. Headstrong killed the redcap with a knife, then held the body over the bucket to collect the blood.

Rook turned to look at Blue. The redcap rocked in place, the muscles in his jaw twitching. Only minutes before, he had ordered Tipple to kill two of his own people, but now tears spilled down his cheeks.

"Why don't the others do anything?" Winter asked.

"Because it would take at least twenty of them to overpower that ogre," said Sterling. "Not to mention whatever death Yog can hurl at them from her hut."

"Anyone see the nymph?" Rook asked.

The others shook their heads.

"Skye hates caves," said Blue. "Smoke gets too thick. No way to fly away."

"Are we sure Yog's in the hut?" asked Tipple.

Winter shrugged. "Where else would she be?"

"It's where she feels safest," added Kas.

Blue rocked from side to side. "Spring the trap while Yog takes nap!"

Rook didn't like it. There were too many unknowns. Too many ways the whole plan could turn to shite.

"Let's hurry up and do this," said Tipple. "If we wait here much longer, I'm going to need to duck away to take a piss."

Rook took a second length of rope and began binding Tipple's wrists. "Trick knot. Tug this end and the whole thing comes loose."

"Got it." Tipple lifted his wrists and sighed. "How drunk was I when I agreed to this?"

Rook handed a small knife to Blue. If they expected anyone to believe a redcap had captured a human twice his size, that redcap had to be armed. Rook also made a show of checking his crossbow for Blue's benefit. For once, Blue didn't respond with laughter. He simply nodded, acknowledging the threat, then looked out to where Headstrong was tossing another body onto the pile.

"Thank you, my friends." Kas stared at Yog's hut. "You've proven yourselves true Heroes of Albion."

"As have you. After our victory, we will find a way to restore you to your proper form, and we shall all celebrate together."

Kas hunched lower in Tipple's pocket. "Good thing stone has no sense of smell," he muttered. "All right, you lug. All you have to do is stumble into the water and fall down long enough for me to get out. I don't need to breathe, so I'll just walk along the bottom and climb into Yog's hut. Once I'm there, I should be able to find her life and destroy it. Then all you'll need to do is kill her mortal body. Wait for my signal, then the rest of you do whatever it takes to bring her down."

"What signal?" asked Winter.

"I figured I'd take command of her hut and try to kick the ogre in the head." Kas chuckled. "I haven't tried to control that monstrosity in ages, but I imagine it will come back to me."

With that, Kas vanished into the bottom of Tipple's pocket. Blue tugged the ropes, hauling Tipple into the open.

For his part, Tipple looked to be having far too much fun playing up his role. The instant they emerged from the tunnel, he started yelling, "Yog! Where are you, Yog? I got . . . I've got somethin' to say to you!"

He slurred his words, staggered from side to side, and paused once to let out a belch that echoed through the cavern. He then proceeded to curse Blue, Blue's mother, his brothers and sisters, any children he might have, and his pets. He started to describe exactly what he intended to do to Blue, to Yog, and to everyone else in this "chamber pot of a cave," only to stop in mid rant so he could double over and dry heave like he was trying to hack up his own innards.

Other redcaps swarmed towards them. Blue yanked out his knife and waved it wildly. "Mine! My drunk human!"

A withered crone emerged from the hut and watched from the doorstep, water lapping at her toes. The woman looked like she'd shatter in a stiff breeze, but judging someone by looks alone was a good way to end up dead.

"So much for her nap," Rook said tightly.

"There you are, you clay-headed, misbegotten, greasy-haired ass-canker!" Tipple roared, and started towards the water, dragging Blue along behind him, to the obvious amusement of the watching redcaps. "I had compart—copatriots—I had friends in Grayrock, witch!"

"He's overdoing it," Sterling muttered.

Yog examined Tipple from her cabin. A tangle of grey hair had escaped the red bandanna around her scalp and fallen into her face like a shrivelled tentacle. Overlong fingers stroked the skull that topped her bone cane. She looked like an old woman scratching her favourite cat.

Several redcaps threw small rocks and other debris at Tipple. A cold glare from Yog made them scamper back.

Tipple appeared to trip over his own feet. He went down with an enormous splash at the edge of the pool. Sputtering and cursing, he tried to push himself up, only to slip a second time. Rook couldn't tell if that one had been intentional or not, but it should be enough for Kas to slip free.

"What is this, Blue?" Yog's voice carried throughout the cavern.

"Hero!" Blue raised his knife. "*I* captured him!"

"You captured a sick, drunken fool. I knew these Heroes were pale imitations of the ones I fought before, but I expected better." Her hut walked towards the shore, wooden legs bending like those of a spider.

"Do you think Blue will keep to the plan?" asked Winter.

"No." Sterling slid his sword free. "Primarily because I never shared the real plan with him. Or with you, and for that I beg your forgiveness."

Winter's lips pursed, and the air grew chillier. "You didn't trust him."

"Not him," said Sterling. "*Them*. There was a second message on the skull. A line that read, 'Kas bad.' I think Blue was warning us to expect betrayal."

"You could have mentioned that sooner," said Rook.

"This is the first chance I've had where neither Kas nor Blue could overhear." Sterling shifted his shoulder, loosening his sword arm. "If things fall apart, as they most certainly will, Rook should regroup with the other Heroes in Grayrock. Tell them what's happened, and to prepare for Yog's arrival."

"Grayrock?" whispered Rook. "I thought she was after Brightlodge."

"She is." Sterling grinned. "I intend to divert her."

"You're counting on a double cross. That's a risky game." In Rook's experience, such plans could steal victory from overwhelming odds, but they were just as likely to end in disaster.

Yog's hut stopped a short distance from Jeremiah Tipple. "Search him. Once you're certain he's unarmed, bring him to me."

"Here we go," said Sterling. "Be ready."

Blue tried to haul Tipple back to shore, but the man didn't budge. Tipple grabbed the rope and kicked the redcap's feet out from under him. The instant Blue hit the water, Tipple grabbed him by the ankles and charged the hut, swinging Blue like a club.

His first strike knocked Yog into the water. With a howl of triumph, he tossed Blue aside and threw himself atop Yog, trying to throttle her. His muscles bulged. Any ordinary person would have been dead within seconds.

Sterling pointed. "Rook, try to keep the ogre off our backs. Winter, you're with me. If anything gets too close, freeze it."

"Where are we going?" asked Winter.

Sterling pointed to one of the campfires. "Close enough to grab a burning branch. I don't feel like trying to find one little box Yog's kept hidden for centuries. Easier to burn the whole damn hut, don't you think?"

"I like it! I'll freeze the lake to keep the hut from escaping or ducking underwater."

Bones leaped from the water to assail Tipple, biting and clubbing him into submission. Yog rose, seemingly unharmed. She returned to her hut and pulled herself up while Tipple covered his head and shoulders.

Sterling sprinted out of the tunnel, heading for the closest fire. Winter followed a half step behind. With everyone's attention on Tipple and Yog, they were able to get most of the way there before the first redcap noticed.

Rook's crossbow cut the redcap down before he could cry out. It bought them only a few more seconds before a small stone doll climbed out of the water. Kas scrambled up the hut and shouted to Yog, "The redcap betrayed you, my love! Beware the tunnels!"

"Bloody hell." Rook gripped his crossbow in both hands and bellowed the Strangers' war cry, a deep-throated sound of hunger and rage. He stomped into the cavern and shot the nearest redcap in the face.

As a rule, the sight of a Stranger charging into battle with a heavy, repeating crossbow was enough to make any sane foe think twice. Unfortunately, these redcaps didn't even bother with the first thought. They simply attacked. Some scooped up rocks and weapons. Others charged bare-handed. Rook reloaded, used the stock of his crossbow to knock one redcap into the path of the rest, shot a second, then ran in the opposite direction from Sterling and Winter, trying to draw the redcaps away.

Sterling had Arbiter in one hand and a flaming torch in the other. A pair of frozen redcaps showed that Winter had been busy as well. By the hut, Tipple roared and tried again to reach Yog, but the hut lurched forwards, and one of the stilts swung out to club him in the chest. He flew backwards, hitting the beach hard enough to make Rook wince in sympathy.

"Bring me the Heroes," Yog shouted.

"I was right," Rook muttered. "This was a bloody stupid plan." A sea of redcaps stood between him and the others. They swarmed around Sterling and Winter, cutting them off from Yog's hut.

Headstrong lumbered across the cavern, her attention fixed solely on Rook. She knocked redcaps aside with the flats of her axes.

Rook waited until the ogre was close enough for him to count her oversized yellow teeth. He picked his targets and squeezed the trigger. Two bolts hit a noggin in the mouth and eye. Several more slammed into Headstrong's stomach. Another buried itself in the ear of a different noggin. He concentrated the rest on the ogre's thigh, hoping to make her fall.

It wasn't enough. Rook rolled out of the way of the first swing. He tried to get in another shot while Headstrong recovered, but she was faster than he would have guessed. Instead of lurching to and fro, she used her axes' momentum to spin around for a second swipe that nearly took Rook's head from his body.

He rolled again, then hurled sand and gravel at the ogre's eyes. It wasn't much of an attack, but it distracted Headstrong long enough for him to jump up and smash the butt of his crossbow into the bridge of her nose. The ogre howled and stumbled, but before he could follow up on his advantage, one of her noggins shouted, "To yer left!"

Rook ducked, barely avoiding her blind swing.

"He dropped low!"

The second axe descended towards his head. He dived aside, and the blade smashed into the ground, spraying dirt everywhere.

"Get him into biting range!"

"Try not to kill him," yelled another noggin. "Just maim him a lot. Yog likes her food fresh."

An explosion of snow and ice flung the redcaps back from Winter and Sterling long enough for Sterling to hurl his torch at the hut. One of the stilted legs knocked it into the water, then the redcaps were swarming over them.

All of Rook's training and experience urged him to fight on. Like the Strangers said, you were born alone, but you died together. You fought as one, and you damn well didn't leave a single man, woman, or child behind.

But Sterling claimed to have a plan, and he was counting on Rook to get word to Grayrock.

"Aw, hell." Rook retreated towards the tunnel. Once there, he rammed a new magazine into his crossbow. Yog was out of range and presumably unkillable, since it looked like that ruddy beggar Kas had never had any intention of helping them find and end her life.

He aimed at Headstrong instead. If nothing else, he meant to take down at least one of Yog's Riders today.

A quiet titter carried through the tunnel behind him. Rook whirled and shot the squad of redcaps sneaking up behind him. The bolts exploded, blowing the redcaps apart.

Headstrong was coming too fast for him to reload again. With a curse, Rook slid the strap over his shoulder and fled.

"I *hate* this bloody plan."

chapter 18

GLORY

It was bad enough that Glory, Inga, Shroud, and Leech had been forced to set out in the ridiculously dark, cold, early hours of the night, while Sterling's team enjoyed a good night's sleep. This was the only way to ensure they got Ben to Grayrock in time.

Their unannounced travelling companion was another matter. Glory hadn't come to Brightlodge to be a delivery girl, and she *certainly* hadn't signed up for babysitting duty.

"What happens if Sterling and the others can't stop Yog?" asked Greta. "She'll come after us next, right?"

"After your brother, to be specific," said Glory. Greta had sneaked out of Brightlodge and followed them. She'd done a good job too, making it almost an hour before Shroud spotted her. By then it was too late to turn around. "Remind me why we didn't send you marching back to Brightlodge?"

"Are you daft?" asked Inga. "You don't send a helpless child walking through the woods alone."

"I'm not helpless." Greta pulled out the long kitchen knife she had tucked through her belt.

"There you go," said Glory. "She's not helpless."

"She's trying to look after her brother." Inga smiled at the girl.

"Fine, but as her Mayor, I'm ordering her to stay quiet and out of the way. If we run into trouble, we'll have enough to worry about without having to save her neck too."

"Trouble like that?" Greta pointed to a streak of glowing coals crossing the path ahead. In full daylight, it might have looked like dirt or mud, as if a runaway mule had dragged a plough through the woods, but in the darkness it was easy to make out the ripples of orange heat pulsing through the ash.

"It's a foot wide at most." Inga walked to the edge of the smouldering line. "Not much of a barrier."

"Not a barrier. A trip wire. Cross the flames and trigger the trap." Shroud unshouldered his bow and jogged into the woods, heading north. "I'll see how far it stretches."

"Skye did this," Glory guessed. She looked about, searching for the nymph.

"If Winter were here, she could—" Greta began.

"But she's not." Glory scowled. Had something moved in the distance? Skye and her little flaming puppets could be closing in while they stood here like fools, stopped in their tracks by a line on the ground.

"It looks to circle all of Grayrock," Shroud called from the treetops. "Even crosses the river, like some sort of bridge. Also, we've got a pair of greencaps heading this way from the town."

"Good." Glory flexed her fingers and stepped into the open, deliberately making herself a target.

It wasn't long before the greencaps came into view. They moved with a lopsided pace, weapons ready. One appeared to be injured. His arm was held close to his body.

"Is that who I think it is?" asked Greta.

"The Mayor." This got better and better. "I wonder how he escaped the flooding."

The Mayor had recognised Glory, too. She could tell from the way he screamed and charged, waving a pickaxe about his head.

He would have run right through the blackened trap if his fellow greencap hadn't stopped him. Well, not so much "stopped him" as "hit him in the back of the head with a rock."

The Mayor spun and cursed. In addition to the improvised, bloody cap nailed to his scalp, the Mayor had also nailed his broken arm to his ribs. She supposed it was as good a makeshift splint as the creatures were likely to get.

"How does it feel to lose your title and your town both?" Glory called out. She spread her arms. "Care to try to take it back?"

Once again the Mayor started towards her, only to be hit with another rock. Blast that second greencap. Though watching him throw rocks at the Mayor was entertaining.

"Let's play a game," Shroud said from the shadows. "Every trap can be bypassed. Whichever one of you shares the secret wins his life. The other gets the consolation prize of an arrow through the throat." The creak of his bow being drawn punctuated the threat.

"There's nae trap," said the second greencap. "Just a ruse. Cross and see."

"You first," said Glory.

The Mayor snorted. "Doesn't matter. Skye'll burn you all. Pay ye back for destroying my town."

"Skye was trying to destroy Grayrock before we ever got here," Inga pointed out.

"Pah." He threw a rock. A pillar of fire shot up to engulf the rock as it passed over Skye's trap, after which the now-flaming missile bounced harmlessly off Inga's shield.

It was a rather pitiful attack. Standing there, seeing what the man had become—what he had been—Glory almost felt sorry for him. She stepped to the edge of the charred boundary. "You want to be Mayor of Grayrock again?"

The Mayor stilled. His eyes narrowed, and his lips pulled back from his teeth.

"We lost Grayrock because of Yog. She sent Skye to kill your people. *Our* people. She summoned the magestorm that turned you into this. She sent her redcaps over our walls to burn and pillage. We were both Mayors of Grayrock." Glory took a deep breath. "And we both failed to protect our town."

He didn't answer, but he was listening.

"I'll resign," she continued. "You'll be the rightful Mayor of . . . well, of whatever's left. All you have to do is earn it. We couldn't save Grayrock. Help me avenge it."

"Please," added Greta. "For all of us."

For a moment, Glory thought they had gotten through to whatever shred of humanity survived in that twisted body. The Mayor looked over his shoulder at Grayrock. Then he spun and threw another rock, triggering another quick column of fire. Glory twisted to one side and yanked Greta out of the way, letting the rock pass them by.

"It was a good try," said Inga.

"Right, then." Glory stepped back. "Give me the boy."

"What are you doing?" asked Leech.

She snatched the doll from Inga. "We don't have time for greencap games, and I've got a trick they haven't yet seen."

Both greencaps were laughing and taunting them now, slapping their backsides and turning to throw rocks and bones and scraps of wood and who knew what else. As each object passed over the ash boundary, glowing sparks shot up to cling to them. Sticks burst into flame. Bone turned black. She could only imagine what that boundary would do to anyone who crossed it.

Glory did her best to ignore the assault. She moved beyond her rage at these creatures that would mock and delay her. Manifesting her Will into spheres of flame or poison was simple enough. She had mastered that years ago. But it was a poor Hero indeed who limited herself to a single weapon.

"Hold on," she whispered. Ben's stone arms tightened around her wrist.

Glory launched her Will like a noose, snaring the second greencap. The instant she felt a connection, she *pulled*.

Between one heartbeat and the next, she and the greencap swapped places. She appeared on the far side of the smouldering ash, beside the Mayor. The other greencap found himself where Glory had been—directly in the middle of three Heroes.

"Aw, dung." The greencap straightened, but he hadn't gone more than a single step when Inga's fist sent him flying through the air into a tree. He slumped to the ground, unconscious.

Glory smiled at the Mayor, who turned to flee. She hurled a fire apple in front of his path. He shrieked and jumped back, arm flailing for balance. She started towards him, but the moment she moved, her vision darkened around the edges, and the hammering of her heartbeat filled her ears.

"What's wrong?" Ben sounded like he was shouting from a distance.

"Nothing." She wasn't about to admit how much certain spells took out of her. She rubbed her eyes and blinked to see the Mayor charging her with a sword.

A flaming arrow sprouted from the Mayor's arm, and the sword fell away. Glory stepped to the side, and he stumbled past . . . directly onto the ashes.

He had just enough time to shriek and spin towards Glory, as if to beg for help. The blackened path flared to life. All the heat and flame and fury converged on a single point, expending its power in a single pillar of flame that stretched far above the treetops.

"Well," said Leech. "Now we know what Skye's trap did."

Within moments, nothing remained of that trap except for the scorched patch of dirt and weeds where the Mayor had died. Glory threw a stick across the line to the others. Nothing happened. Then, just to be safe, Leech tossed the remaining greencap's unconscious body towards Glory.

"Looks like it expended everything on the Mayor," said Leech.

"And sent up a signal Skye could see from miles away. She's like a spider, and this was her web." Glory started jogging towards the river and the walls of Grayrock. "Keep an eye out for smoke."

Glory spoke mostly for Leech and Inga's benefit. They hadn't been here the last time Skye attacked and might not recognise the sign of her approach.

She checked Ben to make sure he was ready. He wore a pair of small, weighted pouches looped over his shoulders so the straps formed an X on his chest and back. All they had to do was get him through the gate and into the water.

"There she is." Shroud pointed to a slender caped figure standing atop the remains of the southwest watchtower. "Looks like she was waiting for us."

Smoke spilled from Skye's form. Her cape blossomed and grew, swelling over her head, until she lifted into the air. She swooped over the river. Fire and smoke streaked from her hands to the dirt and water below though she was much too far away for her attack to reach Glory or her companions.

"Water is no way to destroy a town," Skye shouted. She flew to and fro, continuing to rain fire. The trees closest to the river began to burn. "Yog was too worried about her precious Kas. She should have let me purge this place. Build a wall of fire and listen to the screams. Watch them trample one another in their panic under the blackened skies!"

At this distance, Glory had to strain to hear Skye's shouts. "Did you catch that last bit?"

"I think she said something about quacking spies," said Inga. "You think she means to attack us with evil ducks?"

Leech shook his head. "I thought it was blackened pies. Maybe she's just a lousy cook."

Shroud held his bow in one hand. With the other, he grabbed a handful of half-rotted leaves and tossed them into the air. "The wind's against us. I'll need to get closer to hit her."

Where Skye's flames struck the ground, creatures of sticks and fire and smoke began to rise, just as had happened the last time they faced her. They spread out to block the way to Grayrock.

Glory glanced at the rising sun. "Inga, how well does your shield do against fire?"

Inga hefted Bulwark. "It stops everything from magic to charging pigs."

"Charming." She watched Skye rise higher, lifted aloft by the smoke filling her cape. More of her flaming minions started towards the Heroes. "Shroud, take Ben. You and Inga head for the wall. Leech and I will see what we can do about Skye and her droppings."

"She'll never let them take Ben back into Grayrock," said Greta. "You can't get to the gates, and if you try to circle around, her sparklings will—"

"Who needs gates?" Glory looked pointedly at Shroud's bow.

Shroud grinned. "Ben doesn't weigh that much, though the lead shot he's carrying will drag the arrow down." He raised his thumb to the wall and squinted with one eye, estimating the distance. "Given the wind . . . if I can get within sixty yards, I'll launch the lad over the wall and into the drink, nice as you please."

"You're going to *shoot my brother*?"

"He should be honoured. He'll be the first person who can say he was shot by Shroud and survived." Shroud snapped the broadhead off an arrow. "Here you go, Ben. Use this to cut yourself free when you hit the water."

The doll held up his wooden limbs. Limbs that were noticeably lacking in fingers.

"Right." Shroud used a length of string to tie the broadhead to Ben's arm. A second bit of string tied Ben to the arrow, making him look like a wooden kebab.

Glory stepped into the clearing and turned her attention to Skye's flaming soldiers. No use attacking them with magical fire, but acid would smother the flame and eat away at the magically animated body within. She conjured two spheres shaped like green apples and hurled them at Skye's creations. The thick poison splashed several of the creatures and clung to them. They staggered back, their bodies spraying smoke and embers.

Leech spread his hands, reaching for whatever false life he might be able to steal as Shroud and Inga ran towards the wall.

"What can I do?" asked Greta.

"Stay out of the way." Glory studied the ground in front of them. Skye wasn't the only one who could set traps. Conjuring death from the earth was harder than summoning it in her hands, but the principle was the same. It was all a matter of Will.

One group had broken away in pursuit of Shroud and Inga. Glory focused on a patch of land in front of them and cast her trap.

Hardly had she finished than the first of the creatures set it off. The ground exploded like a sickly green fountain. Flames died, and the thing collapsed into a sizzling pile of sticks and ash. The poison splashed two others that had been following close behind. Both stumbled to the ground. Neither got back up.

"Lead them towards the river," said Leech.

Glory nodded and started running. Greta followed, as did most of the creatures.

"What are you doing?" Glory shouted.

"Grayrock was my home," said Greta. "I want to help! Winter wouldn't run from a fight, and neither will I!"

"Did you miss the part where Winter almost got herself killed?" Glory hit the water and didn't stop until it was almost to her knees. Her boots would never be the same.

Cold and grey with dust, the river flowed out from the gates of Grayrock and over the old road, disappearing into the woods. It was more a stream than a river, but it was enough to bring beings of living fire to a halt. They stopped at the edge, crowding together until the heat was a palpable pressure against her skin.

Greta stooped and used her hands to splash water at the creatures. It wasn't much, but several hissed and moved away when the water struck.

"Is it me, or does Skye look annoyed?" asked Glory. The nymph was floating towards them, her hands enveloped in fire and black smoke.

Leech tapped Glory's shoulder and pointed. Inga continued to fend off Skye's minions, while Shroud drew back his bowstring. The arrow carrying Ben was little more than a blur that shot up in an arc, clearing the wall by inches before disappearing into Grayrock.

"I hope he's all right," said Greta.

Glory grabbed her by the shoulder and hauled her back as fire streaked down. The river sizzled and steamed where Greta had been standing.

Leech looked like he was trying to bring Skye down, but he wasn't having much luck.

"Greta, follow the stream back into the woods. Skye shouldn't be able to see you through the trees. If you're hit, duck beneath the water." Glory started upriver. "If Leech and I can get through the gates into Grayrock, we'll have some cover against Skye's assault."

That was easier said than done. Skye's animated campfires crowded both sides of the water, and the nymph continued to throw flame from above. One struck Leech on the side. Another singed Glory's arm, setting her sleeve alight. She threw herself into the water, then rolled out of the way of another attack.

An arrow zipped past Skye. Shroud and Inga charged the creatures from behind. Some of them pulled away to intercept this new threat.

"Aim for Skye's cape," Glory shouted. "It's what keeps her aloft!"

Shroud didn't answer, but he pulled a blue-fletched arrow from his quiver, and his next shot ripped through Skye's billowing cape, leaving a fist-sized hole in its wake. Skye shrieked and gripped her shoulders where the cape connected to her gown.

Skye was focusing her assault on Shroud, pouring smoke and fire so thick he was unable to get off another good shot. But he was keeping her busy, and that was all Glory needed. She flung another poison apple to clear a path and waded to land.

"What are you doing?" Leech shouted.

"New plan. Get to the gates. I'm going to hit her from behind."

She ran towards the tower on the northwest part of the wall. Sweat stung her eyes, and her burnt arm throbbed with pain, impossible to ignore. This was where the second wave of redcaps had entered Grayrock during their initial assault on the town. As she had hoped, most of the ropes and ladders they had used were still here. She reached the base and climbed one-handed, rolling onto the observation platform. The tower creaked and shifted under her weight.

A handful of Skye's creations scrambled up the wall after her like rats. Glory dropped another apple on their heads, then turned to check on the others.

Inga had stepped in front of Shroud, using Bulwark to fend off a gout of flame. The instant it stopped, Shroud popped up and put another arrow through Skye's cape. Smoke poured out, forming a cloud around the nymph.

Glory readied her magic, but she couldn't even see Skye anymore. Shroud's bow had gone silent as well. The black fog spread and thickened. The cloud soon stretched out over much of the lake. It looked like Skye intended to drift over the town and flee into the hills, much as she had done after their last encounter.

"Not this time, you don't." Glory ran along the top of the wall, jumping the occasional cracked stone or dead redcap. "Shroud, get ready!"

There were times for precision and care. This wasn't one of them. Glory hurled one flaming apple after another into the cloud. The first explosion dispersed the smoke in a sphere as wide as Glory was tall. The next three thinned the air enough to make out Skye's form. More smoke poured from her gown, like ink from a squid.

Another arrow ripped through Skye's cape. It looked like it had sliced the nymph's arm as well. But it wasn't enough. Skye dipped lower, dropping out of Shroud's line of fire.

Glory reached the edge of the broken dam. Nothing of the town was visible through the grey-brown water, save the tip of the Mayor's tower, jutting up from the centre like a crenulated stone island.

Glory threw another red apple, this time aiming for Skye's cape. If it was enchanted to sail on enchanted smoke, perhaps other forms of magic would work too.

The cape rippled sharply away from the explosion, jerking Skye backwards. She wheeled her arms through the air. Glory's next attack splattered poison on both Skye and the cape. Skye screamed, but the cape seemed unaffected.

The nymph twisted, and fire poured down at Glory. She started to dodge, but the water had turned the rocks slippery. Her right food slid out from beneath her. She hit the dam hard and tried to catch herself, but she couldn't find a handhold.

She rolled off the edge and landed hard in the shallow water next to the falls, where the broken dam had formed a sloping hill into the water. A hill with many hard edges and corners, all of which had left their marks on her bones. A hill that felt far less stable than Glory would have liked.

Her legs and hips were in the water. Very slowly, she reached to either side to try to pull herself up. The rocks shifted beneath her and the water rose past her waist.

The rush of the falls tugged her legs, trying to haul her under. The shock of the water on her burnt arm and back made her lock her jaw to keep from screaming. She blinked back tears and searched for Skye.

The nymph was circling around to finish Glory off. Smoke and fire poured off her skin.

"Kill me if you can," Glory muttered. "But you're coming with me." She saw two options. One involved drowning. The other involved the kind of fowl-brained idea Winter might have come up with . . . which would in all likelihood be followed by drowning.

Skye launched another column of flame.

Glory let go of the rocks. As the water yanked her down, she stretched her Will towards Skye and *pulled,* trying to perform the same swap she had done with the greencap in the woods.

Water covered her head and filled her nose, and a single thought fought to the surface: If she failed, Winter would never let her live this down.

And then she was falling through the air. The world spun around her. She spotted Skye in the water an instant before steam and smoke obscured her from view.

Glory tried to twist into a dive, but she was too exhausted and falling too fast. She slammed into the water hard enough to expel the air from her lungs. Her vision went white, and water rushed into her mouth and nose.

She couldn't see, couldn't tell which way was up. The current from the falls battered her like a leaf in a gale. She tried to fight, but she could barely move. She felt herself falling into night.

"Are you all right? Can you hear me?"

Glory opened her eyes. Greta was staring down at her, water dripping from her hair and face. Glory tried to speak, but her lungs rebelled. Strong hands hoisted her onto her side, and she vomited murky water.

"She's alive!"

"Of course," said Leech. "The dead don't vomit."

Glory could hear the smile behind his mask. "Where . . . ?"

"Don't try to talk yet." Leech put his fingers to her lips. "You busted yourself up pretty good. You managed to damage almost every part of your body. I've been using some of my own life to stabilise you, but there's only so much I can do."

"You're outside Grayrock," said Greta. "Inga carried you out—"

"After Greta here dived in to rescue you." Inga beamed at the younger girl. "She followed you into Grayrock. While the rest of us were finishing off Skye's henchmen, she was saving your life."

"Skye?" asked Glory.

"Dead." Shroud pursed his lips. "She tried to climb out, but her cape dragged her down. The body washed up against the gates a few minutes ago."

"Dibs on the body!" Leech said.

"This is no time to be playing with corpses," said Inga. "If Sterling and the others can't stop Yog, she'll come here next."

"Likely from the south or west." Shroud peered out at the woods. "The mountains make an eastern approach difficult, and the river protects us from the north. If it were me, I'd come through Talondell. The forest will make her as hard to see as a black cat at midnight."

"Yog's not going to be happy," said Greta. "You killed one of her Riders."

Glory closed her eyes. The sun's warmth would dry her clothes, and the way she figured, she'd earned a bit of rest. "Wake me when she gets here and I'll finish her off, too."

chapter 19

STERLING

"If I'd known you had transformed yourself into stone, I would have let Skye burn the bloody town to the ground without fear of losing you," said Yog as she examined a set of knives that looked disturbingly like the tools one might find in a butcher shop. Or at Leech's place. She had spread them out on a small table.

"'Twas sweet of you to worry, love." Kas stepped over one of the knives and reached out to pat Yog's hand.

Sterling sat between Tipple and Winter, his limbs bound in ropes that pricked his skin like thorns. His lips were bruised and swollen, and his mouth tasted like he had been chewing coins all day. His head throbbed, and he didn't think it was just from the beating he had taken in the cavern.

An iron pot hung in the small fireplace, giving off a foul, salt-scented smoke. Sticky red droplets crawling down the side of the pot left little doubt as to its main ingredient. If the mere smell of Yog's brew was enough to make him feel this bad, he had new respect for what Tipple had endured after drinking her poisoned ale.

The hut was like a child's overflowing toy chest, assuming that child was more interested in bones and herbs and old vials than wooden soldiers and pretend swords. Sterling's own sword, along with their other weapons, was piled out of reach in a corner.

What Sterling didn't see was any kind of small, wooden box that looked like it might contain Yog's life. If the box was here, there were a thousand places it could be hidden away. Sterling could have searched the hut for a year without finding it.

"Three Heroes." Yog sounded almost kindly, like the grandmother who was always handing out sweets. "Which of you should I carve up first?"

"The redcap," said Kas. "He tried to betray you to the Heroes."

"What?" Blue jumped to his feet, banging the top of his head on a shelf hard enough to make its contents rattle—the shelf's contents, that was. He pointed at Sterling and his fellow prisoners. "Blue brought three Heroes for Yog! Three to eat or kill or flog!"

"You led them here hoping they would burn Yog's life," Kas snapped.

"Me?" Blue's eyes were round. "*You* promised to sneak in and steal Yog's hut!"

"You miserable little—"

"Enough." Though Yog didn't raise her voice, both Blue and Kas fell silent immediately. Yog turned to study the three Heroes.

Few things disconcerted Sterling, but the sight of Yog's sharpened iron teeth, each one dark and pitted save for the gleaming edge, made his shoulders tense. It was one thing to face a monster or wild animal. Their fangs, no matter how sharp and deadly, were natural. This was something Yog had deliberately done to herself.

He supposed it was possible someone else had forced those teeth upon her. But somehow he doubted it. Feeble-looking as she was, there was a strength to Yog's words and stance that suggested nothing around her happened without her permission.

Sterling adopted his most charming smile. "Those must be a beast to sharpen."

The wrinkles by her eyes grew deeper, an expression that mixed amusement and annoyance. "I file them once a month. My mouth tastes of grit and rust for days afterwards. But they're much better for tearing through bone and sinew."

"Sterling's the talker of the group," said Kas. "All pretty words and speeches. He's handy with that sword of his, though."

Yog picked up Sterling's sword. "Best to eat him first. Bad enough I have to listen to the ogre's incessant squabbling with her noggins. What can you tell me of the others?"

"The big one's strong, but from what little I've seen, he's unreliable. Just as likely to hug you as he is to punch you, depending on how much he's had to drink." Kas turned towards Winter. "Her, on the other hand, she's got some fire to her. So to speak. She's the one who brought down the dam. She's strong willed, but once you overcome that, she'd be a good choice."

"A good choice for what?" asked Winter.

"For one of my Riders." Yog walked to the fireplace and checked the contents of the pot. "It's been centuries since I last broke a Hero."

"Are we exchanging threats now? How fun!" Winter smiled. "Have you ever seen a bad case of frostbite? Would you like to guess which of your extremities will fall off first?"

"Oh, yes. I like her." Yog pointed the sword at Sterling. "Let's see what happens after she's watched her friends die. How long will that defiance last when she's alone, with no hope of rescue, no company save her own failure?"

Winter's nose wrinkled. "You know, it's awfully dusty in here."

Yog blinked. Before she could respond to the seemingly random comment, Winter arched her back and sneezed.

Snow and frost sprayed forth. Kas toppled onto his back, completely encased in ice. Yog raised a hand to shield her face. Ice grew around her like a second skin of glass.

Winter turned towards Blue. "Be a dear and cut us loose."

Blue shook his head and pointed.

Cracks spread through the ice that imprisoned Yog. Large chunks fell away as she flexed her arms.

Winter filled her lungs, but before she could launch another attack Yog stepped forwards and stabbed Arbiter into her shoulder. Whatever power Winter had been gathering was lost to her scream.

"You present me with a dilemma," Sterling said tightly. "I can't decide whether to kill you myself or to allow Winter the pleasure of ending you."

"They're always so defiant in the beginning." Yog yanked the sword free and used the pommel to break the ice holding her husband. "Winter, as a potential Rider, you may choose which of your friends I kill first. Select one and his death will be quick. Refuse to answer and they will both die slowly. Painfully."

Winter's bleeding had slowed. Frost rose from the cut, as if she were chilling and sealing the wound from within. Satisfied that she was in no immediate danger of bleeding to death, Sterling turned his full attention to Yog. "I wouldn't advise killing us just yet."

"And why is that?"

Sterling leaned back, looked Yog in the eye, and smiled.

He had learned at a young age that a smile was as powerful a weapon as any sword. Just as he had practised swordplay until he had mastered every technique, he had done the same with his smile, trying different expressions in the mirror and learning which could earn him an extra dessert, help him escape chores, or deflect punishment. As he grew older, he learned to apply that smile to the local lads and lasses, whoever happened to catch his eye that day. He could stop an angry mob or rally an army with the right smile.

A smile could also threaten. Any oaf could bellow and shout loud enough to frighten a few people. It took *skill* to make your enemies soil themselves with nothing more than a smile.

The smile he used against Yog blended quiet threat with total confidence, and perhaps just a hint of condescension, like Yog was a child scheming to steal a tart from the kitchen, thinking herself clever and never knowing her parents watched from the doorway.

The wild tufts of Yog's eyebrows squeezed together in momentary confusion. She raised the sword to strike, hesitated . . .

"He's stalling," said Kas.

"Are you sure, little man?" Sterling tilted his head, adding a bit more condescension to his smile. "After you went to such trouble to capture us, do you really want to risk wasting our power?"

Yog's jaw tightened. Arbiter wavered in her hand. Through clenched iron teeth she said, "Explain. Quickly."

"All in good time, my dear lady." Sterling made a show of looking around. "I'm curious about this hut. It appears to be larger on the inside."

"It is," said Yog. "It's grown a bit over the years, though the outer shell remains unchanged."

"Fascinating." He glanced at the trio of skulls sitting to one side of the table, each one lit from within by blue candle flame. "When we were talking about you back in Brightlodge, Leech said something interesting. He thinks that in order to best steal a Hero's power, you'd have to act quickly, before the life drained from the body. Which would suggest you have to keep us alive until you're ready to consume us. And *that* means you can't kill us until the curse is lifted. What would happen if you tried, by the way? Is that how you lost your original teeth?"

"Grayrock is gone," Yog snapped. "The town lies at the bottom of a lake. None remain but corpses."

"Are you absolutely certain?" Sterling leaned back. "It would be a shame to waste a perfectly good Hero."

Yog stabbed the sword into the floor. "What are you saying?"

"I have a few more questions first," Sterling said. "Then I'll explain."

"Like how'd Kas persuade you not to eat him?" Tipple piped up. "'Cause that's the kind of knowledge some of us might soon find useful."

Yog scowled. "I wasn't always the twisted crone you see before you. In my day, before Grayrock's curse, I was considered quite stunning."

"I told the truth about setting out to slay her," said Kas. "But it was years before William Grayrock came along. Yog was too powerful for me. I soon recognised the inevitable and surrendered. I knew enough of her reputation to understand my fate, the same fate that had befallen others of my kind. I asked for a single boon before she went about taking my life: a kiss from the loveliest woman I'd ever laid eyes upon."

"Must've been some kiss!" said Tipple.

"It was." Yog smiled again, and in that moment she looked—not younger, but slightly less evil and haggard. Aside from the iron teeth.

"If it's a kiss you desire, then untie me, my lady." Sterling winked. "Let my friends go and I'll—"

"Will you just kill him already?" Kas snapped.

"Perhaps later."

Sterling's smile never faltered. "So it was William Grayrock who cast the curse, not Kas? Then how did Kas end up shrunken and buried in that box?"

"Grayrock again," said Kas. "Yog attempted to transform him, but the curse was already weakening her. The bastard managed to deflect her spell onto me. I went searching for a way to restore Yog to her former self, but the villagers caught me. They buried me alive."

Sterling shook his head in exaggerated dismay. "The redcap I can forgive. Madness is part of his nature. But you, sir, knew exactly what Yog was. You had seen what she did. You helped her anyway."

"Because he understood what you never will." Yog stepped

closer. "I lived through the Fallow Wars. I saw the Old Kingdom collapse into myth. I watched Heroes fall. Throughout that time, only one thing remained constant. Not honour or glory. Not Heroes, whose names were forgotten within a generation or two. Only power."

It wasn't the response Sterling had expected. The Old Kingdom and the Fallow Wars were little more than myth and fairy tale, stories told by parents to lull children to sleep, or by cruel older siblings to plant the seeds of nightmares in their younger brothers and sisters. "The Pitch Black Ages," he whispered. "You lived through the darkest days of Albion's history, saw the suffering and the death, and you thought of nothing but your own power?"

"What I saw was impermanence," said Yog. "The peace and prosperity brought about by the first Hero was an eyeblink in the existence of the world. Your Gathering of Heroes will fade into nothingness. Brightlodge will topple over the falls and be lost to history. A hundred years from now, the three of you will be dust, and it will be as if you never existed."

Winter looked up at Yog. "That's the most dismal thing I've ever heard. When was the last time you got out and enjoyed yourself? I recommend dancing, myself. What's life without dance?"

"Or drink?" added Tipple.

"Or a partner beneath the covers?" said Sterling.

"You know nothing of life," said Yog. "You're each so young, so full of noble intentions, setting out to protect the innocent and fight the darkness. But over time, you'll gain a taste for power. Well, either that or you get yourselves killed. For those who live, who begin to grow in strength, your arrogance will soon be revealed. You're not truly interested in protecting others. You do this for your own glory. For the way they look at you afterwards. For their eagerness to warm your bed. And for that secret knowledge that you're *better* than they are."

There was just enough truth in her words to pierce Sterling's guard, scoring the point as neatly as his first fencing master. He regained his composure in an instant, but Yog's knowing smile told him she had seen through the mask.

"All Heroes walk a narrow path," Sterling conceded. "It's easy to stumble. Nobility and honour aren't badges you receive with your first blade; they're journeys. Choices we make each day of our lives. The true test of the Hero is to recognise the allure of that darker path and to turn away."

"Oh, well said," cheered Winter. "Much better than your usual speeches."

Tipple simply belched.

"Tell me, Yog," Sterling pressed. "If corruption is as inevitable as you say, what of yourself? You've stolen the power of countless Heroes. What have you become?"

"A twisted, bitter, lonely hag," Yog said easily. "A survivor. A murderess a thousand times over. Unlike you, I've no illusions about what I am."

"You've seen the world in its glory, and you've seen it at its darkest."

"I've seen enough to know that Albion will never truly escape that darkness."

"You could have *been* the light." Sterling leaned forwards. "You could have led and inspired the people of Albion. I've listened to stories of Heroes all my life, stories that taught me to be a better man. Nobility and leadership aren't about smiting those who block your path. They're about lifting people up, showing them a better path."

Yog stepped closer, gripping Arbiter with both hands. "No more pretty words. My beloved is right. You're stalling."

"Before you strike, I believe I promised you an explanation," said Sterling. "Do you remember Ben from Grayrock? His sister called him Hedgehog. Skye brought him to you, and you transformed him into a doll. You forced his sister to spy for you."

Yog nodded, her forehead furrowed.

Both Winter and Tipple were staring at him now, along with Yog, Kas, and Blue. There was nothing in the world like a rapt audience. In that moment, ropes meant nothing; they were all prisoners of his words. "Like most of the town's residents, he was a descendant of William Grayrock."

Slowly, Yog withdrew the sword.

"I sent him home this morning," Sterling continued cheerfully. "Along with an escort to make sure he arrived safely. Just in case Kas or Blue betrayed us. By now, he should be back in his house under the lake, probably sorting through the mess and looking for valuables. Thanks to your magic, Ben doesn't need to breathe. He can hide out underwater for as long as it takes."

"Heroes gloat," said Blue, "but wood floats!"

"Yes, that's true," Sterling admitted. "Which is why Shroud prepared lead weights to help him sink. We got the idea from watching your redcaps search the lake."

"You're lying," said Kas.

"Maybe. You could send one of your Riders out to check. Or just go ahead and start your feast. But as long as a descendant of Grayrock lives within that town, your curse will go on."

Sterling shrugged. "Or who knows, maybe the curse has worn off after all these years and you can once again consume the flesh of Heroes without injury. Maybe it won't rip those nasty metal teeth from your gums." He leaned forwards. "Try it. It *probably* won't kill you . . ."

Yog's response was in a language Sterling didn't know, though he guessed the meaning was anything but civilised. She threw his sword to the ground—out of his reach, unfortunately—and spun towards the three skulls. She sat down in front of them and began barking orders to whoever was listening on the other side of her spell.

The hut lurched into motion. Wooden bowls and dishes spilled from the shelves. The curtains hanging over the shelves kept most of the more fragile items in place. One lumbering step at a time, the hut began to march.

"What makes you think I won't simply remove the spell on the boy and let him drown?" Yog asked.

"From this distance?" Winter laughed. "You haven't even restored your husband. You *might* have the strength of Will to change Ben back in person, but not from here."

"There's a simple solution," Kas said. "Skye was supposed to be guarding Grayrock. Simply ask her whether the other Heroes have truly returned to—"

"Skye . . . is not responding to my summons." Yog glared at Sterling.

"Maybe she stopped by the pub," Tipple suggested.

Yog ignored him and reached into one of the skulls—the blackened one—to remove the burning candle. She brought the flame towards Winter's face. "There are those who have begged for the chance to serve me. Take the fire into yourself. The power you've known is but a shadow of your potential."

Winter pursed her lips and blew. The flame rippled but refused to die. She frowned and tried again. This time, frost and snow swirled from her lips, but still the candle burned.

Yog turned away and set the candle on the table. It remained upright, despite the rocking motion of the hut that spilled rivulets of wax with each step. "When the boy lies dead and you see the fate that awaits your companions, you'll choose differently. Young Heroes are all the same. So willing to sacrifice themselves to save another. In the end, I will allow you to surrender your Will to mine, and in exchange, one of your friends may go free. But which one, I wonder. For whom will you sacrifice yourself?"

"Winter won't break." Sterling gave Winter a reassuring smile, then leaned back against the wall. "I imagine she'll enjoy killing you, though. Assuming I don't get the chance first."

"Such arrogance," said Kas.

"Not at all, my diminutive friend. But I would wager on any of my companions over you and your withered wife."

"And why is that?" Yog asked, sounding amused.

"Because they're Heroes."

chapter 20

LEECH

Leech sat atop the southern wall of Grayrock, examining the nymph's remains. The uneven stone wall was a far cry from his dissection table back in Brightlodge, but it provided a relatively flat surface with plenty of sunlight, and the angle drained any run-off down the outside.

"I've seen nine hundred sixteen and a half dead bodies in my time." Shroud's casual comment made Leech jump. The man had come up behind him without a sound. "This is the first time I've seen one burned from the inside. Well, the second if we're counting acid burns."

"She drowned and burned at the same time." Leech set his knives aside and stretched his back and shoulders. Hunching over the corpse for so long was doing bad things to his spine. "It was a quick death, and a fascinating one. But it makes a proper autopsy a challenge. How's Glory doing?"

"Still sleeping. Inga and Greta are with her." Shroud crouched to study the corpse more closely. Of all the Heroes Leech had met, Shroud came closest to sharing Leech's interest in the body's workings. "Have you found anything useful?"

"Wait 'til you see this." Leech touched Shroud's arm.

"What are you doing?"

"Watch and see. It's pretty exciting." Leech drained a sliver of Shroud's life energy and channelled it into the body: specifically, into the right arm.

The nymph's hand twitched.

An arrow slammed into the corpse. Shroud had drawn and shot in less time than it took to inhale.

"It's all right," Leech said quickly. "Stop shooting the dead body!"

Shroud returned the second arrow to his quiver. "Just making sure. You know, when a Conclave assassin kills someone, they stay dead."

"She is dead. Mostly." Leech turned away to grab a sack of bones he had brought along from Brightlodge. He dumped them in a pile. "I'd been playing around earlier with the fragments from Yog's skeletal fence."

Leech picked up a jawbone and held it out to Shroud, who took it without flinching. "Look at those teeth. Chompers that loose should've popped right out the first time the skull tried to bite someone. But we've seen 'em chew through rope and leather, not to mention flesh. When Yog sends her bones against us, her Will must take the place of gums, muscle, and other connective tissue."

"Makes sense." Shroud tossed the jawbone back.

Leech transferred another drop of life into the jawbone. The teeth clicked and rattled. "I'd already figured out how to drain the energy from the bones, to protect us from another attack. But it works both ways. I think this is how she animates them, by siphoning some of her own excess life and power into the bones."

"And this helps us how?"

"By itself? It doesn't. But isn't it fascinating?" He pointed to the nymph. "Yog's done the same thing with her Riders. Skye's life is gone, but a bit of Yog's energy remains. I wouldn't be surprised if Skye's bones eventually joined the rest in Yog's fence."

Shroud's expression brightened. "Does that mean if we kill Skye—again—we'd be killing part of Yog?"

"I don't think so. But I discovered something else." He set the jaw aside and picked up a finger bone. As before, he fed the bone just enough to start it twitching, but this time he didn't stop. The bone twitched more violently, then—

Leech pointed triumphantly to the other bones. "Did you see?"

"I see that finger bone jumping about like . . ." Shroud fell quiet as the pile of bones shifted.

Leech hurled the finger bone into the lake. Several tiny bones hopped out of the pile and clacked against the stone, like fledgling birds trying to follow their mother.

"I'm not sure, but I think the bones that reacted were from the same body. Before Yog turned them into a fence, like. They're still connected."

"Any chance you can control them the way Yog does?" asked Shroud.

"I doubt it." He picked up part of a skull. "But if any of this fellow is in Yog's fence, I might be able to disrupt that part of her assault. The same goes for the rest of these bony bits and bobs."

Leech glanced out over the lake, wondering how Ben was doing. "When Yog cast her spell on Kas and Ben, do you think she transformed their true bodies into doll form? If we chiselled Kas open, would we find miniature stone lungs and intestines inside? Or did she rip the mind from the flesh and transfer it into a pre-made doll? If that's the case, you've got to wonder what became of the original bodies."

Shroud was staring at him.

"Sorry. Just thinking out loud."

"Something's wrong." Shroud pointed to the ground below, where Inga was running towards them, sword drawn.

"We've got visitors!" Inga bellowed.

Shroud unravelled a climbing rope, secured it to the crenulations, and slid down the outside of the wall. He jogged to the edge of the woods and scaled a tree, nimbly disappearing into the foliage. From there, he would have a clear shot at anyone approaching the town.

Leech gathered his bones and followed, albeit less gracefully. "Is it Yog?"

"We'll know soon enough," said Inga.

Leech could hear raucous laughter in the distance, too faint to discern the details. "Sounds like redcaps."

He and Inga made for the river. Inga moved ahead. Leech drew a deboning knife and waited. This could be part of Yog's assault, or it could just be a band of redcaps who had heard about the fall of Grayrock and were coming to plunder and cause mischief, not necessarily in that order.

A single figure jogged through the shadows. He moved like a human, not a redcap. "Wait!" Leech squinted. "That's Rook."

"Are you sure?" asked Inga. "I can't see his face from here."

"I can." Leech was already running. "A good surgeon needs good eyesight."

Inga followed, but the weight of her equipment slowed her down, meaning Leech was the first to see the extent of Rook's injuries. That many cuts, bruises, and what looked like at least one dislocation would have killed a lesser man; Rook simply looked peeved.

"Leech. Good man." Rook pointed to his right shoulder, which bulged a good three inches from where it should have been. "Fix that for me so I can finish whipping these dogs."

"What's after you?"

"Just redcaps. Though I imagine Yog will be on her way soon enough." He shook his head. "I hate this plan."

Leech put his knife in his teeth long enough to grasp Rook's arm, pull it out, and pop the shoulder back into place. Rook's jaw tightened, but he didn't make a sound.

"What about the others?" asked Inga.

"Alive, last I knew."

Leech took the knife from his mouth and stepped past Rook as the redcaps closed in. "Ever wondered whether redcaps' hearts are as twisted as the rest of their bodies?" He took a small vial from a padded pouch at his belt, removed the stopper, and carefully dipped the blade into the blue-black goo inside. "Let's find out."

One of Shroud's arrows took the first redcap. Leech's knife spun through the air to lodge in the abdomen of the second.

The redcap looked down at the knife. It wasn't a fatal wound, but the skin around the blade quickly began to darken and blister. "Och. A'm feelin' a bit wabbit."

His eyes rolled up in his head, and he collapsed. That was when Inga charged past like a bull, using her shield to send three more redcaps flying into the river.

Another tried to get behind Inga and stab her with a short sword. Leech pulled the life from that one, making him stagger, and transferred the energy into Rook's body. It wasn't enough to kill the redcap, but it slowed him enough for Inga to whirl and finish the job with her own sword.

The fighting ended as swiftly as it had begun. Leech brushed his hands together and turned back to Rook.

"What was that?" Rook asked, nodding at the diseased and dying redcap.

"A particularly nasty infection. You don't want to know the details. Just make sure you don't touch the body. Or the ground around him. In fact, we should probably burn the corpse to be safe." He poked and prodded at Rook's injuries. "You're bleeding internally. You'd have dropped dead before the day was over."

Rook shrugged his good shoulder. "I should have died in the Deadlands more times than I can count."

Leech found two more redcaps who weren't dead yet and used their remaining life to stop the bleeding, mend several bones, and seal some of the cuts covering Rook's body. "You'll live, but you need rest."

"I'll rest when I'm dead."

"Which will be sooner than you expect if you try to fight in this condition," Leech said.

"What happened?" asked Inga.

"Kas betrayed us. Sterling saw it coming. He got the others into Yog's hut so they can try to figure out where the old witch is hiding her life." Rook touched his left eye, which was swollen halfway shut. "This might all be going to Sterling's plan, but when we're through, I still intend to put that doll to a grindstone and wear him down to sand."

Nothing Leech said would persuade Rook to rest. Inga had to threaten to physically tie Rook up and carry him off before the man grudgingly agreed.

"He's as mule-headed as my cousin," Inga said fondly.

They set him up a small shelter just inside the wall, atop a floating wardrobe Shroud lashed to the gates. Rook groaned as he settled back. He placed his crossbow at his side. The gates and the assorted debris would give him cover while allowing him to shoot anything that approached.

"How long do you think we have before Yog arrives?" asked Inga. They had gathered a short distance beyond the wall. Shroud was sketching traps and ambush points in the mud and muttering to himself about the most efficient way of cutting down an approaching force.

"Depends on how fast a walking hut can travel." Leech looked out at the woods. "She can't kill the others 'til she deals with Ben."

"We won't let that happen." Inga peered over Shroud's shoulder. "Maybe we should wake Glory up and have her start laying down her own traps."

"Good thinking," said Shroud. "I passed Greta as she was leaving, and she told me Glory looked to be resting more comfortably."

"What do you mean leaving?" Inga searched the surrounding land. "Where did she go?"

"She said something about bringing a pike to Founder's Hill for luck."

"Are you thick in the head? You thought nothing of an unarmed child's walking off alone while we're waiting for Yog and her army to come crashing down on our heads?"

Shroud shrugged. "That child was old enough to follow us through the woods, and levelheaded enough to save Glory's life."

"Leech and I are going after her."

"We are?" asked Leech.

"If she's run into trouble, she'll need healing." To Shroud she said, "We'll be quick as we can. Signal if you see Yog."

With that, Inga set off running. Fortunately, they didn't have far to go. A well-trod path led northwest into a small clearing in the forest, where Greta sat in front of an old stone marker. Moss and dirt covered much of the rectangular stone.

"What are you doing out here?" Inga demanded.

Greta jumped and bit back a cry. "Oh. Inga. I didn't hear you."

"She clanks like a kitchen mishap, and you didn't hear her?" asked Leech.

"I was thinking." Greta's face was pale, and her eyes red. Judging from the streaks through the dirt on her cheeks, she'd been crying. "I just needed a little time alone. I thought I'd lay a pike on Grayrock's grave. It's stupid, I know, but they say it brings you luck. Only I didn't have a pike, so I drew one in the dirt."

Inga softened. "There, there. Don't worry, Inga's here. What's really troubling you, lass?"

"After I pulled Glory out of the lake, I started shaking." Greta looked away.

"Seems like a normal reaction to chilly water," said Leech.

"It wasn't that. I was afraid. Seeing my home destroyed, and Skye trying to kill us all . . . I tried not to let the rest of you see. Heroes aren't supposed to get scared. But then those redcaps arrived, and I saw how hurt your friend Rook was . . ."

"I know!" crowed Leech. "Did you see that dislocation? His arm was popped out enough, you probably could've twisted the whole thing right off!"

Inga glared. "Why don't you check around to make sure nothing sneaks up on us, and I'll take care of Greta here."

Leech shrugged and left the two of them alone. There wasn't much to see. A few old stumps from when the site had been cleared. A ring of pine trees with their blue-green branches intertwined.

He pushed through the pines, but found nothing save for a black squirrel, a half-rotted log, and a small hornets' nest. A mosquito landed on his wrist. The bite was finer than any needle or blade. Leech had barely felt a thing when it bit him.

He carried the mosquito back to the clearing, still watching it feed, and sat down on one of the stumps. On a whim, he drained the life from the mosquito—it seemed only fair—and tried to transfer that life into the tree stump. He had never been able to tap the energy of plants the way he did. . . .

"What is it?" asked Inga.

He dropped to one knee and placed both hands on the stump. He could see where each stroke of the axe had bitten into the wood. "Dead trees. Dead bones."

"You sound like Blue. What are you talking about?"

Leech reached for the darkness, searching for that tiny, short-lived spark that had lingered—if only for a moment—within the stump. Greta whimpered and backed away. He must have let his shadow aspect show for a moment there. "We have to get back to Grayrock." Leech beamed. "I know where Yog hid her life."

chapter 21

INGA

"The hut?" Inga used Bulwark to shove a low-hanging branch out of the way.

"Isn't it obvious? Yog hid her life in a wooden box," said Leech. "Nobody said it had to be a *small* box, hey? Wood has no animate life of its own, but her hut tromps around the woods like an animal. She must have found a way to infuse her life into her home."

"Take down the hut and we take down Yog." Inga grinned. "I've never fought a hut before."

"We'll have to be careful," said Leech. "Tipple and the others are still inside."

A high-pitched whistle tore through the air.

"What was that?" asked Greta.

"Shroud's signal arrow." Inga picked up speed, positioning herself in front of the others. When they emerged from the woods, there was no sign of Shroud. No doubt he was hiding like a mountain lion, waiting to pounce.

Inga took Greta by the shoulder. "Get inside and keep an eye on Rook and Glory."

"Or just Rook." Leech pointed to the slender figure standing atop the wall by the gates.

"Aren't you supposed to be resting?" Inga shouted.

Glory conjured a ball of flame. "As if you lot stand a chance against Yog without my help."

"She sounds like herself again." Leech took Greta by the hand and led her to where a section of wall had crumbled. Water trickled over the hill of broken stone.

That wall had been standing a short time before. The water must have eroded the foundation. At this rate, how long would it be before the last of Grayrock fell and washed away?

Inga waited until the others were both safely behind the walls—"safe" being a relative thing—then climbed up to find a good place to wait.

There was no subtlety to Yog's approach. Inga heard the tromp of the wooden hut smashing through the trees long before it came into view.

The redcaps were first to emerge from the forest. They were a far cry from Yog's earlier forces, numbering less than a dozen. The frontmost redcap suddenly howled and clutched his foot. A second pointed and laughed, but did the same two steps later. Inga chuckled, remembering Shroud's plans. The redcaps had reached Shroud's caltrops, then.

The rest slowed their approach, spreading outward, where another tripped over a line that set off a flash bomb directly in her face. One of Shroud's arrows finished her off.

Inga stood atop the broken section of wall, Bulwark in one hand, her sword in the other. The stone blocks created a pile of cracks and corners that would snap your ankle like kindling if you weren't careful. She shifted position, testing her footing.

"Tipple will be furious about missing this fight," Glory yelled.

"Maybe we can save a few stragglers for him," Inga called back.

Headstrong and the enchanted hut came next. The ogre waved a pair of enormous axes, one in each hand, while her noggins shouted what might have been a war cry. Though it could just as easily have been indigestion, assuming those things actually ate. Inga's granddaddy used to make similar noises after eating too much trout.

A swarm of skulls flew towards her, their eyes burning with blue flame. Inga smashed the first out of the air with her sword. Bulwark blocked the next, but there were too many to stop them all. Teeth clamped onto her leg. Another skull tangled in her hair, jaw clacking.

Both skulls suddenly fell away and clattered down the rocks, dead. Deader, rather. She spared a quick nod towards Leech.

Headstrong and the hut split up. The ogre charged directly at Inga, while the hut circled to Inga's left, climbing the rocks as easily as a mountain goat.

Inga shifted one leg back and dug her toe beneath a broken fragment of stone. She focused on the ogre's eyes, letting her peripheral vision track the movement of both axes. The instant Headstrong drew back to strike, Inga kicked the stone upwards. It hit the ogre directly on the mouth. It wasn't enough to stop her, but it startled her long enough for Inga to lunge forwards and land a cut along the front of her thigh.

The ogre didn't seem to notice. She kicked Inga's shield. Inga fell back, her shoulder throbbing. Even for an ogre, Headstrong was ridiculously strong.

"Watch that shield," cried one of the noggins.

"Mind the rocks," said another. "If you fall, you'll crush old Scratcher."

"Hit her with the axe! Then hit her with the other one!"

Inga twirled her blade overhead to draw Headstrong's attention. At the same time, Bulwark's power warmed her arm. The phantom shield smashed forwards, sending the ogre tumbling hard onto the rocks below. It looked like Bulwark had bloodied the noses of at least two noggins.

"I *told* you to watch the shield!" grumbled one.

Muffled shouts came from the noggin Headstrong had landed on. Inga guessed that would be Scratcher. She shifted her stance and redoubled her assault, using the higher ground to add power to her strikes.

"Hit her legs," said the same noggin. "Chop her down like a tree, then split her for kindling!"

"Naw, take out the ground under her," argued another.

Headstrong jumped back and swung low, striking the stone beneath Inga's feet. The blow chipped the blade of the axe, but the rocks shifted. Inga staggered, off balance.

"Now!" yelled the first noggin.

Inga blocked the next swing, but the impact knocked her onto her back. She slid down several feet, which put her directly into the path of the second axe. She braced Bulwark.

It felt like a horse had landed on her. If not for Bulwark's power, Inga had no doubt the blow would have split her and the shield both.

A second strike followed, and when that too failed to kill her, Headstrong simply threw herself atop Bulwark and Inga. The weight crushed the air from her lungs. Her sword was useless from this angle. She didn't have enough power to penetrate the ogre's thick hide.

"Granny warned me about days like this." Each time she exhaled, it got harder to draw another breath. The noggins were shouting and laughing. Sparks flashed at the edge of her vision.

She dropped her sword, reached past Bulwark, tightened her fist around the ogre's ear, and twisted hard.

Headstrong howled, and the pressure eased.

"Like Old Farmer Bristles used to say, control the head and the body will follow." Inga yanked down and to the side, twisting her fingers deeper into the greasy cartilage of the ogre's ear. Headstrong rolled off her. Unfortunately, she rolled right onto Inga's discarded sword. Had Inga been a luckier woman, the ogre would have run herself through in the process. Instead, she simply trapped the blade where Inga couldn't get to it.

Inga pushed herself up and kicked the ogre in the side of the head. The impact nearly broke her toes. "That bloody *hurts.*"

"I'll show you bloody," Headstrong roared, and climbed to her feet.

Inga jumped back to avoid another swipe of those axes. "What's Yog doing?" she shouted, keeping her attention on the ogre. She had lost track of the hut during the fight.

"She's on the wall, circling the lake," Leech yelled. "Probably searching for the boy. Glory's holding her back. I'm trying to keep her bones off us."

Headstrong kicked Inga's sword away. She and her noggins wore disturbingly similar smiles, hungry and sadistic. "You got her now," said one. "Take your time. Don't get stupid."

"Too late," crowed another. Headstrong thumped that one with the handle of her axe.

Inga used the opening to jump forwards and seize the haft of the axe. She tried to twist it out of Headstrong's hand, but the ogre's grip was like iron. Inga had to let go or be pulled off her feet.

"That's it," said the one-eyed noggin. "Slow and steady."

Inga snatched up a broken fragment of rock and threw it at the noggin, breaking the bulbous nose.

"Kill that bloody human!" it roared.

Headstrong raised both weapons and smashed them down on Inga's shield.

Inga still had the high ground, giving her leverage against Headstrong's greater strength. More important, it put Headstrong at just the right height for Inga to force the shield higher, then ram the lower edge into the ogre's throat.

Headstrong staggered and dropped one of her axes.

"Way to go, lard-fingers," said another noggin.

Inga followed up with her shield, knocking Headstrong back, then snatched up her sword. Both she and the ogre were breathing hard. Sweat painted wisps of hair to Inga's face. She readied her sword—

"Ben!"

The cry came from Greta, and she sounded terrified. Inga kicked Headstrong in the eye, then scrambled to the top of the wall and looked in at the lake.

Ben was bobbing in the water, fully human once more. Yog's hut perched like an insect on the edge of the dam. Yog must have transformed him to his natural shape, and from the looks of it, he wasn't much of a swimmer. Either that or he was having trouble controlling his limbs after his time as a doll.

She heard the stone crunching under Headstrong's feet and spun to ward off that enormous axe. "Leech, can you get to Ben?"

"Not without losing control of Yog's bones," Leech shouted.

Glory was too busy flinging magic at Yog's hut. If she went after Ben, who knew what the old witch would do.

Inga was confident she could beat Headstrong in time, but Ben didn't have time. Yet she couldn't retreat, either. If she tried to disengage, that axe would split her spine.

There was a sharp thump, and the ogre's head jerked to the side. A black-shafted arrow pierced her nose like an obscenely misplaced moustache. Headstrong's yellow eyes crossed, trying to focus.

"I've got this!" Shroud nocked another arrow as he jogged along the top of the wall towards them. "Go!"

Inga started running. Greta was swimming towards her brother, but a group of redcap skullchuckers had spotted her from the ruins of the watchtower. Bone and rock splashed the water.

Behind Inga, another arrow thudded into the ogre, who roared.

Inga sheathed her sword and made her way to the watchtower. She pulled herself up onto the platform behind the redcaps, who were laughing and pointing at the struggling children.

Ben bobbed in the water, his arms pressing down at his sides, his mouth dipping below the surface again and again. His efforts grew noticeably weaker, but Greta was almost there. A redcap picked up a skull with some sort of explosive mixture inside and looked about, presumably searching for a way to light the fuse.

Inga cleared her throat. The four redcaps jumped, with one nearly falling off the tower.

"Those kids are friends of mine." Inga couldn't recall the last time she had been this angry. Fighting was one thing, but to make sport out of trying to kill two children . . .

"Aw, yoos all banter," said the closest redcap. "Attack!"

Inga smiled and raised her shield. She could feel Bulwark's fury, as hot as her own and begging for release. The shield began to glow.

The redcaps hesitated.

Phantom shields shot out, smashing redcaps and the remnants of the tower alike. Splintered wood and screaming redcaps flew in all directions. Two redcaps splashed into the water. The others hit the ground outside. One exploded on impact.

Inga jumped after the two in the water. It was a bit of a drop, but she used a redcap to break her fall. She landed in the knee-deep water, snatched the other by the shirt, and threw him against the wall.

Greta had reached her brother and was struggling towards the shore, but she was bleeding from a cut on her forehead, and Ben was flailing. His panic could drown them both.

"Come on, Bulwark," said Inga. "Let's bring them in."

A spectral fist reached over the water to grasp both children. Inga normally used this trick to haul her enemies in for a good thrashing, but this time the shield was far more careful. Within seconds, Inga was helping Ben and Greta out of the water. She pulled them towards the collapsed section of wall. Ben coughed and gagged, but he was alive.

"Well done, Greta." Inga wrapped the girl in a one-armed hug. "You're as heroic as anyone I've met back in Wendleglass Hall."

"Thanks." Greta was shivering, but her voice sounded stronger, more confident.

Inga looked around. The other Heroes were keeping Yog busy. As for Headstrong—Inga craned her head, but there was no sign of Shroud or the ogre. "Can you walk?"

Greta nodded. Inga scooped Ben up in one arm and waded along the inside of the wall, towards the gates. Greta kept a hand on Bulwark for support.

Rook sat with his crossbow in hand, with several extra quivers piled beside him. He didn't ask any questions. He simply nodded and said, "I'll keep them safe."

"Stay inside the gates." Inga ran a hand over her scalp, pushing her hair from her face. So long as Ben and Greta were within Grayrock's walls, Yog's curse should remain. "Don't worry. We won't let Yog hurt either of you again."

Inga returned to the top of the wall. While she had been helping save Ben, the hut had gotten the upper hand—upper stilt, rather—with Leech and Glory, knocking them off the wall and chasing them into the clearing outside. Each of the wooden legs was as thick as a man's arm, but they moved as fast as whips.

Skulls were scattered over the ground. Others floated away in the river. It looked like Leech had stopped more than half of Yog's skeletal defences. The rest clung to the walls of the hut, the bones lending strength and armour of a sort to her walking home. Glory's magical assault didn't appear to be slowing the hut down. Each strike flowed past bone and wood like grease from a hot frying pan.

"I'll be right there," Inga shouted.

The hut caught Leech in the leg, knocking him down. His femur was visibly broken, but he didn't cry out. He stretched out one hand, placed the other against the break, and shoved. "Soon would be good, if it's all the same to you!"

When she was a child, Inga would have charged headfirst into battle to protect her friends, punching and kicking until either she or her opponent—usually the latter—went down and stayed there. True, she did that a lot as an adult, too. But what good would a sword be against an enemy like this? You didn't cut down a tree with a pocketknife.

Inga searched the rocks where she had battled Headstrong. The ogre had dropped one of her axes. If it remained . . .

There, half-buried in the rocks. Inga grabbed the handle and yanked it free.

An ogre could wield this thing one-handed, but if Inga wanted any power or control, she would need both. Reluctantly, she removed Bulwark from her arm and set it on the ground. She gripped the axe with both hands and tested its weight.

"This ought to do it." *Now* she charged headfirst into the battle.

A bruised and bloody redcap saw her coming, squeaked in alarm, and fled for the woods.

Inga raised her axe as she neared the hut, but the hut lashed out with one of its rear legs before she could swing. She twisted, and the blow grazed her ribs.

"It's quicker than it looks," Glory warned.

"I can see that, thanks." Inga fell back from a second attack. With four legs, the hut could only strike with one at a time without losing its balance. Inga kept her distance, trying to get a sense of its rhythm. There was a pause after each swing to recover.

A pair of skulls detached from the edge of the roof and flew towards her. One dropped and rolled into the mud, thanks to Leech. Inga shattered the other with her axe.

She darted left, then right, getting inside the hut's reach long enough to slam the axe into the closest leg. The blade bit the wood, then the hut twisted, nearly wrenching the weapon from her hands. Inga held tight. The blade ripped loose. Inga stumbled back, off balance. The hut lashed out again, and she fell.

Her back hit the ground, and the air exploded from her chest. Her armour had likely saved her from a broken back, but she would be feeling that in her spine for the next few days. "This is why Mum wanted me to stay home."

She pushed herself up and moved towards the hut. There was no way of sneaking up on it, as the thing had no front or back. She couldn't tell which leg she'd struck, let alone target a second attack to the same spot. She needed to find a way to take this thing down in one swing.

"Stay back," she called to Leech and Glory. She slowed her breathing, trying to let the sounds of battle flow past her. The laughter of the few remaining redcaps. The creaks and thuds of the hut, and the clattering of its contents. Her focus narrowed, like she was watching the hut through a sighting tube. The sky, the river, the trees beyond, everything else faded from her awareness.

Three of her friends were imprisoned inside that hut. They would die at Yog's hands if she didn't take it down.

Bones peeled away and flew towards the gates. Towards Ben and Greta.

Inga tightened her grip and waited. One leg hummed through the air, close enough for her to feel the wind. She backed away, drawing Yog in. Let Yog think she was injured and retreating.

She focused on a single leg, watching it bend and straighten. There were no knees or hinges, but the wood bent most sharply in two places, both near the centre. Each joint was marked by a round knot. She chose the higher of the two.

One hand gripped the axe high, the other low. The moment the hut stepped closer, Inga charged. There would be no swerving this time, no dodging aside. The hut swung, and Inga blocked with the haft of her weapon. The impact jarred her shoulders, but this axe had endured an ogre's power and ferocity without breaking. Inga spun in a full circle, adding the axe's weight to her own strength and momentum, concentrating only on that dark knot in the wood.

The axe cut cleanly through the leg, sending splinters flying. The weight of the blow spun Inga off her feet. She rolled out of the hut's reach. Behind her, Leech gave a cheer as the hut staggered, off balance.

Inga had seen her share of crippled animals growing up. Most of them got along just fine with a missing leg. Her favourite had been a little black pup who was born without front legs but had learned to hop from house to house, begging for scraps.

But the hut's centre of balance was higher than that of an animal, and it didn't seem to understand what had happened. It toppled to the left, trying to catch itself on its missing leg. An indignant shriek came from the inside. The remaining legs continued to kick, but it couldn't get itself upright again. Instead, it simply dragged itself in a slow circle. The remaining bones flew away like rats from a sinking ship.

"Nice hit," said Glory.

"Thanks." Inga wondered how long the hut would keep spinning before it tired. The remaining legs could still break bone if anyone got too close.

Leech braced his leg with one hand as he downed a potion. The tension in his body visibly eased. "What happened to Shroud?"

"He went after Headstrong." Inga shouldered the axe. "Why don't you two finish off the last of Yog's flying bones while I crack open this walnut and get our friends back?"

chapter 22

SHROUD

Shroud crouched to touch a dark stain in the dirt. He brought his fingers to the tip of his tongue. The salty-iron taste of blood confirmed Headstrong had come this way.

The Conclave wants this ogre dead. Why didn't you put an arrow through her neck when you had the chance instead of just giving her the world's ugliest nose jewellery?

Shroud had hit her several times, but none of his shots had severed any major arteries. Judging from the amount of blood on the trail, all he had likely accomplished so far was to make her angry.

She's playing it smart, taking the fight to an environment that will neutralise the advantage of your bow. And you're letting her lead you along like a cow to the butcher.

Headstrong had fled north, running through the woods until she reached a spot where the river was shallow enough to cross, at which point she'd doubled back into the hills. The landscape grew steadily steeper, with a drop-off to Shroud's left.

Your orders come directly from the Conclave. If you want them to take you seriously, finish the job. Eliminate the target and bring back proof of the kill. Otherwise, the next warrant will list you *as the target.*

Shroud checked every tree and outcropping for signs of an ambush. Most ogres didn't bother with traps, but then, this was no ordinary ogre, was it? Watching her fight Inga had confirmed it. The way she brought both axes together to block Inga's sword, or the transition into a Low Cat stance when she started to lose her balance. Though those moves had been clumsy and poorly executed, Shroud still recognised them from the Conclave's Martial Doctrine. But how had an ogre learned them?

He felt the pressure of the trip wire against his shin. Instinct and training propelled him into a leaping roll as a dart tore through the hem of his cloak. Poisoned and barbed, no doubt. He rose into a crouch, knives in both hands.

The odds of a hastily set trip wire killing a Conclave-trained assassin were slim, which meant Headstrong was trying either to slow him down so she could escape, or else to distract him in order to get the drop on him. And she didn't strike Shroud as one to run away if there was any chance to inflict more bloodshed.

By the time he consciously registered the sound of shifting pebbles ahead, he was already throwing himself to the ground. The rock that would have crushed his skull flew over his head to crack a sapling that clung to the rise behind him. Shroud spun so his feet were pointed at the approaching ogre and flung both knives.

One clanked harmlessly from the head of Headstrong's axe. The other stuck in her left biceps.

The ogre roared and charged.

Shroud was already slipping his bow from his shoulder. He jumped to his feet and backed away as he fitted an arrow to the string. He aimed at Headstrong's eye, waited for her to bring her axe up to block, then dropped his aim. The arrow thudded into her stomach.

The gut is one of the only parts of an ogre not protected by bone. It's a slow kill, though. If you want to bring her down, aim for the mouth, throat, or an eye.

Headstrong had picked a good spot for an ambush. There were few trees here for Shroud to hide behind. To one side was a steep drop. To the other, a wall of rock and dirt. The ledge was perhaps ten feet wide, enough room for her to fight, but minimising the advantage of Shroud's greater agility.

"Careful of this one," said one of the noggins. "He's a Conclave assassin."

Headstrong snorted. "He won't be the first I've killed."

Had the Conclave sent others to deal with Headstrong, only to fail? Or had the ogre targeted one of the Conclave's own, and that was the reason for the blood order?

Focus!

Headstrong charged. Her power was in hand-to-hand fighting. Shroud was a distance killer. He had to keep out of reach long enough to bring her down. He grabbed an unlit bomb and hurled it at her face. She blocked it automatically, and the pot shattered in a cloud of foul-smelling powders and chemicals. Shroud knew from experience how they would burn the eyes, nose, and throat. Her eyes would water, rendering her effectively blind, and woe unto her if she tried to rub her face before washing her hands.

He switched back to his bow and put an arrow into her leg. He fired the next at her foot, hoping to pin her in place, but the arrowhead failed to penetrate her boot.

"He's right in front of us," one of the heads shouted. Tears streamed down its eyes as well, but it hadn't taken as much of the bomb's powder as Headstrong. The ogre leaped forwards and swung. The axe blade nicked his bow.

Shroud cursed. The wood creaked and cracked when he tested the string. He tossed the bow away. What good did it do to blind an ogre when she had other heads to see for her? He yanked a sharpened metal star from a hidden pocket on his sleeve, waited for that noggin to try to talk again, and hurled the star into its open mouth.

Forget the noggins. Take down the ogre!

"Humans are so fragile," said Headstrong. "One squeeze and your little heads just pop off and die. Too bad. You'd've made a good noggin." She advanced, her axe slashing to and fro, following the guidance of her remaining noggins. There was no pattern to her attacks. She was deliberately random, making it impossible for him to anticipate and take advantage.

He threw another knife, sticking this one in her right thigh. She didn't seem to notice. Her size was too great an advantage in a fight like this. He had to turn it into a weakness.

He pulled a thick punching dagger with his left hand and a hooked blade on a chain with his right. The chain blade was a particularly challenging weapon he had acquired down in Crowsgate. Fling the blade correctly and the chain would slide between the finger and thumb, allowing you to snap it back before it fully extended, or to manipulate it into a complex series of arcs. A master could slit a target's throat from around a corner. Smaller hooks at the base of the blade allowed it to be used as a makeshift grappling hook for getting over walls and fences.

So far, he had discovered thirty-one ways to kill a man from ten feet away.

"There's one thing I can't decide," he said as Headstrong moved towards him. "Do I count you as a single kill, or do I tally up each noggin separately?"

He moved to the edge and glanced down. There were trees a short distance away, but the ground closest to the cliff was barren. The drop was about sixty feet, give or take. He studied Headstrong, calculating how her size and weight would affect the size of the blood spatter.

Headstrong approached more cautiously this time. She bled from dozens of wounds, and at least one of her noggins looked to be dead.

"Watch the chain blade," said the head resting near Headstrong's left armpit. "Could be poisoned."

Only an idiot uses poison on a chain blade. Too difficult to control. One wrong move and you've killed yourself with your own weapon. Who wants to risk that kind of embarrassment?

"No Conclave assassin would be fool enough to poison a chain blade," snapped the one-eyed noggin, echoing Shroud's thoughts.

"What's your name?" asked Shroud.

"Headstrong." The ogre's eyes were red, but her vision had cleared enough to follow Shroud's movements.

Shroud chuckled. "Not you. The noggin. She's the only one worth talking to."

"Night Axe." In addition to the eye, Night Axe was also missing most of an ear.

"How did Headstrong manage to kill you?"

"She didn't," said Night Axe. "I was my sister's noggin 'til a Conclave killer named Peril came along. Killed her and took me as a trophy. Kept me for years, 'til Yog helped old Headstink kill him."

With that, the pieces began sliding into place. The Conclave wouldn't bother to avenge an assassin who got himself offed by an ogre. Such failures were an embarrassment to the Conclave's masters, who had proclaimed that allowing yourself to be killed was a crime punishable by death.

But how much had Night Axe seen and heard in her time with a Conclave assassin? How many secrets had she learned? No wonder the Conclave wanted Headstrong and her noggins eliminated.

Headstrong roared and jumped forwards, her axe swinging down on a path that would separate his hand from his arm. Shroud jerked back, but twisting out of the way left him off balance. Headstrong backhanded him on the side of the head.

Shroud's foot slipped off the edge.

He didn't try to stop his fall. Instead, he whipped the chain blade at the ogre's leg. He deliberately overshot, so the chain hit her leg below the knee. The blade whipped around and crossed the chain. One of the barbs hooked tight.

His dagger fell away. He grabbed the chain with both hands. It jerked taut, slamming him against the cliff side.

Headstrong shouted again, this time from pain. Shroud braced both feet against the cliff and pulled hard. An enormous, warty foot came into view.

He had intended to drive the punching dagger into the cliff and use it as a makeshift handhold while the ogre plummeted to her death. Then he would pull himself back onto the ledge and make his way safely down to retrieve proof of the kill.

Always have a plan. Always be prepared for that plan to go to hell at any given moment.

Headstrong's entire right leg hung over the edge now.

"Forget the stupid axe," yelled one of her noggins. "Grab something! Anything!"

There were small trees and shrubs up there. If she got hold of one, she might be able to shake him free.

Shroud let go with his right hand and retrieved the last of his throwing stars. He extended both legs against the cliff to get a better angle, then hurled the star directly into the ogre's backside.

Headstrong howled and tumbled over the edge.

Shroud pushed away from the cliff as he fell, releasing the chain and launching himself towards the trees he had seen below.

There was no chance of a controlled landing. Wind rushed past his ears. Smaller branches whipped his body, and larger ones battered his bones. Others broke away from the trees, their jagged ends tearing clothes and skin. The earth and sky spun around him. He saw the ground rushing up and had just enough time to exhale and contort his body, hoping to roll with the landing.

He heard the impact quite clearly, which struck him as odd. Everything went white. There was no pain. Why wasn't there pain? A beating like that should have—

Wait for it.

He didn't have the breath to scream. All he could manage was a pained whimper as his body registered the abuse it had suffered. He spat blood and pine needles. At least two teeth had come loose. Blood dribbled from his nose. When he tried to focus on the tree towering over him, his eyes couldn't decide which of the two identical trees wavering past one another was real.

Take a slow, careful breath. Check for broken ribs or a punctured lung.

It felt like he might have dislocated a rib or two in the back, but thankfully, he didn't feel any stabbing pain in his chest. He tested his arms and fingers, then carefully pushed himself into a seated position. Two fingers on his right hand were broken, and the knuckles were scraped bloody. But considering the height of the fall, he had been lucky.

Wait until you try to get out of bed tomorrow morning.

Headstrong hadn't been so fortunate. She'd landed a short distance away. All that mass and muscle had worked against her, and she hadn't managed to break her fall on the way down. Shroud was amazed she was still breathing. Considering the odd angle of her neck and the blood bubbling between her lips, that wouldn't continue much longer.

Slowly and carefully, Shroud untwisted himself from his cloak and stood. A broken branch as thick as his thumb jutted from his left thigh, but the leg would still support his weight. He hobbled towards Headstrong and collapsed on the ground beside her, careful to stay well out of reach. He didn't think she was a threat anymore, but he hadn't survived this long by making assumptions.

Her axe sat in the dirt about ten feet away. Headstrong had landed on several of her noggins. If the impact hadn't finished them off, they'd suffocate soon enough. Shroud couldn't have rolled her off them if he'd wanted to. Only one noggin, Night Axe, appeared conscious. She just blinked up at him, her bloodied eyes crossed.

Shroud's arrow was still stuck through Headstrong's nose. He found that oddly funny. The fall had broken the ogre, but his arrow had survived intact.

Night Axe's eyes tried to focus on Shroud. She licked her lips and said, "Nice move with the chain blade. Who taught you that?"

"Desperation."

Night Axe snorted, spraying blood down her chin. "Good teacher."

Headstrong's breath echoed wetly in her chest. Shroud had seen enough deaths to know she had only minutes left. Maybe less.

"Peril was a good master," said Night Axe. "Made sure I got fed. Let me watch plenty of violence. And he didn't smell half as bad as an ogre. Then Yog came along, forced me to serve this clod. Headstrong was tough. Yog needed us to make her smart."

"'Smart' being a relative term."

"She said if I didn't help her, she'd have me tied to a stick like poor Scratcher. Only I wouldn't be scratching. My new name would be Wiper."

"I might have broken too," Shroud admitted. Headstrong's chest had stopped moving. The ogre was dead.

"Go ahead and finish me," Night Axe said. "I'm dying anyway. But at least I outlived Headstrong."

Shroud gripped the stick embedded in his leg, clenched his jaw, and twisted it free. One hand clamped the wound to slow the bleeding. With the other, he tore a strip from his shirt and wadded it into a ball. He jammed the rag into the wound, then tore a second strip and knotted the makeshift bandage into place. He'd need to cut himself a walking stick to make it back to Grayrock.

He limped over to retrieve Headstrong's weapon. One edge of the axe was badly chipped from the impact, but the other remained sharp and smooth.

The weight of the axe made his shoulder cry out in pain, but that same weight made it the weapon most likely to penetrate an ogre's skull.

"There's six gold in Headstrong's belt pouch. They're yours if you'll do me a favour."

"I've been known to give discounts in the past," said Shroud. "As a professional courtesy."

"Yog took me away from a good life." Night Axe closed her eyes. "Make sure she dies, will you?"

"It will be my pleasure," he said, and brought the axe down.

chapter 23

WINTER

The hut lay on its side. Bottles and herbs and half-carved dolls had fallen onto the wall. Fortunately, the table and other heavy furniture appeared to be secured to the floor. Otherwise it would have crushed them.

Winter could feel the hut trying futilely to crawl with its stilted legs. She heard Inga shouting through the broken door frame.

To either side, Sterling and Tipple tried to right themselves. Blue sat overhead, perched on the edge of the desk. Yog was struggling to open a storage compartment in the wall, a task made more difficult by the pile of knickknacks and other junk blocking the door.

"Winter!" Sterling squirmed onto his side. "Are you all right?"

"I've had better days," she admitted.

"This is your final chance," said Yog. "Serve me, and become stronger than you ever imagined. Or refuse, and die with your friends."

Winter nodded and leaned back. "I'll take death, thank you."

"You're a child," Yog said, her words dripping with disdain. "You can't possibly understand—"

"I understand that no matter how powerful your Riders might be, they don't seem to have much fun." Her arms and legs were still tied. She looked around, hoping perhaps a knife had fallen among the other clutter. "Well, aside from Skye and her cape. I wouldn't mind being able to fly around like that."

Something slammed into the side of the hut.

"Look at the redcap," Winter continued. "Does he look happy to you? Your Riders don't even get uniforms. If I ever turned to evil, I'd do it in style. Black furs trimmed in gold, a tall crown of gold and crystal, and a truly wicked-looking sceptre. The whole works."

"Forget her," Kas yelled, digging himself out of a pile of salt from a broken pot. "They're attacking the hut."

Yog scowled, her lips peeling back from her rusted teeth. She grabbed the cabinet door with both hands and heaved it open.

The cabinet was larger than it should have been. Yog hauled an iron cauldron out as if it weighed nothing. She grabbed Kas in one hand and climbed into the cauldron. "Blue, guard the hut and watch the Heroes. If one of them tries anything, kill the others."

The cauldron lurched into the air and hovered briefly in the middle of the hut. Yog crouched until only the tangled nest of her hair was visible. The cauldron tilted sideways and shot up like a stone from a catapult, cracking the door frame on the way out.

"Where's she off to, do you think?" Winter asked.

"Probably to kill Ben," said Sterling. "She turned him human while you were napping."

"We can't have that. Not after we worked so hard to rescue him." Winter stretched her shoulders. "Who else is ready to get out of this dump?"

Blue jumped down and pointed a knife at Tipple's throat. "Yog said no!"

The hut was still spinning though it had slowed somewhat when Yog left. Blue wobbled in place, and the knife's tip came dangerously close to Tipple's face.

"Watch it, redcap!"

A collection of glass pots spilled down on them, releasing what could have been anything from rare spices to powdered bull parts.

"Take it easy, Blue," said Winter. "You don't want to hurt him."

Blue cocked his head to the side.

"Right, maybe you do," she conceded. "The thing is, if you so much as scratch either of my friends, I'll freeze the blood in your veins until your heart shatters like glass." She pursed her lips and blew frost over his nose.

Blue grimaced and rubbed his face.

"You told me you wanted your freedom," said Sterling. "You can choose to keep living in fear, a slave forced to hunt and kill your own kind. Or you can help us punish the one who did this to you."

"Yog will never let you be free," Winter added. "You'll never be able to rejoin your people. Never be able to explore, to see the world and spread your mischief wherever you choose."

Blue stared at the knife in his hand. "Free or flee or kill the three."

She blew a puff of cold over the ropes at her wrists, turning them brittle. Her sweat turned to ice that clung to her skin. She flexed her arms, and the ropes snapped. "I can't promise we'll survive if we go after Yog. I can't promise victory. But I *can* promise you something even better."

Blue leaned closer.

Winter winked. "I give you my word that helping us will be much more fun."

Slowly, the redcap began to giggle.

Winter jumped to grab the broken doorway. She pulled herself up onto the still-spinning hut and searched the sky until she spotted Yog swooping about in her flying cauldron, flinging enchanted bones at the remaining Heroes. She seemed to be focusing her assault on Rook, who was crouched just inside the gates. Inga stood atop the rubble by the old tower. Leech and Glory were on the wall to the south, and both looked ready to collapse. There was no sign of Shroud. She hoped he hadn't fallen.

Winter blasted ice at the flailing legs of the hut, freezing them to the ground. Once it stopped moving, she jumped down and made her way to the edge of the river.

Crossbow bolts pinged off Yog's cauldron with no effect. Bones and blue fire poured down. With a curse Winter could hear even from this distance, Rook wrenched open the gates. He, Greta, and a boy jumped into the water flowing out of Grayrock just before a new assault shattered the makeshift platform where they'd been resting.

It took her a moment to recognise the boy as Ben. She had only seen him as a doll, but the spiked mess of his hair was unmistakable.

They were exposed and vulnerable, but Yog didn't seem to care. She swooped back towards the hut. "Blue! The children have fled. Grayrock is lost. Quickly, bring me the flesh of a Hero!"

The redcap poked his head out of the door. The sun silhouetted his cap as he climbed carefully out of the hut. The broken door frame was at a steep angle, and a misstep would send him tumbling into the dirt. He jumped down, arms spinning wildly.

"Bring me their flesh!" Yog shouted again.

Instead, Blue turned around, dropped his pants, and waved his naked arse in Yog's direction, laughing maniacally the whole time.

Winter couldn't see Yog's face from here, but the outrage and fury in her cry echoed across the lake.

Sterling and Tipple were climbing out after Blue. Yog retreated towards the quarry. The remaining bones flew from the hut to orbit her flying cauldron.

"The hut!" Inga shouted. "That's where she's hidden her life."

"We know that," Tipple yelled back. "We've not found it yet."

"Not inside the hut. The hut itself!"

Winter's smile grew. "Hey, Blue! How would you like to help Sterling and Tipple with a little home demolition?"

Blue chortled so hard he toppled over. "Wag my butt then break the hut!"

"Rip it apart. I'm going after Yog." Winter released her Will, freezing a path over the water. She strode up the river and through the gates of Grayrock. Fog swirled at her feet. She sucked the air through her teeth. Icicles formed in her hands, razor sharp and magically hardened.

A pair of skulls flew at her. She met them with a blast of arctic wind, and they tumbled harmlessly into the water to either side. Step by step, she strode through the gates and onto the lake, towards Yog.

"Your minions are gone or turned against you." Winter threw one of her icicles towards Yog. It struck the cauldron, spreading a patch of ice over the metal. "Your time ended long ago."

Her second icicle followed. Winter formed two more from the moisture in the air. Yog sent more of her bones to attack, but they tumbled into the water, their power stolen by Leech.

"You're old and weak, Yog," she called. "The autumn of your life has been long, but it's time Winter brought that autumn to an end."

Yog slumped, and for a moment Winter thought she might give up. She looked so weary, like it was taking all of her strength simply to hold her body up. Yog looked at her hut, trapped in the ice, then at the Heroes arrayed against her.

"Surrender," shouted Sterling. He had climbed onto the wall, where he cut quite the dashing figure. Winter wondered how long he had spent finding just the right angle for that pose, so the sun would highlight his hair and gleam off his drawn sword. "You had the power of a Hero once. Find your courage. The heart of a Hero still beats within you."

"No," said Yog, almost too quietly to hear. "Not yet." She grabbed Kas from within the cauldron and clenched the stone doll in her fist. "I'm sorry, my love."

Kas seemed confused at first, but when she brought the doll towards her jaws, he began to scream.

Winter grimaced as iron teeth crunched through stone, and the screaming was abruptly cut off.

"Did she just . . . ?" Shroud asked. Winter hadn't heard him walking along the path of ice behind her.

"Yes." Winter felt ill. Despite everything, she had been sceptical of Yog's story. The idea of literally consuming someone's power . . . it was ridiculous, and that was coming from a girl who had sneezed her pet dog to a wall.

Watching Yog now removed any doubt about her claims. Her spine straightened. She spread her fingers, and even from here, Winter could see the stiffness vanish from her joints. Yog clapped her hands, and fire erupted from the skulls orbiting her cauldron. The flames resolved into manlike shapes, warriors of blue fire topped with bone. Other bones merged with the fire, forming partial skeletons.

"They should pose an interesting challenge," Shroud commented.

"What's that?" Winter pointed to an oversized, foul-smelling sack tied to Shroud's hip.

"Souvenir." He leaned on a hastily cut crutch, and seemed to have lost his bow.

"I don't suppose you have any more tricks inside that cloak of yours?"

"Let me check." He began rooting through his pockets.

Winter hurled a blast of cold at the closest of the skeletons. The flames weakened, and a layer of ice began to form over the skull, but the instant she broke off her attack the ice turned to steam, and the flames flared up like the fur of an angry cat.

"Try this?" Shroud handed her a small pot with a fuse sticking out of the top. "Most of them got smashed to pieces when I fell."

"Fell from where?" Winter shook her head. "Never mind. How many do you have left?"

"Four."

How many explosives did Shroud typically carry around with him? "Take them to the others. Toss them into the hut and shut the door. I'll take care of Yog."

The ice at Winter's feet crackled with new cold, the path growing wider and deeper. She was a child of the north. A creature of the dark, frigid nights. Her breath was the wind, her skin frost. Her body took on the glassy shine of new-frozen ice.

The skeleton attacked again. Fingers of blue fire reached for Winter's throat, only to shy away at the last moment. It stepped back, and the skull tilted to one side as it studied her.

Winter smiled and reached into the flames to seize the skull. The heat seared her hands, boiling off her protective armour of ice, but that barrier of steam prevented the creature from burning her flesh.

She stepped to the edge of her ice and dragged the skull down into the frigid lake. The water erupted like a living thing, hissing and bubbling. The ice cracked beneath her, but she held on, forcing her cold into the porous bone, until finally the body of blue fire dissolved into smoke. The skull and remaining bones drifted apart, lifeless.

"That's one down." Winter pushed herself onto her back. Her hands were red and blistered. Sweat stung her eyes as she looked up at Yog and the swarm of burning warriors awaiting her command. "Oh, hell."

Winter jumped to her feet and ran, sliding over the ice towards the gates. Two of the burning figures swooped to intercept her.

Cold blasted from her hands, forming a ramp of ice. She pushed herself faster, using her magic to propel her forwards. She hit the ramp and launched into the air over Yog's minions. She landed hard and lost her balance, but continued to slide through the open gates and down the river, freezing the water as she went, until she reached solid ground.

"How's it going with those bombs?" she yelled.

"No good." Shroud stood atop the hut, along with Sterling and Tipple. Blue cowered behind the fallen hut. "I set off all four, and it hardly even belched. I think it got stronger when Yog did."

Rook stood at the edge of the woods, his crossbow ready. She didn't see Greta or Ben anywhere. Hopefully they would remain hidden. Glory and Leech were trying to bring down the remainder of the flaming skeletons, but Yog's power was too much for them.

Inga ran at the hut, an enormous axe clutched in both hands. She slammed the blade down, and the shaft cracked in her hands. The weapon had sunk about an inch into the wood, but it wasn't enough to do any real damage.

"The Conclave has an arsenal of barrel-sized explosives," Shroud commented. "They're not subtle, but they certainly make an impression. The latest design is packed with nails and scrap iron. Kills anything within a fifty-foot radius. I wish we had a few of those with us."

"And if wishes were bacon, we'd all die fat," said Inga. "Unless you have a barrel or two hidden away in one of those pockets?"

"Left them in my other cloak, I'm afraid."

Winter hurried to join them as the burning skeletons closed in. Sterling lunged at the closest, jabbing Arbiter through an eye socket. He gripped the hilt with both hands, using the blade like a lever to pry the skull free.

Tipple grabbed a chair from the hut. He smashed it over another of Yog's warriors, battering it until the bones splintered.

Inga's shield tossed two more back, but it wasn't enough. The air around them rippled from the heat. Tipple's makeshift weapon burned to ash in his hands, and Sterling's sleeve was on fire. Winter extinguished him before the flames could spread.

Yog circled overhead, laughing. A lucky throw by Shroud put a knife square in the centre of her throat, but she tore it free and tossed it aside like it was nothing. Dark clouds slowly swirled together, a maelstrom, with Yog at its heart.

So long as the hut survived, Yog was unstoppable. Winter studied the hut, still twitching on the ground. The broken door frame looked to be slowly healing, the slivers of wood knitting together. "Inga, I've seen your shield push enemies about like toys. Can it pull them in as well?"

"Sure."

"Oh, good." Winter pointed. "Do me a favour and bring that cauldron down here. I'd like to have a word with Yog."

Inga's sword knocked another skeleton back, then she raised her shield to the sky. A glowing chain shot upwards to wrap around Yog's cauldron. Like a fisherman fighting a shark, Inga slowly hauled the cauldron lower. Winter half expected to see Inga tossed through the air, but though her boots slid through the mud, Bulwark kept her grounded.

"That's it." Inga's neck muscles were taut as steel. "That's all I can give you."

The cauldron was still a good ten feet overhead. Winter spun. "Tipple, give a lass a boost?"

He grinned and laced his hands together. Winter put one foot on the makeshift platform, grabbed his head for balance, and braced herself.

"Punch her lights out for me," Tipple said, and tossed her skyward.

Winter caught the lip of the cauldron and reached for Yog. Cold sprayed from her fingers, but Yog grabbed her wrist and squeezed. She was as strong as an ogre.

The cauldron tore free of Bulwark's magic and shot skyward. Yog leaned out and twisted her other hand into Winter's shirt. Winter tried to hold on to the cauldron, but Yog jerked her loose.

"Pathetic,"Yog taunted her. "Will it break your friends to see you dashed against the rocks, do you think? Perhaps your death will persuade one of them to accept a place as my Rider. That one, Glory, has potential. I could see her leading my assault on Brightlodge."

"Oh, sure. Because Glory is *such* a follower." Winter rolled her eyes.

"It doesn't matter. They will all burn. If they won't serve me in life, I'll feed on their flesh and let their bones serve me in death. But first . . ."

She bared her teeth. Gleaming scratches cut through the dull iron surface where she had bitten into the stone doll that was once her husband. She pulled Winter closer.

Winter gathered the last of her Will and focused it into the tip of one finger, a finger she touched to Yog's exposed iron teeth. Pain blinded her, but she felt the cold spreading through the metal and into Yog's tongue and cheeks, locking the jaw in place. A whimper escaped Yog's throat, then that too died.

Winter caught the edge of the cauldron with one hand as she fell. Though her muscles screamed, she dragged her other arm over the edge. The lip dug painfully into her armpit as she reached out to grab Yog's leg. Ice spread over the ragged clothing and down to the bottom of the cauldron.

It would be so easy to let go. Every part of her body was exhausted. Her hands burned with the effort of holding on.

Yog's face was frozen into a snarl. Even her eyes were frosted over. The cold would have killed anyone else. Winter didn't know how long it would stop Yog.

She pulled herself higher. She hooked one leg over the edge and tumbled into the cauldron. "How do you steer this thing?"

Aside from a few broken pieces of Kas, the cauldron's only contents were an old, wooden club about the length of Winter's leg. She grabbed it by one end and the cauldron lurched to the side.

Winter let out a whoop, her pains momentarily forgotten as she flew through the air. Flaming skulls raced to intercept her, but she ducked and let the cauldron batter through them.

She yanked the end of the club to the left, jerking the cauldron sideways. "You might want to get away from that hut!"

As the Heroes scattered, she looped the cauldron around and flew higher, climbing towards the clouds until her friends were indistinguishable specks on the ground below.

Ice cracked. Yog grabbed Winter's wrist.

"Ah, well. Looks like the ride is over." Winter slammed the club downwards.

Her stomach lurched as the cauldron began to fall—no, to *fly* at the ground below. She concentrated her Will on her own body, turning her skin to ice. She nudged the club to one side, lining it up with the hut, then blew every last bit of power she had over Yog. It wasn't much, but if it held her a few seconds longer . . .

Her ice-slick arm slipped from Yog's grip, and she jumped from the cauldron. It continued to accelerate, like an iron boulder flung from the world's most powerful catapult.

The hut exploded. In the cloud of dirt and wood, Winter couldn't see what had happened to Yog, but it couldn't have been pretty.

The ground rushed to meet her, then a glowing shield bumped hard against her side. She tried to cling to Bulwark's projection. Her grip gave way, and the shield shifted into an enormous hand, wrapping around her body and guiding her down.

She crashed hard into Inga, and the two of them toppled to the ground.

"Winter? Can you hear me?" That was Sterling's voice. "Why is she laughing?"

Winter turned to look at him. "That was *fun*!" She lay back, remembering the wind roaring past. Everything hurt, and her head felt like an ice tiger had escaped inside her skull, but she didn't care. "If Yog had offered to let me fly around in her cauldron, I'd have signed up to be a Rider right then."

Glory sniffed. "Have you ever come up with a plan that *didn't* involve almost getting yourself killed?"

"Sure," said Winter. "But they're boring."

A hunched figure raced towards them. Inga raised her weapon, then laughed. Blue the redcap circled them all, spinning and dancing and laughing. "Dead! Dead and broken and dead!"

"I'd better check to make sure," said Shroud.

"Looks like her bony friends all collapsed when the cauldron hit the rocks." Tipple used a slender bone to scratch between his shoulder blades. "I think the redcap's right. Yog's done for."

"Never assume." Shroud walked purposefully towards the now-flattened cauldron, which sat in the middle of a crater. "Ah, yes. She's quite dead. The deadest I've seen in quite some time." He pulled a knife and tossed it down, presumably into the body.

"What'd you do that for?" asked Tipple.

"Just making sure."

"What do we do with him?" Sterling asked, cocking his head towards Blue.

"Do?" Blue scowled. "Blue helped. Saved stupid Heroes!"

"The little bugger also peopled those poisons—he poisoned those people in Brightlodge," said Tipple.

"As Heroes of Albion, our duty is clear," said Sterling. "Blue must be brought to Brightlodge to face the consequences of his actions."

"But we said—," Winter started.

"You offered him freedom. I merely promised him the chance to help bring his tormentor to justice." Sterling turned to Blue. "You've committed numerous crimes against the people of Brightlodge. As a Hero of Albion, I cannot in good faith ignore those actions. But your actions today *will* be taken into consideration."

"That's not fair," said Inga. "You can't judge him for what he did when he was enslaved to Yog."

"Judge *this,*" Blue crowed, and kicked Sterling square in the groin. Sterling doubled over. Tipple roared with laughter. Glory smirked.

Leech just shook his head and said, "I'm not healing that."

Blue sprinted towards the woods and disappeared. Nobody seemed inclined to pursue him.

Winter smiled and closed her eyes, enjoying the cool of the rocks and dirt, and listened to the laughter and outrage of her fellow Heroes.

chapter 24

TIPPLE

Jeremiah Tipple slammed his mug down on the bar. "And that, my friends, is how we rid Albion of a flying cannibal witch and her multitude of minstrous mon—of monstrous minions."

"That's total chicken crap," said the man to his right, who had been listening raptly for the past hour. He was one of several people who had been buying Tipple drinks all night long. "The greencaps, sure. We all saw them. But an old witch flying around in a cauldron, eating stone dolls? Pah."

"You callin' me a liar?" Tipple pointed to the other Heroes gathered around a nearby table. "Ask any of that lot. They'll tell you."

"What's going to happen to the refugees from Grayrock?" asked the woman pressed comfortably close to Tipple's left side.

"Not much left of that place to go back to," he admitted, sliding one arm around her waist. "The rain last week took out another chunk of the dam. Soon there won't be anything left but the river. The survivors seem to be settling into Brightlodge, though. I hear one of them got caught trying to fix the chicken races just last night."

"I never even heard of a town called Grayrock," said the first man.

Tipple laughed and clapped him on the back, just hard enough to remind him who he was challenging. "When's the last time you set foot outside Brightlodge, friend?"

"Leave Brightlodge?" He stared, as horrified as if Tipple had asked permission to set him on fire. "Do you know the kind of things that live in those woods?"

"That's all well and good," said another woman. "But Grayrock fell more than a week ago. What about the rest of Albion's troubles? The White Lady's still out there, you know. Not to mention trolls, balverines, hollow men, and that greencap dog that keeps stealing scraps from the butcher. When are you Heroes going to take care of all that?"

"Leech's been working to fix the remaining greencaps. Those who are still alive." Tipple didn't understand half of what Leech was doing, but he trusted the man's cleverness. It sounded like he'd worked out most of the ingredients in Yog's cure. "As for the rest, don't you worry. We'll be setting out first thing in the morning. Why d'you think I'm drinking tonight?"

That met with a roar of approval.

"What happened to Ben and his sister Greta?" asked another voice.

Tipple looked pointedly at his empty mug. Moments later, someone swapped it out for a full one. He grinned and nodded in thanks. "Back with their family, safe and sound. Greta wants to go into the wood-carving business. Turns out she has a knack for it, and Ben had an idea for a line of dolls designed like Heroes."

He reached into his pocket and pulled out a wooden doll. The painting was a bit uneven, and there was an unsightly knot on the face that looked like a nasty black eye, but it was as solid a toy as any. "By month's end, you'll all be able to buy your own miniatau—minatiu—your own Tiny Tipple!"

He took another draught of ale, then looked around the Cock and Bard. Some of his fellow Heroes had retired for the night. Sterling and Winter were dancing to the tunes of an inebriated fiddler. From the way Sterling was jumping and kicking his heels, Blue's kick hadn't done him any lasting harm.

Shroud sat in a corner by the door, his back to the wall. He'd disappeared for several days after they returned, saying it was "Conclave business," but had returned to Wendleglass Hall as determined as ever to explore Albion and find new and interesting ways of killing its inhabitants. He'd spent the evening diagramming Yog's death and trying to calculate just how fast she'd been going when she hit the hut.

Leech was talking to a man who looked faintly ill. Knowing Leech, he was probably describing the anatomical effects of freezing a witch's head from the inside out, or talking about the best way to remove the heart of a still-living balverine.

"'Scuse me." Tipple grabbed another mug and made his way towards Leech's table. His guesses had been good, but not quite correct. Leech was deep into a lecture about the cranial structure of ogre and redcap skulls.

Tipple grabbed Leech in a one-armed hug. "You need another drink, my friend!"

Leech's captive audience took that opportunity to make a break for it. He stopped only to whisper to Tipple, "Get away while you can. This fellow's not right in the head."

Tipple's good cheer vanished. He set down his mug, caught the man by the collar, and hoisted him into the air. "I'll give you the count of one to apologise. Leech took me into his home when I had redcap poison eating away at my guts. He's faced redcaps and smugglers and flaming skeletons and nightmares you can't imagine. You should be grateful he's more tolerant of idiots than I am."

Tipple grabbed the man's belt with his left hand and lifted him overhead, fully prepared to toss him headfirst out the door.

"Jeremiah, stop." Leech folded his arms. "Put him down."

Tipple grimaced, but dropped the man, who fled into the street.

"How's your gut feeling?"

Tipple settled into the chair beside Leech. "Full to bursting, and all the better for it."

Leech grinned and tapped his mug to Tipple's. "Did I tell you what I learned about redcap brains? They look like ours, all pale and wrinkly, but the texture is very different. More gelatinous, with a thicker skin. Slide a nail into 'em and they just kind of ooze around the metal like soft cheese. There's damage, but significantly less than you'd get with yours or mine."

Tipple peered into his mug and wondered if he should order another. He figured he'd need it by the time this conversation was through. "Forget redcaps. What can you tell me about balverines. They're saying some idiot tried to make a zoo of the things. Naturally, they've escaped and started killing everything in sight. There are even rumours of hybrids."

Leech's face lit up. "The balverines are crossbreeding?" He leaned in, his drink forgotten. "I assume you know the basics of balverine anatomy. Teeth, claws, fur, and so on. What really distinguishes them from other predators are their more human traits. Take the hip bones, for example. They're shaped like those of a human, allowing balverines to walk and fight on two legs."

Tipple chuckled and stretched out to listen, crossing his feet on an unoccupied chair to his right. He doubted he'd remember a quarter of what Leech was telling him come morning, but that didn't matter. They'd beaten Yog, protected Brightlodge, and saved . . . well, most of the people from Grayrock, at any rate. And Tipple had stories enough to keep people paying his tab for weeks.

Tonight was for celebrating. Tomorrow he would head out with his friends and do it all over again.

It was the life of a Hero, and Jeremiah Tipple wouldn't have traded it for anything.

PHOTO: © DENISE LEIGH

JIM C. HINES made his professional debut in 1998 with "Blade of the Bunny," an award-winning story that appeared in *Writers of the Future XV.* Since then, his short fiction has been featured in more than fifty magazines and anthologies. He's written ten books, including *Libriomancer, The Stepsister Scheme,* and the humorous Goblin Quest series. He promises that no chickens were harmed in the making of this book.

jimchines.com
Facebook.com/jimhines
@jimchines

ABOUT THE TYPE

This book was set in Bembo, a typeface based on an old-style Roman face that was used for Cardinal Pietro Bembo's tract *De Aetna* in 1495. Bembo was cut by Francesco Griffo (1450–1518) in the early sixteenth century for Italian Renaissance printer and publisher Aldus Manutius (1449–1515). The Lanston Monotype Company of Philadelphia brought the well-proportioned letterforms of Bembo to the United States in the 1930s.